The End of the World

THE

Classic Tales *of* Apocalyptic
Science Fiction

END

Compiled by
Michael Kelahan

OF THE

WORLD

FALL RIVER PRESS

This 2010 edition published by Fall River Press

Book design by Michele Trombley

Fall River Press
122 Fifth Avenue
New York, NY 10011

ISBN: 978-1-4351-2592-6

Printed and bound in the United States of America

1 3 5 7 9 10 8 6 4 2

To
Everett F. Bleiler,
whose scholarship has kept science fiction visionary.

CONTENTS

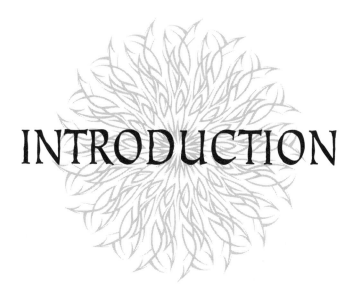

INTRODUCTION

In the nineteenth and early twentieth centuries, the fate of the world and its people was extremely precarious. With unsettling frequency, the Earth endured comet strikes that caused cataclysmic earthquakes and floods. Rogue celestial bodies regularly entered our solar system, threatening to destabilize the Earth's orbit. Meteors plunged into the sun, raising temperatures on the planet's surface to life-endangering levels—that is, on the days when the sun wasn't flaring its last feeble flame before shepherding its satellites into the lightless chill of the interstellar void. Even when the planet itself was safe, humanity repeatedly faced extinction from pestilence, famine, cosmic clouds of noxious vapors, mad scientists, and heedless businessmen whose greedy schemes depleted the planet's supply of life-sustaining elements.

Of course none of these extreme events actually happened, and the risks that they *might have* were no greater then than they are today. But you couldn't have guessed that from the prevalence of doomsday scenarios in the literature and popular fiction of the day. Apocalypse seems to have been very much on the minds writers of speculative fiction in the century or so that separates the publication of Mary Shelley's *Frankenstein* in 1818 and the debut in 1926 of *Amazing Stories*, the pulp magazine that gave science fiction its name. If you consider those to be the years marking the gestation of the science fiction genre, you could almost say that science fiction began (in part) with the end of the world.

Why this dismal theme should have been so prevalent is not hard to understand. The nineteenth century was an era of great scientific and technological advancement. Significant strides were made in astronomy, biology, chemistry, and other scientific disciplines. Increasing scientific sophistication fueled the Industrial Revolution which transformed the pace and proficiency of the civilized world. Comparing their progress to that of earlier ages, the leading nations of the day had every reason to believe that they had achieved the pinnacle of perfection, and were the undisputed masters of the world.

But not all prognoses for the advancement of civilization were so optimistic. Expanding avenues of scientific inquiry enhanced humankind's understanding of its place in the universe, but also increased uncertainty about our centrality to it. The publication of Charles Darwin's *On the Origin of Species* in 1859 rocked the foundations of the civilized world with its suggestion that humans were not divinely ordained Lords of Creation but merely one of countless species that had arrived at their current station through evolutionary processes governed by randomness and chance. Darwin's theory led some thinkers to a pessimistic sense of humanity's ordinariness, and the understanding that the same blind natural processes that elevated the species to its present height might just as easily sweep it away. In his poem "Dover Beach" (1867) Matthew Arnold evoked a haunting metaphor that poignantly captured the despair of those who had lost faith in their significance in the natural order:

> *the world, which seems*
> *To lie before us like a land of dreams,*
> *So various, so beautiful, so new,*
> *Hath really neither joy, nor love, nor light,*
> *Nor certitude, nor peace, nor help for pain;*
> *And we are here as on a darkling plain*
> *Swept with confused alarms of struggle and flight,*
> *Where ignorant armies clash by night.*

This volume collects twenty stories and one poem published between 1816 and 1921 all of whose authors contemplated the frailty and vulnerability of humankind and imagined various ways in which our world might end. Although the contents are representative, they are by no means exhaustive. Doomsday scenarios ran to the length of full novels published in this interval, among them Mary Shelley's *The Last Man* (1826), Camille Flammarion's *La Fin du Monde* (1893), and J. H. Rosny's *La Morte del la Terre* (1910). With the exception of Robert Duncan Milne's diptych "Into the Sun" and "Plucked from the Burning," I have limited selections to one story per author, although apocalyptic scenarios were a subspecialty in the repertoire of several writers, notably H. G. Wells who reflected on it as an inevitable consequence of cosmic entropy in *The Time Machine* (1895), a possible outcome of extraterrestrial invasion in *The War of the Worlds* (1898), and a catastrophe that could occur as the result of any number of other unforeseeable events in many works of short fiction. I have included several stories whose themes deal more with the end of civilization or the collapse of society as the Victorians knew it, rather than the destruction of the planet or its peoples. The nineteenth century was a particularly rich time for futuristic dystopias such as Samuel Butler's *Erewhon* (1872), a transparent satire of Victorian society, and post-apocalyptic tales such as Richard Jeffries' *After London* (1885), in which society reverts to a more primitive feudal form in the wake of catastrophic disaster. The thrust of these and other such stories is that the world will go on in the wake of the overthrow or destruction of civilization, albeit in a form very different from the comfortable and reassuring order we have known before. Several stories collected here feature disasters that are experienced more as local than global phenomena, yet nevertheless convey the sense of a hitherto safe and secure world convulsed by catastrophe.

The book opens with the remarkable poem "Darkness" by Lord Byron, one of the greatest of the British Romantic poets. The Romantics were prone to depict Nature with a near-religious reverence in their poetry, but in Byron's poem awe at the majesty of Nature shades over into terror as the narrator contemplates a universe entropically running down. Written in July of 1816, Byron's poem was likely inspired by an actual natural catastrophe. The year before, Mount Tambora, an active volcano in the Indonesian islands, had erupted. It was the most powerful volcanic eruption in recorded history up to that time, and the volcanic ash it spewed into the atmosphere unnaturally darkened the sky and disrupted weather patterns as far away as Europe and North America, precipitating "The Year without a Summer," as 1816 was known. The ensuing failure of crops and death of livestock was responsible for deadly famine in parts of the northern hemisphere. It is surely not a coincidence that Byron wrote this poem the same summer that Mary Shelley conceived the idea for her novel *Frankenstein* and John Polidori the idea for his landmark tale "The Vampyre," while all were housebound by inclement weather during their shared sojourn on Lake Geneva in Switzerland. The Gothic impulse that inspired these stories was an outgrowth of the European Romantic movement and its rebellion against the rationalism and reason of the Age of Enlightenment. The spirit that infuses these works of Gothic horror can be traced in some of this volume's more scientifically reasoned stories.

It is not surprising that comets are the agents of apocalypse in a significant number of stories. S. Austin, Jr.'s "The Comet" and Edgar Allan Poe's "The Conversation of Eiros and Charmion" both are concerned with devastating consequences of Earth's collision with a comet, while Robert Duncan Milnes's "Into the Sun" and "Plucked from Burning" and Simon Newcomb's "The End of the World" tell of destructive increases in radiant energy caused by a comet's plunge into the sun. H. G. Wells's "The Star" parallels these tales with its description of the disturbing effects of a renegade celestial body passing through out solar system. In the nineteenth century, there were a number of notable comet sightings, starting with the Great Comet of 1811 which, though it did not pass close to the Earth to threaten danger, was of such considerable size that it was visible to the naked eye for more than two-thirds of the year. Halley's Comet appeared on its 75-to-76 year orbit in 1835, and 1858 saw the spectacular appearance of Donati's Comet, the most brilliant comet of the century and the first to be photographed. Other notable comets appeared in 1861 and 1882. Though none of this book's stories can be related to the appearance of any of these comets specifically, the nineteenth century is the first century in which comets begin appearing in literature as phenomena with scientifically explicable causes and consequences, rather than as portents of mostly supernatural significance. Indeed, it is impossible to read a story such as Austin's and *not* marvel at its provocative philosophical discussion about how an Earth-destroying comet strike mocks entrenched beliefs that humanity is somehow a special or divinely favored species. Less than half a century later, Newcomb presents the destruction wrought on Earth by a comet's plunge into the sun as a sort of baptism by fire for a world in need of a jolt out of its evolutionary inertia.

Some writers imagined different yet equally menacing celestial phenomena for their doomsday stories. Both George C. Wallis, in "The Last Days of Earth," and Edwin A. Start, in "The Last Sunset," envision a point in the future where our sun is a dying star whose energy to generate life-sustaining warmth is exhausted. Sir Arthur Conan Doyle's short novel "The Poison Belt" imagines the earth sweeping unavoidably through a cloud of cosmic gas toxic to organic life. One of the more ingenious if fanciful tales concerned with a cosmic threat to Earth, Frank Lillie Pollock's "Finis," proposes the existence of a central universal sun so remote from the Earth that its infernally hot rays have only just begun to penetrate our solar system at the start of the twentieth century. All of these stories present the Earth which, has nurtured and sustained life for billions of years, as the ultimate inescapable trap when deadly phenomena on a cosmic scale overwhelms the planet.

Among several stories of mad science and experiments run amok with world-threatening consequences, Robert Cromie's "The Crack of Doom," with it's cabal of philosophical nihilists intent on harnessing the power of the atom to destroy the universe, is the most interesting for being the first work of fiction to explore the ramifications of unleashed nuclear energy. George Griffith's "A Corner in Lightning" and Robert Barr's "Within an Ace of the End of the World" both offer wry commentary on the excesses and misguided values of unchecked industrialization in their depictions of irresponsible businessmen who nearly destroy the world through greedy entrepreneurial schemes. Like Jack London's "The Scarlet Plague," about a pandemic that reverts civilization back to primitivism and overturns the social order, these stories are steeped in a type of class-consciousness that critiques elitism and wealth as expressions of a selfishness inimical to the fate of the human race. These tales can be read as the more sober counterbalances to Nathaniel Hawthorne's "Earth's Holocaust" and Ambrose Bierce's "For the Ahkoond," which satirize humankind's worst self-destructive tendencies.

No matter what threat to the world they envision, how current or far in the future they are set, how imaginative their science fiction conceits, or whether they are played for drama or humor, the selections in this volume all have one thing in common: their depiction of how human beings would face the unthinkable prospect of their extinction and brace for its horrors. In these stories, the best and worst of human nature come out under duress and, for the most part, it is the best that triumphs. Their coldly rational scientific speculations and intellectual arguments notwithstanding, these stories are reminders that emotions, traits, and behaviors that define us as humans—compassion, sympathy, dignity, courage, fortitude, self-sacrifice, love—may not save the world from annihilation, but that without them the world might not be worth living in anyway.

—*Michael Kelahan*
New York, 2010

DARKNESS

LORD BYRON

George Gordon, Lord Byron (1788–1824) was one of the best-known literary figures of his day. Like his fellow romantic poets, he frequently laced his verse with images of the awesome and the sublime. "Darkness," written in 1816, is an unusually bleak meditation on the end of the world that, for its time, seems surprisingly modern.

I had a dream, which was not all a dream.
The bright sun was extinguish'd, and the stars
Did wander darkling in the eternal space,
Rayless, and pathless, and the icy earth
Swung blind and blackening in the moonless air;
Morn came and went—and came, and brought no day,
And men forgot their passions in the dread
Of this their desolation; and all hearts
Were chilled into a selfish prayer for light.
And they did live by watchfires—and the thrones,

The palaces of crowned kings—the huts,
The habitations of all things which dwell,
Were burnt for beacons; cities were consumed,
And men were gather'd round their blazing homes
To look once more into each other's face:
Happy were those which dwelt within the eye
Of the volcanoes, and their mountain-torch;
A fearful hope was all the world contained;
Forests were set on fire—but hour by hour
They fell and faded—and the crackling trunks
Extinguished with a crash—and all was black.
The brows of men by the despairing light
Wore an unearthly aspect, as by fits
The flashes fell upon them; some lay down
And hid their eyes and wept; and some did rest
Their chins upon their clenched hands, and smiled;
And others hurried to and fro, and fed
Their funeral piles with fuel, and look'd up
With mad disquietude on the dull sky,
The pall of a past world; and then again
With curses cast them down upon the dust,
And gnash'd their teeth and howl'd. The wild birds shriek'd,
And, terrified, did flutter on the ground,
And flap their useless wings; the wildest brutes
Came tame and tremulous; and vipers crawled
And twined themselves among the multitude,
Hissing, but stingless—they were slain for food.
And War, which for a moment was no more,
Did glut himself again;—a meal was bought
With blood, and each sate sullenly apart
Gorging himself in gloom: no love was left;
All earth was but one thought—and that was death,
Immediate and inglorious; and the pang
Of famine fed upon all entrails—men
Died, and their bones were tombless as their flesh;
The meagre by the meagre were devour'd,
Even dogs assail'd their masters, all save one,

And he was faithful to a corse, and kept
The birds and beasts and famish'd men at bay,
Till hunger clung them, or the dropping dead
Lured their lank jaws; himself sought out no food,
But with a piteous and perpetual moan,
And a quick desolate cry, licking the hand
Which answer'd not with a caress—he died.
The crowd was famished by degrees; but two
Of an enormous city did survive,
And they were enemies: they met beside
The dying embers of an altar-place
Where had been heap'd a mass of holy things
For an unholy usage: they raked up,
And shivering scraped with their cold skeleton hands
The feeble ashes, and their feeble breath
Blew for a little life, and made a flame
Which was a mockery; then they lifted up
Their eyes as it grew lighter, and beheld
Each other's aspects—saw, and shriek'd, and died—
Even of their mutual hideousness they died,
Unknowing who he was upon whose brow
Famine had written Fiend. The world was void,
The populous and the powerful was a lump,
Seasonless, herbless, treeless, manless, lifeless—
A lump of death—a chaos of hard clay.
The rivers, lakes, and ocean all stood still,
And nothing stirr'd within their silent depths;
Ships sailorless lay rotting on the sea,
And their masts fell down piecemeal; as they dropp'd
They slept on the abyss without a surge—
The waves were dead; the tides were in their grave,
The Moon, their mistress, had expired before;
The winds were wither'd in the stagnant air,
And the clouds perished! Darkness had no need
Of aid from them—She was the Universe.

THE LAST MAN

ANONYMOUS

This anonymously bylined story was first published in England's popular fiction periodical Blackwood's Magazine. *It appeared in the March issue of 1826, the same year that saw the publication of Mary Shelley's similarly titled novel of a future world ravaged by plague. In this story, the end of the world is less a reality than a state of mind inspired by a mood of Gothic dread.*

I awoke as from a long and deep sleep. Whether I had been in a trance, or asleep, or dead, I knew not; neither did I seek to inquire. With that inconsistency that may often be remarked in dreams, I took the whole as a matter of course, and awoke with the full persuasion that the long sleep or trance in which I had been laid, had nothing in it either new or appalling. That it *had* been of long continuance I doubted not; indeed I thought that I knew that months and years had rolled over my head while I was trapped in mysterious slumbers. Yet my recollection of the occurrences that had taken place before I had been lulled to sleep was perfect; and I had the most accurate remembrance of the spot on which I lay, and the plants and flowers that had been budding around me. Still there was all the mistiness of a vision cast over the time, and the cause of my having laid myself down. It was one of the vagaries of a dream, and I thought on it without wondering.

The spot on which I was lying was just at the entrance of a cave, that I fancied had been the scene of some of my brightest joys and my deepest sorrows. It was known to none save me, and to me it had been a place of refuge and a defence, for in the wildness of my dream I thought that I had been persecuted and hunted from the society of man; and that in that lone cave, and that romantic valley, I had found peace and security.

I lay with my back on the ground, and my head resting on my arm, so that when I opened my eyes, the first objects that I gazed on were the stars and the full moon; and the appearance that the heavens presented to me was so extraordinary, and at the same time so awful, because so unlike the silvery brightness of the sky on which I had last gazed, that I raised my head on my hand, and, leaning on my elbow, looked with a long and idiot stare on the moon and the stars, and the black expanse of ether.

There was a dimness in the air—an unnatural dimness—not a haze or a thin mantle of clouds stretching over and obscuring the atmosphere—but a darkness—a broad shadow—spreading over, yet obscuring nothing, as if above the heavenly bodies had been spread an immense covering of clouds, that hid from them the light in which they moved and had their being.

The moon was large and dark. It seemed to have approached so near the earth, that had it shown with its usual lustre, the seas, and the lands, and the forests, that I believed to exist in it, would have been all distinctly visible. As it was, it had no longer the fair round shape that I had so often gazed on without wonder. The few rays of light that it emitted seemed thrown from hollow and highland—from rocks and from rugged declivities. It glared on me like a monstrous inhabitant of the air, and, as I shuddered beneath its broken light, I fancied that it was descending nearer and nearer to the earth, until it seemed about to settle down and crush me slowly and heavily to nothing. I turned from that terrible moon, and my eyes rested on stars and on planets, studded more thickly than imagination can conceive. They too were larger, and redder, and darker than they had been, and they shone more steadily through the clear darkness of the mysterious sky. They did not twinkle with varying and silvery beams—they were rather like little balls of smouldering fire, struggling with a suffocating atmosphere for existence.

I started up with a loud cry of despair,—I saw the whole reeling around me,—I felt as if I had been delirious,—mad,—I threw myself again on the flat rock, and again closed my eyes to shut out the dark fancies that on every side seemed to assail me,—a thousand wild ideas whirled through my brain,—I was dying,—I was dead,—I had perished at the mouth of that mossy cave,—I was in the land of spirits,—myself a spirit, and waiting for final doom in one of the worlds that I had seen sparkling around me. No, no,—I had not felt the pangs of dissolution, and my reason seemed to recall unto me all that I had suffered, and all that I had endured,—I repeated the list of my miseries,—it was perfect, but Death was not there.

I was delirious,—in a mad fever,—I felt helpless and weak, and the thought flashed across my mind that there I was left to die alone, and to struggle and fight with death in utter desolation,—the cave was known to none save me, and—as I imagined in my delirium—to one fair being whom I had loved, and who had visited my lonely cave as the messenger of joy and gladness. Then all the unconnected imaginations of a dream came rushing into my mind, and overwhelming me with thoughts of guilt and sorrow,—indistinctly marked out, and darkly understood, but pressing into my soul with all the freshness of a recent fact,—and I shrieked in agony; for I thought that I had murdered her, my meek and innocent love, and that now with my madness I was expiating the foulness of my crime.—No, no, no,—these visions passed away, and I knew that I had not been guilty,—but I thought—and I shook with a strong convulsion as I believed it to be true—I thought that I had sunk to sleep in her arms, and that the last sounds that I heard were the sweet murmurs of her voice.—Merciful heavens! She too is dead,—or she has deserted me,—my shrieks, my convulsive agony, would else have aroused her. But *no*—I shook off these fancies with a strong effort, and again I hoped. I prayed that I might still be asleep, and still only suffering from the pressure of an agonizing dream. I roused myself—I called forth all my energies, and I again opened my eyes, and again saw the moon and the stars, and the unnatural heaven glaring on me through the darkness of the night, and again overpowered with the strong emotions that shook my reason, I fell to the ground in a swoon.

When I recovered, the scene was new. The moon and the stars had set, and the sun had arisen,—but still the same dark atmosphere, and the same mysterious sky. As yet, I saw not the sun, for my face was not in the direction of his rising. My courage was, however, revived, and I began to hope that all had been but one of the visions of the night. But when I raised my head, and looked around, I was amazed,— distracted,—I had lain down in a woody and romantic glen,—I looked around for the copse and hazel that sheltered me,—I looked for the clear wild stream that fell in many a cascade from the rocks,—I listened for the song of the birds, and strained my ear to catch one sound of life or animation; no tree reared its green boughs to the morning sun,—all was silent, and lone, and gloomy,—nothing was there but grey rocks, that seemed fast hastening to decay, and the old roots of some immense trees, that seemed to have grown, and flourished, and died there.

I raised myself until I sat upright. Horrible was the palsy that fell on my sense when I saw the cave—the very cave that I had seen covered with moss, and the wild shrubs of the forest, standing as grim and as dark as the grave, without one leaf of verdure to adorn it, without one single bush to hide it; there it was, grey and mouldering; and there lay the beautiful vale, one dreadful mass of rocky desolation, with a wide, dry channel winding along what had once been the foot of a green valley.

I looked around on that inclosed glen as far as my eye could reach, but all was dark and dreary, all seemed alike hastening to decay. The rocks had fallen in huge fragments, and among these fragments appeared large roots and decayed trunks of trees, not clothed with moss, or with mushrooms, springing up from the moist wood, but dry, and old, and wasted. I well remembered, that in that valley no tree of larger growth than the hazel, or the wild rose, had found room or nourishment, yet there lay large trees among the black masses of rock, and it was evident that there they had grown and died.

Some dreadful convulsion must have taken place—yet it was not the rapid devastation of an earthquake. The slow finger of time was there, and every object bore marks of the lapse of years—ay, of centuries.

Rocks had mouldered away—young trees and bushes had grown up, and come to maturity, and perished, while I was wrapped in oblivion. And yet, now that I saw, and knew that it was only through many a year having passed by, that all these changes had been effected, even now my sense recovered in some measure from the delirious excitement of the first surprise, and, such is the inconsistency of a dream, I almost fancied that all this desolation had been a thing to be looked for and expected, for *then,* for the first time, I remembered that during my long sleep I thought that I knew, that days, and months, and years, were rolling over me in rapid and noiseless succession.

No sooner had this idea seized my mind—no sooner did I conceive that I had indeed slept—that I had indeed lain in silent insensibility, until wood, and rock, and river, had dried up, or fallen beneath the hand of time—that the moon and the stars—and, prepared as I was for wonders, I started, as at that instant I instinctively turned towards the part of the heavens in which the sun was to make his appearance; prepared as I was, I started when I beheld his huge round bulk heaving slowly above the barrier of rocks that surrounded me. His was no longer the piercing ray, the dazzling, the pure and colourless light, that had shed glory and radiance on the world on which I had closed my eyes—he was now a dark round orb of reddish flame. He had sunk nearer the earth as he approached nearer the close of his career, and he too seemed to share with the heaven and the earth the symptoms of decay and dissolution.

When I saw universal nature thus worn out and exhausted—thus perishing from old age, and expiring from the sheer want of renewing materials, then I thought that surely my frail body must likewise have waxed old and infirm—surely I too must be bowed down with age and weariness.

I raised myself slowly and fearfully from the earth, and at length I stood upright. There I stood unscathed by time—fresh and vigorous as when last I walked on the surface of a green and beautiful world—my frame as firmly knit, and my every limb as active as if a few brief hours, instead of many long years, had witnessed me extended on that broad platform of rock.

At first a sudden gleam of joy broke on my soul, when I thought that here I stood unharmed by time—that I at least had lost nothing of life by the wonderful visitation that had befallen me.

I felt as if I could fly away from this scene of devastation, and in other climes seek for fresher skies and more verdant vales. Alas! alas! I soon and easily gained the top of the rising bank, and fixed my eyes on the wide landscape of a desolate and unpeopled world. Desolation! Desolation! I knew that it was to be dreaded as a fearful and a terrible thing, and I had felt the sorrows of a lone and helpless spirit—but never, never had I conceived the full misery that is contained in that one awful word, until I stood on the brow of that hill, and looked on the wide and wasted world that lay stretched in one vast desert before me.

Then despair and dread indeed laid hold of me—then dark visions of woe and of loneliness rose indistinctly before me—thoughts of nights and days of never-ending darkness and cold—and then the miseries of hunger and of slow decay and starvation, and hopeless destitution—and then the hard struggle to live, and the still harder struggle of youth and strength to die—Dark visions of woe, where fled ye? before what angel of light hid ye your diminished heads? The sum of my miseries seemed to overwhelm me—a loud sound, as one universal crash of dissolving nature, rung in my ears—I gave one wild shriek—one convulsive struggle—and—*awoke*—and there stood my man John, with my shaving-jug in the one hand, and my well-cleaned boots in the other—his mouth open, and his eyes rolling hideously at thus witnessing the frolics of his staid and quiet master.

By his entrance were these visions dispelled, else Lord knows how long I might have lingered out my existence in that dreary world, or what woes and unspeakable miseries had been in store for me.

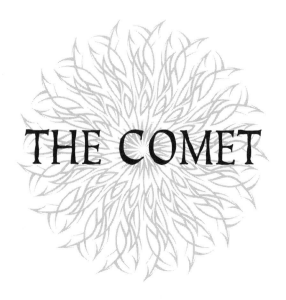

THE COMET

S. AUSTIN, JR.

This remarkable story appeared in the 1839 edition of The Token and Atlantic Souvenir, *an American literary miscellany published annually at Christmas time. It is one of the earliest known stories to speculate on the fate of the Earth following a comet strike. Its provocative philosophical arguments notwithstanding, it is almost impossible not to be moved by the poignance of its depiction of humanity's last gasp.*

It was a fine clear night, in the summer of 18**. A party of serenaders were abroad in the city. One of them, remarking upon the brilliancy of the heavens, discovered a small star, of unusual color and singular appearance.

"It is unlike a star, comet, or planet," said he, showing it to his companions.

" 'T is the lost Pleiad," said one, "in search of her sisters."

"Yes," said another, "our music has led her astray;

'For music shall untune the spheres.' ''

"Let the stars look to the matter," said a third; " 't is no concern of ours. What is Hecuba to us? Come! it is after midnight and we have yet three places to visit."

A sentimentalist sat at his window.—There was the grandeur of the midnight firmament; the sublime silence of the scene; "the poetry of heaven."

He saw a star with a red and scowling aspect. Its eye, contrasted with those around, was unlike, strange, unnatural. It was a blemish upon night's escutcheon.

A wagoner trudged by the side of his team. They stopped to drink at a lonely brook. He looked round upon the sky; "My eyes, what a power o' stars!" There was one, a strange and queer-looking sort of a star. "It looks like a scarecrow in a cornfield!"

There appeared, a few days after, in one of the public journals, in a column of unimportant items, a short paragraph; "A small comet has appeared in the southwest part of the heavens, visible about midnight."

The serenader and his friends were lounging abroad.

"I was right," said he, "in my conjecture the other night; it was a comet which we saw."

"And what then?" said his friend.

"Why, then, my vision is more acute than yours."

"And what then?" said his friend.

"Why, then, I advise you to procure a tub, and live like your prototype of old, Diogenes."

"Is there any thing new in the gay world?" said the sentimentalist, to a lovely young lady; "any thing to amuse

'the mind of desultory man;
Studious of change, and pleased with novelty?' ''

"Oh yes," said she; "we have a stranger come to town."

"And who may he be?"

"One who comes under very suspicious circumstances; he brings letters to no one; his face is flushed, and he indicates intemperance; and his course has been very erratic."

"He is not likely to meet with an excess of hospitality," said the sentimentalist.

"Indeed he may, though," said she; "for he increases every hour in public estimation; and, were you near him, you would at once acknowledge the warmth and ardor of his temperament."

"A man of talents?"

"I cannot say, precisely; but he is acknowledged to be very quick and brilliant."

"It is plain, that I am not so; otherwise, I should not have been so long in discovering, that you were amusing yourself at my expense."

"Oh, by no means," said she, laughing; "how could I be more explicit or unequivocal; 't is the comet, about which I am talking.

"Yes, very explicit and unequivocal, indeed; but do you know this same comet belongs to me."

"Ah, indeed!"

"Yes, by right of discovery. I saw it last Tuesday, near midnight, and, I suspect, before anyone else."

"Well," said she, "I apprehend no one will come to disturb you in your salamander kingdom."

"Landlord! what news are you reading on?" said the wagoner, in the bar-room.

"Why, they say a comet's come."

"A comet! faith, the very same," said the wagoner; "I saw it first, I'll bet; I was coming over the turnpike last Tuesday night, and just afore I got to Brown's Corner, I turned off Lily Brook, to water; and I went to push up my hat, to see if the moon wasn't ris, and I broke my tobacco pipe, which I had stuck in my hat-band, confound it; and, as I was looking about, I see a queer looking sort of comet-like star; I knew 't was a comet; it looked like a star jest blown out; and I see it afore the printer, or any body else, I'll bet.—I say, landlord, you've got this 'ere toddy a leetle too sweet, I guess."

Meantime the earth kept onward; wheeling her rapid and sublime flight round the sun; regardless of the little, bustling creature, man, upon the surface; and heeding not a small, fiery body, which lay in ambush amongst a cluster of stars, in a remote part of the heavens.

Richmond was a young astronomer, who had distinguished himself in the science. He was an enthusiast, and surveyed the heavens as his own; and with all the complacency of conscious skill and knowledge. He regarded the earth, merely as a travelling observatory. He was the first to discover the comet, prowling near the borders of the solar system. Every night, equipped with sextant and telescope, he sallied out to reconnoiter the enemy. He quickly perceived there was danger.

As yet, the far-off comet was not present to the world of men's thoughts. Matters of immediate concernment filled their minds; for present necessity, the power which rules the destinies of mortals, exacts undivided, unceasing devotion.

From his distant abode, the comet was eyeing the solar system;

"Watching, in grim repose, his evening prey."

By and by he set himself in motion; and the astronomers could see him a great way off, moving in a solitary grandeur through the wilds of distant space. His pace accelerated; and his course was right onward toward the earth. His aspect was a pale red; and he looked like an angry man, rushing with fell purpose upon his object.

The astronomers were alarmed; they saw the danger, and awakened the press. "It is now," said one of the public journals, "nearly three weeks since the comet was first discernible; its increase has been rapid, beyond all former precedent; and in size, it much exceeds the great comet of 1680. We could, last night at midnight, distinctly read a book printed in small character. An anxious feeling pervades the whole community; it is indeed remarkable, that none of our leading astronomers have developed its elements and course; we trust, that another week will not pass, without some relief to the general anxiety on this subject." "Last night," said another journal, "the heavens were unclouded, and the comet was out in great pomp. He has ceased to be the grand, and is now the terrible. His nightly increase is appalling, and his nucleus nearly as large as the sun. A gloomy foreboding has seized the public mind. We have not as yet seen any calculations from those who profess much skill in astronomy, but in the result of such as have appeared, there is a fearful and alarming coincidence." "A ship," said a third, "arrived last night; all Europe was in consternation at the progress of the comet. It was the general belief, it would approach so near the earth, as to endanger every animated existence, and that a universal catastrophe was at hand."

The comet was now advancing from the southern part of the heavens, and drove onward with fierce careering and deadly menace toward the earth. Every night he came out with augmented splendor. The stars seemed to recede before the blaze of his fire. He overthrew the dominion of night, and scattered its shades before him. His disc and shining train appeared like the shield of a warrior, with the red horsehair streaming from his helmet. The timid became anxious and talkative; men of firm nerves were silent. The churches were filled, and charities abundant. The booksellers sold great numbers of astronomical treatises, and essays on comets, heat, gravity, density. Solicitude, the younger sister of Fear, had thrown her checkered mantle over all;—all but childhood, happy with its marbles, tops, and balls, and its ignorance of to-morrow.

"This," said Richmond to his friend Vivian, "this is the astronomical 'reign of terror'; and has a mighty influence on the conduct of men. There is an absence of crime, and a punctilious performance of duty; knavery is obsolete, and honesty in fashion. Fear is a wonderful quickener of the moral principle."

"Yes," said Vivian, "and is an energy impelling man in almost all his actions. Above, below, around, the power of fear is universal. In heaven he is the prime agent of Jove, and all the lesser gods are subjected to his sway. On earth he is the Atlas, and grand conservative principle, of the moral world. He is the presiding demon in the infernal regions and makes them hell. If, however, your comet is as potent as many think he is, the empire of fear 'now totters to its fall,' as well as every other empire."

"I am a little skeptical on that point," said Richmond; "my belief is, that the comet will approach near the earth without coming in contact; we shall probably be singed, and frightened, but not annihilated. There must be an actual collision of the bodies, to destroy animal life entirely.—Ah, a lucky coincidence! here comes Dr. H——, whose scientific ability makes him a sort of an oracle in the present crisis. He can enlighten us."

The Doctor came up, and saluted.

"I am very happy to meet you, gentlemen," said he; "and, without pretending to the power of divination, I venture to assert, your conversation is about the universal subject, the comet; and, in that belief, will take the liberty to continue it. I have heard, Mr. Richmond, that you have made many observations on its course, with a view of determining its nearest approach to the earth. Pray, is such the case?"

"It is even so, Sir," replied Richmond.

"I have great confidence in their accuracy," said the Doctor, "and my object, this morning, was to propose, that we meet tomorrow, and compare what we have done. I have made several observations myself; but I find it an injury to my eyes to continue them. I have no doubt, however, that the observations we both have made, furnish sufficient data to determine the distance of the comet at its nearest approach to the earth."

"Then you do not believe in the probability of a collision of the two bodies," said Vivian.

"No," replied the Doctor, "I have no such fears. I am a firm believer in the permanence of the solar system."

"I shall not fail to be present, Sir, to-morrow," said Richmond.

"Mr. Vivian, you must also be with us," said the Doctor; "we have all a common interest in the result."

Vivian bowed; he should be most happy to be present.

During the three preceding nights the heavens had been overcast; yet the light of the comet struck through the clouds, and showed its near presence and great power; the next night the clouds broke away, and partly disclosed its disc. It had trebled in size during that short period, and the position of its train still continued the same, indicating the directness of its course upon the earth. The tides had rapidly increased; and that night they rushed in with great violence; and no cause could be assigned but the attraction of the comet.

"We hope to be able," said the press of next morning, "to state to our readers conclusive and satisfactory information relative to the future course of the comet. We have ascertained that Dr. H——, and another gentleman of astronomical skill, have appointed a meeting for the purpose of determining it; and, whatever the result of their calculations may be, we shall present it forthwith to our readers. The most fatal certainty can scarce be so harassing as the present anxious suspense."

The next day Vivian met the Doctor at the appointed place. He was alone, walking the room, and impatient at the absence of Richmond.

"Where is Mr. Richmond?" said he.

"I do not know," replied Vivian; "it is but just the time agreed on; he will be here immediately, without doubt.—Have you no apprehension of a catastrophe from the comet?"

"No," replied the Doctor, "my faith is unshaken in the permanence of our system; yet, in my observations last night upon the comet, I was particularly struck with the near coincidence of its orbit with that of the earth's; and also with its density, as indicated by its power over the tides. It may come quite near the earth, however, without doing us mischief; nothing but actual contact would destroy the existing order of things on our planet; and of this contact I think there is very little probability."

"What is your opinion of the recent theory of the asteroids in our system,—Vesta, Ceres, Juno, and Pallas?"

"I have examined the facts and reasonings relative to that theory," said the Doctor; "and think the inference, that these bodies were originally a comet, and planet, split by concussion, is ingenious and plausible, but not conclusive. I should have almost given it credence, but for a prejudice I am sensible I entertain against any theory which unsettles the solar system."

Richmond entered at this moment; he took his seat at the table without speaking; the Doctor did the same.

"Are you not about to attempt the solution of the problem of three bodies?" said Vivian, "since the moon, as well as the earth and comet, must enter into your reasoning."

"No," replied the Doctor: "we shall neglect the moon's agency; she is in such a position, that her influence will not be material."

The observations precisely made by the Doctor and Richmond were fully compared; they differed but little; and the mean was taken; and on this datum each undertook the solution of the problem, to find the distance at which the comet would be from the earth at the point of its nearest approach.

Vivian was leaning over the back of a chair in front of the table. He remarked the feverish and agitated manner of the doctor, after he had made some progress in the solution. The fate of the world seemed to be involved in a combination of figures and diagrams.

They had been some time engaged at the work; and the Doctor was unconsciously carrying on his solution in an audible voice and hurried manner. They overset the inkstand; neither of them heeded it; they dipped their pens in the puddle on the table. The work continued with feverish intensity.

"Good God!" said the doctor, of a sudden; "is it possible?"

His solution was astounding. It brought the comet into actual concussion with the earth; and within five days.

"It cannot be so," said he, striking his first upon the table, " 't is impossible."

He caught at the solution which Richmond had just completed. It did not agree with his own. "Hah!" said he, "I was confident I was in error. I knew I was wrong."

His eyes glanced rapidly over the calculation.—But his countenance soon changed and fell.

"You have made an error, Mr. Richmond; this denominator has changed placed with its numerator."

Richmond took his solution, with some chagrin, to correct it. The Doctor walked the room, endeavoring to suppress his excitement.

"It cannot be so," said he; "there must be error somewhere,—so overwhelming,—impossible!" He twice approached the table and recast his calculations.—"Mr. Vivian, do me the favor to review this solution; I am rather confused this morning."

Vivian did so. It was correct; and agreed, by a slight difference only, with the one Richmond had just completed.

"Have you any other reason to doubt the accuracy of these results," said Vivian, "than the universal ruin they develop?"

"That is sufficient, surely," replied the Doctor. "I cannot reconcile myself to such a dreadful catastrophe,—actual contact!—impossible!— There must be error somewhere; we might as well assert, that the Deity had made a blunder in the solar system; this moral inference is sufficient to show we are wrong."

After a short pause, he suddenly turned to Richmond;

"What table of logarithms have we been using?"

"Sherwin's."

"Sherwin's!" said he, quickly; "there is the error, beyond a doubt." He wrote a note and called a lad. "Carry this to my house; they will deliver you a book; bring it back immediately.—Sherwin! I have no faith in Sherwin; obsolete and full of errors. Yes, yes, it lies there, beyond a doubt. I have known frequent errors in the first figure of his decimals. He, or his printer, has done much mischief in his day."

He continued walking and soliloquizing; and had quite convinced himself, that error existed in the tables of logarithms, when the boy returned with the book. The Doctor seized it instantly.

"Mr. Richmond," said he, "let us take out all the logarithms we have used from Sherwin, and compare them with the tables of Gardener, which I have before me, and we shall detect an error somewhere."

The logarithms, which had been used, were carefully taken out, one by one, and compared with those in the new tables. It so happened that they all agreed, each with the other, to the lowest place of figures. Not a doubt or hope remained. There was a short pause.

The Doctor was a man, who had placed himself in the first rank in scientific attainment and celebrity. He had fame, friends, and fortune; besides the consciousness, that he owed none of these to accidental circumstance. A stupefying amazement came over him, when he saw all the ties about to be violently rent asunder. He stood for a few moments with a bewildered air, leaning against the table; and then, without speaking, walked mechanically out of the room.

"Five days," said Vivian, "is rather a short notice, in which to settle up one's temporal matters."

"Yes, and five days," said Richmond, "is what we make a maximum;—confound my eagerness! the Doctor rather carried it over me in the solution."

"It will not matter much," said Vivian, "at the end of your maximum."

"Very true; but it will vex me until then."

It was known to many, the purpose for which the Doctor and Richmond had met; and a great number had collected round the door, to know the result. As soon as the Doctor appeared, they pressed around him with earnest inquiry, "Pray what is the result?"

His countenance, full of anxiety, answered the question he endeavoured to evade. "We must hope for the best."

"Then there is hope?" said they.

"Whilst there is life, there is hope," said the Doctor.

"But how long will there be life?"

"That is a question which no man can answer," said the Doctor, and passed on.

Those around, excited by the doctors evasion, pressed into the room, where they knew Richmond was. "Mr. Richmond," said the foremost, "you are aware of the universal solicitude in this matter; pray inform us, at what conclusion yourself and the Doctor have arrived? Is there no reason to hope the threatened catastrophe will be averted?"

Richmond was closely intent upon his figures and diagrams; reviewing his calculations,—"Fluxion and attraction of P. is as $ax"x^{\star"}$—"why," said he, "the Doctor and myself differ materially about the result,—we differ materially."

"But to what does this difference relate?" said the interrogator, impatiently.

"Relates to time," said Richmond. "We differ four minutes, two seconds, a third."

"But about what?"

"Oh, about moment of contact."

"Moment of contact! Moment of contact, did you say?"

"Yes, moment of contact," said Richmond; "that is to say, the instant when they touch."

His words struck the ear of those around like the sentence of death. One by one they slunk away in silence.

At this period, the moon, in her progress round the earth, had gotten within the influence of the comet; and that night, when she rose, she was seen oscillating on her centre; and displacing a portion of her sphere, which had been hidden from man since the creation. Her vibrations quickened, as she continued to rise; and she seemed conscious of the grasp of some ruthless and tremendous power. Men felt the presence of an evil genius. It was upon them like a nightmare oppression. No eye was closed; and the night passed in baffled slumbers, feverish prayer, and sharp anxiety.

Cleon was at his quarters. There were present his friends Richmond, Stuart, and Vivian,—idleness and conversation.

"Behold," said Stuart,

> "creation uncreated,
> The gods in terrors, and the skies on fire;
> The earth affrighted, faltering in her course;
> And Death himself aghast, and doomed to die.

> Man of astronomy (to Richmond), involved in starry
>   mysteries,
> Speak! and, in the surrounding pomp of verse heroic,
> Declare the purpose and intent of fate."

"Within thirty hours," replied Richmond, "every animated existence upon the face of this earth shall be destroyed. Here you have it, in plain prose."

"Methinks," said Stuart, "the when the doom of the earth is pronounced, 't is more fitting it be done in sounding hexameters."

"So speak the gods," said Richmond; "but, as we are mere mortals, and soon to be less, let humble prose suffice."

"Whether 't is said or sung, in prose or verse," said Stuart, "I have still a lurking skepticism about a fatal result, notwithstanding your oracular response."

"Your skepticism may continue thirty hours," said Richmond, "but not longer."

"We shall see," said Stuart. "A primary object of the Deity, in our creation, seems to be the gradual perfection of the intellectual part of it. Every comparison of the past with the present, indicates an improvement in the moral and physical condition of man. That the Deity, under these circumstances, should arrest and destroy his own work and purpose, is an act of such egregious caprice as is absolutely irreconcilable with all our ideas of his wisdom and consistency. It is much more probable, that man is in error in his calculations or inferences, than that the essential attributes of the Deity are changed or annihilated.'

"Let me reply in your own style," said Richmond. "We have before us destruction, irresistible and overwhelming. No man can mistake its instant and final character. It is confirmed by every calculation, which has been applied to the subject. It is much more probable, that some of the premises of your argument are incorrect, than that that, which is manifest to sense, and demonstrated by science, should be fallacious."

"The error appears to me," said Vivian, "to be in the assertion that the condition of mankind is progressively improving. Where are the proofs?"

"The proofs," said Cleon, "are in the condition of man at the present time, as contrasted with any previous period. Let the contrast be made, and the improvement is manifest. Even if we were ignorant of the former condition of human society, we should still be justified in inferring its improvement from the many and continued discoveries in art and science."

"And still more," said Stuart, "from the greater diffusion of knowledge, and the progress of liberal opinions, and free institutions. It strikes me that the improvement in the condition of the human race proceeds in something like a geometrical progress. Almost every new discovery or invention may be combined or modified with many of those already in existence; and such combinations are themselves new discoveries, which may be again modified or compounded. And the greater also our stock of facts, which are every day accumulating, and the greater certainty in our conclusions, and the more varied and efficient are invention and discovery. And, as the condition of man is so closely connected with the state of art and science, the principle, here asserted, is most animated to the philanthropist; for it must, eventually, carry man to the highest point of perfection, of which his nature is susceptible."

"And then the millennium commences," said Vivian.

"Yes," said Stuart, "the millennium commences, if you please; or an indefinite period during which man exists in a state near to moral and physical perfection.

"To say," said Cleon, " that man is to remain as he now is, seems to me to impeach the purpose of the benevolence of the Deity; for with what design has man been created, if he is to continue to all eternity in his present imperfect condition? No; we may say, that sound theology, the nature of the human mind, and past experience, all concur in proof of the assertion, that the condition of mankind is, and has been, progressively improving."

"I am not at issue with you," said Vivian, "and do not believe, that the general condition of man is now, or ever has been, susceptible of much improvement. 'T is experience alone which can decide the question. The arguments from mind and theology are abstract and metaphysical, and fall before the power of experience, if experience is opposed to them. And this I assert to be the case in the present instance. Beginning at the empire of China, and traversing the whole of Asia, we search in vain for any historical proofs, that the condition of its inhabitants is better at the present period, than it was three thousand years ago. If we proceed into the dominion of the Turk, what a melancholy contrast to the state of the ancient Greek and Egyptian. Looking northward, you can scarce hesitate to prefer the condition of the ancient free, wild, roving Scythian, to that of his miserable descendant, the Russian boor, bound down in everlasting chains to feudal bondage. Diverging south we are in Africa; and although she shows us but a few centuries of her history, 't is for our purpose. No sooner had the civilized European discovered America, than forthwith, for the purposes of slavery, he converted the plains of Africa into one vast field of war, rapine, and violence. Whatever may have been the former state of Africa, it could not have been worse than since the days of Columbus."

"Crossing to South America, we find it possessed by blacks, whites, and mulattoes, in slavery and misrule, in the place of the 'Children of the Sun,' and the patriarchal government of the Incas. Proceeding north, we pass the West India isles. Let the history of Hispaniola suffice; its ancient people, though savage, yet gentle, hospitable, and unoffending. Their Evil Genius leads the Europeans to their shores; and forthwith two millions of its happy, simple-hearted inhabitants, are torn in pieces and butchered, by dogs and Christian Spaniards. A deed unrivalled in atrocity! The delight and boast of Hell. What are those islands now? What! but the pens and stalls of selfishness and slavery. North America remains; its aborigines, so few and unknown, that we can scarce institute a comparison with those who now possess it. But we know, that it is still a mooted point among philosophers, whether the additional wants, cares, and vexations of civilized life make it much more desirable than the savage state, and whether the individuals in each are not under equal sufferance.

"Europe, the eye of the world, is the last which stands before us, with her science, arts, vices and refinement, misery and pageantry. The great mass of her population struggling to obtain a bare subsistence. Their ancestors, the Goth, Vandal, Gaul, Spaniard, must, at least, have obtained as much, with this difference, that, as they were more thinly scattered, they were more addicted to agricultural pursuits, than the present crowded population of Europe, who are, therefore, from necessity, partly commercial and manufacturing. And you well know, how much in simplicity of character, in independence, and in the means of obtaining a subsistence, an agricultural is superior to a commercial or manufacturing population.

"So much for the past and present state of man. On whatsoever side we turn, we search in vain for proofs of any amelioration of his hard condition; and yet you propose to carry on the present order of things, in the hope, mind you, not in the certainty, that you may at last bring human nature near to a state of perfection. But, gracious heavens! at what a waste of human suffering is the experiment to be continued! an experiment, I repeat, which has been tried under such varied circumstances of government, climate, manners, customs, for six thousand years, upon two hundred generations of men, and found so utterly incompatible with human happiness. To prove that moral and physical discoveries have improved the condition of the race, you must take the microcosm of man and not great masses of his species. Is he not assailed by as many vexations now as in ancient days? Do not the same wants, which urged him yesterday, press him to-day? Is not the struggle to get bread, and to get power, just as hard, and as eager as ever? Is there less of ennui besetting wealth? less solicitude in middle life? less suffering in poverty now, than there was three thousand years ago? Answer me that. Even admitting, that you might carry man to the highest point of perfection, of which his nature is capable, there still remain enough of natural evil beyond your control, to make life, at best, a mere dull sufferance. Many will still be born with physical constitutions ill adapted to their condition in life; with mental constitutions too much alive to external impressions, too sensitive to life's jarring discords. Sickness and accident will occasionally assail every one. Some experience will still be necessary to success in life; but the natural order of things, relating to youth, manhood, and age, pushes man into active life and compels him to act, before he has attained that experience. Miscarriage and its effects follow him in middle life; and in old age there is little of value in success; whilst defeat and poverty are doubly distressing.

"These are a few, and but a few, of those natural evils, which no human ingenuity can counteract or destroy. What countless myriads must be subjected to their cruelty and tyranny, if the present system is continued! Who loses, if 't is now destroyed? Not ourselves, who have seen something of what life is. Not posterity, a non-existent, and therefore not susceptible of loss or gain. No, the intractableness of matter has almost baffled the benevolence of the Deity; and now, in the plenitude of his power, yes, and of his benevolence too, he stretches forth his arm to annihilate a system, which experience has shown to be quite at variance with human happiness. You emphasize on the discoveries of the past century, as tending to ameliorate the condition of man. But let me remind you, that one of those discoveries or developments is of a principle, which confounds and paralyzes all the rest. 'T is, that population constantly and severely presses upon the supply of food; and that poverty and disease are the harsh agents appointed to keep it down; that the primary effect of any improvement in physics, morals, or government, is to augment the supply of food; this augments the members of society, until their increase has again overtaken the augmented supply of food, and presses upon it with the same intensity as before. The relative condition of the different classes in society is then the same as at the outset, but with this difference, that the numbers of the outer circle, or those immediately exposed to the severity of the checks to population, have been increased in direct proportion to the extent and value of the discovery, which gave the first impulse. This is the principle, which baffles every attempt to improve the condition of man. 'T is the curse with which the race was 'baptized' from the beginning. And is this the system you would perpetuate?—into the very texture of which evil is interwoven, warp and woof. Fie on such a system; the sooner the present impending destruction burst upon it the better.

"This is rabid misanthropy," said Stuart; "the offspring of a morbid sensibility, too keenly alive to the petty troubles of life. Experience, upon which you so much rely, in order to be efficient, must be recorded and generally available. This can only be done through the medium of printing. It is not three centuries since that art has been in existence. We may say, therefore, that during that short period only men have read its lessons. Greater developments and improvements, as you well know, have been made during that period, not merely in physics, but in morals and legislation, than during all preceding ages. The same results could not continue to be produced, without eventually exalting man far above his original and present condition. Intemperance, for instance, becomes a strong passion; yet we have seen how much, in modern days, it has been circumscribed and repressed by the united power of the press and public opinion.

Why may we not infer, that hereafter every other pernicious passion may in like manner be tamed or destroyed?"

"Will man then be happy?" said Vivian.

"Ah, that is the final question," said Cleon. "I think with you, Stuart, that man may ultimately be carried very near to perfection. But I think also with Vivian, that it does not necessarily follow, that he would be happy; and, if he is not, why then the labor of creating and continuing this mundane sphere is lost. I have not much concern for the fate of the earth, or the race she bears; and am quite content the comet should do its office. My sympathies are for the moon."

"The moon?" said Stuart, "what concern have you for the moon? The patroness of rogues, and the mother of fools."

"Observe," replied Cleon, "the serenity of her aspect, and the apparent absence of sudden change in her elements. I thence infer a like serenity in the minds of the Lunarians, and that they are therefore more enviably circumstanced than ourselves; for the mind takes its impress from outward objects, and is the mere image or transcript of that which surrounds it; and in these I conjecture, the inhabitants of the moon have much the advantage of us."

"A happy thought, Cleon," said Vivian; "let us pursue it. Let us suppose an intelligent being placed midway between the earth and moon, and ignorant of what is doing on their surfaces. He turns to the moon, and remarks the perpetual sunshine, which radiates on her surface; the slow gradation of her monthly night and day; her poles fixed, and the entire absence of change of temperature; the dignified serenity of her aspect. 'Surely,' he would say, 'if there are sentient beings there, their minds must partake of the nature of these elements, calm, equable, constant. The sunshine of content must be a part of them.' He now turns to the earth, and behold everything of an opposite character; spinning round her axis once in twenty-four hours; her poles shifting, and exposing any point on her surface to extremes of temperature; her disc ever varying, now dark and cloudy, now irradiated by the sun, and now diversified. By parity of inference, he would say, 'If there are intelligent beings there, these elements must influence, and be typical of their natures; an ever-varying, feverish, harassed race.' How true such an inference is, we, alas! who are part of that race, can well testify. It almost confirms your first inference,

Cleon, that the inhabitants of the moon are superior in their natures and condition to ourselves. The Lunarian, as he looks abroad on the heavens through his pure and cloudless sky, sees no change or apparent disorder, unless in the varying disc and fitful elements of our earth. It is not extravagant to suppose, that in his mythology this planet is designated as the abode of outcasts, perhaps as the purgatory of the solar system. In the coming encounter among the celestials, pray, Richmond, arrange matters, so as to bring off the moon unscathed. The moon! the most celestial of all the celestials!"

"Here is the valedictory of the press," said Stuart, taking up one of the public journals and reading. " 'We shall discontinue our journal after to-day. The universal consternation unfits ourselves, as well as our readers, to sustain it. We rely on the mercy and goodness of a Divine Providence to resume it as soon as the menaced evil is passed. It is now quite apparent that the comet will cause a general deluge; the rapid and fearful increase of the tides the past two days places this beyond a doubt. The greatest security we think is on shipboard; but as very few can obtain it, we recommend the construction of rafts, the materials for which may be found in every dwelling. If the waters rise and subside without commotion, most of us may yet escape. We confide in the belief, that the benevolence of the Deity will yet preserve this fair creation, and turn aside the uplifted arm of the destroying angel.' "

"All this availeth nothing," said Richmond,

" 'For Fate and the dooming gods are deaf to tears.'

There is more piety than philosophy in what you have read."
"Why so?"
"Because it appears to me, that the heat of the comet, which is now so palpable, will so rarefy the atmosphere, that this, together with its attraction at the point over which it may be vertical, will cause such a rush of the ocean and atmosphere towards that point, as to produce a whirlwind and deluge such as man never saw, and render utterly unavailing all human effort to escape from it."

"Within about twenty-nine hours," said Vivian, "every animated existence on the face of this earth shall be destroyed. The knell of the human race is tolling."

"Ah!" said Stuart, "that thought must be grateful to the wormwood of your misanthropy."

"Rather, say," replied Vivian, "to my sympathy for human suffering, which must so soon have an end."

"When," said Stuart,

> " 'When will you three meet again?' "

"That will be," said Richmond,

> " 'When wrapped in flames, in ruin hurled,
> Sinks the fabric of the world.' "

"We cannot choose in the matter," said Cleon; "let us agree when next we meet 'to sup with Pluto.' "

They separated.

All that night the house-tops and high places were filled with people, watching in anxious silence the fiery spectre in the heavens. Its flight toward the earth was so rapid, that they could see its disc enlarge and expand with the naked eye. The spirit of man, as he gazed at it, died away within him. The thought of to-morrow fell like a palsy on the soul.

The dawn of the day discovered man almost exhausted with watching and dismay; yet Hope still stood by his side, and once more rallied him to action. Everywhere he was seen, in anxious haste, constructing rafts; the streets and highways were blocked up with whatever was buoyant; all the vessels had been moored off the quays and wharves, and were filled with men, endeavouring to beat off others, who attempted to get on board. The crowd broke into the naval arsenal, and seized three great ships; they overset two of them in rushing on board; the third sunk under her load. Here might be seen, by the streets, and way-side, women praying in loud and fervent accents. The sick, now deserted, were seen, with their pallid faces thrust from some window, imploring help, in feeble wailing. Along the shore, there was a contest to get possession of the boats and small vessels. The tide, which had risen to an unprecedented height, now began to recede, and continued to do so, until the whole of the great bay in front of the city was quite bare. There were seen boxes and bales, drowned men and sunken vessels. The waters receded so far, that no part of the ocean was visible from the city.

The sun had risen, and was just above the horizon. His eye was dim and lustreless. He had seen man, for six thousand years, struggling with adverse destinies, and he now came a lagging and unwilling witness to his death. The tide had begun to return, and the waves, at the summons of the comet, came rushing with tumultuous violence to the shore, overlapping each other, and the sea appearing like a rolling wall of waters. The people stood by their boats, rafts, and frail machines, in fearful solicitude, and in the hope they would be borne up, and subside without commotion, until the catastrophe had passed. At this period it was discovered, that the city was on fire. The waters had flowed into buildings containing lime, which slaked and inflamed. The fire, unopposed and impelled by the rising wind, strode across the city, driving every thing before it. The city was built upon a peninsula. On one side of the road, along the isthmus, was the public cemetery, the tombs built up from a level with the road. The tide of the preceding day had swept across, overthrown the walls, and scattered coffins and dead bodies in every direction. Here might be seen the body recently entombed, and in the white bridal dress in which it had wedded death; the ghastly, half-consumed corpse; the grinning skeleton; and broken coffins; scattered promiscuously along the road. Over this stratum of the dead swept the living tide of men, women, and children, driven by the flames and flood, to the highlands beyond the city. The lowlands were quickly overflowed; and the waves rushed through the valleys, bearing down every thing before them.

The comet was now risen. His coming was preceded by incessant flashes of light,—the banners of the destroying angel,—darting up from north to south, along the whole of the eastern horizon. His disc covered nearly a fourth part of the heavens. It was of a fiery intensity, increasing every instant, and glowing like molten iron. The power of gravity was gradually diminishing; and, as the comet mounted toward the meridian, a strange sensation of lightness was perceptible. The wind blew with frightful violence, and smote down all before it. The waves struck against the foot of the hills, and rebounded to a prodigious height, leaping upwards to the giant attraction of the comet. Its light resembled the sun's, when seen through a smoked glass; it threw a brassy glare over the whole scene. The dome of heaven appeared as if on fire; for the body of the comet shot off incessant streams of light, which the attraction of the earth drew down to every part of the horizon. The soul seemed to dilate to the magnificence of the occasion; for the scene was unspeakably grand; and Death lost half his terrors in its splendid sublimity.

It was now about eleven o'clock, and the comet nearly half way up the heavens. The wrath of the storm every moment increased. It sprung at, and overwhelmed, a miserable remnant of men, who had fled to the highlands. But a single mountain remained, on which was a massive stone tower. The top of the mountain was a flat of many acres. On this was huddled a dense mass of human beings, all striving to get into the tower. The mountain itself stood up like a colossal altar, its top covered with victims, a huge sacrifice at the coming obsequies of Nature. The force of the tempest struck off the tops of the waves, and made the whole sea foam and seethe like a boiling cauldron. It drove the sea-birds against the tower with such force, that they dropped dead at its base. The noise of the whirlwind was a trumpet-roar. It sounded like a shrill, continuous, rattling peal of thunder. The demon of destruction, with his terrible energies, put forth the whole of his blasting power. He rioted in the savage fury of the elements. The foundations of nature were rent asunder at his hands. The solid earth seemed to stagger before his power. Men stood as if in the presence of an angered Deity. They were confounded and paralyzed at the appalling sublimity of the scene.

Meantime the ocean lashed round the sides of the mountain with inconceivable fury. At each heave its ferocious rush swept off some of the outer circle of women and children. The men in the centre seemed to be seized with the spirit of the storm, and in their infuriate struggle to get into the tower. A ship from the ocean, the last of her kind, came flying in affright before the blast; the crew clinging to the shrouds and broken topmasts. She dashed into the valley below, rolled over, and was annihilated in an instant. On the top of the mountain all was rife with horror and distress. The ocean, as it rose, narrowed the circle, and swept off its victims one after another into the foaming vortex. The upheaving waves had now risen to a level with the height of the mountain; and one, a little higher than the rest, lifted up, overwhelmed, and scattered this doomed remnant of the human race. A sharp shriek, faintly heard through the roar of the elements, was the last energy of animated nature.

THE CONVERSATION OF EIROS AND CHARMION

EDGAR ALLAN POE

*The gothic spirit doom and gloom that suffuses much of the poetry
and prose of Edgar Allan Poe (1809–1849) takes a science-fictional
turn in "The Conversation of Eiros and Charmion," which appeared
in the December 1839 issue of* Burton's Gentleman's Magazine,
*then under Poe's editorship. Its description of the earth destroyed by
a comet strike uncannily parallels that in S. Austin's "The Comet,"
which first appeared in print at virtually the same time.*

Πυρ σοι προσοισω
I will bring fire to thee.
Euripides—ANDROM:

EIROS.

Why do you call me Eiros?

CHARMION.

So henceforward will you always be called. You must forget, too, *my* earthly name, and speak to me as Charmion.

EIROS.

This is indeed no dream!

CHARMION.

Dreams are with us no more;—but of these mysteries anon. I rejoice to see you looking life-like and rational. The film of the shadow has already passed from off your eyes. Be of heart, and fear nothing. Your allotted days of stupor have expired; and, to-morrow, I will myself induct you into the full joys and wonders of your novel existence.

EIROS.

True—I feel no stupor—none at all. The wild sickness and the terrible darkness have left me, and I hear no longer that mad, rushing, horrible sound, like the "voice of many waters." Yet my senses are bewildered, Charmion, with the keenness of their perception of *the new*.

CHARMION.

A few days will remove all this;—but I fully understand you, and feel for you. It is now ten earthly years since I underwent what you undergo—yet the remembrance of it hangs by me still. You have now suffered all of pain, however, which you will suffer in Aidenn.

EIROS.

In Aidenn?

CHARMION.

In Aidenn.

EIROS.

Oh God!—pity me, Charmion!—I am overburdened with the majesty of all things—of the unknown now known—of the speculative Future merged in the august and certain Present.

CHARMION.

Grapple not now with such thoughts. To-morrow we will speak of
this. Your mind wavers, and its agitation will find relief in the exercise
of simple memories. Look not around, nor forward—but back. I am
burning with anxiety to hear the details of that stupendous event which
threw you among us. Tell me of it. Let us converse of familiar things, in
the old familiar language of the world which has so fearfully perished.

EIROS.

Most fearfully, fearfully!—this is indeed no dream.

CHARMION.

Dreams are no more. Was I much mourned, my Eiros?

EIROS.

Mourned, Charmion?—oh deeply. To that last hour of all, there hung a
cloud of intense gloom and devout sorrow over your household.

CHARMION.

And that last hour—speak of it. Remember that, beyond the naked
fact of the catastrophe itself, I know nothing. When, coming out
from among mankind, I passed into Night through the Grave—at that
period, if I remember aright, the calamity which overwhelmed you
was utterly unanticipated. But, indeed, I knew little of the speculative
philosophy of the day.

EIROS.

The individual calamity was, as you say, entirely unanticipated; but
analogous misfortunes had been long a subject of discussion with
astronomers. I need scarce tell you, my friend, that, even when you
left us, men had agreed to understand those passages in the most holy
writings which speak of the final destruction of all things by fire, as
having reference to the orb of the earth alone. But in regard to the
immediate agency of the ruin, speculation had been at fault from that
epoch in astronomical knowledge in which the comets were divested
of the terrors of flame. The very moderate density of these bodies
had been well established. They had been observed to pass among the

satellites of Jupiter, without bringing about any sensible alteration either in the masses or in the orbits of these secondary planets. We had long regarded the wanderers as vapory creations of inconceivable tenuity, and as altogether incapable of doing injury to our substantial globe, even in the event of contact. But contact was not in any degree dreaded; for the elements of all the comets were accurately known. That among *them* we should look for the agency of the threatened fiery destruction had been for many years considered an inadmissible idea. But wonders and wild fancies had been, of late days, strangely rife among mankind; and, although it was only with a few of the ignorant that actual apprehension prevailed, upon the announcement by astronomers of a *new* comet, yet this announcement was generally received with I know not what of agitation and mistrust.

The elements of the strange orb were immediately calculated, and it was at once conceded by all observers, that its path, at perihelion, would bring it into very close proximity with the earth. There were two or three astronomers, of secondary note, who resolutely maintained that a contact was inevitable. I cannot very well express to you the effect of this intelligence upon the people. For a few short days they would not believe an assertion which their intellect, so long employed among worldly considerations, could not in any manner grasp. But the truth of a vitally important fact soon makes its way into the understanding of even the most stolid. Finally, all men saw that astronomical knowledge lied not, and they awaited the comet. Its approach was not, at first, seemingly rapid; nor was its appearance of very unusual character. It was of a dull red, and had little perceptible train. For seven or eight days we saw no material increase in its apparent diameter, and but a partial alteration in its color. Meantime, the ordinary affairs of men were discarded and all interests absorbed in a growing discussion, instituted by the philosophic, in respect to the cometary nature. Even the grossly ignorant aroused their sluggish capacities to such considerations. The learned *now* gave their intellect—their soul—to no such points as the allaying of fear, or to the sustenance of loved theory. They sought—they panted for right views. They groaned for perfected knowledge. *Truth* arose in the purity of her strength and exceeding majesty, and the wise bowed down and adored.

That material injury to our globe or to its inhabitants would result from the apprehended contact, was an opinion which hourly lost ground among the wise; and the wise were now freely permitted to rule the reason and the fancy of the crowd. It was demonstrated, that the density of the comet's *nucleus* was far less than that of our rarest gas; and the harmless passage of a similar visitor among the satellites of Jupiter was a point strongly insisted upon, and which served greatly to allay terror. Theologists, with an earnestness fear-enkindled, dwelt upon the biblical prophecies, and expounded them to the people with a directness and simplicity of which no previous instance had been known. That the final destruction of the earth must be brought about by the agency of fire, was urged with a spirit that enforced every where conviction; and that the comets were of no fiery nature (as all men now knew) was a truth which relieved all, in a great measure, from the apprehension of the great calamity foretold. It is noticeable that the popular prejudices and vulgar errors in regard to pestilences and wars—errors which were wont to prevail upon every appearance of a comet—were now altogether unknown. As if by some sudden convulsive exertion, reason had at once hurled superstition from her throne. The feeblest intellect had derived vigor from excessive interest.

What minor evils might arise from the contact were points of elaborate question. The learned spoke of slight geological disturbances, of probable alterations in climate, and consequently in vegetation; of possible magnetic and electric influences. Many held that no visible or perceptible effect would in any manner be produced. While such discussions were going on, their subject gradually approached, growing larger in apparent diameter, and of a more brilliant luster. Mankind grew paler as it came. All human operations were suspended.

There was an epoch in the course of the general sentiment when the comet had attained, at length, a size surpassing that of any previously recorded visitation. The people now, dismissing any lingering hope that the astronomers were wrong, experienced all the certainty of evil. The chimerical aspect of their terror was gone. The hearts of the stoutest of our race beat violently within their bosoms. A very few days sufficed, however, to merge even such feelings in sentiments more unendurable. We could no longer apply to the strange orb any *accustomed* thoughts. Its *historical* attributes had disappeared. It oppressed us with a hideous *novelty* of emotion. We saw it not as an astronomical phenomenon in the heavens, but as an incubus upon our hearts, and a shadow upon our brains. It had taken, with inconceivable rapidity, the character of a gigantic mantle of rare flame, extending from horizon to horizon.

Yet a day, and men breathed with greater freedom. It was clear that we were already within the influence of the comet; yet we lived. We even felt an unusual elasticity of frame and vivacity of mind. The exceeding tenuity of the object of our dread was apparent; for all heavenly objects were plainly visible through it. Meantime, our vegetation had perceptibly altered; and we gained faith, from this predicted circumstance, in the foresight of the wise. A wild luxuriance of foliage, utterly unknown before, burst out upon every vegetable thing.

Yet another day—and the evil was not altogether upon us. It was now evident that its nucleus would first reach us. A wild change had come over all men; and the first sense of *pain* was the wild signal for general lamentation and horror. This first sense of pain lay in a rigorous constriction of the breast and lungs, and an insufferable dryness of the skin. It could not be denied that our atmosphere was radically affected; the conformation of this atmosphere and the possible modifications to which it might be subjected, were now the topics of discussion. The result of investigation sent an electric thrill of the intensest terror through the universal heart of man.

It had been long known that the air which encircled us was a compound of oxygen and nitrogen gases, in the proportion of twenty-one measures of oxygen, and seventy-nine of nitrogen, in every one hundred of the atmosphere. Oxygen, which was the principle of combustion, and the vehicle of heat, was absolutely necessary to the support of animal life, and was the most powerful and energetic agent in nature. Nitrogen, on the contrary, was incapable of supporting either animal life or flame. An unnatural excess of oxygen would result, it had been ascertained, in just such an elevation of the animal spirits as we had latterly experienced. It was the pursuit, the extension of the idea, which had engendered awe. What would be the result of *a total extraction of the nitrogen?* A combustion irresistible, all-devouring, omni-prevalent, immediate;—the entire fulfillment, in all their minute and terrible details, of the fiery and horror-inspiring denunciations of the prophecies of the Holy Book.

Why need I paint, Charmion, the now disenchained frenzy of mankind? That tenuity in the comet which had previously inspired us with hope, was now the source of the bitterness of despair. In its impalpable gaseous character we clearly perceived the consummation of Fate. Meantime a day again passed—bearing away with it the last shadow of Hope. We gasped in the rapid modification of the air. The red blood bounded tumultuously through its strict channels. A furious delirium possessed all men; and, with arms rigidly outstretched towards the threatening heavens, they trembled and shrieked aloud. But the nucleus of the destroyer was now upon us;—even here in Aidenn, I shudder while I speak. Let me be brief—brief as the ruin that overwhelmed. For a moment there was a wild lurid light alone, visiting and penetrating all things. Then—let us bow down Charmion, before the excessive majesty of the great God!—then, there came a shouting and pervading sound, as if from the mouth itself of HIM; while the whole incumbent mass of ether in which we existed, burst at once into a species of intense flame, for whose surpassing brilliancy and all-fervid heat even the angels in the high Heaven of pure knowledge have no name. Thus ended all.

EARTH'S HOLOCAUST

NATHANIEL HAWTHORNE

In his stories and novels, Nathaniel Hawthorne (1804–1864) often explored the impact of early America's Puritan heritage on the behavior of ordinary men and women. Much of his fiction is allegorical, including this parable first published in the May 1844 issue of Graham's Lady's and Gentleman's Magazine. *Hawthorne lodged his tongue firmly in cheek when he wrote this satirical account of a bonfire of the vanities that represents the destruction of civilization for its moral improvement.*

Once upon a time—but whether in the time past or time to come is a matter of little or no moment—this wide world had become so overburdened with an accumulation of worn-out trumpery, that the inhabitants determined to rid themselves of it by a general bonfire. The site fixed upon at the representation of the Insurance Companies, and as being as central a spot as any other on the globe, was one of the broadest prairies of the West, where no human habitation would be endangered by the flames, and where a vast assemblage of spectators might commodiously admire the show. Having a taste for sights of this kind, and imagining, likewise, that the illumination of the bonfire might reveal some profundity of moral truth, heretofore hidden in mist or darkness, I made it convenient to journey thither and be present. At my arrival, although the heap of condemned rubbish was as yet comparatively small, the torch had already been applied. Amid that boundless plain, in the dusk of the evening, like a far-off star alone in the firmament, there was merely visible one tremulous gleam, whence none could have anticipated so fierce a blaze as was destined to ensue. With every moment, however, there came foot-travellers, women holding up their aprons, men on horseback, wheelbarrows, lumbering baggage-wagons, and other vehicles, great and small, and from far and near, laden with articles that were judged fit for nothing but to be burned.

"What materials have been used to kindle the flame?" inquired I of a bystander; for I was desirous of knowing the whole process of the affair from beginning to end.

The person whom I addressed was a grave man, fifty years old or thereabout, who had evidently come thither as a looker-on; he struck me immediately as having weighed for himself the true value of life and its circumstances, and therefore as feeling little personal interest in whatever judgment the world might form of them. Before answering my question, he looked me in the face, by the kindling light of the fire.

"O, some very dry combustibles," replied he, "and extremely suitable to the purpose,—no other, in fact, than yesterday's newspapers, last month's magazines, and last year's withered leaves. Here now comes some antiquated trash that will take fire like a handful of shavings."

As he spoke, some rough-looking men advanced to the verge of the bonfire, and threw in, as it appeared, all the rubbish of the Herald's Office; the blazonry of coat-armor, the crests and devices of illustrious families; pedigrees that extended back, like lines of light, into the mist of the dark ages; together with stars, garters, and embroidered collars; each of which, as paltry a bauble as it might appear to the uninstructed eye, had once possessed vast significance, and was still, in truth, reckoned among the most precious of moral or material facts by the worshippers of the gorgeous past. Mingled with this confused heap, which was tossed into the flames by armsfull at once, were innumerable badges of knighthood; comprising those of all the

European sovereignties, and Napoleon's decoration of the Legion of Honor, the ribands of which were entangled with those of the ancient order of St. Louis. There, too, were the medals of our own Society of Cincinnati, by means of which, as history tells us, an order of hereditary knights came near being constituted out of the king-quellers of the Revolution. And, besides, there were the patents of nobility of German counts and barons, Spanish grandees, and English peers, from the worm-eaten instruments signed by William the Conqueror down to the bran-new parchment of the latest lord who has received his honors from the fair hand of Victoria.

At sight of the dense volumes of smoke, mingled with vivid jets of flame, that gushed and eddied forth from this immense pile of earthly distinctions, the multitude of plebeian spectators set up a joyous shout, and clapped their hands with an emphasis that made the welkin echo. That was their moment of triumph, achieved, after long ages, over creatures of the same clay and the same spiritual infirmities, who had dared to assume the privileges due only to Heaven's better workmanship. But now there rushed towards the blazing heap a gray-haired man, of stately presence, wearing a coat, from the breast of which some star, or other badge of rank, seemed to have been forcibly wrenched away. He had not the tokens of intellectual power in his face; but still there was the demeanor, the habitual and almost native dignity, of one who had been born to the idea of his own social superiority, and had never felt it questioned till that moment.

"People," cried he, gazing at the ruin of what was dearest to his eyes with grief and wonder, but nevertheless with a degree of stateliness— "people, what have you done! This fire is consuming all that marked your advance from barbarism, or that could have prevented your relapse thither. We, the men of the privileged orders, were those who kept alive from age to age the old chivalrous spirit; the gentle and generous thought; the higher, the purer, the more refined and delicate life! With the nobles, too, you cast off the poet, the painter, the sculptor—all the beautiful arts; for we were their patrons, and created the atmosphere in which they flourish. In abolishing the majestic distinctions of rank, society loses not only its grace, but its steadfastness—"

More he would doubtless have spoken; but here there arose an outcry, sportive, contemptuous, and indignant, that altogether drowned the appeal of the fallen nobleman; insomuch that, casting one look of despair at his own half-burnt pedigree, he shrunk back into the crowd, glad to shelter himself under his new-found insignificance.

"Let him thank his stars that we have not flung him into the same fire!" shouted a rude figure, spurning the embers with his foot. "And, henceforth, let no man dare to show a piece of musty parchment as his warrant for lording it over his fellows. If he have strength of arm, well and good; it is one species of superiority. If he have wit, wisdom, courage, force of character, let these attributes do for him what they may; but from this day forward no mortal must hope for place and consideration, by reckoning up the mouldy bones of his ancestors! That nonsense is done away."

"And in good time," remarked the grave observer by my side—in a low voice however— "if no worse nonsense comes in its place; but, at all events, this species of nonsense has fairly lived out its life."

There was little space to muse or moralize over the embers of this time-honored rubbish; for, before it was half burnt out, there came another multitude from beyond the sea, bearing the purple robes of royalty, and the crowns, globes, and sceptres of emperors and kings. All these had been condemned as useless baubles; playthings, at best, fit only for the infancy of the world or rods to govern and chastise it in its nonage; but with which universal manhood, at its full-grown stature, could no longer brook to be insulted. Into such contempt had these regal insignia now fallen, that the gilded crown and tinselled robes of the player king from Drury Lane Theatre, had been thrown in among the rest, doubtless as a mockery of his brother-monarchs on the great stage of the world. It was a strange sight, to discern the crown-jewels of England, glowing and flashing in the midst of the fire. Some of them had been delivered down from the time of the Saxon princes; others were purchased with vast revenues, or perchance ravished from the dead brows of the native potentates of Hindostan; and the whole now blazed with a dazzling lustre, as if a star had fallen in that spot and been shattered into fragments. The splendor of the ruined monarchy had no reflection save in those inestimable precious-stones. But, enough on this subject! It were but tedious to describe how the Emperor of Austria's mantle was converted to tinder, and how the posts and pillars of the French throne became a heap of coals, which it was impossible to distinguish from those of any other wood. Let me add, however, that I noticed one of the exiled Poles stirring up the bonfire with the Czar of Russia's sceptre, which he afterwards flung into the flames.

"The smell of singed garments is quite intolerable here," observed my new acquaintance, as the breeze enveloped us in the smoke of a royal wardrobe. "Let us get to windward and see what they are doing on the other side of the bonfire."

We accordingly passed around, and were just in time to witness the arrival of a vast procession of Washingtonians—as the votaries of temperance call themselves now-a-days—accompanied by thousands of the Irish disciples of Father Mathew, with that great apostle at their head. They brought a rich contribution to the bonfire; being nothing less than all the hogsheads and barrels of liquor in the world, which they rolled before them across the prairie.

"Now, my children," cried Father Mathew, when they reached the verge of the fire— "one shove more, and the work is done. And now let us stand off, and see Satan deal with his own liquor."

Accordingly, having placed their wooden vessels within reach of the flames, the procession stood off at a safe distance, and soon beheld them burst into a blaze that reached the clouds and threatened to set the sky itself on fire. And well it might. For here was the whole world's stock of spirituous liquors, which, instead of kindling a frenzied light in the eyes of individual topers as of yore, soared upwards with a bewildering gleam that startled all mankind. It was the aggregate of that fierce fire which would otherwise have scorched the hearts of millions. Meantime, numberless bottles of precious wine were flung into the blaze, which lapped up the contents as if it loved them, and grew, like other drunkards, the merrier and fiercer for what it quaffed. Never again will the insatiable thirst of the fire-fiend be so pampered! Here were the treasures of famous bon-vivants—liquors that had been tossed on ocean, and mellowed in the sun, and hoarded long in the recesses of the earth—the pale, the gold, the ruddy juice of whatever vineyards were most delicate—the entire vintage of Tokay—all mingling in one stream with the vile fluids of the common pot-house, and contributing to heighten the self-same blaze. And while it rose in a gigantic spire, that seemed to wave against the arch of the firmament, and combine itself with the light of stars, the multitude gave a shout as if the broad earth were exulting in its deliverance from the curse of ages.

But the joy was not universal. Many deemed that human life would be gloomier than ever when that brief illumination should sink down. While the reformers were at work I overheard muttered expostulations from several respectable gentlemen with red noses, and wearing gouty shoes; and a ragged worthy, whose face looked like a hearth where the fire is burnt out, now expressed his discontent more openly and boldly.

"What is this world good for," said the Last Toper, "now that we can never be jolly any more? What is to comfort the poor man in sorrow and perplexity? —how is he to keep his heart warm against the cold winds of this cheerless earth? —and what do you propose to give him, in exchange for the solace that you take away? How are old friends to sit together by the fireside without a cheerful glass between them? A plague upon your reformation! It is a sad world, a cold world, a selfish world, a low world, not worth an honest fellow's living in, now that good fellowship is gone forever!"

This harangue excited great mirth among the bystanders; but, preposterous as was the sentiment, I could not help commiserating the forlorn condition of the Last Toper, whose boon-companions had dwindled away from his side, leaving the poor fellow without a soul to countenance him in sipping his liquor, nor, indeed, any liquor to sip. Not that this was quite the true state of the case; for I had observed him at a critical moment, filch a bottle of fourth-proof brandy that fell beside the bonfire, and hide it in his pocket.

The spirituous and fermented liquors being thus disposed of, the zeal of the reformers next induced them to replenish the fire with all the boxes of tea and bags of coffee in the world. And now came the planters of Virginia, bringing their crops of tobacco. These, being cast upon the heap of inutility, aggregated it to the size of a mountain, and incensed the atmosphere with such potent fragrance, that methought we should never draw pure breath again. The present sacrifice seemed to startle the lovers of the weed more than any that they had hitherto witnessed.

"Well; —they've put my pipe out," said an old gentleman, flinging it into the flames in a pet. "What is this world coming to? Everything rich and racy—all the spice of life—is to be condemned as useless. Now that they have kindled the bonfire, if these nonsensical reformers would fling themselves into it, all would be well enough!"

"Be patient," responded a stanch conservative; — "it will come to that in the end. They will first fling us in, and finally themselves."

From the general and systematic measures of reform, I now turn to consider the individual contributions to this memorable bonfire. In many instances these were of a very amusing character. One poor fellow threw in his empty purse, and another, a bundle of counterfeit or insolvable banknotes. Fashionable ladies threw in their last season's bonnets, together with heaps of ribbon, yellow lace, and much other half-worn milliner's ware; all of which proved even more evanescent in the fire, than it had been in the fashion. A multitude of lovers, of both sexes—discarded maids or bachelors, and couples, mutually weary of one another—tossed in bundles of perfumed letters and enamored sonnets. A hack-politician, being deprived of bread by the loss of office, threw in his teeth, which happened to be false ones. The Rev. Sydney Smith—having voyaged across the Atlantic for that sole purpose—came up to the bonfire with a bitter grin and threw in certain repudiated bonds, fortified though they were with the broad seal of a sovereign state. A little boy of five years old, in the premature manliness of the present epoch, threw in his playthings; a college-graduate, his diploma; an apothecary, ruined by the spread of homœopathy, his whole stock of drugs and medicines; a physician, his library; a parson, his old sermons; and a fine gentleman of the old school, his code of manners, which he had formerly written down for the benefit of the next generation. A widow, resolving on a second marriage, slyly threw in her dead husband's miniature. A young man, jilted by his mistress, would willingly have flung his own desperate heart into the flames, but could find no means to wrench it out of his bosom. An American author, whose works were neglected by the public, threw his pen and paper into the bonfire, and betook himself to some less discouraging occupation. It somewhat startled me to overhear a number of ladies, highly respectable in appearance, proposing to fling their gowns and petticoats into the flames, and assume the garb, together with the manners, duties, offices, and responsibilities, of the opposite sex.

What favor was accorded to this scheme I am unable to say, my attention being suddenly drawn to a poor, deceived, and half-delirious girl, who, exclaiming that she was the most worthless thing alive or dead, attempted to cast herself into the fire amid all that wrecked and broken trumpery of the world. A good man, however, ran to her rescue.

"Patience, my poor girl!" said he, as he drew her back from the fierce embrace of the destroying angel. "Be patient, and abide Heaven's will. So long as you possess a living soul, all may be restored to its first freshness. These things of matter and creations of human fantasy are fit for nothing but to be burnt, when once they have had their day; but your day is Eternity!"

"Yes," said the wretched girl, whose frenzy seemed now to have sunk down into deep despondency; — "yes; and the sunshine is blotted out of it!"

It was now rumored among the spectators, that all the weapons and munitions of war were to be thrown into the bonfire; with the exception of the world's stock of gunpowder, which, as the safest mode of disposing of it, had already been drowned in the sea. This intelligence seemed to awaken great diversity of opinion. The hopeful philanthropist esteemed it a token that the millennium was already come; while persons of another stamp, in whose view mankind was a breed of bulldogs, prophesied that all the old stoutness, fervor, nobleness, generosity, and magnanimity of the race would disappear; these qualities, as they affirmed, requiring blood for their nourishment. They comforted themselves, however, in the belief that the proposed abolition of war was impracticable for any length of time together.

Be that as it might, numberless great guns, whose thunder had long been the voice of battle—the artillery of the Armada, the battering trains of Marlborough, and the adverse cannon of Napoleon and Wellington—were trundled into the midst of the fire. By the continual addition of dry combustibles, it had now waxed so intense that neither brass nor iron could withstand it. It was wonderful to behold how these terrible instruments of slaughter melted away like playthings of wax. Then the armies of the earth wheeled around the mighty furnace, with their military music playing triumphant marches, and flung in their muskets and swords. The standard-bearers, likewise, cast one look upward at their banners, all tattered with shot-holes, and inscribed with the names of victorious fields; and, giving them a last flourish on the breeze, they lowered them into the flame, which snatched them upward in its rush towards the clouds. This ceremony being over, the world was left without a single weapon in its hands, except possibly a few old king's arms and rusty swords and other trophies of the Revolution in some of our State armories. And now the drums were beaten and the trumpets brayed all together, as a prelude to the proclamation of universal and eternal peace and the announcement that glory was no longer to be won by blood; but that it would henceforth be the contention of the human race to work out the greatest mutual good, and that beneficence, in the future annals of the earth, would claim the praise of valor. The blessed tidings were accordingly promulgated, and caused infinite rejoicings among those who had stood aghast at the horror and absurdity of war.

But I saw a grim smile pass over the seared visage of a stately old commander—by his war-worn figure and rich military dress, he might have been one of Napoleon's famous marshals—who, with the rest of the world's soldiery, had just flung away the sword that had been familiar to his right hand for half-a-century.

"Aye, aye!" grumbled he. "Let them proclaim what they please; but, in the end, we shall find that all this foolery has only made more work for the armorers and cannon-founderies."

"Why, Sir," exclaimed I, in astonishment, "do you imagine that the human race will ever so far return on the steps of its past madness, as to weld another sword, or cast another cannon?"

"There will be no need," observed, with a sneer, one who neither felt benevolence nor had faith in it. "When Cain wished to slay his brother, he was at no loss for a weapon."

"We shall see," replied the veteran commander. — "If I am mistaken, so much the better; but in my opinion—without pretending to philosophize about the matter—the necessity of war lies far deeper than these honest gentlemen suppose. What! Is there a field for all the petty disputes of individuals? and shall there be no great law-court for the settlement of national difficulties? The battle-field is the only court where such suits can be tried."

"You forget, general," rejoined I, "that, in this advanced stage of civilization, Reason and Philanthropy combined will constitute just such a tribunal as is requisite."

"Ah, I had forgotten that, indeed!" said the old warrior, as he limped away.

The fire was now to be replenished with materials that had hitherto been considered of even greater importance to the well-being of society, than the warlike munitions which we had already seen consumed. A body of reformers had travelled all over the earth in quest of the machinery by which the different nations were accustomed to inflict the punishment of death. A shudder passed through the multitude as these ghastly emblems were dragged forward. Even the flames seemed at first to shrink away, displaying the shape and murderous contrivance of each in a full blaze of light, which of itself was sufficient to convince mankind of the long and deadly error of human law. Those old implements of cruelty—those horrible monsters of mechanism—those inventions which it seemed to demand something worse than man's natural heart to contrive, and which had lurked in the dusky nooks of ancient prisons, the subject of terror-stricken legend—were now brought forth to view. Headsmen's axes, with the rust of noble and royal blood upon them, and a vast collection of halters that had choked the breath of plebeian victims, were thrown in together. A shout greeted the arrival of the guillotine, which was thrust forward on the same wheels that had borne it from one to another of the bloodstained streets of Paris. But the loudest roar of applause went up, telling the distant sky of the triumph of the earth's redemption, when the gallows made its appearance. An ill-looking fellow, however, rushed forward, and putting himself in the path of the reformers, bellowed hoarsely, and fought with brute fury to stay their progress.

It was little matter of surprise, perhaps, that the executioner should thus do his best to vindicate and uphold the machinery by which he himself had his livelihood, and worthier individuals their death. But it deserved special note that men of a far different sphere—even of that consecrated class in whose guardianship the world is apt to trust its benevolence—were found to take the hangman's view of the question.

"Stay, my brethren!" cried one of them. "You are misled by a false philanthropy!—you know not what you do. The gallows is a heaven-oriented instrument. Bear it back, then, reverently, and set it up in its old place; else the world will fall to speedy ruin and desolation!"

"Onward, onward!" shouted a leader in the reform. "Into the flames with the accursed instrument of man's bloody policy! How can human law inculcate benevolence and love, while it persists in setting up the gallows as its chief symbol? One heave more, good friends, and the world will be redeemed from its greatest error."

A thousand hands, that nevertheless loathed the touch, now lent their assistance, and thrust the ominous burden far, far into the centre of the raging furnace. There its fatal and abhorred image was beheld, first black, then a red coal, then ashes.

"That was well done!" exclaimed I.

"Yes; it was well done," replied—but with less enthusiasm than I expected—the thoughtful observer, who was still at my side; "well done, if the world be good enough for the measure. Death, however, is an idea that cannot easily be dispensed with, in any condition between the primal innocence and that other purity and perfection which, perchance, we are destined to attain after travelling round the full circle. But, at all events, it is well that the experiment should now be tried."

"Too cold!—too cold!" impatiently exclaimed the young and ardent leader in this triumph. "Let the heart have its voice here, as well as the intellect. And as for ripeness—and as for progress—let mankind always do the highest, kindest, noblest thing that, at any given period, it has attained the perception of; and surely that thing cannot be wrong nor wrongly timed."

I know not whether it were the excitement of the scene, or whether the good people around the bonfire were really growing more enlightened every instant; but they now proceeded to measures, in the full length of which I was hardly prepared to keep them company. For instance, some threw their marriage-certificates into the flames, and declared themselves candidates for a higher, holier, and more comprehensive union than that which had subsisted from the birth of time under the form of the connubial tie. Others hastened to the vaults of banks, and to the coffers of the rich—all of which were opened to the first comer on this fated occasion—and brought entire bales of paper-money to enliven the blaze, and tons of coin to be melted down by its intensity. Henceforth, they said, universal benevolence, uncoined and exhaustless, was to be the golden currency of the world. At this intelligence, the bankers, and speculators in the stocks, grew pale; and a pick-pocket, who had reaped a rich harvest among the crowd, fell down in a deadly fainting-fit. A few men of business burned their day-books and legers, the notes and obligations of their creditors, and all other evidences of debts due to themselves; while perhaps a somewhat larger number satisfied their zeal for reform with the sacrifice of any uncomfortable recollection of their own indebtment. There was then a cry, that the period was arrived, when the title-deeds of landed property should be given to the flames, and the whole soil of the earth revert to the public, from whom it had been wrongfully abstracted, and most unequally distributed among individuals. Another party demanded, that all written constitutions, set forms of government, legislative acts, statute-books, and everything else on which human invention had endeavored to stamp its arbitrary laws, should at once be destroyed, leaving the consummated world as free as the man first created.

Whether any ultimate action was taken with regard to these propositions, is beyond my knowledge; for, just then, some matters were in progress that concerned my sympathies more nearly.

"See!—see!—what heaps of books and pamphlets!" cried a fellow, who did not seem to be a lover of literature. "Now we shall have a glorious blaze!"

"That's just the thing," said a modern philosopher. "Now we shall get rid of the weight of dead men's thought, which has hitherto pressed so heavily on the living intellect that it has been incompetent to any effectual self-exertion. Well done, my lads! Into the fire with them! Now you are enlightening the world, indeed!"

"But what is to become of the Trade?" cried a frantic bookseller.

"Oh, by all means, let them accompany their merchandise," coolly observed an author. "It will be a noble funeral-pile!"

The truth was, that the human race had now reached a stage of progress so far beyond what the wisest and wittiest men of former ages had ever dreamed of, that it would have been a manifest absurdity to allow the earth to be any longer encumbered with their poor achievements in the literary line. Accordingly, a thorough and searching investigation had swept the booksellers' shops, hawkers' stands, public and private libraries, and even the little book-shelf by the country fireside, and had brought the world's entire mass of printed paper, bound or in sheets, to swell the already mountain-bulk of our illustrious bonfire. Thick, heavy folios, containing the labors of lexicographers, commentators, and encyclopediasts, were flung in, and, falling among the embers with a leaden thump, smouldered away to ashes, like rotten wood. The small, richly-gilt French tomes of the last age, with the hundred volumes of Voltaire among them, went off in a brilliant shower of sparkles and little jets of flame; while the current literature of the same nation burned red and blue, and threw an infernal light over the visages of the spectators, converting them all to the aspect of parti-colored fiends. A collection of German stories emitted a scent of brimstone. The English standard authors made excellent fuel, generally exhibiting the properties of sound oak logs. Milton's works, in particular, sent up a powerful blaze, gradually reddening into a coal, which promised to endure longer than almost any other material of the pile. From Shakespeare there gushed a flame of such marvellous splendor that men shaded their eyes as against the sun's meridian glory; nor, even when the works of his own elucidators were flung upon him did he cease to flash forth a dazzling radiance from beneath the ponderous heap. It is my belief, that he is still blazing as fervidly as ever.

"Could a poet but light a lamp at that glorious flame," remarked I, "he might then consume the midnight oil to some good purpose."

"That is the very thing which modern poets have been too apt to do—or, at least, to attempt," answered a critic. "The chief benefit to be expected from this conflagration of past literature, undoubtedly is, that writers will henceforth be compelled to light their lamps at the sun or stars."

"If they can reach so high," said I. "But that task requires a giant, who may afterwards distribute the light among inferior men. It is not every one that can steal the fire from Heaven, like Prometheus; but, when once he had done the deed, a thousand hearths were kindled by it."

It amazed me much to observe how indefinite was the proportion between the physical mass of any given author and the property of brilliant and long-continued combustion. For instance, there was not a quarto volume of the last century—nor, indeed, of the present—that could compete in that particular with a child's little gilt-covered book, containing *Mother Goose's Melodies*. *The Life and Death of Tom Thumb* outlasted the biography of Marlborough. An epic, indeed a dozen of them, was converted to white ashes before the single sheet of an old ballad was half-consumed. In more than one case, too, when volumes of applauded verse proved incapable of anything better than a stifling smoke, an unregarded ditty of some nameless bard—perchance in the corner of a newspaper—soared up among the stars with a flame as brilliant as their own. Speaking of the properties of flame, methought Shelley's poetry emitted a purer light than almost any other productions of his day; contrasting beautifully with the fitful and lurid gleams, and gushes of black vapor, that flashed and eddied from the volumes of Lord Byron. As for Tom Moore, some of his songs diffused an odor like a burning pastille.

I felt particular interest in watching the combustion of American authors, and scrupulously noted, by my watch, the precise number of moments that changed most of them from shabbily printed books to indistinguishable ashes. It would be invidious, however, if not perilous, to betray these awful secrets; so that I shall content myself with observing that it was not invariably the writer most frequent in the public mouth that made the most splendid appearance in the bonfire. I especially remember that a great deal of excellent inflammability was exhibited in a thin volume of poems by Ellery Channing; although, to speak the truth, there were certain portions that hissed and spluttered in a very disagreeable fashion. A curious phenomenon occurred in reference to several writers, native as well as foreign. Their books, though of highly respectable figure, instead of bursting into a blaze or even smouldering out their substance in smoke, suddenly melted away, in a manner that proved them to be ice.

If it be no lack of modesty to mention my own works, it must here be confessed, that I looked for them with fatherly interest, but in vain. Too probably they were changed to vapor by the first action of the heat; at best, I can only hope that, in their quiet way, they contributed a glimmering spark or two to the splendor of the evening.

"Alas, and woe is me!" thus bemoaned himself a heavy-looking gentleman in green spectacles. "The world is utterly ruined, and there is nothing to live for any longer. The business of my life is snatched from me. Not a volume to be had for love or money!"

"This," remarked the sedate observer beside me, "is a book-worm—one of those men who are born to gnaw dead thoughts. His clothes, you see, are covered with the dust of libraries. He has no inward fountain of ideas; and, in good earnest, now that the old stock is abolished, I do not see what is to become of the poor fellow. Have you no word of comfort for him?"

"My dear sir," said I, to the desperate book-worm, "is not Nature better than a book? —is not the human heart deeper than any system of philosophy?—is not life replete with more instruction than past observers have found it possible to write down in maxims? Be of good cheer! The great book of Time is still spread wide open before us; and, if we read it aright, it will be to us a volume of eternal Truth."

"Oh, my books, my books, my precious, printed books!" reiterated the forlorn bookworm. "My only reality was a bound volume; and now they will not leave me even a shadowy pamphlet!"

In fact, the last remnant of the literature of all the ages was now descending upon the blazing heap in the shape of a cloud of pamphlets from the press of the New World. These likewise were consumed in the twinkling of an eye, leaving the earth, for the first time since the days of Cadmus, free from the plague of letters,—an enviable field for the authors of the next generation!

"Well!—and does anything remain to be done?" inquired I, somewhat anxiously. "Unless we set fire to the earth itself, and then leap boldly off into infinite space, I know not that we can carry reform to any farther point."

"You are vastly mistaken, my good friend," said the observer. "Believe me, the fire will not be allowed to settle down, without the addition of fuel that will startle many persons, who have lent a willing hand thus far."

Nevertheless there appeared to be a relaxation of effort, for a little time, during which, probably, the leaders of the movement were considering what should be done next. In the interval, a philosopher threw his theory into the flames; a sacrifice, which, by those who knew how to estimate it, was pronounced the most remarkable that had yet been made. The combustion, however, was by no means brilliant. Some indefatigable people, scorning to take a moment's ease, now employed themselves in collecting all the withered leaves and fallen boughs of the forest, and thereby recruited the bonfire to a greater height than ever. But this was mere by-play.

"Here comes the fresh fuel that I spoke of," said my companion.

To my astonishment, the persons who now advanced into the vacant space, around the mountain of fire, bore surplices, and other priestly garments, mitres, crosiers, and a confusion of popish and protestant emblems, with which it seemed their purpose to consummate the great act of faith. Crosses, from the spires of old cathedrals, were cast upon the heap, with as little remorse as if the reverence of centuries, passing in long array beneath the lofty towers had not looked up to them as the holiest of symbols. The font in which infants were consecrated to God; the sacramental vessels, whence Piety received the hallowed draught; were given to the same destruction. Perhaps it most nearly touched my heart, to see, among these devoted relics fragments of the humble communion-tables and undecorated pulpits which I recognized as having been torn from the meeting-houses of New England. Those simple edifices might have been permitted to retain all of sacred embellishment that their Puritan founders had bestowed, even though the mighty structure of St. Peter's had sent its spoils to the fire of this terrible sacrifice. Yet I felt that these were but the externals of religion, and might most safely be relinquished by spirits that best knew their deep significance.

"All is well," said I, cheerfully. "The wood-paths shall be the aisles of our cathedral—the firmament itself shall be its ceiling. What needs an earthly roof between the Deity and his worshipper? Our faith can well afford to lose all the drapery that even the holiest men have thrown around it, and be only the more sublime in its simplicity."

"True," said my companion; "but will they pause here?"

The doubt implied in his question was well-founded. In the general destruction of books, already described, a holy volume—that stood apart from the catalogue of human literature, and yet, in one sense, was at its head—had been spared. But the Titan of innovation— angel or fiend, double in his nature, and capable of deeds befitting both characters—at first shaking down only the old and rotten shapes of things, had now, as it appeared, laid his terrible hand upon the main pillars, which supported the whole edifice of our moral and spiritual state. The inhabitants of the earth had grown too enlightened to define their faith within a form of words, or to limit the spiritual by any analogy to our material existence. Truths, which the Heavens trembled at, were now but a fable of the world's infancy. Therefore, as the final sacrifice of human error, what else remained to be thrown

upon the embers of that awful pile, except the Book, which, though
a celestial revelation to past ages, was but a voice from a lower sphere
as regarded the present race of man? It was done! Upon the blazing
heap of falsehood and worn-out truth—things that the earth had never
needed, or had ceased to need, or had grown childishly weary of—fell
the ponderous church-Bible, the great old volume, that had lain so long
on the cushion of the pulpit, and whence the pastor's solemn voice had
given holy utterance on so many a Sabbath day. There, likewise, fell the
family-Bible, which the long-buried patriarch had read to his children—
in prosperity or sorrow, by the fireside, and in the summer-shade of
trees—and had bequeathed downward as the heirloom of generations.
There fell the bosom-Bible, the little volume that had been the soul's
friend of some sorely tried Child of Dust, who thence took courage,
whether his trial were for life or death, steadfastly confronting both in
the strong assurance of Immortality.

All these were flung into the fierce and riotous blaze; and then a
mighty wind came roaring across the plain, with a desolate howl, as
if it were the angry lamentation of the earth for the loss of Heaven's
sunshine; and it shook the gigantic pyramid of flame, and scattered the
cinders of half-consumed abominations around upon the spectators.

"This is terrible!" said I, feeling that my check grew pale, and seeing
a like change in the visages about me.

"Be of good courage yet," answered the man with whom I had so
often spoken. He continued to gaze steadily at the spectacle, with a
singular calmness, as if it concerned him merely as an observer.—"Be
of good courage—nor yet exult too much; for there is far less both
of good and evil in the effect of this bonfire than the world might be
willing to believe."

"How can that be?" exclaimed I, impatiently.—"Has it not consumed
everything? Has it not swallowed up, or melted down, every human
or divine appendage of our mortal state that had substance enough to
be acted on by fire? Will there be anything left us, tomorrow morning,
better or worse than a heap of embers and ashes?"

"Assuredly there will," said my grave friend. "Come hither tomorrow
morning, or whenever the combustible portion of the pile shall be
quite burnt out—and you will find among the ashes everything really
valuable that you have seen cast into the flames. Trust me; the world

of tomorrow will again enrich itself with the gold and diamonds which have been cast off by the world of to-day. Not a truth is destroyed—nor buried so deep among the ashes, but it will be raked up at last."

This was a strange assurance. Yet I felt inclined to credit it; the more especially as I beheld, among the wallowing flames, a copy of the Holy Scriptures, the pages of which, instead of being blackened into tinder, only assumed a more dazzling whiteness, as the finger-marks of human imperfection were purified away. Certain marginal notes and commentaries, it is true, yielded to the intensity of the fiery test, but without detriment to the smallest syllable that had flamed from the pen of inspiration.

"Yes;—there is the proof of what you say," answered I, turning to the observer. "But, if only what is evil can feel the action of the fire, then, surely, the conflagration has been of inestimable utility. Yet, if I understand aright, you intimate a doubt whether the world's expectation of benefit would be realized by it."

"Listen to the talk of these worthies," said he, pointing to a group in front of the blazing pile.—"Possibly they may teach you something useful, without intending it."

The persons, whom he indicated, consisted of that brutal and most earthy figure, who had stood forth so furiously in defence of the gallows—the hangman, in short—together with the Last Thief and the Last Murderer; all three of whom were clustered about the Last Toper. The latter was liberally passing the brandy-bottle, which he had rescued from the general destruction of wines and spirits. This little convivial party seemed at the lowest pitch of despondency; as considering that the purified world must needs be utterly unlike, the sphere that they had hitherto known, and therefore but a strange and desolate abode for gentlemen of their kidney.

"The best counsel for all of us, is," remarked the hangman, "that—as soon as we have finished the last drop of liquor—I help you, my three friends, to a comfortable end upon the nearest tree, and then hang myself on the same bough. This is no world for us any longer."

"Poh, poh, my good fellows!" said a dark-complexioned personage, who now joined the group—his complexion was indeed fearfully dark, and his eyes glowed with a redder light than that of the bonfire— "Be not so cast down, my dear friends; you shall see good days yet. There is one thing that these wiseacres have forgotten to throw into the fire, and without which all the rest of the conflagration is just nothing at all—yes; though they had burnt the earth itself to a cinder."

"And what may that be?" eagerly demanded the Last Murderer.

"What but the human heart itself?" said the dark-visaged stranger, with a portentous grin. "And, unless they hit upon some method of purifying that foul cavern, forth from it will re-issue all the shapes of wrong and misery—the same old shapes or worse ones—which they have taken such a vast deal of trouble to consume to ashes. I have stood by this livelong night, and laughed in my sleeve at the whole business. Oh, take my word for it, it will be the old world yet!"

This brief conversation supplied me with a theme for lengthened thought. How sad a truth, if true it were—that Man's age-long endeavor for perfection had served only to render him the mockery of the Evil Principle, from the fatal circumstance of an error at the very root of the matter! The Heart—the Heart—there was the little, yet boundless sphere, wherein existed the original wrong of which the crime and misery of this outward world were merely types. Purify that inward sphere; and the many shapes of evil that haunt the outward, and which now seem almost our only realities, will turn to shadowy phantoms and vanish of their own accord. But, if we go no deeper than the Intellect, and strive, with merely that feeble instrument, to discern and rectify what is wrong, our whole accomplishment will be a dream, so unsubstantial that it matters little whether the bonfire, which I have so faithfully described, were what we choose to call a real event, and a flame that would scorch the finger—or only a phosphoric radiance, and a parable of my own brain.

INTO THE SUN

ROBERT DUNCAN MILNE

This story from San Francisco-based writer Robert Duncan Milne (1844–1899) will surely put readers in mind of the fiction of Jules Verne, in which hot-air ballooning was a technologically sophisticated means of transcontinental transportation. It appeared in the November 18, 1882 issue of The Argonaut, *and readers dismayed by its cliffhanger ending will be happy to know that Milne published a sequel (reprinted directly after this story) less than a month later.*

A nd so you think, doctor, that the comet which has just been reported from South America is the same as last year's comet—the one discovered first by Cruls at Rio Janeiro, I mean, and which was afterward so plainly visible to us here all through the month of October?"

"Judging from the statement in the papers regarding its general appearance, and the course which it is traveling, I do not see to what other conclusion we can come. It is approaching the sun from the same quarter as last year's comet; it resembles it in appearance; it's rate of motion is as great, if not greater; all these things are very strong arguments of identity."

"But, then, how do you account for so speedy a return? This is only the end of August, and last year's comet was computed to have passed its perihelion about the eighteenth of September—scarcely a year ago. Even Encke's and Biela's comets, which are denizens of our solar system, so to speak, have longer periods than that."

"I account for it simply on the hypothesis that this comet passes so close to the sun that its motion is retarded, and its course consequently changed after every such approach. I believe, with Mr. Proctor and Professor Boss, that this is the comet of 1843 and 1880; that it is moving in a succession of eccentric spirals, the curvatures of which have reduced its periods of revolution from perhaps many hundreds of years to—at its last recorded return—thirty-seven years, then to two and a fraction, and now to less than one; and that its ultimate destination is to be precipitated into the sun."

"This is certainly startling, supposing your hypothesis to be correct; and should such a casualty happen, what result would you anticipate?"

"That demands some consideration. Take another cigar, and we shall look into the matter."

The foregoing conversation took place in the rooms of my friend Dr. Arkwright, upon Market Street; the time was about eleven o'clock at night; the date, the twenty-seventh of August; the interrogation had been mine and the answers the Doctor's; I may add that the doctor was a chemist of no mean attainments, and took great interest in all scientific discussions and experiments.

"The effect of a collision of a comet with the sun," observed the doctor, as he lit his cigar, "would depend upon a good many conditions. It would depend primarily upon the mass, momentum, and velocity of the comet—something, too, upon its constitution. Let me see that paragraph again. Ah, here it is," and the doctor proceeded to read from the paper:

" 'RIO JANEIRO, August 18th.—The comet was again visible last evening, before and after sunset, about thirty degrees from the sun. Mr. Cruls pronounces it identical with the comet of last year. It is approaching the sun at the rate of two and a half degrees a day. R.A., at noon yesterday, 178 degrees, 24 minutes; Dec. 83 degrees, 40 minutes, S.'

"Now this," he went on, "corresponds exactly with the position and motion of last year's comet. It came from a point nearly due south of the sun, consequently was invisible to the northern before perihelion."

"Pardon me," I interrupted, "but you remember the newspaper predictions regarding last year's comet were to the effect that it would speedily become invisible to us here, whereas it continued to adorn the morning skies for weeks, till it faded away in the remote distance."

"That was because the nature of its orbit was not distinctly understood. The plane of the comet's orbit cut the plane of the earth's orbit nearly at right angles, but the major axis or general direction of the orbit in space, was also inclined some fifty degrees to our plane; and so it came about that while the approach of the comet was from a point somewhat east of south, its return journey into space was along a line some twenty degrees south of west, which threw its course nearly along the line of the celestial equator; consequently, last year's comet was visible in the early morning, not only to us, but to every inhabitant of the earth between the sixtieth parallel north and the south pole, until the vast distance caused it to disappear. But, as I was going to say when you interrupted me, if the distance of the comet from the sun was only thirty degrees when observed at Rio Janeiro, nine days ago, and its speed was then two and a half degrees a day, it can not be far from perihelion now, especially as its speed increases as it approaches the sun."

"Suppose it should strike the sun this time," said I. "What results would you predict?"

"A solid globe," replied the doctor, "of the size of our earth, if falling upon the sun with the momentum resulting from direct attraction from its present position in space, would engender sufficient heat to maintain the solar fires at their existing standard, without further supply, for about ninety years. This calculation does not involve great scientific or mathematical knowledge, but, on the contrary, is as simple as it is reliable, because we have positive data to go upon in the mass and momentum of our planet. But with a comet the case is different. We do not know what elements its nucleus is composed of. It is true we do not know the value of its momentum; but what does that tell us if we do not know its density or mass? A momentum of four hundred miles a second—the estimated rate of speed of the present comet at perihelion—would undoubtedly engender fierce combustion were the comet a ponderable body. On the other hand large bodies composed of fluid matter highly volatilized might collide with the sun without any appreciable effect."

"Have we any data to go upon this matter?" I inquired.

"With regard to our own sun," replied the doctor, "we have not; but several suggestive circumstances have occurred in the case of other suns which lead us to infer that something similar might happen to our own. Some years ago, a star in the constellation Cygnus was observed to suddenly blaze out with extraordinary brilliancy, its lustre increasing from that of a star of the sixth magnitude—but faintly distinguishable to the unaided eye—to that of a star of the first. This brilliancy was maintained for several days, when it resumed its original condition. Now, it is fair to infer that this great increase of light may have been caused by the precipitation of some large solid body—a planet, a comet, or perhaps another sun—upon the sun in question; and, as light and heat are now understood to be merely different modes or expressions of the same quality of motion, it is fair to infer further that the increment of heat corresponded to that of light."

"What, then, do you suppose would be the natural effect upon ourselves, here, on this planet, by some such catastrophe as you have just imagined happening to our own sun!" I asked.

"The light and heat of our luminary might be increased a hundred fold, or a thousand fold, according to the nature of the collision. One can conceive of combustion so fierce as to evaporate all of our oceans in one short minute, or even to volatilize the solid matter of our planet in less than that time, like a globule of mercury in a hot-air chamber. 'Large' and 'small' are not absolute, but relative, terms in Nature's vocabulary; both are equally amenable to her laws," sententiously observed the doctor.

"A comforting reflection, certainly," I remarked. "Let us hope we shall not be favored with any such experience."

"Who can tell?" rejoined the doctor, as he rose from his seat. "Excuse me for a minute. You know there is a balloon ascension from Woodwards Gardens to-morrow, and there is a new ingredient I am going to introduce at the inflation. The stuff wants a little more mixing. Take another cigar. I won't be a minute."

I sat back and meditated as I listened to the retreating footsteps of the doctor, as he passed into an adjoining room. I looked at the clock. It was half past eleven. It was a warm night for San Francisco in August—remarkably so, in fact. I got up to open the window, and as I did so the doctor entered the room again.

"What is that?" I exclaimed involuntarily, as I threw up the sash. And the spectacle which met my gaze as I did so, certainly warranted the exclamation.

Doctor Arkwright's rooms were on the north side of Market Street, and the inferior height of the buildings opposite afforded an uninterrupted view of the horizon of the south and east. Over the tops of the houses to the east could be seen a thin, livid line, marking the waters of the bay, and beyond it the serrated outline of the Alameda hills. All this was normal and just as I had seen it a hundred times before, but in the northeast the sky was lit up with a lurid, dull red glow, which extended northward along the horizon in a broadening arc, till the view was shut out by the street line to our left. This light resembled in all respects the *aurora borealis* except that of color. Instead of the cold, clear radiance of the northern light, we were confronted with an angry, blood-red glare which ever and anon shot forks, and tongues, and streamers of fire upward toward the zenith. It was as if some vast conflagration were in progress to our north. But what, I asked myself, could produce so extensive, so powerful an illumination? Vast forest fires, or the burning of large cities, make themselves manifest by a sky-reflected glare for great distances, but they do not display the regularity—or the harmony, so to speak—which was apparent in the present instance. The conclusion was inevitable that the phenomenon was not local in its source.

As we looked out the window we could see that the scene had arrested the attention of others besides ourselves. Little knots of people had collected on the sidewalk; larger knots at the street corners; and the passers-by kept turning their heads to gaze at the strange spectacle. At the same time the air was growing heavier and more sultry every minute. There was not a breath stirring, but an ominous and preternatural calm seemed to brood over the city, like that in which some climates is the precursor of a storm, and which here is frequently known as "earthquake weather."

The doctor broke the silence.

"This is something quite out of the run of common events," he exclaimed. "The light in the north must have a cause. All the Sonoma and Mendocino redwoods, with the pineries of Oregon and Washington Territory thrown in, would not make such a blaze as that. Besides, that is not the sort of sky-reflection a forest fire would cause."

"Just my own idea," I asserted.

"Let us see if we can not connect it with a wider origin. It is now nearly midnight. That light is in the north. The sun's rays are now illuminating the other side of the globe. It is, therefore, sunrise on the Atlantic, noon in Eastern Europe, and sunset in western Asia. When you came here, scarcely an hour ago, the heavens were clear, and the temperature normal. Whatever has given rise to this extraordinary phenomenon has done so within the last hour. Even since we began to look I see that the extremity of the illuminated arc has shifted further to the east. That light has its origin in the sun, but it altogether passes the bounds of experience."

"Might we not connect it with the comet we have just been speaking about?" I suggested. "It should now be near its perihelion point."

"That must be it," acquiesced the doctor. "Who knows but that the fiery wanderer has actually come in contact with the sun? Let us go out."

We put on our hats, and left the building. All along the sidewalks we came upon excited groups staring at the strange light, and speculating upon its cause. The general expression of opinion referred it so some vast forest fire, though there were not wanting religious enthusiasts who saw in it a manifestation of divine wrath, or a portent of the predicted consummation of all things; for in the uninformed human mind there is no middle ground between the grossly practical and the purely fanatical. We hurried along Market Street and turned down Kearney, where the crowds were even denser and more anxious-looking. Arrived at the *Chronicle* office, I noticed that a succession of messengers from the various telegraph offices were encountering each other on the stairs of the building.

"If you will wait a minute," I said to the doctor, "I will run upstairs and find out what is the matter."

"Strange news from the East," said the telegraphic editor, hurriedly, in answer to my question, at the same time pointing to a little pile of dispatches. "These have been coming in for the last half hour from all points of the Union."

I took up one, and read the contents:

NEW YORK, 3:15 A.M.—Extraordinary light just broke out over the eastern horizon. Very red and threatening. Seems to proceed from a great distance out at sea. People unable to assign cause.

Another ran as follows:

NEW ORLEANS, 4:10 A.M.—vivid conflagration reflected in the sky, a little north of east. General sentiment that vast fires have sprung up in the cane-brakes. Population abroad and anxious.

"There are a score more," remarked the editor, "from Chicago, Memphis, Canada—everywhere, in fact—all to the same purpose. What do you make of it?"

"The phenomenon is evidently universal," I said. "It must have its origin in the sun. Do you notice how hot and stifling the air is getting? Have you any dispatches from Europe?"

"None yet. Ah, here is a cablegram repeated from New York," said the editor, taking a dispatch from the hand of a messenger who just then entered. "This may tell us something. Listen:

"LONDON, 7:45 A.M.—Five minutes ago sun's heat became overpowering. Business stopped. People falling dead in streets. Thermometer risen from 52 degrees to 113. Still rising. Message from Greenwich Observatory says'—

"The dispatch stops abruptly there," interpolated the editor, "and the New York operator goes on thus: 'Message cut short. Nothing more through cable. Intense alarm everywhere. Light and heat increasing."

"Well," said I, "it must be as Doctor Arkwright suggested. The comet observed again at Rio Janeiro, ten days ago, has fallen into the sun. Heaven only knows what we had better do."

"I shall edit these dispatches and get the paper out, at any rate," said the editor with determination. "Ah, here comes the ice for the printers," as half a dozen men filed past the door, each with a sack upon his shoulder. "The paper must come out if the earth burns for it. I fancy we can hold out until sunrise, and before then the worst may be over."

I left the office, rejoined the doctor in the street, and told him the news.

"There is no doubt about it," he remarked at once. "The comet of last year has fallen into the sun. All the telegraphic messages were nearly identical in time, as it is now just midnight here, and consequently about four o'clock in New York, and eight o'clock in England."

"What had we better do?" queried I.

"I do not think there is any cause for immediate alarm," replied the doctor. "We shall see whether the heat increases materially between now and sunrise, and take measures accordingly. Meanwhile, let us look about us."

The scenes of alarm were intensified in the streets as we passed along. It seemed as if half the population of the city had left their houses, and gathered in the most public places. Thousands of people were pushing and jostling each other in the neighborhood of the various newspaper offices in frantic endeavors to get a glimpse of the bulletin boards, where the substance of the various telegrams was posted up as fast as they came in. Multitudes of hacks and express wagons were driving hither and thither, crowded with family parties seemingly intent upon leaving the city, and probably without any definite aim or accurate comprehension of what they were doing or whither they were going.

As the hours wore on toward morning the angry red arch moved farther along the horizon, its outlines grew bolder and brighter, and its flaming crest towered higher in the heavens. Nothing could be conceived more ominous or ghastly, more calculated to produce feelings of brutish terror, and to convince the spectator of his utter powerlessness to cope with an inevitable and inexorable event, than this blood-red arch of flame which spread over one fourth of the apparent horizon. The air, too, was momentarily growing heavier and more stifling. A glance at a thermometer in one of the hotels gave a temperature of 114 degrees.

Between two and three o'clock four successive alarms of fire were sounded from the lower quarters of the city. Two large wholesale houses and a liquor store, in three contiguous blocks, caught fire, evidently the work of incendiaries. Multitudes of the worst rabble collected, as if by concert, in the business quarters. Shops and warehouses were broken into and looted—the police force, though working vigorously, not being strong enough to arrest the work of pillage, backed as it was by the moral terrors of the night, and the general paralysis which unnerved the better class of citizens. Strange scenes were being enacted at every corner and on every street. Groups of women kneeling upon sidewalks, and rending the air with prayers and lamentations, were jostled aside by ruffians wild and furious with liquor. A procession of religious fanatics, chanting shrill and discordant hymns, and bearing lanterns in their hands, passed unheeded through the crowded streets, and we could afterward watch them threading their way up the steep side of Telegraph Hill. In short, the terrible and bizarre effects of that fearful night would overtax the pen of a Dante to describe, or the pencil of a Doré to portray.

"Let us go home," said the doctor, looking at his watch. "It is now half past three. The temperature of the atmosphere is evidently rising. The chances are that it will become unbearable after sunrise. We must consider what is best to do."

We pushed our way back through the crowded streets, past despairing and terror-stricken men and wailing women; but as we passed the bulletin boards at the corner of Bush and Kearny streets, it was encouraging to mark that at least one earthly industry would continue to go on till the mechanism could run no longer, and the world would, at any rate, get full particulars of its approaching doom, so long as wires could transmit them, compositors set them in type, and pressmen print them. I felt that the power and grandeur of the press had never been more fully exemplified than in the regular and ceaseless pulsations of its machinery as the daily issue was being thrown off, with the news that the other hemisphere was in conflagration, and that a few short hours would in all probability witness the same catastrophe in our town.

The last two wagons which had driven up with ice for the employees had been boarded and sacked by the thirsty mob, and, looking down into the press room as I entered the building, I could see the pressman stripped to the waist in that terrible hot air bath, while upstairs the telegraphic editor was in similar *deshabille*, with the additional feature of a wet towel round his temples. He motioned to the latest dispatch from New York as I entered. I took it up and read as follows:

NEW YORK, 6:00 A.M.—Sun just risen. Heat terrible. Air suffocating. People seeking shade. Thousands bathing off the docks. Thousands killed by sunstroke.

"Almost a recapitulation of the London message of three hours ago," I said as I hurried out. "Three hours hence we may expect the same here."

I rejoined the doctor in the street, and together we proceeded to his apartments.

"Now," said he, as I told him the purport of the last message, "there is only one thing to be done if we wish to save our lives. It is a chance if even this plan will succeed, but at all events there *is* a chance.

"What is it?" I asked eagerly.

"I take it," answered he, "that the increase of heat and light which will accrue as soon as the sun rises above the horizon must prove fatal to all animal life beneath the influence of his beams. The population of Europe, and by this time, I doubt not, all of this country east of the Mississippi, is next to annihilated. With us it is but a question of time unless—"

"Unless what?" I exclaimed excitedly, as he paused meditatively.

"Unless we are willing to run a great risk," he added. "You are a philosopher enough to know that heat and light are simply modes of motion—expressions, so to speak, of the same molecular action of the elements they pass through or agitate. They have no intrinsic being in themselves, no entity, no existence, as it were, independent of outside matter. In their case the two forms of outside matter affected by them are the ether pervading space and the atmosphere of our planet. Do you follow?"

"Certainly," I replied impatiently, for I dreaded one of the doctor's disquisitions at such a critical moment as this. "But my dear sir, what is the practical application of your theorem? How can we apply it to the case in point?"

"In this wise," he went on: "heat—that is, the heat we will have to do with now—is caused by the action of the sun's rays upon our atmosphere. If we get beyond the limits of that atmosphere, what then?

Simply, we have no heat. Ascend to a different altitude, even under the cloudless rays of a vertical sun, and you will freeze to death. The limit of perpetual snow is not an extreme one?"

"I catch your idea perfectly," I assented. "I concede the accuracy of your premise. But what does it avail us? The Sierra Nevada mountains are practically as far off as the peaks of the Himalayas."

"There are other means," rejoined the doctor, "of attaining the necessary altitude. A balloon ascension, you are aware, was to have taken place from Woodward's Gardens. I was going to assist at the inflation, to test a new method of generating gas. I now propose that we endeavor to gain possession of the balloon and make the ascension. I do not think we shall be anticipated or thwarted in doing so."

"We must remember that the risk of the balloon bursting, through the expansion of the gas, is great; for we shall be exposed, not only to its normal expansion, should we penetrate the upper atmospheric strata, but to its abnormal expansion through heat, should we fail to do so in time."

"It is shaking the dice with death in any case," I answered and proceeded to assist the doctor in packing the apparatus and chemicals he had prepared over night; and having done so, we left the building and hastened southward along Market Street. The cars were not running, and the carriages we saw paid no heed to our importunities; so the precious time seemed to fly past while we swiftly covered the mile which separated us from the gardens. The gates were luckily open, and none of the employees visible, so we made for the spot where the balloon, half-inflated, lay like some slimy antediluvian monster in its lair. We adjusted the apparatus and arranged the ropes as speedily as possible, and waited anxiously while the great bag slowly swelled and shook, rearing itself and falling back by turns, but gradually assuming more and more spherical proportions.

Meanwhile, we had again opportunity to observe the condition of the atmosphere and the heavens. It was already half past four, and in less than an hour the sun would spring up in the east. The pale, bluish tints of daybreak were beginning to assert themselves beside the lurid semi-circle which flamed above them. This latter changed to a hard, coppery hue as daylight became stronger, but preserved its contour unchanged. The heat became more oppressive, the thermometer we had brought with us now registering 133 degrees. Strange sounds were wafted in from the city—meaningless, indeed, but rendered fearfully suggestive by the circumstances of the morning. The animals howled unceasingly from their cages, and we could hear their frantic struggles for liberty. One cat-like form that had made good its escape shot past us in the gloom. Had the whole menagerie been set free at that moment, we should have had nothing to fear from them, so great is the influence elemental crises exert over brute creation.

We had at last the satisfaction of seeing the great globe swing clear of the ground, though not yet full inflated, and tug at the ropes which moored it. We had already placed the ballast-bags and other necessary articles in the car, when, perspiring at every pore, we simultaneously cut the last ropes, and rose heavily into the air. There was not a breath of wind stirring, but our course was guided slightly east in the direction of the bay.

It was now broad daylight, and the upper limb of the sun appeared above the horizon as we estimated our altitude from surrounding objects at about a thousand feet. As the full orb appeared the heat became more intense, and by the doctor's direction we swathed out heads in flannel, sprinkled sparingly with a preparation of ether and alcohol, the swift evaporation of which imparted coolness for a short time. The sky had now assumed the appearance of a vast brazen dome, and the waters of the ocean to the west and the bay beneath us reflected the dull, dead, pitiless glare with horrible fidelity. We had taken the precaution to hang heavy blankets upon the ropes sustaining the car, and these we kept sparingly moistened with water. Our own thirst was as intense as our perspiration was profuse, and we had divested ourselves of everything but our woolen underclothing—wool being a non-conductor, and therefore as effective in excluding heat as retaining it. We were provided with a powerful ship telescope, and also a large binocular glass of long range, and so far as the discomforts of the situation would permit us we took observations of the prospect beneath. To the unaided eye the city simply presented a patch of little rectangles at the end of a brown peninsula, but through our glasses the streets and houses became surprisingly plain. Little squat black forms were to be seen moving, falling down, and lying in the streets. Down by the city front the wharves were seen to be lined with nude or semi-nude bodies, which dived into the water and remained submerged, with the exception of their heads, though these disappeared at short intervals below the surface. Thousands upon thousands of people were thus engaged. The spectacle would have been utterly absurd and ludicrous had it not been tremendous in its awful suggestiveness.

"The mortality will be terrible, I fear," said the doctor, "if things do not change for the better soon, and I see no prospect of that. Our thermometer already marks 147 degrees even at this altitude. We are in the *tepidarium* of a thrice-heated Turkish bath. And if this is the case at a barometric altitude of eleven thousand feet—nearly two perpendicular miles—what must it be down there? It is too terrible to contemplate!"

"It is only seven o'clock yet," I remarked, looking at my watch. "The sun is scarcely an hour high."

"We must throw out more ballast," said the doctor, "and reach the highest strata at all hazards." He threw out a forty-pound bag of sand."

We shot upward with tremendous velocity for several minutes, when our ascent again became regular. We now remarked, with intense relief, that the thermometer did not rise—that, in fact, it had fallen about two degrees; though this relief was counterbalanced by the extreme difficulty of breathing the rarefied air at this immense altitude, which we estimated by the barometer at twenty-five thousand feet, or nearly five perpendicular miles. We therefore opened the valve and discharged a quantity of gas, and presently descended into a stratum of dense fog. This fog reminded me of the steam which rises from tropical vegetation during the rainy season, and I mentioned the fact to the doctor.

"If these fogs," replied he, "would only rest upon the city, they might shield it from destruction, but in a case of this kind we have no meteorological data to go on. No one can estimate either the amount of heat or the meteorological results it is now producing on the surface of the earth five miles below us."

The stratum of fog in which we now were was dense and impenetrable. We lay in it as in a steam-bath, the balloon not seeming to drift, but swaying sluggishly from side to side, like a sail flapping idly against a mast in a calm.

Hour after hour passed like this, the temperature still ranging from 130 to 140 degrees Fahrenheit. The doctor preserved his wonted equanimity.

"I have grave apprehensions," he remarked impressively as if in answer to my thoughts, "that the fiery cataclysm, a foreboding of which has run through all systems of philosophies and religions through all ages, and which seems to be, as it were, ingrained in the inner consciousness of man, is now upon us. I am determined, however, not to fall a victim to the fiery energy that has been evoked, and shall anticipate such a fate by an easier and less disagreeable one," and as she spoke he motioned significantly toward his right hip.

"Do you think, then," said I, "that an act under such circumstances"—designedly employing a vague periphrasis on such an unpleasant topic—"is morally defensible?"

"What can it matter?" returned the doctor, with a shrug. "Of two alternatives, both leading to the same end, common sense accepts the easier. A refusal to touch the hemlock would not have saved Socrates."

In spite of the terrible forebodings which filled me, the exigencies of the situation seemed to render any brain preternaturally concentrated and abnormally active. The surrounding stillness, the lack of sound of any description, the dreamy warmth of the dense mist in which we lay, exercised a sedative influence, and rendered the mind peculiarly impressionable to action from within.

"We have no means, then, of calculating the probable intensity of the heat at the earth's surface?" I asked.

"None whatever," replied the doctor. "We are now at an indicated elevation, by barometrical pressure, of twenty-two thousand feet. We are probably actually much higher, as the steam in which we lie is acting on the barometer. Atmospheric conditions like the present, at such an altitude, are totally beyond the experience of science. They might be, and probably are, caused by the action of intense heat upon hotter surfaces below us. To the fact of their presence, however, we owe our existence. This atmosphere, though peculiarly favorable to the passage of heat rays through it, is incapable of retaining them."

"Supposing," I went on, in a wildly speculative mood, engendered by the excitement of the occasion, "supposing that the heat of the surface of the earth were sufficiently intense to melt metals—iron, for instance—the most refractory substances, in fact. Take a further flight: supposing that such heat were ten times intensified, what would be its effect on our planet?"

"The solid portions—the crust with everything upon it—would be the first to experience the effects of such a catastrophe. Then the oceans would boil, and their surface waters, at any rate, be converted into steam."

"What then?" I continued.

"This steam would ascend to the upper regions of the atmosphere till it reached an equilibrium of rarefaction, when its expansion would cool it, upon which rapid condensation would follow, and it would descend to earth in the form of rain. The more sudden and energetic the heat, the sooner would this result be accomplished, and the more copious the precipitation of the succeeding rain. After the first terrible crisis, the grand compensation of natural law would come into play, and the face of the planet would be protected from further harm by the shield of humid vapor—the *vis medicatrix naturae*, so to speak. Equilibrium would be restored, but most organisms would meanwhile have perished.

"Most organisms, you say," I repeated, inquiringly.

"It is possible," said the doctor, "that ocean infusoria, and even some of the comparatively higher forms of ocean life, might survive. It is also possible that terrestrial animals occupying high altitudes—mountaineers, for example, whose homes are deep snow and glaciers, denizens of the frozen zone, and beings similarly situated—might escape. This would altogether depend upon the intensity and duration of the heat. We must remember that *size*, looked at from a universal point of view, is merely relative. If we consider our planet as a six-inch ball, our oceans, with their significant average depth of a few miles, would be aptly represented by a film of the finest writing paper. How long, think you, would a watery film, such as that, last a few feet from a suddenly stirred fire?"

I bowed acquiescence to the conclusion drawn from the simile, and the doctor proceeded:

"There can be no longer any doubt that the present elemental convulsion is due to the collision of the comet with the sun. Knowing what we do of its orbit from last year's computation, its precipitation upon the solar surface has taken place on the side farthest from our own position in space. We do not, therefore, experience so sudden and so fierce atmospherical excitement as would otherwise have followed. It now remains to be seen what the duration of the effect will be."

During the latter portion of our conversation a low moaning sound, which had been heard for the past few minutes, was growing more pronounced and seemingly coming nearer. At the same time the barometer was observed to be falling rapidly.

"That is the sound of wind," I exclaimed. "I have heard it on tropical deserts and on tropical seas. I can not be mistaken. It comes from the east."

"The hot air from the parched continent is approaching," said the doctor. "Scientifically speaking, atmospheric convection is taking place, and we shall bear the brunt of it."

As he spoke the balloon was seized with a violent tremor. It vibrated from apex to car, and the next moment was struck by the most terrific tornado it is possible to imagine. The blast was like the torrid breath of a furnace, and we involuntarily covered our heads with out blankets, and clutched convulsively to the frail bulwarks of the car, which was being dragged on at a tremendous velocity, and at a horribly acute angle, by the distended gas-bag which towered ahead of us. Luckily we had both clutched mechanically at the railing on the side whence the wind came, to let go which hold would have meant instant precipitation over the opposite side of the car into the yawning gulf beneath. For less than a minute, so far as my stricken and scattered senses could compute, we were borne on by this terrific simoom, when, suddenly, we found ourselves, as before, in the midst of a preternatural calm. We had evidently drifted into an eddy of the cyclone; for I could hear its sullen and awful roar at some distance to our right. Hardly had we composed ourselves when the blast struck us again; this time on the opposite side of the car. Again we were hurled forward by the resistless elemental fury, but this time in a sensibly downward direction. The blast had struck us from above, and was hurling us before it—down, down, to inevitable destruction. Fortunately, the comparative bulk of the balloon offered more resistance than the car to this downward progress. Down, down, we sped, till, of a sudden, we emerged from the cloud-strata and obtained a brief and abrupt glimpse of the scene below. The counterblasts of the past few minutes had apparently compensated each other's action, for we found ourselves just over the city.

The city? There was no city. I recognized, indeed, the contour of the peninsula, and the well-known outlines of the bay and islands, through

casual rifts in the dense clouds of steam which rose in volumes from
below. Well nigh stupefied and maddened as I was by the intense heat,
a horrible curiosity seized me to peer into the dread mystery beneath
and while with one scorched and writhing hand I held the blankets,
which had not yet parted with the moisture gathered from the clouds
above, to my aching head and temples, with the other I raised the
powerful binocular to my eyes. Through drifting rifts of steam-
clouds that obscured the scene, I caught glimpses which filled me
with unutterable and nameless horror. Neither streets nor buildings
were decipherable where the city once had been. The eye rested upon
nothing but irregular and misshapen piles of vitrified slag and calcined
ashes. Everything was as scarred in a ruinous silence as the ruined
surface of the moon. There was neither flame nor fire to be seen.
Things seemed to have long passed the stage of active combustion,
as though all the elements necessary to sustain flame had already
been abstracted from them. Here and there an ominous dark red
glow showed, however, that the lava into which the fair city had been
transformed was still incandescent. The sand dunes to the west shone
like glaciers or dull mirrors through the steam fissures, and long
shapeless masses of what resembled charred wood were strewn here
and there over the surface of the bay. Less than five seconds served to
reveal all that I have taken so long to describe. The binocular, too hot
to hold, dropped from my hand. At the same moment the balloon was
again struck by the cyclone, and dashed eastward with the same fury as
before. The doctor caught convulsively at the railing of the car, missed
his hold, and with a wild, despairing shriek, outstretched arms, and
starting eyes fixed upon mine, disappeared headlong into the abyss.

★ ★ ★

I am alone in the balloon—perhaps alone in the world. My companion
has been hurled to a fiery death below. His awful shriek still rings in
my ears. It sounds over the sullen roar of the cyclone. I am whirled
resistlessly onward.

The blast shifts. Again the balloon pauses in one of the strange eddies
formed by this strange simoom. The wind dies away to a moan. It rises
again. It writhes around the car like convulsive struggles of some giant

reptile in the throes of death. It seizes me again in its resistless clutch. The balloon is being whirled toward the earth.

I am falling. But no—it seems to me that the earth—the plutonic, igneous earth—is rising toward me. With lightning-like rapidity it seems to hurl itself up through the air to meet me. I hear the roar of flames mingling with the roar of the blast. I see the seething, bubbling waste of waters through rifts in the clouds of steam.

I am nearing the molten surface. My feeling has changed. I am conscious that it has ceased to rise. I feel that I am falling now—falling into the fiery depths below. Nearer—nearer yet; scorched and blackened by the awful heat as I approach—I fall—down—down—down—

PLUCKED FROM THE BURNING

ROBERT DUNCAN MILNE

This direct sequel to Milne's "Into the Sun" appeared in the December 16, 1882 issue of The Argonaut. *Though it shows the horrendous aftermath of the worldwide conflagration caused by that story's comet plunge into the sun, its unusually upbeat ending is surprisingly progressive.*

W here am I?" I exclaimed, as I rubbed my eyes and looked around me, gazing with mingled curiosity and awe on the unaccustomed objects which I saw.

There responded a long-bearded and grey-serged man in an unknown tongue, as he bent over the pallet on which I was lying, and proceeded to anoint my skin, (I perceived that I was naked), with an unguent that recalled the fancied perfume of some oriental nard that I had read of, but could not at the moment identify.

I tried to raise my head from the pillow, but the muscles refused to respond to the action of the will. Helplessly I dropped my eyes to the inferior portion of my frame and beheld, with sickening apprehension that I was scarred and blistered from neck to foot. At the same I perceived that that I was lying upon robes or sheets of the finest silk. Such extraordinary care contrasted strangely with the paltry surroundings of the chamber, and such luxury applied to myself—for the extent of it I could appreciate—strangely with the seemingly ascetic poverty of the person who stood beside me. I had no difficulty, however, in determining from the architectural points of the chamber, and the features, dress, and intonation of my companion, that I was in some Mongolian settlement—how or where was an inconceivable mystery. Memory, for the moment, was a blank. Suddenly a flood of thoughts surged through my brain. In an instant I recalled the events of that fearful day in San Francisco—the ascent in the balloon, the aspect of the ruined city, the tragic death of the doctor, and my own imminent destruction when I became senseless.

How long I had lain in a comatose condition, I, of course, do not know; but, judging from the extraordinary distance traversed in the interim, either time must have been considerable, or I must have been hurled with inconceivable velocity, in the heart of the storm, to where I now lay.

To cross an ocean and hundreds of leagues of continent in a condition of insensibility does not fall to the lot of every one, and my astonishment may be imagined when I at last discovered how I had been found by the monks of the Buddhist monastery of Badid upon the northern slopes of the Himalayas, on a plateau near by, lying apparently dead, near the fragments of what had once been the balloon and the car.

My theory is that my balloon was caught up by a body of heated air of vast volume, when about to plunge into the fiery abyss, and that this body of air, naturally rising to an upper stratum, was, in its turn, pressed forward by an air-current of tremendous velocity, naturally following the westward course of the sun. My strange appearance and extraordinary manner in which I had reached their neighborhood, coupled with the recent tremendous spectacle which they had witnessed in the nocturnal heavens—for by the time the sun had risen upon Central Asia the force of the comet's collision had been spent, and the heat experienced at this altitude had been barely sufficient to melt a few feet of the everlasting snows—the entire circumstances attending my advent among them, I repeat, had caused them to regard me with a certain superstitious awe, and to treat me with the consideration I have already referred to.

So far as this portion of our earth was concerned, the fierce and fiery cataclysm which had wrought such ruin upon those regions subjected to the full potency of the blazing orb had been represented only by the terrible auroral display, which, according to the monks, had traveled round the half circuit of the heavens from west to east in blood-red anger, but had faded away before the first beams of morning brightened the sky. They regarded it, I also learned, as a presage of the second coming of the original Buddha.

The seclusion of the Thibetan highlanders is so great, and their intercourse with the outside world so limited and infrequent, that it was weeks before the vague and terrible rumors which were wafted faintly from the lowlands of China began to impress them more strongly with the possible truth of the terrible story which I had attempted to convey to them by signs and broken expressions.

Day by day the desire became more intense within me to revisit the haunts of men, and learn the worst regarding the catastrophe. I had already acquired, during my two months' sojourn at the monastery, a sufficient acquaintance with the Thibetan tongue to enable me to express my self upon ordinary topics with considerable fluency, and my representations exercised such an effect upon Dchiamdcham, one of the most enlightened monks, that he yielded to my solicitations and consented to persuade the rest to make a journey of exploration. As by degrees I gained greater command of the language, and Dchiamdcham and myself managed to reach the intellects of the monks, blinded as they were by ignorance and prejudice, and blurred by superstition, it became evidence that their curiosity was becoming piqued as fast as their feelings were becoming interested. When the spring opened, and the snows melted away upon the surrounding slopes, they were ready to accompany me on an expedition to the plains.

Dchiamdcham had not in vain employed his arguments and exhausted his store of rhetoric in convincing his brethren that one of their main duties lay, in a case of this sort, in assisting mankind. Accordingly, a troop of thirty of the youngest members of the society were drafted for the expeditions, the rest, including the older and weaker of the brethren, being left to guard the several interests of the fraternity. The villages and settlements we passed upon our way for the first two days were tenanted by natives who repeated the strange tales we had previously heard.

A day or two later, after crossing many spurs and mountain ranges, we debouched upon the valley of Kinsha Kiang, or, as it is called during its lower course, the Yangtze-Kiang. As we gradually descended from the higher plateaus we entered regions where the vegetation was parched and lifeless. Houses and villages were either desolate or tenanted only by half-famished creatures who answered our questions in a dazed and bewildered way. Despair seemed to have settled on them. Their flocks and herds seemed scarcely able to sustain existence upon the scant and desiccated herbage. A calamity which they were able neither to comprehend or cope with had fallen upon them and deprived them of heart and courage.

We had remarked for the past few days that the climate had changed to a greater degree than would, under ordinary circumstances, have been the case. Humidity was its prevailing feature. Dense cloud masses rolled over our heads and obscured the sun. As we neared the Chinese lowlands rain fell almost incessantly. The same scenes met our gaze which we had encountered in the more mountainous country, only intensified by their ghastly significance. Dead and decaying bodies of men, women, children, and domestic animals lay promiscuously about at every turn, and in every conceivable posture, as if they had been stricken by some fell pestilence.

As we gazed, the heavens shed sluggish rain-drops as though weeping. It was only too convincing, the awful thought that here, at the western limit of the vast realm of China, we stood at the gates of a tremendous cemetery, rich with the steaming remains of hundreds of millions of human creatures, and countless myriads of species of the animal and vegetable kingdom.

After two weeks of travel we reached the plains. No living thing was there. The earth, however, was clad in verdure. In some mysterious manner it was evident that the germs of certain forms of vegetable life had survived. Wheat, rice, poppies, and weeds grew up together in luxurious confusion, as though sown broadcast over the land. The scene reminded me of some vast Western prairie. The croaking of frogs, heard by night, proved that, at all events, this form of amphibious life had survived the elemental crisis. Fish, too, abounded in the rivers.

It is needless to relate at length the details of our progress to the sea. In the course of six weeks we reached the seaport of Macao on the southern coast. Here everything was wrecked, ruined, and scorched, as though subjected to a blast furnace. Merchandise and commodities of all sorts were baked into utter desiccation. The shipping in the harbor, where it had not been absolutely wrecked or sunk, rose and fell with the pulsations of the waves, planks and timbers yawning and starting from their places. Still, this city had not experienced the same terrible fate that had befallen San Francisco. The force of the convulsion had been spent before its effects had reached this quarter of the globe, though so far as animal life was concerned the results had been identical in both cases. An iron steamer was found in the harbor which it was possible to refit, and, after several weeks' work, she was rendered seaworthy, while her engines had not suffered materially from the heat. Having stocked this vessel with fuel from a coal-yard whose contents had been converted into excellent coke by the solar action, and a sufficient cargo of rice, also luckily found but little parched, in the month of September, about a year after the cometary crisis, the vessel, manned by this strange crew of amateur sailors, and under such singular auspices, steamed slowly out of the harbor of Macao with the determination of visiting other portions of the earth.

The vessel was called the *Euphemia*, and her crew numbered thirty-one, all told. The monk Dchiamdcham, as was natural, was chosen captain of the expedition, while the control of the engine-room was assigned to myself. Luckily, for the first week or more we encountered no severe weather, by which time the monks had opportunity to acquire use of their sea-legs, and to make themselves familiar with the unaccustomed duties of sailor-life. Their duties naturally consisted in keeping things clean, and attending to the furnaces rather than in seamanship, though Dchiamdcham's capacity, combined with such little instruction as I was able to offer, gradually taught them the use of the ropes and the management of the sails, (some of which we had fortunately found uninjured), which was an essential requirement for the prosecution of our enterprise, as we could not tell when we might ever fall in with another supply of coal.

It had been a moot question in which direction we should travel after leaving Macao. Prudence had suggested to me that our wisest course would be westward, to those Asiatic countries which had presumably escaped the full effects of the elemental visitation. We accordingly steered, as nearly as I could calculate, in a southerly direction for the Indian Archipelago, hoping sooner or later to find the Straits of Anjer of the Gilolo Passage. But the fates had decreed otherwise. For the first ten days we experienced mild and favorable weather, and our dead reckoning, as well as the increasing declination of the Pole Star, showed that we were approaching the Islands, when we encountered one of those typhoons which are of by no means rare occurrence on the China Sea. By the time the violence of the gale was spent we had been driven far eastward, over the waters of the Pacific—how far, we had no means of ascertaining. In the absence of a chronometer and almanac, it was impossible to approximate the longitude.

From the sun's meridian altitude, I determined that we were about twenty degrees north of the equator; also, that, judging from an estimated dead reckoning, the nearest land in our proposed course was the Sandwich Islands. The desire was strong within me to revisit California and learn the full extent of the catastrophe I had witnessed from the balloon. Not many days after, the eastern horizon resolved itself into a long line of cloud, and I had no difficulty in recognizing the contour of the Coast Range Mountains to the south of the town of Monterey. The aspect of the beech, of the headlands, of the white surf of the bay was perfectly familiar, and the brown appearance of plain and highland was just as might have been expected at that season of the year. The sea was destitute of ships. No sea-birds were to be seen; nor did the white and glistening houses at either extremity of the bay suggest the looks of Monterey and Santa Cruz. Instead of this, irregular ruins seemed to mark the sites of these well-known watering places. On the afternoon of the following day, we sighted the Golden Gate. It was a calm and cloudless day—such a day as, a year ago, would have called out innumerable vehicles to the ocean beach. We steamed slowly north, past the spot where the Ocean House had once been. The sudden turning of a point brought us in full view of the Cliff House, or rather the spot it had once occupied, for no building of any kind was to be seen. The outline of Sea Rock rose from the water, with the spray dashing white against its sides, but the glossy colony that had once sported there was gone. No difference was apparent in the bare and russet aspect of the bluffs overlooking the entrance to the bay. It is true that there were no signs of living vegetation visible, but that was normal for California in summer time. Our vessel steamed onward to the harbor, and came abreast of Fort Point. No fierce bombardment could have produced a spectacle of completer ruin. The fiery heat which failed to melt rocks, could nevertheless crumble mortar and cement to powder, and a shapeless pile of brick, with here and there a mass of iron showing through it, was all that remained of that solid structure once bristling with heavy ordnance. The officers' quarters and the Presidio barracks presented a similar spectacle of desolation. Alcatraz was also dismantled, while of the houses and streets which covered the hills between the Presidio and the city scarce a vestige could be seen.

At length we steamed round Black Point and came in full view of the site of the city. The destruction that had fallen upon the ponderous brick fortifications has visited with redoubled force the wooden structures which composed the bulk of the streets. Only the lines of the broadest thoroughfares were defined. Those running east and west from the wharves to the hills were indistinguishable. Piles of charred timber demonstrated the extent and intensity of the conflagration. The wharves were burned nearly to the water's edge, the tops of the piles, however, showing that the tide was lower now than at the time of the catastrophe. The shipping seemed to have shared the general fate, as not a vessel was to be seen, though the bay, with its islands and the shores lining it, looked as normal as ever.

At sundown we cast anchor in the stream about a mile from what was once the city front, Dchiamdcham and myself determining to go ashore in the morning and inspect the ruined city. After dark I was pacing the deck, when a sight from the direction of the city arrested my attention. There, in the heart of it, among the ruins, shone and twinkled a light. I mentally endeavored to locate it, and came to the conclusion that it originated in the neighborhood of Montgomery or Kearny Streets, and in the line of California or Pine. My surprise was still further increased when I presently beheld a second, but much dimmer light, leaving the first and traveling slowly from it. This light stopped, shone for a few minutes, and finally disappeared. Evidently, I reasoned, those lights indicated the presence of human beings.

Accordingly, next morning, Dchiamdcham and myself left the ship's side in our only boat, and landed where the Oakland ferry depot, at the foot of Market Street, used to stand. After mooring the boat to the remnant of a pile formerly belonging to one of the slips, we clambered over the debris of the railroad offices and succeeded in gaining firm footing on the shore. The open area in front of the company's offices, where the various city cars converge to a terminus, presented a space comparatively free from debris, but the lines of all the streets running cityward, from Sacramento to Pacific, were literally choked and rendered impassable by charred and formless ruins. Market Street alone, by reason of its great breadth, was practicable for a pedestrian, though even on this wide thorough fare, blocks of masonry from the lofty warehouses which had once adorned it, necessitated either climbing over or making a circuit around them.

We pushed on as best we could, Dchiamdcham and myself, till we reached the intersection of Montgomery Street. Here our farther progress was arrested by a gigantic mass of masonry which had once composed the Palace Hotel. Such a pile of awful and indescribable confusion as was here witnessed in the destruction of one of the largest edifices on earth struck dismay to the soul of even the philosophical Dchiamdcham. The material of the vast rectangle had toppled over an area of at least two acres, choking not only its own proper ground, but also the surrounding thoroughfares for many yards. Masses of charred furniture and rusty iron were dispersed through the heterogeneous pile, while here and there a ghastly skeleton seemed striving to free itself from its encumbering tomb, or a fleshless skull grinned mockingly through the environment of a blackened window-sash like a hideous painting from its frame. Even as we looked, the sudden lapse of a crumbling fragment frightened from their lairs a horde of sleek and whiskered rats, which glared at us with keen eyes, as though undecided whether to hazard an attack. Life, such as it was, had evidently survived in some of the forms best suited to the exigencies of the case—a terrible travesty on the doctrine of the survival of the fittest.

Sick at heart and shuddering at the spectacle, we turned abruptly to the right, and groped our way as best we could down the line of

Montgomery Street. Past what I recognized as some mullions from the Masonic Temple at the corner of Post Street; past the spot where once stood the Lick House; past the shapeless piles of brick and stone which once belonged to the Occidental Hotel and Russ House blocks, we neared the intersection of Pine Street. Here a peculiar sound arrested my attention. I stopped to listen. It was a regular, monotonous, dull, clinking sound. I had heard it thousands of times before, and it thrilled my soul to hear it. I clutched Dchiamdcham by the arm and dragged him over a pile of rubbish that lay in front of what had once been Nevada Block. As we gained the top of the pile I beheld a sight so unaccountable, so utterly at variance with my surroundings and my preconceived notions of what I might expect, that I stood transfixed and speechless. There, directly on the ruins of the Nevada Bank, I saw two men in conventional miner's garb; one sitting on a convenient block and leaning on his pick, the other standing and wielding the same implement to the sound I had already heard.

An involuntary exclamation of surprise escaped me, at which the men looked up. Their astonishment was equal to our own, and mutual explanations were in order. It seemed that these men had been working on a shift in the fourteen-hundred-foot level of one of the Comstock mines on the day of the cometary catastrophe. At sunrise, when the heat became more oppressive, a signal had been given from the surface for the miners to ascend. These two men were working in an out-of-the-way drift at the time, and did not hear the signal. At noon they discovered the departure of their comrades, but could not divine the reason. Finding themselves alone in the mine, they signaled to be taken up. No notice was taken of their signal, and next day, becoming thoroughly alarmed, they had perilously climbed up the bucket-rope from level to level until they gained the surface. Nothing but corpses of the dead and ruined buildings met their gaze, nor could they account for the condition of things by any natural means. The very accident of having been forgiven in the mines saved them; for the heat there, always oppressive, had not been materially augmented at such a depth below the surface of the earth.

By the time they emerged the elemental crisis was over. Bewildered, they wandered forth to find the country ghastly with death. Instinctively they sought the mountains, and had found upon the higher slopes of

the Sierra Nevadas a hunter's hut that had survived the melting of
the everlasting snows. They discovered, too, that a few more beings,
like themselves, had survived what they now perceived to have been
a natural convulsion, though they could not, of course, have any idea
of its extent. They subsisted during the winter on roots and ground
animals which had been protected by snow. A potato patch similarly
protected had luckily been found.

Early in the year they struck out for San Francisco where, in spite
of ghastly surroundings, the old mining passion seized them, and they
determined to prospect the basement of the Nevada Bank, trusting
to luck for the means of hereafter utilizing what they might acquire.
But they could not live without food, and several months had now
been expended in trips to the mountains to accomplish the result
of a thriving potato patch in what had formerly been a millionaire's
garden. They had scarcely commenced operations on our arrival, and
immediately offered us equal shares in the recovered bullion if we
would assist them and afterward carry them off.

The extraordinary recital of these men convinced me that, after all,
the destructive effects of the conflagration were not as wide-spread
as, at first sight, they would seem to be. It would, however, be tedious
to relate the explorations we made in this and other countries. The
general result was the same, though details varied, of course, with
conditions. Suffice it to say that to-day, at a distance of ten years
from that disastrous day, in the summer of 1893, the earth smiles and
blossoms once more, though they are the smiles and blossoms of a
wilderness. Our men and our women are fewer, but they are simpler,
handsomer, and hardier. Our domestic animals and our cultivated
crops follow the same rule. We have no arts or sciences, for we have
no use for them. Dchiamdcham and his brother monks have forsaken
asceticism in view of the novel requirements of life, and though we
follow no formulated religion, and have no laws, we are all good,
because there is no interest in being bad.

UTOPIA, 1893.

FOR THE AHKOOND

AMBROSE BIERCE

This jeux d'esprit *about the destruction of civilization by disease and a second Ice Age comes from the pen of Ambrose Bierce (1842–1914?), who frequently larded his tales of fantasy and the macabre with satire. "For the Ahkoond" is one of several stories (including "Ashes of the Beacon" and "John Smith Liberator") in which Bierce used futuristic fantasy to comment on flaws and foibles of people of his time.*

In the year 4591 I accepted from his gracious Majesty the Ahkoond of Citrusia a commission to explore the unknown region lying to the eastward of the Ultimate Hills, the range which that learned archaeologist, Simeon Tucker, affirms to be identical with the "Rocky Mountains" of the ancients. For this proof of his Majesty's favor I was indebted, doubtless, to a certain distinction that I had been fortunate enough to acquire by explorations in the heart of Darkest Europe. His Majesty kindly offered to raise and equip a large expeditionary force to accompany me, and I was given the widest discretion in the matter of outfit; I could draw upon the royal treasury for any sum that I might require, and upon the royal university for all the scientific apparatus and assistance necessary to my purpose. Declining these encumbrances, I took my electric rifle and a portable waterproof case containing a few simple instruments and writing materials and set out. Among the instruments was, of course, an aerial isochronophone which I set by the one in the Ahkoond's private dining-room at the palace. His Majesty invariably dined alone at 18 o'clock, and sat at table six hours: it was my intention to send him all my reports at the hour of 23, just as dessert would be served, and he would be in a proper frame of mind to appreciate my discoveries and my services to the crown.

At 9 o'clock on the 13th of Meijh I left Sanf Rachisco and after a tedious journey of nearly fifty minutes arrived at Bolosson, the eastern terminus of the magnetic tube, on the summit of the Ultimate Hills. According to Tucker this was anciently a station on the Central Peaceful Railway, and was called "German," in honor of an illustrious dancing master. Prof. Nupper, however, says it was the ancient Nevraska, the capital of Kikago, and geographers generally have accepted that view.

Finding nothing at Bolosson to interest me except a fine view of the volcano Carlema, then in active eruption, I shouldered my electric rifle and with my case of instruments strapped upon my back plunged at once into the wilderness, down the eastern slope. As I descended the character of the vegetation altered. The pines of the higher altitudes gave place to oaks, these to ash, beech and maple. To these succeeded the tamarack and such trees as affect a moist and marshy habitat; and finally, when for four months I had been steadily descending, I found myself in a primeval flora consisting mainly of giant ferns, some of them as much as twenty *surindas* in diameter. They grew upon the margins of vast stagnant lakes which I was compelled to navigate by means of rude rafts made from their trunks lashed together with vines.

In the fauna of the region that I had traversed I had noted changes corresponding to those in the flora. On the upper slope there was nothing but the mountain sheep, but I passed successively through the habitats of the bear, the deer and the horse. This last mentioned creature, which our naturalists have believed long extinct, and which

Dorbley declares our ancestors domesticated, I found in vast numbers on high table lands covered with grass upon which it feeds. The animal answers the current description of the horse very nearly, but all that I saw were destitute of the horns, and none had the characteristic forked tail. This member, on the contrary, is a tassel of straight wiry hair, reaching nearly to the ground—a surprising sight. Lower still I came upon the mastodon, the lion, the tiger, hippopotamus and alligator, all differing very little from those infesting Central Europe, as described in my "Travels in the Forgotten Continent."

In the lake region where I now found myself, the waters abounded with ichthyosauri, and along the margins the iguanodon dragged his obscene bulk in indolent immunity. Great flocks of pterodactyls, their bodies as large as those of oxen and their necks enormously long, clamored and fought in the air, the broad membranes of their wings making a singular musical humming, unlike anything that I had ever heard. Between them and the ichthyosauri there was incessant battle, and I was constantly reminded of the ancient poet's splendid and original comparison of man to

> *dragons of the prime*
> *That tare each other in their slime.*

When brought down with my electric rifle and properly roasted, the pterodactyl proved very good eating, particularly the pads of the toes.

In urging my raft along the shore line of one of the stagnant lagoons one day I was surprised to find a broad rock jutting out from the shore, its upper surface some ten *coprets* above the water. Disembarking, I ascended it, and on examination recognized it as the remnant of an immense mountain which at one time must have been 5,000 *coprets* in height and doubtless the dominating peak of a long range. From the striations all over it I discovered that it had been worn away to its present trivial size by glacial action. Opening my case of instruments, I took out my petrochronologue and applied it to the worn and scratched surface of the rock. The indicator at once pointed to K 59 xpc ½! At this astonishing result I was nearly overcome by excitement: the last erosions of the ice-masses upon this vestige of a stupendous mountain range which they had worn away, had been made as recently as the year 1945! Hastily applying my nymograph, I found that the name of this particular mountain at the time when it began to be enveloped in the mass of ice moving down upon it from the north, was "Pike's Peak." Other observations with other instruments showed that at that time the country circumjacent to it had been inhabited by a partly civilized race of people known as Galoots, the name of their capital city being Denver.

That evening at the hour of 23 I set up my aerial isochronophone and reported to his gracious Majesty the Ahkoond as follows:

"*Sire:* I have the honor to report that I have made a startling discovery. The primeval region into which I have penetrated, as I informed you yesterday—the ichthyosaurus belt—was peopled by tribes considerably advanced in some of the arts almost within historic times: in 1920. They were exterminated by a glacial period not exceeding one hundred and twenty-five years in duration. Your Majesty can conceive the magnitude and violence of the natural forces which overwhelmed their country with moving sheets of ice not less that 5,000 *coprets* in thickness, grinding down every eminence, destroying (of course) all animal and vegetable life and leaving the region a fathomless bog of detritus. Out of this vast sea of mud Nature has had to evolve another creation, beginning *de novo*, with her lowest forms. It has long been known, your Majesty, that the region east of the Ultimate Hills, between them and the Wintry Sea, was once the seat of an ancient civilization, some scraps and shreds of whose history, arts and literature have been wafted to us across the gulf of time; but it was reserved for your gracious Majesty, through me, your humble and unworthy instrument, to ascertain the astonishing fact that these were a pre-glacial people—that between them and us stands, as it were, a wall of impenetrable ice. That all local records of this unfortunate race have perished your Majesty needs not to be told: we can supplement our present imperfect knowledge of them by instrumental observation only."

To this message I received the following extraordinary reply:

"All right—another bottle of—ice goes: push on—this cheese is too— spare no effort to—hand me those nuts—learn all you can—damn you!"

His most gracious Majesty was being served with dessert, and served badly.

I now resolved to go directly north toward the source of the ice-flow and investigate its cause, but examining my barometer found that I was more than 8,000 *coprets* below the sea-level; the moving ice had not only ground down the face of the country, planing off the eminences and filling the depressions, but its enormous weight had caused the earth's crust to sag, and with the lessening of the weight from evaporation it had not recovered.

I had no desire to continue in this depression, as I should in going north, for I should find nothing but lakes, marshes and ferneries, infested with the same primitive and monstrous forms of life. So I continued my course eastward and soon had the satisfaction to find myself meeting the sluggish current of such streams as I encountered in my way. By vigorous use of the new double-distance telepode, which enables the wearer to step eighty *surindas* instead of forty, as with the instrument in popular use, I was soon again at a considerable elevation above the sea-level and nearly 200 *prastams* from "Pike's Peak." A little farther along the water courses began to flow to the eastward. The flora and fauna had again altered in character, and now began to grow sparse; the soil was thin and arid, and in a week I found myself in a region absolutely destitute of organic life and without a vestige of soil. All was barren rock. The surface for hundreds of *prastams*, as I continued my advance, was nearly level, with a slight dip to the eastward. The rock was singularly striated, the scratches arranged concentrically and in helicoidal curves. This circumstance puzzled me and I resolved to take some more instrumental observations, bitterly regretting my improvidence in not availing myself of the Ahkoond's permission to bring with me such apparatus and assistants as would have given me knowledge vastly more copious and accurate than I could acquire with my simple pocket appliances.

I need not here go into the details of my observations with such instruments as I had, nor into the calculations of which these observations were the basic data. Suffice it that after two months' labor I reported the results to his Majesty in Sanf Rachisco in the words following:

"*Sire:* It is my high privilege to apprise you of my arrival on the
western slope of a mighty depression running through the center
of the continent north and south, formerly known as the Mississippi
Valley. It was once the seat of a thriving and prosperous population
known as the Pukes, but is now a vast expanse of bare rock, from which
every particle of soil and everything movable, including people, animals
and vegetation, have been lifted by terrific cyclones and scattered afar,
falling in other lands and at sea in the form of what was called meteoric
dust! I find that these terrible phenomena began to occur about the
year 1860, and lasted, with increasing frequency and power, through a
century, culminating about the middle of that glacial period which saw
the extinction of the Galoots and their neighboring tribes. There was,
of course, a close connection between the two malefic phenomena,
both, doubtless, being due to the same cause, which I have been unable
to trace. A cyclone, I venture to remind your gracious Majesty, is a
mighty whirlwind, accompanied by the most startling meteorological
phenomena, such as electrical disturbances, floods of falling water,
darkness and so forth. It moves with great speed, sucking up everything
and reducing it to powder. In many days' journey I have not found
a square *copret* of the country that did not suffer a visitation. If any
human being escaped he must speedily have perished from starvation.
For some twenty centuries the Pukes have been an extinct race, and
their country a desolation in which no living thing can dwell, unless,
like me, it is supplied with Dr. Blobob's Condensed Life-pills."

The Ahkoond replied that he was pleased to feel the most poignant
grief for the fate of the unfortunate Pukes, and if I should by chance find
the ancient king of the country I was to do my best to revive him with
the patent resuscitator and present him the assurances of his Majesty's
distinguished consideration; but as the politoscope showed that the
nation had been a republic I gave myself no trouble in the matter.

My next report was made six months later and was in substance this:

"*Sire:* I address your Majesty from a point 430 *coprets* vertically above
the site of the famous ancient city of Buffalo, once the capital of a
powerful nation called the Smugwumps. I can approach no nearer
because of the hardness of the snow, which is very firmly packed.

For hundreds of *prastams* in every direction, and for thousands to the north and west, the land is covered with this substance, which, as your Majesty is doubtless aware, is extremely cold to the touch, but by application of sufficient heat can be turned into water. It falls from the heavens, and is believed by the learned among your Majesty's subjects to have a sidereal origin.

"The Smugwumps were a hardy and intelligent race, but they entertained the vain delusion that they could subdue Nature. Their year was divided into two seasons—summer and winter, the former warm, the latter cold. About the beginning of the nineteenth century according to my archaethermograph, the summers began to grow shorter and hotter, the winters longer and colder. At every point in their country, and every day in the year, when they had not the hottest weather ever known in that place, they had the coldest. When they were not dying by hundreds from sunstroke they were dying by thousands from frost. But these heroic and devoted people struggled on, believing that they were becoming acclimated faster than the climate was becoming insupportable. Those called away on business were even afflicted with nostalgia, and with a fatal infatuation returned to grill or freeze, according to the season of their arrival. Finally there was no summer at all, though the last flash of heat slew several millions and set most of their cities afire, and winter reigned eternal.

"The Smugwumps were now keenly sensible of the perils environing them, and, abandoning their homes, endeavored to reach their kindred, the Californians, on the western side of the continent in what is now your Majesty's ever-blessed realm. But it was too late: the snow growing deeper and deeper day by day, besieged them in their towns and dwellings, and they were unable to escape. The last one of them perished about the year 1943, and may God have mercy on his fool soul!"

To this dispatch the Ahkoond replied that it was the royal opinion that the Smugwumps were served very well right.

Some weeks later I reported thus:

"*Sire:* The country which your Majesty's munificence is enabling your devoted servant to explore extends southward and southwestward from Smugwumpia many hundreds of *prastams*, its eastern and southern borders being the Wintry Sea and the Fiery Gulf, respectively. The population in ancient times was composed of Whites and Blacks in about equal numbers and of about equal moral worth—at least that is the record on the dial of my ethnograph when set for the twentieth century and given a southern exposure. The Whites were called Crackers and the Blacks known as Coons.

"I find here none of the barrenness and desolation characterizing the land of the ancient Pukes, and the climate is not so rigorous and thrilling as that of the country of the late Smugwumps. It is, indeed, rather agreeable in point of temperature, and the soil being fertile exceedingly, the whole land is covered with a dense and rank vegetation. I have yet to find a square *smig* of it that is open ground, or one that is not the lair of some savage beast, the haunt of some venomous reptile, or the roost of some offensive bird. Crackers and Coons alike are long extinct, and these are their successors.

"Nothing could be more forbidding and unwholesome than these interminable jungles, with their horrible wealth of organic life in its most objectionable forms. By repeated observations with the necrohistoriograph I find that the inhabitants of this country, who had always been more or less dead, were wholly extirpated contemporaneously with the disastrous events which swept away the Galoots, the Pukes and the Smugwumps. The agency of their effacement was an endemic disorder known as yellow fever. The ravages of this frightful disease were of frequent recurrence, every point of the country being a center of infection; but in some seasons it was worse than in others. Once in every half century at first, and afterward every year* it broke out somewhere and swept over wide areas with such fatal effect that there were not enough of the living to plunder the dead; but at the first frost it would subside. During the ensuing two or three months of immunity the stupid survivors returned to the infected homes from which they had fled and were ready for the next outbreak. Emigration would have saved them all, but although the Californians (over whose happy and prosperous descendants your Majesty has the goodness to reign) invited them again

---

*At one time it was foolishly believed that the disease had been eradicated by slapping the mosquitoes which were thought to produce it; but a few years later it broke out with greater violence than ever before, although the mosquitoes had left the country.

and again to their beautiful land, where sickness and death were hardly known, they would not go, and by the year 1946 the last one of them, may it please your gracious Majesty, was dead and damned."

Having spoken this into the transmitter of the aerial isochronophone at the usual hour of 23 o'clock I applied the receiver to my ear, confidently expecting the customary commendation. Imagine my astonishment and dismay when my master's well-remembered voice was heard in utterance of the most awful imprecations on me and my work, followed by appalling threats against my life!

The Ahkoond had changed his dinner-time to five hours later and I had been speaking into the ears of an empty stomach!

THE CRACK OF DOOM

ROBERT CROMIE

Irish writer Robert Cromie (1856–1907) wrote several science fiction novels late in the nineteenth century, including A Plunge into Space *(1890), which Jules Verne admired enough to write a preface to. In his short novel* The Crack of Doom, *first published in 1895, he endows a group of philosophical nihilists with a grasp of atomic theory that makes their insane ambition to disintegrate the planet seem scientifically feasible.*

PREFACE

The rough notes from which this narrative has been constructed were given to me by the man who tells the story. For obvious reasons I have altered the names of the principals, and I hereby pass on the assurance which I have received, that the originals of such as are left alive can be found if their discovery be thought desirable. This alteration of names, the piecing together of somewhat disconnected and sometimes nearly indecipherable memoranda, and the reduction of the mass to consecutive form, are all that has been required of me or would have been permitted to me. The expedition to Labrador mentioned by the narrator has not returned, nor has it ever been definitely traced. He does not undertake to prove that it ever set out. But he avers that all which is hereafter set down is truly told, and he leaves it to mankind to accept the warning which it has fallen to him to convey, or await the proof of its sincerity which he believes the end of the century will produce.

I. THE UNIVERSE A MISTAKE!

"The Universe is a mistake!"

Thus spake Herbert Brande, a passenger on the *Majestic*, making for Queenstown Harbour, one evening early in the past year. Foolish as the words may seem, they were partly influential in leading to my terrible association with him, and all that is described in this book.

Brande was standing beside me on the starboard side of the vessel. We had been discussing a current astronomical essay, as we watched the hazy blue line of the Irish coast rise on the horizon. This conversation was interrupted by Brande, who said, impatiently:

"Why tell us of stars distant so far from this insignificant little world of ours—so insignificant that even its own inhabitants speak disrespectfully of it—that it would take hundreds of years to telegraph to some of them, thousands to others, and millions to the rest? Why limit oneself to a mere million of years for a dramatic illustration, when there is a star in space distant so far from us that if a telegram left the earth for it this very night, and maintained for ever its initial velocity, it would never reach that star?"

He said this without any apparent effort after rhetorical effect; but the suddenness with which he had presented a very obvious truism in a fresh light to me made the conception of the vastness of space absolutely oppressive. In the hope of changing the subject I replied:

"Nothing is gained by dwelling on these scientific speculations. The mind is only bewildered. The Universe is inexplicable."

"The Universe!" he exclaimed. "That is easily explained. The Universe is a mistake!"

"The greatest mistake of the century, I suppose," I added, somewhat annoyed, for I thought Brande was laughing at me.

"Say, of Time, and I agree with you," he replied, careless of my astonishment.

I did not answer him for some moments.

This man Brande was young in years, but middle-aged in the expression of his pale, intellectual face, and old—if age be synonymous with knowledge—in his ideas. His knowledge, indeed, was so exhaustive that the scientific pleasantries to which he was prone could always be justified, dialectically at least, by him when he was contradicted. Those who knew him well did not argue with him. I was always stumbling into intellectual pitfalls, for I had only known him since the steamer left New York.

As to myself, there is little to be told. My history prior to my acquaintance with Brande was commonplace. I was merely an active, athletic Englishman, Arthur Marcel by name. I had studied medicine, and was a doctor in all but the degree. This certificate had been dispensed with owing to an unexpected legacy, on receipt of which I determined to devote it to the furtherance of my own amusement. In the pursuit of this object, I had visited many lands and had become familiar with most of the beaten tracks of travel. I was returning to England after an absence of three years spent in aimless roaming. My age was thirty-one years, and my salient characteristic at the time was to hold fast by anything that interested me, until my humour changed. Brande's conversational vagaries had amused me on the voyage. His extraordinary comment on the Universe decided me to cement our shipboard acquaintance before reaching port.

"That explanation of yours," I said, lighting a fresh cigar, and returning to a subject which I had so recently tried to shelve, "isn't it rather vague?"

"For the present it must serve," he answered absently.

To force him into admitting that his phrase was only a thoughtless exclamation, or induce him to defend it, I said:

"It does not serve any reasonable purpose. It adds nothing to knowledge. As it stands, it is neither academic nor practical."

Brande looked at me earnestly for a moment, and then said gravely:

"The academic value of the explanation will be shown to you if you will join a society I have founded; and its practicalness will soon be made plain whether you join or not."

"What do you call this club of yours?" I asked.

"We do not call it a club. We call it a Society—the *Cui Bono* Society," he answered coldly.

"I like the name," I returned. "It is suggestive. It may mean anything—or nothing."

"You will learn later that the Society means something; a good deal, in fact."

This was said in the dry, unemotional tone which I afterwards found was the only sign of displeasure Brande ever permitted himself to show. His arrangements for going on shore at Queenstown had been made early in the day, but he left me to look for his sister, of whom I had seen very little on the voyage. The weather had been rough, and as she was not a good sailor, I had only had a rare glimpse of a very dark and handsome girl, whose society possessed for me a strange attraction, although we were then almost strangers. Indeed, I regretted keenly, as the time of our separation approached, having registered my luggage (consisting largely of curios and mementoes of my travels, of which I was very careful) for Liverpool. My own time was valueless, and it would have been more agreeable to me to continue the journey with the Brandes, no matter where they went.

There was a choppy sea on when we reached the entrance to the harbour, so the *Majestic* steamed in between the Carlisle and Camden forts, and on to the man-of-war roads, where the tender met us. By this time, Brande and his sister were ready to go on shore; but as there was a heavy mail to be transhipped, we had still an hour at our disposal. For some time we paced the deck, exchanging commonplaces on the voyage and confidences as to our future plans. It was almost dark, but not dark enough to prevent us from seeing those wonderfully green hills which landlock the harbour. To me the verdant woods and hills were delightful after the brown plains and interminable prairies on which I had spent many months. As the lights of Queenstown began to speck the slowly gathering gloom, Miss Brande asked me to point out Rostellan Castle. It could not be seen from the vessel, but the familiar legend was easily recalled, and this led us to talk about Irish tradition with its weird romance and never failing pathos. This interested her. Freed now from the lassitude of sea-sickness, the girl became more fascinating to me every moment. Everything she said was worth listening to, apart from the charming manner in which it was said.

To declare that she was an extremely pretty girl would not convey the strange, almost unearthly, beauty of her face—as intellectual as her brother's—and of the charm of her slight but exquisitely moulded figure. In her dark eyes there was a sympathy, a compassion, that was new to me. It thrilled me with an emotion different from anything that my frankly happy, but hitherto wholly selfish life had known. There was only one note in her conversation which jarred upon me. She was apt to drift into the extraordinary views of life and death which were interesting when formulated by her eccentric brother, but pained me coming from her lips. In spite of this, the purpose I had contemplated of joining Brande's Society—evoked as it had been by his own whimsical observation—now took definite form. I would join that Society. It would be the best way of keeping near to Natalie Brande.

Her brother returned to us to say that the tender was about to leave the ship. He had left us for half an hour. I did not notice his absence until he himself announced it. As we shook hands, I said to him:

"I have been thinking about that Society of yours. I mean to join it."

"I am very glad," he replied. "You will find it a new sensation, quite outside the beaten track, which you know so well."

There was a shade of half-kindly contempt in his voice, which missed me at the moment. I answered gaily, knowing that he would not be offended by what was said in jest:

"I am sure I shall. If all the members are as mad as yourself, it will be the most interesting experience outside Bedlam that any man could wish for."

I had a foretaste of that interest soon.

As Miss Brande was walking to the gangway, a lamp shone full upon her gypsy face. The blue-black hair, the dark eyes, and a deep red rose she wore in her bonnet, seemed to me an exquisite arrangement of harmonious colour. And the thought flashed into my mind very vividly, however trivial it may seem here, when written down in cold words: "The queen of women, and the queen of flowers." That is not precisely how my thought ran, but I cannot describe it better. The finer subtleties of the brain do not bear well the daylight of language.

Brande drew her back and whispered to her. Then the sweet face, now slightly flushed, was turned to me again.

"Oh, thank you for that pretty thought," she said with a pleasant smile. "You are too flattering. The 'queen of flowers' is very true, but the 'queen of women!' Oh, no!" She made a graceful gesture of dissent, and passed down the gangway.

As the tender disappeared into the darkness, a tiny scrap of lace waved, and I knew vaguely that she was thinking of me. But how she read my thought so exactly I could not tell.

That knowledge it has been my fate to gain.

II. A STRANGE EXPERIMENT

Soon after my arrival in London, I called on Brande, at the address he had given me in Brook Street. He received me with the pleasant affability which a man of the world easily assumes, and his apology for being unable to pass the evening with me in his own house was a model of social style. The difficulty in the way was practically an impossibility. His Society had a meeting on that evening, and it was imperative that he should be present.

"Why not come yourself?" he said. "It is what we might call a guest night. That is, visitors, if friends of members, are admitted, and as this privilege may not be again accorded to outsiders, you ought to come before you decide finally to join us. I must go now, but Natalie" (he did not say "Miss Brande") "will entertain you and bring you to the hall. It is very near—in Hanover Square."

"I shall be very glad indeed to bring Miss Brande to the hall," I answered, changing the sentence in order to correct Brande's too patronising phrase.

"The same thing in different words, is it not? If you prefer it that way, please have it so." His imperturbability was unaffected.

Miss Brande here entered the room. Her brother, with a word of renewed apology, left us, and presently I saw him cross the street and hail a passing hansom.

"You must not blame him for running off," Miss Brande said. "He has much to think of, and the Society depends almost wholly on himself."

I stammered out that I did not blame him at all, and indeed my disclaimer was absolutely true. Brande could not have pleased me better than he had done by relieving us of his company.

Miss Brande made tea, which I pretended to enjoy in the hope of pleasing her. Over this we talked more like old and well proven friends than mere acquaintances of ten days' standing. Just once or twice the mysterious chord which marred the girl's charming conversation was touched. She immediately changed the subject on observing my distress. I say distress, for a weaker word would not fittingly describe the emotion I felt whenever she blundered into the pseudo-scientific nonsense which was her brother's favourite affectation. At least, it seemed nonsense to me. I could not well foresee then that the theses which appeared to be mere theoretical absurdities, would ever be proven—as they have been—very terrible realities. On subjects of ordinary educational interest my hostess displayed such full knowledge of the question and ease in dealing with it, that I listened, fascinated, as long as she chose to continue speaking. It was a novel and delightful experience to hear a girl as handsome as a pictorial masterpiece, and dressed like a court beauty, discourse with the knowledge, and in the language, of the oldest philosopher. But this was only one of the many surprising combinations in her complex personality. My novitiate was still in its first stage.

The time to set out for the meeting arrived all too soon for my inclination. We decided to walk, the evening being fine and not too warm, and the distance only a ten minutes' stroll. At a street crossing, we met a crowd unusually large for that neighbourhood. Miss Brande again surprised me. She was watching the crowd seething and swarming past. Her dark eyes followed the people with a strange wondering, pitying look which I did not understand. Her face, exquisite in its expression at all times, was now absolutely transformed, beatified. Brande had often spoken to me of mesmerism, clairvoyance, and similar subjects, and it occurred to me that he had used his sister as a medium, a clairvoyante. Her brain was not, therefore, under normal control. I determined instantly to tell him on the first opportunity that if he did not wish to see the girl permanently injured, he would have to curtail his hypnotic influence.

"It is rather a stirring sight," I said so sharply to Miss Brande that she started. I meant to startle her, but did not succeed as far as I wished.

"It is a very terrible sight," she answered.

"Oh, there is no danger," I said hastily, and drew her hand over my arm.

"Danger! I was not thinking of danger."

As she did not remove her hand, I did not infringe the silence which followed this, until a break in the traffic allowed us to cross the street. Then I said:

"May I ask what you were thinking of just now, Miss Brande?"

"Of the people—their lives—their work—their misery!"

"I assure you many are very happy," I replied. "You take a morbid view. Misery is not the rule. I am sure the majority are happy."

"What difference does that make?" the girl said with a sigh. "What is the end of it all—the meaning of it all? Their happiness! *Cui Bono?*"

We walked on in silence, while I turned over in my mind what she had said. I could come to no conclusion upon it save that my dislike for her enigmatic aberrations was becoming more intense as my liking for the girl herself increased. To change the current of her thoughts and my own, I asked her abruptly:

"Are you a member of the *Cui Bono* Society?"

"I! Oh, no. Women are not allowed to join—for the present."

"I am delighted to hear it," I said heartily, "and I hope the rule will continue in force."

She looked at me in surprise. "Why should you mind? You are joining yourself."

"That is different. I don't approve of ladies mixing themselves up in these curious and perhaps questionable societies."

My remark amused her. Her eyes sparkled with simple fun. The change in her manner was very agreeable to me.

"I might have expected that." To my extreme satisfaction she now looked almost mischievous. "Herbert told me you were a little—"

"A little what?"

"Well, a little—you won't be vexed? That is right. He said a little—mediæval."

This abated my appreciation of her sense of humour, and I maintained a dignified reticence, which unhappily she regarded as mere sullenness, until we reached the Society's room.

The place was well filled, and the company, in spite of the extravagantly modern costumes of the younger women, which I cannot describe better than by saying that there was little difference in it from that of ordinary male attire, was quite conventional in so far as the interchange of ordinary courtesies went. When, however, any member of the Society mingled with a group of visitors, the conversation was soon turned into a new channel. Secrets of science, which I had been accustomed to look upon as undiscoverable, were bandied about like the merest commonplaces of education. The absurdity of individuality and the subjectivity of the emotions were alike insisted on without notice of the paradox, which to me appeared extreme. The Associates were altruistic for the sake of altruism, not for the sake of its beneficiaries. They were not pantheists, for they saw neither universal good nor God, but rather evil in all things—themselves included. Their talk, however, was brilliant, and, with allowance for its jarring sentiments, it possessed something of the indefinable charm which followed Brande. My reflections on this identity of interest were interrupted by the man himself. After a word of welcome he said:

"Let me show you our great experiment; that which touches the high-water mark of scientific achievement in the history of humanity. It is not much in itself, but it is the pioneer of many marvels."

He brought me to a metal stand, on which a small instrument constructed of some white metal was placed. A large number of wires were connected with various portions of it, and these wires passed into the side-wall of the building.

In appearance, this marvel of micrology, so far as the eye-piece and upper portions went, was like an ordinary microscope, but its magnifying power was to me unbelievable. It magnified the object under examination many thousand times more than the most powerful microscope in the world.

I looked through the upper lens, and saw a small globe suspended in the middle of a tiny chamber filled with soft blue light, or transparent material. Circling round this globe four other spheres revolved in orbits, some almost circular, some elliptical, some parabolic. As I looked, Brande touched a key, and the little globules began to fly more rapidly round their primary, and make wider sweeps in their revolutions. Another key was pressed, and the revolving spheres slowed down and drew closer until I could scarcely distinguish any movement. The globules seemed to form a solid ball.

"Attend now!" Brande exclaimed.

He tapped the first key sharply. A little grey cloud obscured the blue light. When it cleared away, the revolving globes had disappeared.

"What do you think of it?" he asked carelessly.

"What is it? What does it mean? Is it the solar system or some other system illustrated in miniature? I am sorry for the misadventure."

"You are partly correct," Brande replied. "It is an illustration of a planetary system, though a small one. But there was no misadventure. I caused the somewhat dangerous result you witnessed, the wreckage not merely of the molecule of marsh gas you were examining—which any educated chemist might do as easily as I—but the wreckage of its constituent atoms. This is a scientific victory which dwarfs the work of Helmholtz, Avogadro, or Mendelejeff. The immortal Dalton himself" (the word "immortal" was spoken with a sneer) "might rise from his grave to witness it."

"Atoms—molecules! What are you talking about?" I asked, bewildered.

"You were looking on at the death of a molecule—a molecule of marsh gas, as I have already said. It was caused by a process which I would describe to you if I could reduce my own life work—and that of every scientific amateur who has preceded me since the world began—into half a dozen sentences. As that would be difficult, I must ask you to accept my personal assurance that you witnessed a fact, not a fiction of my imagination."

"And your instrument is so perfect that it not only renders molecules and atoms but their diffusion visible? It is a microscopic impossibility. At least it is amazing."

"Pshaw!" Brande exclaimed impatiently. "My instrument does certainly magnify to a marvellous extent, but not by the old device of the simple microscope, which merely focused a large area of light rays into a small one. So crude a process could never show an atom to the human eye. I add much to that. I restore to the rays themselves the luminosity which they lost in their passage through our atmosphere. I give them back all their visual properties, and turn them with their full etheric blaze on the object under examination. Great as that achievement is, I deny that it is amazing. It may amaze a Papuan to see his eyelash magnified to the size of a wire, or an uneducated Englishman to see a cheese-mite magnified to the size of a midge. It should not amaze you to see a simple process a little further developed."

"Where does the danger you spoke of come in?" I asked with a pretence of interest. Candidly, I did not believe a single word that Brande had said.

"If you will consult a common text-book on the physics of the ether," he replied, "you will find that one grain of matter contains sufficient energy, if etherised, to raise a hundred thousand tons nearly two miles. In face of such potentiality it is not wise to wreck incautiously even the atoms of a molecule."

"And the limits to this description of scientific experiment? Where are they?"

"There are no limits," Brande said decisively. "No man can say to science 'thus far and no farther.' No man ever has been able to do so. No man ever shall!"

III. "IT IS GOOD TO BE ALIVE"

Amongst the letters lying on my breakfast-table a few days after the meeting was one addressed in an unfamiliar hand. The writing was bold, and formed like a man's. There was a faint trace of a perfume about the envelope which I remembered. I opened it first.

It was, as I expected, from Miss Brande. Her brother had gone to their country place on the southern coast. She and her friend, Edith Metford, were going that day. Their luggage was already at the station. Would I send on what I required for a short visit, and meet them at eleven o'clock on the bridge over the Serpentine? It was enough for me. I packed a large portmanteau hastily, sent it to Charing Cross, and spent the time at my disposal in the park, which was close to my hotel.

Although the invitation I had received gave me pleasure, I could not altogether remove from my mind a vague sense of disquietude concerning Herbert Brande and his Society. The advanced opinions I had heard, if extreme, were not altogether alarming. But the mysterious way in which Brande himself had spoken about the Society, and the still more mysterious air which some of the members assumed when directly questioned as to its object, suggested much. Might it not be a revolutionary party engaged in a grave intrigue—a branch of some foreign body whose purpose was so dangerous that ordinary disguises were not considered sufficiently secure? Might they not have adopted the jargon and pretended to the opinions of scientific faddists as a cloak for designs more sinister and sincere? The experiment I witnessed might be almost a miracle or merely a trick. Thinking it over thus, I could come to no final opinion, and when I asked myself aloud, "What are you afraid of?" I could not answer my own question. But I thought I would defer joining the Society pending further information.

A few minutes before eleven, I walked towards the bridge over the Serpentine. No ladies appeared to be on it. There were only a couple of smartly dressed youths there, one smoking a cigarette. I sauntered about until one of the lads, the one who was not smoking, looked up and beckoned to me. I approached leisurely, for it struck me that the boy would have shown better breeding if he had come toward me, considering my seniority.

"I am sorry I did not notice you sooner. Why did you not come on when you saw us?" the smallest and slimmest youth called to me.

"In the name of—Miss—Miss—" I stammered.

"Brande; you haven't forgotten my name, I hope," Natalie Brande said coolly. "This is my friend, Edith Metford. Metford, this is Arthur Marcel."

"How do you do, Marcel? I am glad to meet you; I have heard 'favourable mention' of you from the Brandes," the second figure in knickerbockers said pleasantly.

"How do you do, sir—madam—I mean—Miss—" I blundered, and then in despair I asked Miss Brande, "Is this a *tableau vivant*? What is the meaning of these disguises?" My embarrassment was so great that my discourteous question may be pardoned.

"Our dress! Surely you have seen women rationally dressed before!" Miss Brande answered complacently, while the other girl watched my astonishment with evident amusement.

This second girl, Edith Metford, was a frank, handsome young woman, but unlike the *spirituelle* beauty of Natalie Brande. She was perceptibly taller than her friend, and of fuller figure. In consequence, she looked, in my opinion, to even less advantage in her eccentric costume, or rational dress, than did Miss Brande.

"Rationally dressed! Oh, yes. I know the divided skirt, but—"

Miss Metford interrupted me. "Do you call the divided skirt atrocity rational dress?" she asked pointedly.

"Upon my honour I do not," I answered.

These girls were too advanced in their ideas of dress for me. Nor did I feel at all at my ease during this conversation, which did not, however, appear to embarrass them. I proposed hastily to get a cab, but they demurred. It was such a lovely day, they preferred to walk, part of the way at least. I pointed out that there might be drawbacks to this amendment of my proposal.

"What drawbacks?" Miss Metford asked.

"For instance, isn't it probable we shall all be arrested by the police?" I replied.

"Rubbish! We are not in Russia," both exclaimed.

"Which is lucky for you," I reflected, as we commenced what was to me a most disagreeable walk. I got them into a cab sooner than they wished. At the railway station I did not offer to procure their tickets. To do so, I felt, would only give offence. Critical glances followed us as we went to our carriage. Londoners are becoming accustomed to varieties, if not vagaries, in ladies' costumes, but the dress of my friends was evidently a little out of the common even for them. Miss Metford was just turning the handle of a carriage door, when I interposed, saying, "This is a smoking compartment."

"So I see. I am going to smoke—if you don't object?"

"I don't suppose it would make any difference if I did," I said, with unconscious asperity, for indeed this excess of free manners was jarring upon me. The line dividing it from vulgarity was becoming so thin I was losing sight of the divisor. Yet no one, even the most fastidious, could associate vulgarity with Natalie Brande. There remained an air of unassumed sincerity about herself and all her actions, including even her dress, which absolutely excluded her from hostile criticism. I could not, however, extend that lenient judgment to Miss Metford. The girls spoke and acted—as they had dressed themselves—very much alike. Only, what seemed to me in the one a natural eccentricity, seemed in the other an unnatural affectation.

I saw the guard passing, and, calling him over, gave him half-a-crown to have the compartment labelled, "Engaged."

Miss Brande, who had been looking out of the window, absently asked my reason for this precaution. I replied that I wanted the compartment reserved for ourselves. I certainly did not want any staring and otherwise offensive fellow-passengers.

"We don't want all the seats," she persisted.

"No," I admitted. "We don't want the extra seats. But I thought you might like the privacy."

"The desire for privacy is an archaic emotion," Miss Metford remarked sententiously, as she struck a match.

"Besides, it is so selfish. We may be crowding others," Miss Brande said quietly.

I was glad she did not smoke.

"I don't want that now," I said to a porter who was hurrying up with a label. To the girls I remarked a little snappishly, "Of course you are quite right. You must excuse my ignorance."

"No, it is not ignorance," Miss Brande demurred. "You have been away so much. You have hardly been in England, you told me, for years, and—"

"And progress has been marching in my absence," I interrupted.

"So it seems," Miss Metford remarked so significantly that I really could not help retorting with as much emphasis, compatible with politeness, as I could command:

"You see I am therefore unable to appreciate the New Woman, of whom I have heard so much since I came home."

"The conventional New Woman is a grandmotherly old fossil," Miss Metford said quietly.

This disposed of me. I leant back in my seat, and was rigidly silent.

Miles of green fields stippled with daisies and bordered with long lines of white and red hawthorn hedges flew past. The smell of new-mown hay filled the carriage with its sweet perfume, redolent of old associations. My long absence dwindled to a short holiday. The world's wide highways were far off. I was back in the English fields. My slight annoyance passed away. I fell into a pleasant day-dream, which was broken by a soft voice, every undulation of which I already knew by heart.

"I am afraid you think us very advanced," it murmured.

"Very," I agreed, "but I look to you to bring even me up to date."

"Oh, yes, we mean to do that, but we must proceed very gradually."

"You have made an excellent start," I put in.

"Otherwise you would only be shocked."

"It is quite possible." I said this with so much conviction that the two burst out laughing at me. I could not think of anything more to add, and I felt relieved when, with a warning shriek, the train dashed into a tunnel. By the time we had emerged again into the sunlight and the solitude of the open landscape I had ready an impromptu which I had been working at in the darkness. I looked straight at Miss Metford and said:

"After all, it is very pleasant to travel with girls like you."

"Thank you!"

"You did not show any hysterical fear of my kissing you in the tunnel."

"Why the deuce would you do that?" Miss Metford replied with great composure, as she blew a smoke ring.

When we reached our destination I braced myself for another disagreeable minute or two. For if the great Londoners thought us quaint, surely the little country station idlers would swear we were demented. We crossed the platform so quickly that the wonderment we created soon passed. Our luggage was looked after by a servant, to whose care I confided it with a very brief description. The loss of an item of it did not seem to me of as much importance as our own immediate departure.

Brande met us at his hall door. His house was a pleasant one, covered with flowering creeping plants, and surrounded by miniature forests. In front there was a lake four hundred yards in width. Close-shaven lawns bordered it. They were artificial products, no doubt, but they were artificial successes—undulating, earth-scented, fresh rolled every morning. Here there was an isolated shrub, there a thick bank of rhododendrons. And the buds, bursting into floral carnival, promised fine contrasts when their full splendour was come. The lake wavelets tinkled musically on a pebbly beach.

Our host could not entertain us in person. He was busy. The plea was evidently sincere, notwithstanding that the business of a country gentleman—which he now seemed to be—is something less exacting than busy people's leisure. After a short rest, and an admirably-served lunch, we were dismissed to the woods for our better amusement.

Thereafter followed for me a strangely peaceful, idyllic day—all save its ending. Looking back on it, I know that the sun which set that evening went down on the last of my happiness. But it all seems trivial now.

My companions were accomplished botanists, and here, for the first time, I found myself on common ground with both. We discussed every familiar wild flower as eagerly as if we had been professed field naturalists. In walking or climbing my assistance was neither requisitioned nor required. I did not offer, therefore, what must have been unwelcome when it was superfluous.

We rested at last under the shade of a big beech, for the afternoon
sun was rather oppressive. It was a pleasant spot to while away an hour.
A purling brook went babbling by, singing to itself as it journeyed
to the sea. Insects droned about in busy flight. There was a perfume
of honeysuckle wafted to us on the summer wind, which stirred
the beech-tree and rustled its young leaves lazily, so that the sunlight
peeped through the green lattice-work and shone on the faces of these
two handsome girls, stretched in graceful postures on the cool sward
below—their white teeth sparkling in its brilliance, while their soft
laughter made music for me. In the fulness of my heart, I said aloud:

"It is a good thing to be alive."

IV. GEORGE DELANY—DECEASED

"It is a good thing to be alive," Natalie Brande repeated slowly, gazing, as
it were, far off through her half-closed eyelids. Then turning to me and
looking at me full, wide-eyed, she asked: "A good thing for how many?"

"For all; for everything that is alive."

"Faugh! For few things that are alive. For hardly anything. You say it
is a good thing to be alive. How often have you said that in your life?"

"All my life through," I answered stoutly. My constitution was a good
one, and I had lived healthily, if hardily. I voiced the superfluous vitality
of a well nourished body.

"Then you do not know what it is to feel for others."

There was a scream in the underwood near us. It ended in a short,
choking squeak. The girl paled, but she went on with outward calm.

"That hawk or cat feels as you do. I wonder what that young rabbit
thinks of life's problem?"

"But we are neither hawks nor cats, nor even young rabbits," I
answered warmly. "We can not bear the burthens of the whole animal
world. Our own are sufficient for us."

"You are right. They are more than sufficient."

I had made a false move, and so tried to recover my lost ground.
She would not permit me. The conversation which had run in
pleasant channels for two happy hours was ended. Thenceforth,
in spite of my obstructive efforts, subjects were introduced which
could not be conversed on but must be discussed. On every one Miss
Brande took the part of the weak against the strong, oblivious of

every consideration of policy and even ethics, careful only that she championed the weak because of their weakness. Miss Metford abetted her in this, and went further in their joint revolt against common sense. Miss Brande was argumentative, pleading. Miss Metford was defiant. Between the two I fared ill.

Of course the Woman question was soon introduced, and in this I made the best defence of time-honoured customs of which I was capable. But my outworks fell down as promptly before the voices of these young women as did the walls of Jericho before the blast of a ram's horn. Nothing that I had cherished was left to me. Woman no longer wanted man's protection. ("Enslavement" they called it.) Why should she, when in the evolution of society there was not now, or presently would not be, anything from which to protect her? ("Competing slaveowners" was what they said.) When you wish to behold protectors you must postulate dangers. The first are valueless save as a preventive of the second. Both evils will be conveniently dispensed with. All this was new to me, most of my thinking life having been passed in distant lands, where the science of ethics is codified into a simple statute—the will of the strongest.

When my dialectical humiliation was within one point of completion, Miss Metford came to my rescue. For some time she had looked on at my discomfiture with a good-natured neutrality, and when I was metaphorically in my last ditch, she arose, stretched her shapely figure, flicked some clinging grass blades from her suit, and declared it was time to return. Brande was a man of science, but as such he was still amenable to punctuality in the matter of dinner.

On the way back I was discreetly silent. When we reached the house I went to look for Herbert Brande. He was engaged in his study, and I could not intrude upon him there. To do so would be to infringe the only rigid rule in his household. Nor had I an opportunity of speaking to him alone until after dinner, when I induced him to take a turn with me round the lake. I smoked strong cigars, and made one of these my excuse.

The sun was setting when we started, and as we walked slowly the twilight shadows were deepening fast by the time we reached the further shore. Brande was in high spirits. Some new scientific experiment, I assumed, had come off successfully. He was beside himself. His conversation was volcanic. Now it rumbled and roared with suppressed fires. Anon, it burst forth in scintillating flashes and shot out streams of quickening wit. I have been his auditor in the three great epochs of his life, but I do not think that anything that I have recollected of his utterances equals the bold impromptus, the masterly handling of his favourite subject, the Universe, which fell from him on that evening. I could not answer him. I could not even follow him, much less suppress him. But I had come forth with a specific object in view, and I would not be gainsaid. And so, as my business had to be done better that it should be done quickly. Taking advantage of a pause which he made, literally for breath, I commenced abruptly:

"I want to speak to you about your sister."

He turned on me surprised. Then his look changed to one of such complete contempt, and withal his bearing suggested so plainly that he knew beforehand what I was going to say, that I blurted out defiantly, and without stopping to choose my words:

"I think it an infernal shame that you, her brother, should allow her to masquerade about with this good-natured but eccentric Metford girl—I should say Miss Metford."

"Why so?" he asked coldly.

"Because it is absurd; and because it isn't decent."

"My dear Abraham," Brande said quietly, "or is your period so recent as that of Isaac or Jacob? My sister pleases herself in these matters, and has every right to do so."

"She has not. You are her brother."

"Very well, I am her brother. She has no right to think for herself; no right to live save by my permission. Then I graciously permit her to think, and I allow her to live."

"You'll be sorry for this nonsense sooner or later—and don't say I didn't warn you." The absolute futility of my last clause struck me painfully at the moment, but I could not think of any way to better it. It was hard to reason with such a man, one who denied the fundamental principles of family life. I was thinking over what to say next, when Brande stopped and put his hand, in a kindly way, upon my shoulder.

"My good fellow," he said, "what does it matter? What do the actions of my sister signify more than the actions of any other man's sister? And what about the Society? Have you made up your mind about joining?"

"I have. I made it up twice to-day," I answered. "I made it up in the morning that I would see yourself and your Society to the devil before I would join it. Excuse my bluntness; but you are so extremely candid yourself you will not mind."

"Certainly, I do not mind bluntness. Rudeness is superfluous."

"And I made it up this evening," I said, a little less aggressively, "that I would join it if the devil himself were already in it, as I half suspect he is."

"I like that," Brande said gravely. "That is the spirit I want in the man who joins me."

To which I replied: "What under the sun is the object of this Society of yours?"

"Proximately to complete our investigations—already far advanced— into the origin of the Universe."

"And ultimately?"

"I cannot tell you now. You will not know that until you join us."

"And if your ultimate object does not suit me, I can withdraw?"

"No, it would then be too late."

"How so? I am not morally bound by an oath which I swear without full knowledge of its consequences and responsibilities."

"Oath! The oath you swear! You swear no oath. Do you fancy you are joining a society of Rechabites or Carmelites, or mediaeval rubbish of that kind. Don't keep so painstakingly behind the age."

I thought for a moment over what this mysterious man had said, over the hidden dangers in which his mad chimeras might involve the most innocent accomplice. Then I thought of that dark-eyed, sweet-voiced, young girl, as she lay on the green grass under the beech-tree in the wood and out-argued me on every point. Very suddenly, and, perhaps, in a manner somewhat grandiose, I answered him:

"I will join your Society for my own purpose, and I will quit it when I choose."

"You have every right," Brande said carelessly. "Many have done the same before you."

"Can you introduce me to any one who has done so?" I asked, with an eagerness that could not be dissembled.

"I am afraid I can not."

"Or give me an address?"

"Oh yes, that is simple." He turned over a note-book until he found a blank page. Then he drew the pencil from its loop, put the point to his lips, and paused. He was standing with his back to the failing light, so I could not see the expression of his mobile face. When he paused, I knew that no ordinary doubt beset him. He stood thus for nearly a minute. While he waited, I watched a pair of swans flit ghost-like over the silken surface of the lake. Between us and a dark bank of wood the lights of the house flamed red. The melancholy even-song of a blackbird wailed out from a shrubbery beside us. Then Herbert Brande wrote in his note-book, and tearing out the page, he handed it to me, saying: "That is the address of the last man who quitted us."

The light was now so dim I had to hold the paper close to my eyes in order to read the lines. They were these—

GEORGE DELANY,
Near Saint Anne's Chapel,
Woking Cemetery.

V. THE MURDER CLUB

"Delany was the last man who quitted us—you see I use your expression again. I like it," Brande said quietly, watching me as he spoke.

I stood staring at the slip of paper which I held in my hand for some moments before I could reply. When my voice came back, I asked hoarsely:

"Did this man, Delany, die suddenly after quitting the Society?"

"He died immediately. The second event was contemporaneous with the first."

"And in consequence of it?"

"Certainly."

"Have all the members who retired from your list been equally short-lived?"

"Without any exception whatever."

"Then your Society, after all your high-flown talk about it, is only a vulgar murder club," I said bitterly.

"Wrong in fact, and impertinent in its expression. It is not a murder club, and—well, you are the first to discover its vulgarity."

"I call things by their plain names. You may call your Society what you please. As to my joining it in face of what you have told me—"

"Which is more than was ever told to any man before he joined—to any man living or dead. And more, you need not join it yet unless you still wish to do so. I presume what I have said will prevent you."

"On the contrary, if I had any doubt, or if there was any possibility of my wavering before this interview, there is none now. I join at once."

He would have taken my hand, but that I could not permit. I left him without another word, or any form of salute, and returned to the house. I did not appear again in the domestic circle that evening, for I had enough upon my mind without further burdening myself with social pretences.

I sat in my room and tried once more to consider my position. It was this: for the sake of a girl whom I had only met some score of times; who sometimes acted, talked, dressed after a fashion suggestive of insanity; who had glorious dark eyes, a perfect figure, and an exquisitely beautiful face—but I interrupt myself. For the sake of this girl, and for the manifestly impossible purpose of protecting her from herself as well as others, I had surrendered myself to the probable vengeance of a band of cut-throats if I betrayed them, and to the certain vengeance of the law if I did not. Brande, notwithstanding his constant scepticism, was scrupulously truthful. His statement of fact must be relied upon. His opinions were another matter. As nothing practical resulted from my reflections, I came to the conclusion that I had got into a pretty mess for the sake of a handsome face. I regretted this result, but was glad of the cause of it. On this I went to bed.

Next morning I was early astir, for I must see Natalie Brande without delay, and I felt sure she would be no sluggard on that splendid summer day. I tried the lawn between the house and the lake shore. I did not find her there. I found her friend Miss Metford. The girl was sauntering about, swinging a walking-cane carelessly. She was still rationally dressed, but I observed with relief that the rational part of her costume was more in the nature of the divided skirt than the plain knickerbockers of the previous day. She accosted me cheerfully by my surname, and not to be outdone by her, I said coolly:

"How d'ye do, Metford?"

"Very well, thanks. I suppose you expected Natalie? You see you have only me."

"Delighted," I was commencing with a forced smile, when she stopped me.

"You look it. But that can't be helped. Natalie saw you going out, and sent me to meet you. I am to look after you for an hour or so. You join the Society this evening, I hear. You must be very pleased—and flattered."

I could not assent to this, and so remained silent. The girl chattered on in her own outspoken manner, which, now that I was growing accustomed to it, I did not find as unpleasant as at first. One thing was evident to me. She had no idea of the villainous nature of Brande's Society. She could not have spoken so carelessly if she shared my knowledge of it. While she talked to me, I wondered if it was fair to her—a likeable girl, in spite of her undesirable affectations of advanced opinion, emancipation or whatever she called it—was it fair to allow her to associate with a band of murderers, and not so much as whisper a word of warning? No doubt, I myself was associating with the band; but I was not in ignorance of the responsibility thereby incurred.

"Miss Metford," I said, without heeding whether I interrupted her, "are you in on the secret of this Society?"

"I? Not at present. I shall be later on."

I stopped and faced her with so serious an expression that she listened to me attentively.

"If you will take my earnest advice—and I beg you not to neglect it—you will have nothing to do with it or any one belonging to it."

"Not even Brande—I mean Natalie? Is she dangerous?"

I disregarded her mischief and continued: "If you can get Miss Brande away from her brother and his acquaintances," (I had nearly said accomplices,) "and keep her away, you would be doing the best and kindest thing you ever did in your life."

Miss Metford was evidently impressed by my seriousness, but, as she herself said very truly, it was unlikely that she would be able to interfere in the way I suggested. Besides, my mysterious warning was altogether too vague to be of any use as a guide for her own action, much less that of her friend. I dared not speak plainer. I could only repeat, in the most emphatic words, my anxiety that she would think carefully over what I had said. I then pretended to recollect an engagement with Brande, for I was in such low spirits I had really little taste for any company.

She was disappointed, and said so in her usual straightforward way. It was not in the power of any gloomy prophecy to oppress her long. The serious look which my words had brought on her face passed quickly, and it was in her natural manner that she bade me good-morning, saying:

"It is rather a bore, for I looked forward to a pleasant hour or two taking you about."

I postponed my breakfast for want of appetite, and, as Brande's house was the best example of Liberty Hall I had ever met with, I offered no apology for my absence during the entire day when I rejoined my host and hostess in the evening. The interval I spent in the woods, thinking much and deciding nothing.

After dinner, Brande introduced me to a man whom he called Edward Grey. Natalie conducted me to the room in which they were engaged. From the mass of correspondence in which this man Grey was absorbed, and the litter of papers about him, it was evident that he must have been in the house long before I made his acquaintance.

Grey handed me a book, which I found to be a register of the names of the members of Brande's Society, and pointed out the place for my signature.

When I had written my name on the list I said to Brande: "Now that I have nominated myself, I suppose you'll second me?"

"It is not necessary," he answered; "you are already a member. Your remark to Miss Metford this morning made you one of us. You advised her, you recollect, to beware of us."

"That girl!" I exclaimed, horrified. "Then she is one of your spies? Is it possible?"

"No, she is not one of our spies. We have none, and she knew nothing of the purpose for which she was used."

"Then I beg to say that you have made a d—d shameful use of her."

In the passion of the moment I forgot my manners to my host, and formed the resolution to denounce the Society to the police the moment I returned to London. Brande was not offended by my violence. There was not a trace of anger in his voice as he said:

"Miss Metford's information was telepathically conveyed to my sister."

"Then it was your sister—"

"My sister knows as little as the other. In turn, I received the information telepathically from her, without the knowledge of either. I was just telling Grey of it when you came into the room."

"And," said Grey, "your intention to go straight from this house to Scotland Yard, there to denounce us to the police, has been telepathically received by myself."

"My God!" I cried, "has a man no longer the right to his own thoughts?"

Grey went on without noticing my exclamation: "Any overt or covert action on your part, toward carrying out your intention, will be telepathically conveyed to us, and our executive—" He shrugged his shoulders.

"I know," I said, "Woking Cemetery, near Saint Anne's Chapel. You have ground there."

"Yes, we have to dispense with—"

"Say murder."

"Dispense with," Grey repeated sharply, "any member whose loyalty is questionable. This is not our wish; it is our necessity. It is the only means by which we can secure the absolute immunity of the Society pending the achievement of its object. To dispense with any living man we have only to will that he shall die."

"And now that I am a member, may I ask what is this object, the secret of which you guard with such fiendish zeal?" I demanded angrily.

"The restoration of a local etheric tumour to its original formation."

"I am already weary of this jargon from Brande," I interrupted. "What do you mean?"

"We mean to attempt the reduction of the solar system to its elemental ether."

"And you will accomplish this triviality by means of Huxley's comet, I suppose?"

I could scarcely control my indignation. This fooling, as I thought it, struck me as insulting. Neither Brande nor Grey appeared to notice my keen resentment. Grey answered me in a quiet, serious tone.

"We shall attempt it by destroying the earth. We may fail in the complete achievement of our design, but in any case we shall at least be certain of reducing this planet to the ether of which it is composed."

"Of course, of course," I agreed derisively. "You will at least make sure of that. You have found out how to do it too, I have no doubt?"

"Yes," said Grey, "we have found out."

VI. A TELEPATHIC TELEGRAM

I left the room and hurried outside without any positive plan for my movements. My brain was in such a whirl I could form no connected train of thought. These men, whose conversation was a jargon fitting only for lunatics, had proved that they could read my mind with the ease of a telegraph operator taking a message off a wire. That they, further, possessed marvellous, if not miraculous powers, over occult natural forces could hardly be doubted. The net in which I had voluntarily entangled myself was closing around me. An irresistible impulse to fly—to desert Natalie and save myself—came over me. I put this aside presently. It was both unworthy and unwise. For whither should I fly? The ends of the earth would not be far enough to save me, the depths of the sea would not be deep enough to hide me from those who killed by willing that their victim should die.

On the other hand, if my senses had only been hocussed, and Messrs. Brande and Grey were nothing better than clever tricksters, the park gate was far enough, and the nearest policeman force enough, to save me from their vengeance. But the girl—Natalie! She was clairvoyante. They practised upon her. My diagnosis of the strange seeing-without-sight expression of her eyes was then correct. And it was clear to me that whatsoever or whomsoever Brande and Grey believed or disbelieved in, they certainly believed in themselves. They might be relied on to spare nothing and no one in their project, however ridiculous or mad their purpose might be. What then availed my paltry protection when the girl herself was a willing victim, and the men omnipotent? Nevertheless, if I failed eventually to serve her, I could at least do my best.

It was clear that I must stand by Natalie Brande.

While I was thus reflecting, the following conversation took place between Brande and Grey. I found a note of it in a diary which Brande kept desultorily. He wrote this up so irregularly no continuous information can be gleaned from it as to his life. How the diary came into my hands will be seen later. The memorandum is written thus:—

Grey—Our new member? Why did you introduce him? You say he cannot help with money. It is plain he cannot help with brains.

Brande—He interests Natalie. He is what the uneducated call good-natured. He enjoys doing unselfish things, unaware that it is for the selfish sake of the agreeable sensation thereby secured. Besides, I like him myself. He amuses me. To make him a member was the only safe way of keeping him so much about us. But Natalie is the main reason. I am afraid of her wavering in spite of my hypnotic influence. In a girl of her intensely emotional nature the sentiment of hopeless love will create profound melancholy. Dominated by that she is safe. It seems cruel at first sight. It is not really so. It is not cruel to reconcile her to a fate she cannot escape. It is merciful. For the rest, what does it matter? It will be all the same in—

Grey—This day six months.

Brande—I believe I shivered. Heredity has much to answer for.

That is the whole of the entry. I did not read the words until the hand that wrote them was dust.

Natalie professed some disappointment when I announced my immediate return to town. I was obliged to manufacture an excuse for such a hasty departure, and so fell back on an old engagement which I had truly overlooked, and which really called me away. But it would have called long enough without an answer if it had not been for Brande himself, his friend Grey, and their insanities. My mind was fixed on one salient issue: how to get Natalie Brande out of her brother's evil influence. This would be better compassed when I myself was outside the scope of his extraordinary influence. And so I went without delay.

For some time after my return to London, I went about visiting old haunts and friends. I soon tired of this. The haunts had lost their interest. The friends were changed, or I was changed. I could not resume the friendships which had been interrupted. The chain of connection had been broken and the links would not weld easily. So, after some futile efforts to return to the circle I had long deserted, I desisted and accepted my exclusion with serenity. I am not sure that I desired the old relationships re-established. And as my long absence had prevented any fresh shoots of friendship being grafted, I found myself alone in London. I need say no more.

One evening I was walking through the streets in a despondent mood, as had become my habit. By chance I read the name of a street into which I had turned to avoid a more crowded thoroughfare. It was that in which Miss Metford lived. I knew that she had returned to town, for she had briefly acquainted me with the fact on a postcard written some days previously.

Here was a chance of distraction. This girl's spontaneous gaiety, which I found at first displeasing, was what I wanted to help me to shake off the gloomy incubus of thought oppressing me. It was hardly within the proprieties to call upon her at such an hour, but it could not matter very much, when the girl's own ideas were so unconventional. She had independent means, and lived apart from her family in order to be rid of domestic limitations. She had told me that she carried a latch-key—indeed she had shown it to me with a flourish of triumph—and that she delighted in free manners. Free manners, she was careful to add, did not mean bad manners. To my mind the terms were synonymous. When opposite her number I decided to call, and, having knocked at the door, was told that Miss Metford was at home.

"Hallo, Marcel! Glad to see you," she called out, somewhat stridently for my taste. Her dress was rather mannish, as usual. In lieu of her out-door tunic she wore a smoking-jacket. When I entered she was sitting in an arm-chair, with her feet on a music-stool. She arose so hastily that the music-stool was overturned, and allowed to lie where it fell.

"What is the matter?" she asked, concerned. "Have you seen a ghost?"

"I think I have seen many ghosts of late," I said, "and they have not been good company. I was passing your door, and I have come in for comfort."

She crossed the room and poured out some whisky from a decanter which was standing on a side-board. Then she opened a bottle of soda-water with a facility which suggested practice. I was relieved to think that it was not Natalie who was my hostess. Handing me the glass, she said peremptorily:

"Drink that. That is right. Give me the glass. Now smoke. Do I allow smoking here? Pah! I smoke here myself."

I lit a cigar and sat down beside her. The clouds began to lift from my brain and float off in the blue smoke wreaths. We talked on ordinary topics without my once noticing how deftly they had been introduced by Miss Metford. I never thought of the flight of time until a chime from a tiny clock on the mantelpiece—an exquisite sample of the tasteful furniture of the whole room—warned me that my visit had lasted two hours. I arose reluctantly.

She rallied me on my ingratitude. I had come in a sorry plight. I was now restored. She was no longer useful, therefore I left her. And so on, till I said with a solemnity no doubt lugubrious:

"I am most grateful, Miss Metford. I cannot tell you how grateful I am. You would not understand—"

"Oh, please leave my poor understanding alone, and tell me what has happened to you. I should like to hear it. And what is more, I like you." She said this so carelessly, I did not feel embarrassed. "Now, then, the whole story, please." Saying which, she sat down again.

"Do you really know nothing more of Brande's Society than you admitted when I last spoke to you about it?" I asked, without taking the chair she pushed over to me.

"This is all I know," she answered, in the rhyming voice of a young pupil declaiming a piece of a little understood and less cared for recitation. "The society has very interesting evenings. Brande shows one beautiful experiments, which, I daresay, would be amazingly instructive if one were inclined that way, which I am not. The men are mostly long-haired creatures with spectacles. Some of them are rather good-looking. All are wholly mad. And my friend—I mean the only girl I could ever stand as a friend—Natalie Brande, is crazy about them."

"Nothing more than that?"

"Nothing more."

The clock now struck the hour of nine, the warning chime for which had startled me.

"Is there anything more than that?" Miss Metford asked with some impatience.

I thought for a moment. Unless my own senses had deceived me that evening in Brande's house, I ran a great risk of sharing George Delany's fate if I remained where I was much longer. And suppose I told her all I knew, would not that bring the same danger upon her too? So I had to answer:

"I cannot tell you. I am a member now."

"Then you must know more than any mere outsider like myself. I suppose it would not be fair to ask you. Anyhow, you will come back and see me soon. By the way, what is your address?"

I gave her my address. She wrote it down on a silver-cased tablet, and remarked:

"That will be all right. I'll look you up some evening."

As I drove to my hotel, I felt that the mesmeric trick, or whatever artifice had been practised upon me by Brande and Grey, had now assumed its true proportion. I laughed at my fears, and was thankful that I had not described them to the strong-minded young woman to whose kindly society I owed so much. What an idiot she would have thought me!

A servant met me in the hall.

"Telegram, sir. Just arrived at this moment."

I took the telegram, and went upstairs with it unopened in my hand. A strange fear overcame me. I dared not open the envelope. I knew beforehand who the sender was, and what the drift of the message would be. I was right. It was from Brande.

> I beg you to be more cautious. Your discussion with Miss
> M. this evening might have been disastrous. I thought all
> was over at nine o'clock.
>
> BRANDE.

I sat down stupefied. When my senses returned, I looked at the table where I had thrown the telegram. It was not there, nor in the room. I rang for the man who had given it to me, and he came immediately.

"About that telegram you gave me just now, Phillips—"

"I beg your pardon, sir," the man interrupted, "I did not give you any telegram this evening."

"I mean when you spoke to me in the hall."

"Yes, sir. I said 'good-night,' but you took no notice. Excuse me, sir, I thought you looked strange."

"Oh, I was thinking of something else. And I remember now, it was Johnson who gave me the telegram."

"Johnson left yesterday, sir."

"Then it was yesterday I was thinking of. You may go, Phillips."

So Brande's telepathic power was objective as well as subjective. My own brain, unaccustomed to be impressed by another mind "otherwise than through the recognised channels of sense," had supplied the likeliest authority for its message. The message was duly delivered, but the telegram was a delusion.

VII. GUILTY!

As to protecting Natalie Brande from her brother and the fanatics with whom he associated, it was now plain that I was powerless. And what guarantee had I that she herself was unaware of his nefarious purpose; that she did not sympathise with it? This last thought flashed upon me one day, and the sting of pain that followed it was so intolerable, I determined instantly to prove its falsity or truth.

I telegraphed to Brande that I was running down to spend a day or two with him, and followed my message without waiting for a reply. I have still a very distinct recollection of that journey, notwithstanding much that might well have blotted it from my memory. Every mile sped over seemed to mark one more barrier passed on my way to some strange fate; every moment which brought me nearer this incomprehensible girl with her magical eyes was an epoch of impossibility against my ever voluntarily turning back. And now that it is all over, I am glad that I went on steadfastly to the end.

Brande received me with the easy affability of a man to whom good breeding had ceased to be a habit, and had become an instinct. Only once did anything pass between us bearing on the extraordinary relationship which he had established with me—the relation of victor and victim, I considered it. We had been left together for a few moments, and I said as soon as the others were out of hearing distance:

"I got your message."

"I know you did," he replied. That was all. There was an awkward pause. It must be broken somehow. Any way out of the difficulty was better than to continue in it.

"Have you seen this?" I asked, handing Brande a copy of a novel which I had picked up at a railway bookstall. When I say that it was new and popular, it will be understood that it was indecent.

He looked at the title, and said indifferently: "Yes, I have seen it, and in order to appreciate this class of fiction fairly, I have even tried to read it. Why do you ask?"

"Because I thought it would be in your line. It is very advanced." I said this to gain time.

"Advanced—advanced? I am afraid I do not comprehend. What do you mean by 'advanced'? And how could it be in my line. I presume you mean by that, on my plane of thought?"

"By 'advanced,' I mean up-to-date. What do you mean by it?"

"If I used the word at all, I should mean educated, evolved. Is this evolved? Is it even educated? It is not always grammatical. It has no style. In motive, it ante-dates Boccaccio."

"You disapprove of it."

"Certainly not."

"Then you approve it, notwithstanding your immediate condemnation?"

"By no means. I neither approve nor disapprove. It only represents a phase of humanity—the deliberate purpose of securing money or notoriety to the individual, regardless of the welfare of the community. There is nothing to admire in that. It would be invidious to blame it when the whole social scheme is equally wrong and contemptible. By the way, what interest do you think the wares of any literary pander, of either sex, could possess for me, a student—even if a mistaken one—of science?"

"I did not think the book would possess the slightest interest for you, and I suppose you are already aware of that?"

"Ah no! My telepathic power is reserved for more serious purposes. Its exercise costs me too much to expend it on trifles. In consequence I do not know why you mentioned the book."

To this I answered candidly, "I mentioned it in order to get myself out of a conversational difficulty—without much success."

Natalie was reserved with me at first. She devoted herself unnecessarily to a boy named Halley who was staying with them. Grey had gone to London. His place was taken by a Mr. Rockingham, whom I did not like. There was something sinister in his expression, and he rarely spoke save to say something cynical, and in consequence disagreeable. He had "seen life," that is, everything deleterious to and destructive of it. His connection with Brande was clearly a rebound, the rebound of disgust. There was nothing creditable to him in that. My first impression of him was thus unfavourable. My last recollection of him is a fitting item in the nightmare which contains it.

The youth Halley would have interested me under ordinary circumstances. His face was as handsome and refined as that of a pretty girl. His figure, too, was slight and his voice effeminate. But there my own advantage, as I deemed it, over him ceased. Intellectually, he was a pupil of Brande's who did his master credit. Having made this discovery I did not pursue it. My mind was fixed too fast upon a definite issue to be more than temporarily interested in the epigrams of a peachy-cheeked man of science.

The afternoon was well advanced before I had an opportunity of speaking to Natalie. When it came, I did not stop to puzzle over a choice of phrases.

"I wish to speak to you alone on a subject of extreme importance to me," I said hurriedly. "Will you come with me to the sea-shore? Your time, I know, is fully occupied. I would not ask this if my happiness did not depend upon it."

The philosopher looked on me with grave, kind eyes. But the woman's heart within her sent the red blood flaming to her cheeks. It was then given to me to fathom the lowest depth of boorish stupidity I had ever sounded.

"I don't mean that," I cried, "I would not dare—"

The blush on her cheek burnt deeper as she tossed her head proudly back, and said straight out, without any show of fence or shadow of concealment:

"It was my mistake. I am glad to know that I did you an injustice. You are my friend, are you not?"

"I believe I have the right to claim that title," I answered.

"Then what you ask is granted. Come." She put her hand boldly into mine. I grasped the slender fingers, saying:

"Yes, Natalie, some day I will prove to you that I am your friend."

"The proof is unnecessary," she replied, in a low sad voice.

We started for the sea. Not a word was spoken on the way. Nor did our eyes meet. We were in a strange position. It was this: the man who had vowed he was the woman's friend—who did not intend to shirk the proof of his promise, and never did gainsay it—meant to ask the woman, before the day was over, to clear herself of knowingly associating with a gang of scientific murderers. The woman had vaguely divined his purpose, and could not clear herself.

When we arrived at the shore we occupied ourselves inconsequently. We hunted little fishes until Natalie's dainty boots were dripping. We examined quaint denizens of the shallow water until her gloves were spoilt. We sprang from rock to rock and evaded the onrush of the foaming waves. We made aqueducts for inter-communication between deep pools. We basked in the sunshine, and listened to the deep moan of the sounding sea, and the solemn murmur of the shells. We drank in the deep breath of the ocean, and for a brief space we were like happy children.

The end came soon to this ephemeral happiness. It was only one of those bright coins snatched from the niggard hand of Time which must always be paid back with usurious charges. We paid with cruel interest.

Standing on a flat rock side by side, I nerved myself to ask this girl the same question I had asked her friend, Edith Metford, how much she knew of the extraordinary and preposterous Society—as I still tried to consider it—which Herbert Brande had founded. She looked so frank, so refined, so kind, I hardly dared to put my brutal question to an innocent girl, whom I had seen wince at the suffering of a maimed bird, and pale to the lips at the death-cry of a rabbit. This time there was no possibility of untoward consequence in the question save to myself—for surely the girl was safe from her own brother. And I myself preferred to risk the consequences rather than endure longer the thought that she belonged voluntarily to a vile murder club. Yet the question would not come. A simple thing brought it out. Natalie, after looking seaward silently for some minutes, said simply:

"How long are we to stand here, I wonder?"

"Until you answer this question. How much do you know about your brother's Society, which I have joined to my own intense regret?"

"I am sorry you regret having joined," she replied gravely.

"You would not be sorry," said I, "if you knew as much about it as I do," forgetting that I had still no answer to my question, and that the extent of her knowledge was unknown to me.

"I believe I do know as much as you." There was a tremor in her voice and an anxious pleading look in her eyes. This look maddened me. Why should she plead to me unless she was guilty? I stamped my foot upon the rock without noticing that in so doing I kicked our whole collection of shells into the water.

There was something more to ask, but I stood silent and sullen. The woods above the beach were choral with bird-voices. They were hateful to me. The sea song of the tumbling waves was hideous. I cursed the yellow sunset light glaring on their snowy crests. A tiny hand was laid upon my arm. I writhed under its deadly if delicious touch. But I could not put it away, nor keep from turning to the sweet face beside me, to mark once more its mute appeal—now more than mere appeal; it was supplication that was in her eyes. Her red lips were parted as though they voiced an unspoken prayer. At last a prayer did pass from them to me.

"Do not judge me until you know me better. Do not hate me without cause. I am not wicked, as you think. I—I—I am trying to do what I think is right. At least, I am not selfish or cruel. Trust me yet a little while."

I looked at her one moment, and then with a sob I clasped her in my arms, and cried aloud:

"My God! to name murder and that angel face in one breath! Child, you have been befooled. You know nothing."

For a second she lingered in my embrace. Then she gently put away my arms, and looking up at me, said fearlessly but sorrowfully:

"I cannot lie—even for your love. I know *all*."

VIII. THE WOKING MYSTERY

She knew all. Then she was a murderess—or in sympathy with murderers. My arms fell from her. I drew back shuddering. I dared not look in her lying eyes, which cried pity when her base heart knew no mercy. Surely now I had solved the maddening puzzle which the character of this girl had, so far, presented to me. Yet the true solution was as far from me as ever. Indeed, I could not well have been further from it than at that moment.

As we walked back, Natalie made two or three unsuccessful attempts to lure me out of the silence which was certainly more eloquent on my part than any words I could have used. Once she commenced:

"It is hard to explain—"

I interrupted her harshly. "No explanation is possible."

On that she put her handkerchief to her eyes, and a half-suppressed sob shook her slight figure. Her grief distracted me. But what could I say to assuage it?

At the hall door I stopped and said, "Good-bye."

"Are you not coming in?"

There was a directness and emphasis in the question which did not escape me.

"I?" The horror in my own voice surprised myself, and assuredly did not pass without her notice.

"Very well; good-bye. We are not exactly slaves of convention here, but you are too far advanced in that direction even for me. This is your second startling departure from us. I trust you will spare me the humiliation entailed by the condescension of your further acquaintance."

"Give me an hour!" I exclaimed aghast. "You do not make allowance for the enigma in which everything is wrapped up. I said I was your friend when I thought you of good report. Give me an hour—only an hour—to say whether I will stand by my promise, now that you yourself have claimed that your report is not good but evil. For that is really what you have protested. Do I ask too much? or is your generosity more limited even than my own?"

"Ah, no! I would not have you think that. Take an hour, or a year—an hour only if you care for my happiness."

"Agreed," said I. "I will take the hour. Discretion can have the year."

So I left her. I could not go indoors. A roof would smother me. Give me the open lawns, the leafy woods, the breath of the summer wind. Away, then, to the silence of the coming night. For an hour leave me to my thoughts. Her unworthiness was now more than suspected. It was admitted. My misery was complete. But I would not part with her; I could not. Innocent or guilty, she was mine. I must suffer with her or for her. The resolution by which I have abided was formed as I wandered lonely through the woods.

When I reached my room that night I found a note from Brande. To receive a letter from a man in whose house I was a guest did not surprise me. I was past that stage. There was nothing mysterious in the letter, save its conclusion. It was simply an invitation to a public meeting of the Society, which was to be held on that day week in the hall in Hanover Square, and the special feature in the letter—seeing that it did not vanish like the telegram, but remained an ordinary sheet of paper—lay in its concluding sentence. This urged me to allow nothing to prevent my attendance. "You will perhaps understand thereafter that we are neither political plotters nor lunatics, as you have thought."

Thought! The man's mysterious power was becoming wearisome. It was too much for me. I wished that I had never seen his face.

As I lay sleepless in my bed, I recommenced that interminable introspection which, heretofore, had been so barren of result. It was easy to swear to myself that I would stand by Natalie Brande, that I would never desert her. But how should my action be directed in order that by its conduct I might prevail upon the girl herself to surrender her evil associates? I knew that she regarded me with affection. And I knew also that she would not leave her brother for my sake. Did she sympathise with his nefarious schemes, or was she decoyed into them like myself?

Decoyed! That was it!

I sprang from the bed, beside myself with delight. Now I had not merely a loophole of escape from all these miseries; I had a royal highway. Fool, idiot, blind mole that I was, not to perceive sooner that easy solution of the problem! No wonder that she was wounded by my unworthy doubts. And she had tried to explain, but I would not listen! I threw myself back and commenced to weave all manner of pleasant fancies round the salvation of this girl from her brother's baneful influence, and the annihilation of his Society, despite its occult powers, by mine own valour. The reaction was too great. Instead of constructing marvellous counterplots, I fell sound asleep.

Next day I found Natalie in a pleasant morning-room to which I was directed. She wore her most extreme—and, in consequence, most exasperating—rational costume. When I entered the room she pushed a chair towards me, in a way that suggested Miss Metford's worst manner, and lit a cigarette, for the express purpose, I felt, of annoying me.

"I have come," I said somewhat shamefacedly, "to explain."

"And apologise?"

"Yes, to apologise. I made a hideous mistake. I have suffered for it as much as you could wish."

"Wish you to suffer!" She flung away her cigarette. Her dark eyes opened wide in unassumed surprise. And that curious light of pity, which I had so often wondered at, came into them. "I am very sorry if you have suffered," she said, with convincing earnestness.

"How could I doubt you? Senseless fool that I was to suppose for one moment that you approved of what you could not choose but know—"

At this her face clouded.

"I am afraid you are still in error. What opinion have you formed which alters your estimate of me?"

"The only opinion possible: that you have unwillingly learned the secret of your brother's Society; but, like myself—you see no way to—to—"

"To what purpose?"

"To destroy it."

"I am not likely to attempt that."

"No, it would be impossible, and the effort would cost your life."

"That is not my reason." She arose and stood facing me. "I do not like to lose your esteem. You know already that I will not lie to retain it. I approve of the Society's purpose."

"And its actions?"

"They are inevitable. Therefore I approve also of its actions. I shall not ask you to remain now, for I see that you are again horrified; as is natural, considering your knowledge—or, pardon me for saying so, your want of knowledge. I shall be glad to see you after the lecture to which you are invited. You will know a little more then; not all, perhaps, but enough to shake your time-dishonoured theories of life—and death."

I bowed, and left the room without a word. It was true, then, that she was mad like the others, or worse than mad—a thousand times worse! I said farewell to Brande, as his guest, for the last time. Thenceforward I would meet him as his enemy—his secret enemy as far as I could preserve my secrecy with such a man; his open enemy when the proper time should come.

In the railway carriage I turned over some letters and papers which I found in my pockets, not with deliberate intention, but to while away the time. One scrap startled me. It was the sheet on which Brande had written the Woking address, and on reading it over once more, a thought occurred to me which I acted on as soon as possible. I could go to Woking and find out something about the man Delany. So long as my inquiries were kept within the limits of the strictest discretion, neither Brande nor any of his executive could blame me for seeking convincing evidence of the secret power they claimed.

On my arrival in London, I drove immediately to the London Necropolis Company's station and caught the funeral train which runs to Brookwood cemetery. With Saint Anne's Chapel as my base, I made short excursions hither and thither, and stood before a tombstone erected to the memory of George Delany, late of the Criminal Investigation Department, Scotland Yard. This was a clue which I could follow, so I hurried back to town and called on the superintendent of the department.

Yes, I was told, Delany had belonged to the department. He had been a very successful officer in ferreting out foreign Anarchists and evil-doers. His last movement was to join a Society of harmless cranks who met in Hanover Square. No importance was attached to this in the department. It could not have been done in the way of business, although Delany pretended that it was. He had dropped dead in the street as he was leaving his cab to enter the office with information which must have appeared to him important—to judge from the cabman's evidence as to his intense excitement and repeated directions for faster driving. There was an inquest and a post-mortem, but "death from natural causes" was the verdict. That was all. It was enough for me.

I had now sufficient evidence, and was finally convinced that the Society was as dangerous as it was demented.

IX. CUI BONO?

When I arrived at the Society's rooms on the evening for which I had an invitation, I found them pleasantly lighted. The various scientific diagrams and instruments had been removed, and comfortable arm-chairs were arranged so that a free passage was available, not merely to each row, but to each chair. The place was full when I entered, and soon afterwards the door was closed and locked. Natalie Brande and Edith Metford were seated beside each other. An empty chair was on Miss Metford's right. She saw me standing at the door and nodded toward the empty seat which she had reserved for me. When I reached it she made a movement as if to forestall me and leave me the middle chair. I deprecated this by a look which was intentionally so severe that she described it later as a malignant scowl.

I could not at the moment seat myself voluntarily beside Natalie Brande with the exact and final knowledge which I had learnt at Scotland Yard only one week old. I could not do it just then, although I did not mean to draw back from what I had undertaken—to stand by her, innocent or guilty. But I must have time to become accustomed to the sensation which followed this knowledge. Miss Metford's fugitive attempts at conversation pending the commencement of the lecture were disagreeable to me.

There was a little stir on the platform. The chairman, in a few words, announced Herbert Brande. "This is the first public lecture," he said, "which has been given since the formation of the Society, and in consequence of the fact that a number of people not scientifically educated are present, the lecturer will avoid the more esoteric phases of his subject, which would otherwise present themselves in his treatment of it, and confine himself to the commonplaces of scientific insight. The title of the lecture is identical with that of our Society—*Cui Bono?*"

Brande came forward unostentatiously and placed a roll of paper on the reading-desk. I have copied the extracts which follow from this manuscript. The whole essay, indeed, remains with me intact, but it is too long—and it would be immaterial—to reproduce it all in this narrative. I cannot hope either to reproduce the weird impressiveness of the lecturer's personality, his hold over his audience, or my own emotions in listening to this man—whom I had proved, not only from his own confession, but by the strongest collateral evidence, to be a callous and relentless murderer—to hear him glide with sonorous voice and graceful gesture from point to point in his logical and terrible indictment of suffering!—the futility of it, both in itself and that by which it was administered! No one could know Brande without finding interest, if not pleasure, in his many chance expressions full of curious and mysterious thought. I had often listened to his extemporaneous brain pictures, as the reader knows, but I had never before heard him deliberately formulate a planned-out system of thought. And such a system! This is the gospel according to Brande.

"In the verbiage of primitive optimism a misleading limitation is placed on the significance of the word Nature and its inflections. And the misconception of the meaning of an important word is as certain to lead to an inaccurate concept as is the misstatement of a premise to precede a false conclusion. For instance, in the aphorism, variously rendered, 'what is natural is right,' there is an excellent illustration of the misapplication of the word 'natural.' If the saying means that what is natural is just and wise, it might as well run 'what is natural is wrong,' injustice and unwisdom being as natural, *i.e.,* a part of Nature, as justice and wisdom. Morbidity and immorality are as natural as health and purity. Not more so, but not less so. That 'Nature is made better by no mean but Nature makes that mean,' is true enough. It is inevitably true. The question remains, in making that mean, has she really made anything that tends toward the final achievement of universal happiness? I say she has not.

"The misuse of a word, it may be argued, could not prove a serious obstacle to the growth of knowledge, and might be even interesting to the student of etymology. But behind the misuse of the word 'natural' there is a serious confusion of thought which must be clarified before the mass of human intelligence can arrive at a just appreciation of the verities which surround human existence, and explain it. To this end it is necessary to get rid of the archaic idea of Nature as a paternal, providential, and beneficent protector, a successor to the 'special providence,' and to know the true Nature, bond-slave as she is of her own eternal persistence of force; that sole primary principle of which all other principles are only correlatives; of which the existence of matter is but a cognisable evidence.

"The optimist notion, therefore, that Nature is an all-wise designer, in whose work order, system, wisdom, and beauty are prominent, does not fare well when placed under the microscope of scientific research.

"Order?

"There is no order in Nature. Her armies are but seething mobs of rioters, destroying everything they can lay hands on.

"System?

"She has no system, unless it be a *reductio ad absurdum,* which only blunders on the right way after fruitlessly trying every other conceivable path. She is not wise. She never fills a pail but she spills a hogshead. All her works are not beautiful. She never makes a masterpiece but she smashes a million 'wasters' without a care. The theory of evolution—her gospel—reeks with ruffianism, nature-patented and promoted. The whole scheme of the universe, all material existence as it is popularly known, is founded upon and begotten of a system of everlasting suffering as hideous as the fantastic nightmares of religious maniacs. The Spanish Inquisitors have been regarded as the most unnatural monsters who ever disgraced the history of mankind. Yet the atrocities of the Inquisitors, like the battlefields of Napoleon and other heroes, were not only natural, but they have their prototypes in every cubic inch of stagnant water, or ounce of diseased tissue. And stagnant water is as natural as sterilised water; and diseased tissue is as natural as healthy tissue. Wholesale murder is Nature's first law. She creates only to kill, and applies the rule as remorselessly to the units in a star-drift as to the tadpoles in a horse-pond.

"It seems a far cry from a star-drift to a horse-pond. It is so in distance and magnitude. It is not in the matter of constituents. In ultimate composition they are identical. The great nebula in Andromeda is an aggregation of atoms, and so is the river Thames. The only difference between them is the difference in the arrangement and incidence of these atoms and in the molecular motion of which they are the first but not the final cause. In a pint of Thames water, we know that there is bound up a latent force beside which steam and electricity are powerless in comparison. To release that force it is only necessary to apply the sympathetic key; just as the heated point of a needle will explode a mine of gunpowder and lay a city in ashes. That force is asleep. The atoms which could give it reality are at rest, or, at least, in a condition of *quasi*-rest. But in the stupendous mass of incandescent gas which constitutes the nebula of Andromeda, every atom is madly seeking rest and finding none; whirling in raging haste, battling with every other atom in its field of motion, impinging upon others and influencing them, being impinged upon and influenced by them. That awful cauldron exemplifies admirably the method of progress stimulated by suffering. It is the embryo of a new Sun and his planets. After many million years of molecular agony, when his season of fission had come, he will rend huge fragments from his mass and hurl them helpless into space, there to grow into his satellites. In their turn they may reproduce themselves in like manner before their true planetary life begins, in which they shall revolve around their parent as solid spheres. Follow them further and learn how beneficent Nature deals with them.

"After the lapse of time-periods which man may calculate in figures, but of which his finite mind cannot form even a true symbolic conception, the outer skin of the planet cools—rests. Internal troubles prevail for longer periods still; and these, in their unsupportable agony, bend and burst the solid strata overlying; vomit fire through their self-made blow-holes, rear mountains from the depths of the sea, then dash them in pieces.

"Time strides on austere.

"The globe still cools. Life appears upon it. Then begins anew the old strife, but under conditions far more dreadful, for though it be founded on atomic consciousness, the central consciousness of the heterogeneous aggregation of atoms becomes immeasurably more sentient and susceptible with every step it takes from homogenesis. This internecine war must continue while any creature great or small shall remain alive upon the world that bore it.

"By slow degrees the mighty milestones in the protoplasmic march are passed. Plants and animals are now busy, murdering and devouring each other—the strong everywhere destroying the weak. New types appear. Old types disappear. Types possessing the greatest capacity for murder progress most rapidly, and those with the least recede and determine. The neolithic man succeeds the palaeolithic man, and sharpens the stone axe. Then to increase their power for destruction, men find it better to hunt in packs. Communities appear. Soon each community discovers that its own advantage is furthered by confining its killing, in the main, to the members of neighbouring communities. Nations early make the same discovery. And at last, as with ourselves, there is established a race with conscience enough to know that it is vile, and intelligence enough to know that it is insignificant. But what profits this? In the fulness of its time the race shall die. Man will go down into the pit, and all his thoughts will perish. The uneasy consciousness which, in this obscure corner, has for a brief space broken the silence of the Universe, will be at rest. Matter will know itself no longer. Life and death and love, stronger than death, will be as though they never had been. Nor will anything that *is* be better or be worse for all that the labour, genius, devotion, and suffering of man have striven through countless generations to effect.

"The roaring loom of Time weaves on. The globe cools out. Life mercifully ceases from upon its surface. The atmosphere and water disappear. It rests. It is dead.

"But for its vicarious service in influencing more youthful planets within its reach, that dead world might as well be loosed at once from its gravitation cable and be turned adrift into space. Its time has not yet come. It will not come until the great central sun of the system to which it belongs has passed laboriously through all his stages of stellar life and died out also. Then when that dead sun, according to the impact theory, blunders across the path of another sun, dead and blind like himself, its time will come. The result of that impact will be a new star nebula, with all its weary history before it; a history of suffering, in which a million years will not be long enough to write a single page.

"Here we have a scientific parallel to the hell of superstition which may account for the instinctive origin of the smoking flax and the fire which shall never be quenched. We know that the atoms of which the human body is built up are atoms of matter. It follows that every atom in every living body will be present in some form at that final impact in which the solar system will be ended in a blazing whirlwind which will melt the earth with its fervent heat. There is not a molecule or cell in any creature alive this day which will not in its ultimate constituents endure the long agony, lasting countless aeons of centuries, wherein the solid mass of this great globe will be represented by a rush of incandescent gas, stupendous in itself, but trivial in comparison with the hurricane of flame in which it will be swallowed up and lost.

"And when from that hell a new star emerges, and new planets in their season are born of him, and he and they repeat, as they must repeat, the ceaseless, changeless, remorseless story of the universe, every atom in this earth will take its place, and fill again functions identical with those which it, or its fellow, fills now. Life will reappear, develop, determine, to be renewed again as before. And so on for ever.

"Nature has known no rest. From the beginning—which never was—she has been building up only to tear down again. She has been fabricating pretty toys and trinkets, that cost her many a thousand years to forge, only to break them in pieces for her sport. With infinite painstaking she has manufactured man only to torture him with mean miseries in the embryonic stages of his race, and in his higher development to madden him with intellectual puzzles. Thus it will be unto the end—which never shall be. For there is neither beginning nor end to her unvarying cycles. Whether the secular optimist be successful or unsuccessful in realising his paltry span of terrestrial paradise, whether the paeans he sings about it are prophetic dithyrambs or misleading myths, no Christian man need fear for his own immortality. That is well assured. In some form he will surely be raised from the dead. In some shape he will live again. But, *Cui bono?*"

X. FORCE—A REMEDY

"Get me out of this, I am stifled—ill," Miss Metford said, in a low voice to me.

As we were hurrying from the room, Brande and his sister, who had joined him, met us. The fire had died out of his eyes. His voice had returned to its ordinary key. His demeanour was imperturbable, sphinx-like. I murmured some words about the eloquence of the lecture, but interrupted myself when I observed his complete indifference to my remarks, and said,

"Neither praise nor blame seems to affect you, Brande."

"Certainly not," he answered calmly. "You forget that there is nothing deserving of either praise or blame."

I knew I could not argue with him, so we passed on. Outside, I offered to find a cab for Miss Metford, and to my surprise she allowed me to do so. Her self-assertive manner was visibly modified. She made no pretence of resenting this slight attention, as was usual with her in similar cases. Indeed, she asked me to accompany her as far as our ways lay together. But I felt that my society at the time could hardly prove enlivening. I excused myself by saying candidly that I wished to be alone.

My own company soon became unendurable. In despair I turned into a music hall. The contrast between my mental excitement and the inanities of the stage was too acute, so this resource speedily failed me. Then I betook myself to the streets again. Here I remembered a letter Brande had put into my hand as I left the hall. It was short, and the tone was even more peremptory than his usual arrogance. It directed me to meet the members of the Society at Charing Cross station at two o'clock on the following day. No information was given, save that we were all going on a long journey; that I must set my affairs in such order that my absence would not cause any trouble, and the letter ended, "Our experiments are now complete. Our plans are matured. Do not fail to attend."

"Fail to attend!" I muttered. "If I am not the most abject coward on the earth I will attend—with every available policeman in London." The pent-up wrath and impotence of many days found voice at last. "Yes, Brande," I shouted aloud, "I will attend, and you shall be sorry for having invited me."

"But I will not be sorry," said Natalie Brande, touching my arm.

"You here!" I exclaimed, in great surprise, for it was fully an hour since I left the hall, and my movements had been at haphazard since then.

"Yes, I have followed you for your own sake. Are you really going to draw back now?"

"I must."

"Then I must go on alone."

"You will not go on alone. You will remain, and your friends shall go on without you—go to prison without you, I mean."

"Poor boy," she said softly, to herself. "I wonder if I would have thought as I think now if I had known him sooner? I suppose I should have been as other women, and their fools' paradise would have been mine—for a little while."

The absolute hopelessness in her voice pierced my heart. I pleaded passionately with her to give up her brother and all the maniacs who followed him. For the time I forgot utterly that the girl, by her own confession, was already with them in sympathy as well as in deed.

She said to me: "I cannot hold back now. And you? You know you are powerless to interfere. If you will not come with me, I must go alone. But you may remain. I have prevailed on Herbert and Grey to permit that."

"Never," I answered. "Where you go, I go."

"It is not really necessary. In the end it will make no difference. And remember, you still think me guilty."

"Even so, I am going with you—guilty."

Now this seemed to me a very ordinary speech, for who would have held back, thinking her innocent? But Natalie stopped suddenly, and, looking me in the face, said, almost with a sob:

"Arthur, I sometimes wish I had known you sooner. I might have been different." She was silent for a moment. Then she said piteously to me: "You will not fail me to-morrow?"

"No, I will not fail you to-morrow," I answered.

She pressed my hand gratefully, and left me without any explanation as to her movements in the meantime.

I hurried to my hotel to set my affairs in order before joining Brande's expedition. The time was short for this. Fortunately there was not much to do. By midnight I had my arrangements nearly complete. At the time, the greater part of my money was lying at call in a London bank. This I determined to draw in gold the next day. I also had at my banker's some scrip, and I knew I could raise money on that. My personal effects and the mementos of my travels, which lay about my rooms in great confusion, must remain where they were. As to the few friends who still remained to me, I did not write to them. I could not well describe a project of which I knew nothing, save that it was being carried out by dangerous lunatics, or, at least, by men who were dangerous, whether their madness was real or assumed. Nor could I think of any reasonable excuse for leaving England after so long an absence without a personal visit to them. It was best, then, to disappear without a word. Having finished my dispositions, I changed my coat for a dressing-gown and sat down by the window, which I threw open, for the summer night was warm. I sat long, and did not leave my chair until the morning sun was shining on my face.

When I got to Charing Cross next day, a group of fifty or sixty people were standing apart from the general crowd and conversing with animation. Almost the whole strength of the Society was assembled to see a few of us off, I thought. In fact, they were all going. About a dozen women were in the party, and they were dressed in the most extravagant rational costumes. Edith Metford was amongst them. I drew her aside, and apologised for not having called to wish her farewell; but she stopped me.

"Oh, it's all right; I am going too. Don't look so frightened."

This was more than I could tolerate. She was far too good a girl to be allowed to walk blindfold into the pit I had digged for myself with full knowledge. I said imperatively:

"Miss Metford, you shall not go. I warned you more than once—and warned you, I firmly believe, at the risk of my life—against these people. You have disregarded the advice which it may yet cost me dear to have given you."

"To tell you the truth," she said candidly, "I would not go an inch if it were not for yourself. I can't trust you with them. You'd get into mischief. I don't mean with Natalie Brande, but the others; I don't like them. So I am coming to look after you."

"Then I shall speak to Brande."

"That would be useless. I joined the Society this morning."

This she said seriously, and without anything of the spirit of bravado which was one of her faults. That ended our dispute. We exchanged a meaning look as our party took their seats. There was now, at any rate, one human being in the Society to whom I could speak my mind.

We travelled by special train. Our ultimate destination was a fishing village on the southern coast, near Brande's residence. Here we found a steam yacht of about a thousand tons lying in the harbour with steam up.

The vessel was a beautiful model. Her lines promised great speed, but the comfort of her passengers had been no less considered by her builder when he gave her so much beam and so high a freeboard. The ship's furniture was the finest I had ever seen, and I had crossed every great ocean in the world. The library, especially, was more suggestive of a room in the British Museum than the batch of books usually carried at sea. But I have no mind to enter on a detailed description of a beautiful pleasure ship while my story waits. I only mention the general condition of the vessel in evidence of the fact which now struck me for the first time—Brande must have unlimited money. His mode of life in London and in the country, notwithstanding his pleasant house, was in the simplest style. From the moment we entered his special train at Charing Cross, he flung money about him with wanton recklessness.

As we made our way through the crowd which was hanging about the quay, an unpleasant incident occurred. Miss Brande, with Halley and Rockingham, became separated from Miss Metford and myself and went on in front of us. We five had formed a sub-section of the main body, and were keeping to ourselves when the unavoidable separation took place. A slight scream in front caused Miss Metford and myself to hurry forward. We found the others surrounded by a gang of drunken sailors, who had stopped them. A red-bearded giant, frenzied with drink, had seized Natalie in his arms. His abettor, a swarthy Italian, had drawn his knife, and menaced Halley and Rockingham. The rest of the band looked on, and cheered their chiefs. Halley was white to the lips; Rockingham was perfectly calm, or, perhaps, indifferent. He called for a policeman. Neither interfered. I did not blame Rockingham; he was a man of the world, so nothing manly could be expected of him. But Halley's cowardice disgusted me.

I rushed forward and caught the Italian from behind, for his knife was dangerous. Seizing him by the collar and waist, I swung him twice, and then flung him from me with all my strength. He spun round two or three times, and then collided with a stack of timber. His head struck a beam, and he fell in his tracks without a word. The red-haired giant instantly released Natalie and put up his hands. The man's attitude showed that he knew nothing of defence. I swept his guard aside, and struck him violently on the neck close to the ear. I was a trained boxer; but I had never before struck a blow in earnest, or in such earnest, and I hardly knew my own strength. The man went down with a grunt like a pole-axed ox, and lay where he fell. To a drunken sailor lad, who seemed anxious to be included in this matter, I dealt a stinging smack on the face with my open hand that satisfied him straightway. The others did not molest me. Turning from the crowd, I found Edith Metford looking at me with blazing eyes.

"Superb! Marcel, I am proud of you!" she cried.

"Oh! Edith, how can you say that?" Natalie Brande exclaimed, still trembling. "Such dreadful violence! The poor men knew no better."

"Poor fiddlesticks! It is well for you that Marcel is a man of violence. He's worth a dozen sheep like—"

"Like whom, Miss Metford?" Rockingham asked, glaring at her so viciously that I interposed with a hasty entreaty that all should hurry to the ship. I did not trust the man.

Miss Metford was not so easily suppressed. She said leisurely, "I meant to say like you, and this over-nervous but otherwise admirable boy. If you think 'sheep' derogatory, pray make it 'goats.'"

I hurried them on board. Brande welcomed us at the gangway. The vessel was his own, so he was as much at home on the ship as in his country house. I had an important letter to write, and very little time for the task. It was not finished a moment too soon, for the moment the last passenger and the last bale of luggage was on board, the captain's telegraph rang from the bridge, and the *Esmeralda* steamed out to sea. My letter, however, was safe on shore. The land was low down upon the horizon before the long summer twilight deepened slowly into night. Then one by one the shadowy cliffs grew dim, dark, and disappeared. We saw no more of England until after many days of gradually culminating horror. The very night which was our first at sea did not pass without a strange adventure, which happened, indeed, by an innocent oversight.

XI. MORITURI TE SALUTANT

We had been sitting on deck chairs smoking and talking for a couple of hours after the late dinner, which was served as soon as the vessel was well out to sea, when Brande came on deck. He was hailed with enthusiasm. This did not move him, or even interest him. I was careful not to join in the acclamations produced by his presence. He noticed this, and lightly called me recalcitrant. I admitted the justice of the epithet, and begged him to consider it one which would always apply to me with equal force. He laughed at this, and contrasted my gloomy fears with the excellent arrangements which he had made for my comfort. I asked him what had become of Grey. I thought it strange that this man should be amongst the absentees.

"Oh, Grey! He goes to Labrador."

"To Labrador! What takes him to Labrador?"

"The same purpose which takes us to the Arafura Sea," Brande answered, and passed on.

Presently there was a slight stir amongst the people, and the word was passed round that Brande was about to undertake some interesting experiment for the amusement of his guests. I hurried aft along with some other men with whom I had been talking, and found Miss Brande and Miss Metford standing hand in hand. Natalie's face was very white, and the only time I ever saw real fear upon it was at that moment. I thought the incident on the quay had unnerved her more than was apparent at the time, and that she was still upset by it. She beckoned to me, and when I came to her she seized my hand. She was trembling so much her words were hardly articulate. Miss Metford was concerned for her companion's nervousness; but otherwise indifferent; while Natalie stood holding our hands in hers like a frightened child awaiting the firing of a cannon.

"He's going to let off something, a rocket, I suppose," Miss Metford said to me. "Natalie seems to think he means to sink the ship."

"He does not mean to do so. He might, if an accident occurred."

"Is he going to fire a mine?" I asked.

"No, he is going to etherize a drop of water." Natalie said this so seriously, we had no thought of laughter, incongruous as the cause of her fears might seem.

At that moment Brande addressed us from the top of the deckhouse, and explained that, in order to illustrate on a large scale the most recent discovery in natural science, he was about to disintegrate a drop of water, at present encased in a hollow glass ball about the size of a pea, which he held between his thumb and forefinger. An electric light was turned upon him so that we could all see the thing quite plainly. He explained that there was a division in the ball; one portion of it containing the drop of water, and the other the agent by which, when the dividing wall was eaten through by its action, the atoms of the water would be resolved into the ultimate ether of which they were composed. As the disintegrating agent was powerless in salt water, we might all feel assured that no great catastrophe would ensue.

Before throwing the glass ball overboard, a careful search for the lights of ships was made from east to west, and north to south.

There was not a light to be seen anywhere. Brande threw the ball over the side. We were going under easy steam at the time, but the moment he left the deckhouse "full speed ahead" was rung from the bridge, and the *Esmeralda* showed us her pace. She literally tore through the water when the engines were got full on.

Before we had gone a hundred yards a great cry arose. A little fleet of French fishing-boats with no lights up had been lying very close to us on the starboard bow. There they were, boatfuls of men, who waved careless adieus to us as we dashed past.

Brande was moved for a moment. Then he shrugged his shoulders and muttered, "It can't be helped now." We all felt that these simple words might mean much. To test their full portent I went over to him, Natalie still holding my hand with trembling fingers.

"Can't you do anything for them?" I asked.

"You mean, go back and sink this ship to keep them company?"

"No; but warn them to fly."

"It would be useless. In this breeze they could not sail a hundred yards in the time allowed, and three miles is the nearest point of safety. I could not say definitely, as this is the first time I have ever tried an experiment so tremendous; but I believe that if we even slowed to half speed, it would be dangerous, and if we stopped, the *Esmeralda* would go to the bottom to-night, as certainly as the sun will rise to-morrow."

Natalie moaned in anguish on hearing this. I said to her sternly:

"I thought you approved of all these actions?"

"This serves no purpose. These men may not even have a painless death, and the reality is more awful than I thought."

Every face was turned to that point in the darkness toward which the foaming wake of the *Esmeralda* stretched back. Not a word more was spoken until Brande, who was standing, watch in hand, beside the light from the deckhouse, came aft and said:

"You will see the explosion in ten seconds."

He could not have spoken more indifferently if the catastrophe he had planned was only the firing of a penny squib.

Then the sea behind us burst into a flame, followed by the sound of an explosion so frightful that we were almost stunned by it. A huge mass of water, torn up in a solid block, was hurled into the air, and there it broke into a hundred roaring cataracts. These, in the brilliant search light from the ship which was now turned upon them full, fell like cataracts of liquid silver into the seething cauldron of water that raged below. The instant the explosion was over, our engines were reversed, and the *Esmeralda* went full speed astern. The waves were still rolling in tumultuous breakers when we got back. We might as well have gone on.

The French fishing fleet had disappeared.

I could not help saying to Brande before we turned in:

"You expect us, I suppose, to believe that the explosion was really caused by a drop of water?"

"Etherized," he interrupted. "Certainly I do. You don't believe it—on what grounds?"

"That it is unbelievable."

"Pshaw! You deny a fact because you do not understand it. Ignorance is not evidence."

"I say it is impossible."

"You do not wish to believe it possible. Wishes are not proofs."

Without pursuing the argument, I said to him:

"It is fortunate that the accident took place at sea. There will be no inquests."

"Oh! I am sorry for the accident. As for the men, they might have had a worse fate. It is better than living in life-long misery as they do. Besides, both they and the fishes that will eat them will soon be numbered amongst the things that have been."

XII. "NO DEATH—SAVE IN LIFE"

For some days afterwards our voyage was uneventful, and the usual shipboard amusements were requisitioned to while away the tedious hours. The French fishing fleet was never mentioned. We got through the Bay with very little knocking about, and passed the Rock without calling. I was not disappointed, for there was slight inducement for going ashore, oppressed as I was with the ever-present incubus of dread. At intervals this feeling became less acute, but only to return, strengthened by its short absences. After a time my danger sense became blunted. The nervous system became torpid under continuous stress, and refused to pass on the sensations with sufficient intensity to the brain; or the weary brain was asleep at its post and did not heed the warnings. I could think no more.

And this reminds me of something which I must tell about young Halley. For several days after the voyage began, the boy avoided me. I knew his reason for doing this. I myself did not blame him for his want of physical courage, but I was glad that he himself was ashamed of it.

Halley came to me one morning and said:

"I wish to speak to you, Marcel. I *must* speak to you. It is about that miserable episode on the evening we left England. I acted like a cad. Therefore I must be a cad. I only want to tell you that I despise myself as much as you can. And that I envy you. I never thought that I should envy a man simply because he had no nervous system."

"Who is this man without a nervous system of whom you speak?" I asked coldly. I was not sorry that I had an opportunity of reading him a lesson which might be placed opposite the many indignities which had been put upon me, in the form mainly of shoulder shrugs, brow elevations, and the like.

"You, of course. I mean no offence—you are magnificent. I am honest in saying that I admire you. I wish I was like you in height, weight, muscle—and absence of nervous system."

"You would keep your own brain, I suppose?" I asked.

"Yes, I would keep that."

"And I will keep my own nervous system," I replied. "And the difference between mine and yours is this: that whereas my own danger sense is, or was, as keen as your own, I have my reserve of nerve force—or had it—which might be relied on to tide me over a sudden emergency. This reserve you have expended on your brain. There are two kinds of cowards; the selfish coward who cares for no interest save his own; the unselfish coward who cares nothing for himself, but who cannot face a danger because he dare not. And there are two kinds of brave men; the nerveless man you spoke of, who simply faces danger because he does not appreciate it, and the man who faces danger because, although he fears it he dares it. I have no difficulty in placing you in this list."

"You place me—"

"A coward because you cannot help it. You are merely out of harmony with your environment. You ought to bring a supply of 'environment' about with you, seeing that you cannot manufacture it off-hand like myself. I wish to be alone. Good-day."

"Before I go, Marcel, I will say this." There were tears in his eyes. "These people do not really know you, with all their telepathic power. You are not—not—"

"Not as great a fool as they think. Thank you. I mean to prove that to them some day."

With that I turned away from him, although I felt that he would have gladly stayed longer with me.

While the *Esmeralda* was sweeping over the long swells of the Mediterranean, I heard Brande lecture for the second time. It was a fitting interlude between his first and third addresses. I might classify them thus—the first, critical; the second, constructive; the third, executive. His third speech was the last he made in the world.

We were assembled in the saloon. It would have been pleasanter on the upper deck, owing to the heat, but the speaker could not then have been easily heard in the noise of the wind and waves. I could scarcely believe that it was Brande who arose to speak, so changed was his expression. The frank scepticism, which had only recently degenerated into a cynicism, still tempered with a half kindly air of easy superiority, was gone. In its place there was a look of concentrated and relentless purpose which dominated the man himself and all who saw him. He began in forcible and direct sentences, with only a faintly reminiscent eloquence which was part of himself, and from which he could not without a conscious effort have freed his style. But the whole bearing of the man had little trace in it of the dilettante academician whom we all remembered.

"When I last addressed this Society," he began, "I laboured under a difficulty in arriving at ultimate truth which was of my own manufacture. I presupposed, as you will remember, the indestructibility of the atom, and, in logical consequence I was bound to admit the conservation of suffering, the eternity of misery. But on that evening many of my audience were untaught in the rudiments of ultimate thought, and some were still sceptical of the *bona fides* of our purpose, and our power to achieve its object. To them, in their then ineptitude, what I shall say now would have been unintelligible. For in the same way that the waves of light or sound exceeding a certain maximum can not be transferred to the brain by dull eyes and ears, my thought pulsations would have escaped those auditors by virtue of their own irresponsiveness. To-night I am free from the limitation which I then suffered, because there are none around me now who have not sufficient knowledge to grasp what I shall present.

"You remember that I traced for you the story of evolution in its journey from the atom to the star. And I showed you that the hypothesis of the indestructibility of the atom was simply a creed of cruelty writ large. I now proceed on the lines of true science to show you how that hypothesis is false; that as the atom *is* destructible—as you have seen by our experiments (the last of which resulted in a climax not intended by me)—the whole scheme of what is called creation falls to pieces. As the atom was the first etheric blunder, so the material Universe is the grand etheric mistake.

"In considering the marvellous and miserable succession of errors resulting from the meretricious atomic remedy adopted by the ether to cure its local sores, it must first be said of the ether itself that there is too much of it. Space is not sufficient for it. Thus, the particles of ether—those imponderable entities which vibrate through a block of marble or a disc of hammered steel with only a dulled, not an annihilated motion, are by their own tumultuous plenty packed closer together than they wish. I say wish, for if all material consciousness and sentiency be founded on atomic consciousness, then in its turn atomic consciousness is founded upon, and dependent on, etheric consciousness. These particles of ether, therefore, when too closely impinged upon by their neighbours, resent the impact, and in doing so initiate etheric whirlwinds, from whose vast perturbances stupendous drifts set out. In their gigantic power these avalanches crush the particles which impede them, force the resisting medium out of its normal stage, destroy the homogeneity of its constituents, and mass them into individualistic communities whose vibrations play with greater freedom when they synchronise. The homogeneous etheric tendencies recede and finally determine.

"Behold a miracle! An atom is born!

"By a similar process—which I may liken to that of putting off an evil day which some time must be endured—the atoms group themselves into molecules. In their turn the molecules go forth to war, capturing or being captured; the vibrations of the slaves always being forced to synchronise with those of their conquerors. The nucleus of the gas of a primal metal is now complete, and the foundation of a solar system—paltry molecule of the Universe as it is—is laid. Thereafter, the rest is easily followed. It is described in your school books, and must not occupy me now.

"But one word I will interpolate which may serve to explain a curious and interesting human belief. You are aware of how, in times past, men of absolutely no scientific insight held firmly to the idea that an elixir of life and a philosopher's stone might be discovered, and that these two objects were nearly always pursued contemporaneously. That is to my mind an extraordinary example of the force of atomic consciousness. The idea itself was absolutely correct; but the men who followed it had slight knowledge of its unity, and none whatever of its proper pursuit. They would have worked on their special lines to eternity before advancing a single step toward their object. And this because they did not know what life was, and death was, and what the metals ultimately signified which they, blind fools, so unsuccessfully tried to transmute. But we know more than they. We have climbed no doubt in the footholds they have carved, and we have gained the summit they only saw in the mirage of hope. For we know that there is no life, no death, no metals, no matter, no emotions, no thoughts; but that all that we call by these names is only the ether in various conditions. Life! I could live as long as this earth will submit to human existence if I had studied that paltry problem. Metals! The ship in which you sail was bought with gold manufactured in my crucibles.

"The unintelligent—or I should say the grossly ignorant—have long held over the heads of the pioneers of science these two great charges: No man has ever yet transmuted a metal; no man has ever yet proved the connecting link between organic and inorganic life. I say *life*, for I take it that this company admits that a slab of granite is as much alive as any man or woman I see before me. But I have manufactured gold, and I could have manufactured protoplasm if I had devoted my life to that object. My studies have been almost wholly on the inorganic plane. Hence the 'philosopher's stone' came in my way, but not the 'elixir of life.' The molecules of protoplasm are only a little more complex than the molecules of hydrogen or nitrogen or iron or coal. You may fuse iron, vaporise water, intermix the gases; but the molecules of all change little in such metamorphosis. And you may slay twenty thousand men at Waterloo or Sedan, or ten thousand generations may be numbered with the dust, and not an ounce of protoplasm lies dead. All molecules are merely arrangements of atoms made under different degrees of pressure and of different ages. And all atoms are constructed of identical constituents—the ether, as I have said. Therefore the ether, which was from the beginning, is now, and ever shall be, which is the same yesterday, to-day, and for ever, is the origin of force, of matter, of life.

"*It is alive!*

"Its starry children are so many that the sands of the sea-shore may not be used as a similitude for their multitude; and they extend so far that distance may not be named in relation to them. They are so high above us and so deep below us that there is neither height nor depth in them. There is neither east nor west in them, nor north and south in them. Nor is there beginning or end to them. Time drops his scythe and stands appalled before that dreadful host. Number applies not to its eternal multitudes. Distance is lost in boundless space. And from all the stars that stud the caverns of the Universe, there swells this awful chorus: Failure! failure and futility! And the ether is to blame!

"Heterogeneous suffering is more acute than homogeneous, because the agony is intensified by being localised; because the comfort of the comfortable is purchasable only by the multiplied misery of the miserable; because aristocratic leisure requires that the poor should be always with it. There is, therefore, no gladness without its overbalancing sorrow. There is no good without intenser evil. There is no death save in life.

"Back, then, from this ill-balanced and unfair long-suffering, this insufficient existence. Back to Nirvana—the ether! And I will lead the way.

"The agent I will employ has cost me all life to discover. It will release the vast stores of etheric energy locked up in the huge atomic warehouse of this planet. I shall remedy the grand mistake only to a degree which it would be preposterous to call even microscopic; but when I have done what I can, I am blameless for the rest. In due season the whole blunder will be cured by the same means that I shall use, and all the hideous experiment will be over, and everlasting rest or *quasi*-rest will supersede the magnificent failure of material existence. This earth, at least, and, I am encouraged to hope, the whole solar system, will by my instrumentality be restored to the ether from which it never should have emerged. Once before, in the history of our system, an effort similar to mine was made, unhappily without success.

"This time we shall not fail!"

A low murmur rose from the audience as the lecturer concluded, and a hushed whisper asked:

"Where was that other effort made?"

Brande faced round momentarily, and said quietly but distinctly:

"On the planet which was where the Asteroids are now."

XIII. MISS MITFORD'S PLAN

We coaled at Port Said like any ordinary steamer. Although I had more than once made the Red Sea voyage, I had never before taken the slightest interest in the coaling of the vessel on which I was a passenger. This time everything was different. That which interested me before seemed trivial now. And that which had before seemed trivial was now absorbing. I watched the coaling—commonplace as the spectacle was—with vivid curiosity. The red lights, the sooty demons at work, every bag of coals they carried, and all the coal dust clouds they created, were fitting episodes in a voyage such as ours. We took an enormous quantity of coal on board. I remained up most of the night in a frame of mind which I thought none might envy. I myself would have made light of it had I known what was still in store for the *Esmeralda* and her company. It was nearly morning when I turned in. When I awoke we were nearing the Red Sea.

On deck, the conversation of our party was always eccentric, but this must be said for it: there was sometimes a scintillating brilliance in it that almost blinded one to its extreme absurdity. The show of high spirits which was very general was, in the main, unaffected. For the rest it was plainly assumed. But those who assumed their parts did so with a histrionic power which was all the more surprising when it is remembered that the origin of their excellent playing was centred in their own fears. I preserved a neutral attitude. I did not venture on any overt act of insubordination. That would have only meant my destruction, without any counter-balancing advantage in the way of baulking an enterprise in which I was a most unwilling participator. And to pretend what I did not feel was a task which I had neither stomach to undertake nor ability to carry out successfully. In consequence I kept my own counsel—and that of Edith Metford.

Brande was the most easily approached maniac I had ever met. His affability continued absolutely consistent. I took advantage of this to say to him on a convenient opportunity: "Why did you bring these people with you? They must all be useless, and many of them little better than a nuisance!"

"Marcel, you are improving. Have you attained the telepathic power? You have read my mind." This was said with a pleasant smile.

"I can not read your mind," I answered; "I only diagnose."

"Your diagnosis is correct. I answer you in a sentence. They are all sympathetic, and human sympathy is necessary to me until my purpose is fulfilled."

"You do not look to me for any measure of this sympathy, I trust?"

"I do not. You are antipathetic."

"I am."

"But necessary, all the same."

"So be it, until the proper time shall come."

"It will never come," Brande said firmly.

"We shall see," I replied as firmly as himself.

Next evening as we were steaming down the blue waters—deep blue they always seemed to me—of the Red Sea, I was sitting on the foredeck smoking and trying to think. I did not notice how the time passed. What seemed to me an hour at most, must have been three or four. With the exception of the men of the crew who were on duty, I was alone, for the heat was intense, and most of our people were lying in their cabins prostrated in spite of the wind-sails which were spread from every port to catch the breeze. My meditations were as usual gloomy and despondent. They were interrupted by Miss Metford. She joined me so noiselessly that I was not aware of her presence until she laid her hand on my arm. I started at her touch, but she whispered a sharp warning, so full of suppressed emotion that I instantly recovered a semblance of unconcern.

The girl was very white and nervous. This contrast from her usual equanimity was disquieting. She clung to me hysterically as she gasped:

"Marcel, it is a mercy I have found you alone, and that there is one sane man in this shipful of lunatics."

"I am afraid you are not altogether right," I said, as I placed a seat for her close to mine. "I can hardly be sane when I am a voluntary passenger on board this vessel."

"Do you really think they mean what they say?" she asked hurriedly, without noticing my remark.

"I really think they have discovered the secret of extraordinary natural forces, so powerful and so terrible that no one can say what they may or may not accomplish. And that is the reason I begged you not to come on this voyage."

"What was the good of asking me not to come without giving me some reason?"

"Had I done so, they might have killed you as they have done others before."

"You might have chanced that, seeing that it will probably end that way."

"And they would certainly have killed me."

"Ah!"

I wondered at the sudden intensity of the girl's sharp gasp when I said this, and marvelled too, how she, who had always been so mannish, nestled close to me and allowed her head to sink down on my shoulder. I pitied the strong-willed, self-reliant nature which had given way under some strain of which I had yet to be told. So I stooped and touched her cheek with my lips in a friendly way, at which she looked up to me with half-closed eyes, and whispered in a voice strangely soft and womanish for her:

"If they must kill us, I wish they would kill us now."

I stroked her soft cheek gently, and urged a less hopeless view. "Even if the worst come, we may as well live as long as we can."

Whereupon to my surprise she, having shot one quick glance into my eyes, put my arm away and drew her chair apart from mine. Her head was turned away from me, but I could not but notice that her bosom rose and fell swiftly. Presently she faced round again, lit a cigarette, put her hands in the pocket of her jacket, and her feet on another chair, and said indifferently:

"You are right. Even if the worst must come, we may as well live as long as we can."

This sudden change in her manner surprised me. I knew I had no art in dealing with women, so I let it pass without comment, and looked out at the glassy sea.

After some minutes of silence, the girl spoke to me again.

"Do you know anything of the actual plans of these maniacs?"

"No. I only know their preposterous purpose."

"Well, I know how it is to be done. Natalie was restless last night— you know that we share the same cabin—and she raved a bit. I kept her in her berth by sheer force, but I allowed her to talk."

This was serious. I drew my chair close to Miss Metford's and whispered, "For heaven's sake, speak low." Then I remembered Brande's power, and wrung my hands in helpless impotence. "You forget Brande. At this moment he is taking down every word we say."

"He's doing nothing of the sort."

"But you forget—"

"I don't forget. By accident I put morphia in the tonic he takes, and he is now past telepathy for some hours at least. He's sound asleep. I suppose if I had not done it by accident he would have known what I was doing, and so have refused the medicine. Anyhow, accident or no accident, I have done it."

"Thank God!" I cried.

"And this precious disintegrating agent! They haven't it with them, it seems. To manufacture it in sufficient quantity would be impossible in any civilised country without fear of detection or interruption. Brande has the prescription, formula—what do you call it?—and if you could get the paper and—"

"Throw it overboard!"

"Rubbish! They would work it all out again."

"What then?" I whispered.

"Steal the paper and—wouldn't it do to put in an extra x or y, or stick a couple of additional figures into any suitable vacancy? Don't you think they'd go on with the scheme and—"

"And?"

"And make a mess of it!"

"Miss Metford," I said, rising from my chair, "I mean Metford, I know you like to be addressed as a man—or used to like it."

"Yes, I used to," she assented coldly.

"I am going to take you in my arms and kiss you."

"I'm hanged if you are!" she exclaimed, so sharply that I was suddenly abashed. My intended familiarity and its expression appeared grotesque, although a few minutes before she was so friendly. But I could not waste precious time in studying a girl's caprices, so I asked at once:

"How can I get this paper?"

"I said steal it, if you recollect." Her voice was now hard, almost harsh. "You can get it in Brande's cabin, if you are neither afraid nor jealous." "I am not much afraid, and I will try it. What do you mean by jealous?"

"I mean, would you, to save Natalie Brande—for they will certainly succeed in blowing themselves up, if nobody else—consent to her marrying another man, say that young lunatic Halley, who is always dangling after her when you are not?"

"Yes," I answered, after some thought. For Halley's attentions to Natalie had been so marked, the plainly inconsequent mention of him in this matter did not strike me. "If that is necessary to save her, of course I would consent to it. Why do you ask? In my place you would do the same."

"No. I'd see the ship and all its precious passengers at the bottom of the sea first."

"Ah! but you are not a man."

"Right! and what's more, I'm glad of it." Then looking down at the rational part of her costume, she added sharply, "I sha'n't wear these things again."

XIV. ROCKINGHAM TO THE SHARKS

At one o'clock in the morning I arose, dressed hurriedly, drew on a pair of felt slippers, and put a revolver in my pocket. It was then time to put Edith Metford's proposal to the proof, and she would be waiting for me on deck to hear whether I had succeeded in it. We had parted a couple of hours before on somewhat chilling terms. I had agreed to follow her suggestion, but I could not trouble my tired brain by guesses at the cause of her moods.

It was very dark. There was only enough light to enable me to find my way along the corridor, off which the state-rooms occupied by Brande and his immediate lieutenants opened. All the sleepers were restless from the terrible heat. As I stole along, a muffled word, a sigh, or a movement in the berths, made me pause at every step with a beating heart. Having listened till all was quiet, I moved on again noiselessly. I was almost at the end of the corridor. So intent had I been on preserving perfect silence, it did not sooner occur to me that I was searching for any special door. I had forgotten Brande's number!

I could no more think of it than one can recall the name of a half-forgotten acquaintance suddenly encountered in the street. It might have been fourteen, or forty-one; or a hundred and fifty. Every number was as likely as it was unlikely. I tried vainly to concentrate my mind. The result was nothing. The missing number gave no clue. To enter the wrong room in that ship at that hour meant death for me. Of that I was certain. To leave the right room unentered gave away my first chance in the unequal battle with Brande. Then, as I knew that my first chance would probably be my last, if not availed of, I turned to the nearest door and quietly tried the handle. The door was not locked. I entered the state-room.

"What do you want?" It was Halley's voice that came from
the berth.

"Pardon me," I whispered, "a mistake. The heat, you know. Went
on deck, and have blundered into your room."

"Oh, all right. Who are you?"

"Brande."

"Good-night. You did not blunder far;" this sleepily.

I went out and closed the door quietly. I had gained something.
I was within one door of my destination, for I knew that Halley was
berthed between Rockingham and Brande. But I did not know on
which side Brande's room was, and I dared not ask. I tried the next
door going forward. It opened like the other. I went in.

"Hallo there!" This time no sleepy or careless man challenged me.
It was Rockingham's voice.

"May I not enter my own room?" I whispered.

"This is not your room. You are?" Rockingham sprang up in his
berth, but before he could leave it I was upon him.

"I am Arthur Marcel. And this iron ring which I press against your
left ear is the muzzle of my revolver. Speak, move, breathe above your
natural breath and your brains go through that porthole. Now, loose
your hold of my arm and come with me."

"You fool!" hissed Rockingham. "You dare not fire. You know
you dare not."

He was about to call out, but my left hand closed on his throat,
and a gurgling gasp was all that issued from him.

I laid down the revolver and turned the ear of the strangling man
close to my mouth. I had little time to think; but thought flies fast
when such deadly peril menaces the thinker as that which I must face
if I failed to make terms with the man who was in my power. I knew
that notwithstanding his intensely disagreeable nature, if he gave his
promise either by spoken word or equivalent sign, I could depend upon
him. There were no liars in Brande's Society. But the word I could not
trust him to say. I must have his sign. I whispered:

"You know I do not wish to kill you. I shall never have another happy
day if you force me to it. I have no choice. You must yield or die. If you
will yield and stand by me rather than against me in what shall follow,
choose life by taking your right hand from my wrist and touching my

left shoulder. I will not hurt you meanwhile. If you choose death, touch me with your left."

The sweat stood on my forehead in big beads as I waited for his choice. It was soon made. He unlocked his left hand and placed it firmly on my right shoulder.

He had chosen death.

So the man was only a physical coward—or perhaps he had only made a choice of alternatives.

I said slowly and in great agony, "May God have mercy on your soul—and mine!" on which the muscles in my left arm stiffened. The big biceps—an heirloom of my athletic days—thickened up, and I turned my eyes away from the dying face, half hidden by the darkness. His struggles were very terrible, but with my weight upon his lower limbs, and my grasp upon his windpipe, that death-throe was as silent as it was horrible. The end came slowly. I could not bear the horror of it longer. I must finish it and be done with it. I put my right arm under the man's shoulders and raised the upper part of his body from the berth. Then a desperate wrench with my left arm, and there was a dull crack like the snapping of a dry stick. It was over. Rockingham's neck was broken.

I wiped away the bloody froth that oozed from the gaping mouth, and tried to compose decently the contorted figure. I covered the face. Then I started on my last mission, for now I knew the door. I had bought the knowledge dearly, and I meant to use it for my own purpose, careless of what violence might be necessary to accomplish my end.

When I entered Brande's state-room I found the electric light full on. He was seated at a writing-table with his head resting on his arms, which hung crossways over the desk. The sleeper breathed so deeply it was evident that the effect of the morphia was still strong upon him. One hand clutched a folded parchment. His fingers clasped it nervelessly, and I had only to force them open one by one in order to withdraw the manuscript. As I did this, he moaned and moved in his chair. I had no fear of his awaking. My hand shook as I unfolded the parchment which I unconsciously handled as carefully as though the thing itself were as deadly as the destruction which might be wrought by its direction.

To me the whole document was a mass of unintelligible formulae. My rusty university education could make nothing of it. But I could not waste time in trying to solve the puzzle, for I did not know what moment some other visitor might arrive to see how Brande fared. I first examined with a pocket microscope the ink of the manuscript, and then making a scratch with Brande's pen on a page of my note-book, I compared the two. The colours were identical. It was the same ink.

In several places where a narrow space had been left vacant, I put 1 in front of the figures which followed. I had no reason for making this particular alteration, save that the figure 1 is more easily forged than any other, and the forgery is consequently more difficult to detect. My additions, when the ink was dry, could only have been discovered by one who was informed that the document had been tampered with. It was probable that a drawer which stood open with the keys in the lock was the place where Brande kept this paper; where he would look for it on awaking. I locked it in the drawer and put the keys into his pocket.

There was something still to do with the sleeping man, whose brain compassed such marvellous powers. His telepathic faculty must be destroyed. I must keep him seriously ill, without killing him. As long as he remained alive his friends would never question his calculations, and the fiasco which was possible under any circumstances would then be assured. I had with me an Eastern drug, which I had bought from an Indian fakir once in Murzapoor. The man was an impostor, whose tricks did not impose on me. But the drug, however he came by it, was reliable. It was a poison which produced a mild form of cerebritis that dulled but did not deaden the mental powers. It acted almost identically whether administered sub-cutaneously or, of course in a larger dose, internally. I brought it home with the intention of giving it to a friend who was interested in vivisection. I did not think that I myself should be the first and last to experiment with it. It served my purpose well.

The moment I pricked his skin, Brande moved in his seat. My hand was on his throat. He nestled his head down again upon his arms, and drew a deep breath. Had he moved again that breath would have been his last. I had been so wrought upon by what I had already done that night, I would have taken his life without the slightest hesitation, if the sacrifice seemed necessary.

When my operation was over, I left the room and moved silently along the corridor till I came to the ladder leading to the deck. Edith

Metford was waiting for me as we had arranged. She was shivering in spite of the awful heat.

"Have you done it?" she whispered.

"I have," I answered, without saying how much I had done. "Now you must retire—and rest easy. The formula won't work. I have put both it and Brande himself out of gear."

"Thank God!" she gasped, and then a sudden faintness came over her. It passed quickly, and as soon as she was sufficiently restored, I begged her to go below. She pleaded that she could not sleep, and asked me to remain with her upon the deck. "It would be absurd to suppose that either of us could sleep this night," she very truly said. On which I was obliged to tell her plainly that she must go below. I had more to do.

"Can I help?" she asked anxiously.

"No. If you could, I would ask you, for you are a brave girl. I have something now to get through which is not woman's work."

"Your work is my work," she answered. "What is it?"

"I have to lower a body overboard without anyone observing me."

There was no time for discussion, so I told her at once, knowing that she would not give way otherwise. She started at my words, but said firmly:

"How will you do that unobserved by the 'watch'? Go down and bring up your—bring it up. I will keep the men employed." She went forward, and I turned again to the companion.

When I got back to Rockingham's cabin I took a sheet of paper and wrote, "Heat—Mad!" making no attempt to imitate his writing. I simply scrawled the words with a rough pen in the hope that they would pass as a message from a man who was hysterical when he wrote them. Then I turned to the berth and took up the body. It was not a pleasant thing to do. But it must be done.

I was a long time reaching the deck, for the arms and legs swung to and fro, and I had to move cautiously lest they should knock against the woodwork I had to pass. I got it safely up and hurried aft with it. Edith, I knew, would contrive to keep the men on watch engaged until I had disposed of my burden. I picked up a coil of rope and made it fast to the dead man's neck. Taking one turn of the rope round a boat-davit, I pushed the thing over the rail. I intended to let go the rope the moment the weight attached to it was safely in the sea, and so lowered away silently, paying out the line without excessive strain owing to the support of the davit round which I had wound it. I had not to wait so long as that, for just as the body was dangling over the foaming wake of the steamer, a little streak of moonlight shot out from behind a bank of cloud and lighted the vessel with a sudden gleam. I was startled by this, and held on, fearing that some watching eye might see my curious movements. For a minute I leaned over the rail and watched the track of the steamer as though I had come on deck for the air. There was a quick rush near the vessel's quarter. Something dark leaped out of the water, and there was a sharp snap—a crunch. The lower limbs were gone in the jaws of a shark. I let go the rope in horror, and the body dropped splashing into that hideous fishing-ground. Sick to death I turned away.

"Get below quickly," Edith Metford said in my ear. "They heard the splash, slight as it was, and are coming this way." Her warning was nearly a sob.

We hurried down the companion as fast as we dared, and listened to the comments of the watch above. They were soon satisfied that nothing of importance had occurred, and resumed their stations.

Before we parted on that horrible night, Edith said in a trembling voice, "You have done your work like a brave man."

"Say rather, like a forger and murderer," I answered.

"No," she maintained. "Many men before you have done much worse in a good cause. You are not a forger. You are a diplomat. You are not a murderer. You are a hero."

But I, being new to this work of slaughter and deception, could only deprecate her sympathy and draw away. I felt that my very presence near her was pollution. I was unclean, and I told her that I was so. Whereupon, without hesitation, she put her arms round my neck, and said clinging closely to me:

"You are not unclean—you are free from guilt. And—Arthur—I will kiss you now."

XV. "IF NOT TOO LATE!"

When I came on deck next morning the coast of Arabia was rising, a thin thread of hazy blue between the leaden grey of the sea and the soft grey of the sky. The morning was cloudy, and the blazing sunlight was

veiled in atmospheric gauze. I had hardly put my foot on deck when
Natalie Brande ran to meet me. I hung back guiltily.

"I thought you would never come. There is dreadful news!" she cried.

I muttered some incoherent words, to which she did not attend, but
went on hurriedly:

"Rockingham has thrown himself overboard in a hysterical fit,
brought on by the heat. The sailors heard the splash—"

"I know they did." This escaped me unawares, and I instantly
prevaricated, "I have been told about that."

"Do you know that Herbert is ill?"

I could have conscientiously answered this question affirmatively
also. Her sudden sympathy for human misadventure jarred upon me, as
it had done once before, when I thought of the ostensible object of the
cruise. I said harshly:

"Then Rockingham is at rest, and your brother is on the road to it."
It was a brutal speech. It had a very different effect to that which
I intended.

"True," she said. "But think of the awful consequences if, now that
Rockingham is gone, Herbert should be seriously ill."

"I do think of it," I said stiffly. Indeed, I could hardly keep from
adding that I had provided for it.

"You must come to him at once. I have faith in you." This gave me
a twinge. "I have no faith in Percival" (the ship's doctor).

"You are nursing your brother?" I said with assumed carelessness.
"Of course."

"What is Percival giving him?"

She described the treatment, and as this was exactly what I myself
would have prescribed to put my own previous interference right, I
promised to come at once, saying:

"It is quite evident that Percival does not understand the case."

"That is exactly what I thought," Natalie agreed, leading me to
Brande's cabin. I found his vitality lower than I expected, and he was very
impatient. The whole purpose of his life was at stake, dependent on his
preserving a healthy body, on which, in turn, a vigorous mind depends.

"How soon can you get me up?" he asked sharply, when my pretended
examination was over.

"I should say a month at most."

"That would be too long," he cried. "You must do it in less."

"It does not depend on me—"

"It does depend on you. I know life itself. You know the paltry science of organic life. I have had no time for such trivial study. Get me well within three days, or—"

"I am attending."

"By the hold over my sister's imagination which I have gained, I will kill her on the fourth morning from now."

"You will—*not*."

"I tell you I will," Brande shrieked, starting up in his berth. "I could do it now."

"You could—*not*."

"Man, do you know what you are saying? You to bandy words with me! A clod-brained fool to dare a man of science! Man of science forsooth! Your men of science are to me as brain-benumbed, as brain-bereft, as that fly which I crush—thus!"

The buzzing insect was indeed dead. But I was something more than a fly. At last I was on a fair field with this scientific magician or madman. And on a fair field I was not afraid of him.

"You are agitating yourself unnecessarily and injuriously," I said in my best professional manner. "And if you persist in doing so you will make my one month three."

In a voice of undisguised scorn, Brande exclaimed, without noticing my interruption:

"Bearded by a creature whose little mind is to me like the open page of a book to read when the humour seizes me." Then with a fierce glance at me he cried:

"I have read your mind before. I can read it now."

"You can—*not*."

He threw himself back in his berth and strove to concentrate his mind. For nearly five minutes he lay quite still, and then he said gently:

"You are right. Have you, then, a higher power than I?"

"No; a lower!"

"A lower! What do you mean?"

"I mean that I have merely paralysed your brain—that for many months to come it will not be restored to its normal power—that it will never reach its normal power again unless I choose."

"Then all is lost—lost—lost!" he wailed out. "The end is as far off, and the journey as long, and the way as hard, as if I had never striven. And the tribute of human tears will be exacted to the uttermost. My life has been in vain!"

The absolute agony in his voice, the note of almost superhuman suffering and despair, was so intense, that, without thinking of what it was this man was grieving over, I found myself saying soothingly:

"No, no! Nothing is lost. It is only your own overstrained nervous system which sends these fantastic nightmares to your brain. I will soon make you all right if you will listen to reason."

He turned to me with the most appealing look which I had ever seen in human eyes save once before—when Natalie pleaded with me.

"I had forgotten," he said, "the issue now lies in your hands. Choose rightly. Choose mercy."

"I will," I answered shortly, for his request brought me back with a jerk to his motive.

"Then you will get me well as soon as your skill can do it?"

"I will keep you in your present condition until I have your most solemn assurance that you will neither go farther yourself nor instigate others to go farther with this preposterous scheme of yours."

"Bah!" Brande ejaculated contemptuously, and lay back with a sudden content. "My brain is certainly out of order, else I should not have forgotten—until your words recalled it—the Labrador expedition."

"The Labrador expedition?"

"Yes. On the day we sailed for the Arafura Sea, Grey started with another party for Labrador. If we fail to act before the 31st December, in the year 1900, he will proceed. And the end of the century will be the date of the end of the earth. I will signal to him now."

His face changed suddenly. For a moment I thought he was dead. Then the dreadful fact came home to me. He was telegraphing telepathically to Grey. So the murder that was upon my soul had been done in vain. Then another life must be taken. Better a double crime than one resultless tragedy. I was spared this.

Brande opened his eyes wearily, and sighed as if fatigued. The effort, short as it was, must have been intense. He was prostrated. His voice was low, almost a whisper, as he said:

"You have succeeded beyond belief. I cannot even signal him, much less exchange ideas." With that he turned his face from me, and instantly fell into a deep sleep.

I left the cabin and went on deck. As usual, it was fairly sprinkled over with the passengers, but owing to the strong head-wind caused by the speed of the steamer, there was a little nook in the bow where there was no one to trouble me with unwelcome company.

I sat down on an arm of the starboard anchor and tried to think. The game which seemed so nearly won had all to be played over again from the first move. If I had killed Brande—which surely would have been justifiable—the other expedition would go on from where he left off. And how should I find them? And who would believe my story when I got back to England?

Brande must go on. His attempt to wreck the earth, even if the power he claimed were not overrated, would fail. For if the compounds of a common explosive must be so nicely balanced as they require to be, surely the addition of the figures which I had made in his formula would upset the balance of constituents in an agent so delicate, though so powerful, as that which he had invented. When the master failed, it was more than probable that the pupil would distrust the invention, and return to London for fresh experiments. Then a clean sweep must be made of the whole party. Meantime, it was plain that Brande must be allowed the opportunity of failing. And this it would be my hazardous duty to superintend.

I returned to Brande's cabin with my mind made up. He was awake, and looked at me eagerly, but waited for me to speak. Our conversation was brief, for I had little sympathy with my patient, and the only anxiety I experienced about his health was the hope that he would not die until he had served my purpose.

"I have decided to get you up," I said curtly.

"You have decided well," he answered, with equal coldness.

That was the whole interview—on which so much depended.

After this I did not speak to Brande on any subject but that of his symptoms, and before long he was able to come on deck. The month I spoke of as the duration of his illness was an intentional exaggeration on my part.

Rockingham was forgotten with a suddenness and completeness that was almost ghastly. The Society claimed to have improved the old

maxim to speak nothing of the dead save what is good. Of the dead
they spoke not at all. It is a callous creed, but in this instance it pleased
me well.

We did not touch at Aden, and I was glad of it. The few attractions
of the place, the diving boys and the like, may be a relief in ordinary sea
voyages, but I was too much absorbed in my experiment on Brande to
bear with patience any delay which served to postpone the crisis of my
scheme. I had treated him well, so far as his bodily health went, but I
deliberately continued to tamper with his brain, so that any return of his
telepathic power was thus prevented. Indeed, Brande himself was not
anxious for such return. The power was always exercised at an extreme
nervous strain, and it was now, he said, unnecessary to his purpose.

In consequence of this determination, I modified the already minute
doses of the drug I was giving him. This soon told with advantage on
his health. His physical improvement partly restored his confidence
in me, so that he followed my instructions faithfully. He evidently
recognised that he was in my power; that if I did not choose to restore
him fully no other man could.

Of the ship's officers, Anderson, who was in command, and Percival,
the doctor, were men of some individuality. The captain was a good
sailor and an excellent man of business. In the first capacity, he was
firm, exacting, and scrupulously conscientious. In the second, his
conscience was more elastic when he saw his way clear to his own
advantage. He had certain rigid rules of conduct which he prided
himself on observing to the letter, without for a moment suspecting
that their *raison d'etre* lay in his own interests. His commercial morality
only required him to keep within the law. His final contract with myself
was, I admit, faithfully carried out, but the terms of it would not have
discredited the most predatory business man in London town.

Percival was the opposite pole of such a character. He was a clever
man, who might have risen in his profession but for his easy-going
indolence. I spent many an hour in his cabin. He was a sportsman
and a skilled *raconteur*. His anecdotes helped to while the weary
time away. He exaggerated persistently, but this did not disturb me.
Besides, if in his narratives he lengthened out the hunt a dozen miles
and increased the weight of the fish to an impossible figure, made the
brace a dozen and the ten-ton boat a man-of-war, it was not because he

was deliberately untruthful. He looked back on his feats through the telescope of a strongly magnifying memory. It was more agreeable to me to hear him boast his prowess than have him inquire after the health and treatment of my patient Brande. On this matter he was naturally very curious, and I very reticent.

That Brande did not entirely trust me was evident from his confusion when I surprised him once reading his formula. His anxiety to convince me that it was only a commonplace memorandum was almost ludicrous. I was glad to see him anxious about that document. The more carefully he preserved it, and the more faithfully he adhered to its conditions, the better for my experiment. A sense of security followed this incident. It did not last long. It ended that evening.

After a day of almost unendurable heat, I went on deck for a breath of air. We were well out in the Indian Ocean, and soundings were being attempted by some of our naturalists. I sat alone and watched the sun sink down into the glassy ocean on which our rushing vessel was the only thing that moved. As the darkness of that hot, still night gathered, weird gleams of phosphorus broke from the steamer's bows and streamed away behind us in long lines of flashing spangles. Where the swell caused by the passage of the ship rose in curling waves, these, as they splashed into mimic breakers, burst into showers of flamboyant light. The water from the discharge-pipe poured down in a cascade, that shone like silver. Every turn of the screw dashed a thousand flashes on either side, and the heaving of the lead was like the flight of a meteor, as it plunged with a luminous trail far down into the dark unfathomable depths below.

My name was spoken softly. Natalie Brande stood beside me. The spell was complete. The unearthly glamour of the magical scene had been compassed by her. She had called it forth and could disperse it by an effort of her will. I wrenched my mind free from the foolish phantasmagoria.

"I have good news," Natalie said in a low voice. Her tones were soft, musical; her manner caressing. Happiness was in her whole bearing, tenderness in her eyes. Dread oppressed me. "Herbert is now well again."

"He has been well for some time," I said, my heart beating fast.

"He is not thoroughly restored even yet. But this evening he was able to receive a message from me by the thought waves. He thinks you are plotting injury to him. His brain is not yet sufficiently strong to show

how foolish this fugitive fancy is. Perhaps you would go to him. He is troubling himself over this. You can set his mind at rest."

"I can—and will—if I am not too late," I answered.

XVI. £5,000 TO DETAIN THE SHIP

Brande was asleep when I entered his cabin. His writing-table was covered with scraps of paper on which he had been scribbling. My name was on every scrap, preceded or followed by an unfinished sentence, thus: "Marcel is thinking— When I was ill, Marcel thought— Marcel means to—" All these I gathered up carefully and put in my pocket. Then I inoculated him with as strong a solution of the drug I was using on him as was compatible with the safety of his life. Immediate danger being thus averted, I determined to run no similar risk again.

For many days after this our voyage was monotonous. The deadly secret shared by Edith Metford and myself drew us gradually nearer to each other as time passed. She understood me, or, at least, gave me the impression that she understood me. Little by little that capricious mood which I have heretofore described changed into one of enduring sympathy. With one trivial exception, this lasted until the end. But for her help my mind would hardly have stood the strain of events which were now at hand, whose livid shadows were projected in the rising fire of Brande's relentless eyes.

Brande appeared to lose interest gradually in his ship's company. He became daily more and more absorbed in his own thoughts. Natalie was ever gentle, even tender. But I chafed at the impalpable barrier which was always between us. Sometimes I thought that she would willingly have ranged herself on my side. Some hidden power held her back. As to the others, I began to like the boy Halley. He was lovable, if not athletic. His devotion to Natalie, which never waned, did not now trouble me. It was only a friendship, and I welcomed it. Had it been anything more, it was not likely that he would have prevailed against the will of a man who had done murder for his mistress. We steamed through the Malay Archipelago, steering north, south, east, west, as if at haphazard, until only the navigating officers and the director of the Society knew how our course lay. We were searching for an island about the bearings of which, it transpired, some mistake had been made. I do not know whether the great laureate ever sailed these seas. But I know that his glorious islands of flowers and islands of fruit, with all their luscious imagery, were here eclipsed by our own islands of foliage. The long lagoons, the deep blue bays, the glittering parti-coloured fish that swam in visible shoals deep down amidst the submerged coral groves over which we passed, the rich-toned sea-weeds and brilliant anemones, the yellow strands and the steep cliffs, the riotous foliage that swept down from the sky to the blue of the sea; all these natural beauties seemed to cry to me with living voices—to me bound on a cruise of universal death.

After a long spell of apparently aimless but glorious steaming, a small island was sighted on our port bow. The *Esmeralda* was steered directly for it, and we dropped anchor in a deep natural harbour on its southern shore. Preparations for landing had been going on during the day, and everything was ready for quitting the ship.

It was here that my first opportunity for making use of the gold I had brought with me occurred. Anderson was called up by Brande, who made him a short complimentary speech, and finished it by ordering his officer to return to England, where further instructions would be given him. This order was received in respectful silence. Captain Anderson had been too liberally treated to demur if the *Esmeralda* had been ordered to the South Pole.

Brande went below for a few minutes, and as soon as he had disappeared I went forward to Anderson and hailed him nervously, for there was not a moment to spare.

"Anderson," I said hurriedly, "you must have noticed that Mr. Brande is an eccentric—"

"Pardon me, sir; it is not my business to comment upon my owner."

"I did not ask you to comment upon him, sir," I said sharply. "It is I who shall comment upon him, and it is for you to say whether you will undertake to earn my money by waiting in this harbour till I am ready to sail back with you to England."

"Have you anything more to say, sir?" Anderson asked stiffly.

"I presume I have said enough."

"If you have nothing more to say I must ask you to leave the bridge, and if it were not that you are leaving the ship this moment, I would caution you not to be impertinent to me again."

He blew his whistle, and a steward ran forward.

"Johnson, see Mr. Marcel's luggage over the side at once." To me he said shortly: "Quit my ship, sir."

This trivial show of temper, which, indeed, had been provoked by my own hasty speech, turned my impatience into fury.

"Before I quit your ship," I said, with emphasis, "I will tell you how you yourself will quit it. You will do so between two policemen if you land in England, and between two marines if you think of keeping on the high seas. Before we started, I sent a detailed statement of this ship, the nature of this nefarious voyage, and the names of the passengers— or as many as I knew—to a friend who will put it in proper hands if anything befalls me. Go back without me and explain the loss of that French fishing fleet which was sunk the very night we sailed. It is an awkward coincidence to be explained by a man who returns from an unknown voyage having lost his entire list of passengers. You cannot be aware of what this man Brande intends, or you would at least stand by us as long as your own safety permitted. In any case you cannot safely return without us."

Anderson, after reflecting for a moment, apologised for his peremptory words, and agreed to stand by night and day, with fires banked, until I, and all whom I could prevail upon to return with me, got back to his vessel. There was no danger of his running short of coal. A ship that was practically an ocean liner in coal ballast would be a considerable time in burning out her own cargo. But he insisted on a large money payment in advance. I had foolishly mentioned that I had a little over £5,000 in gold. This he claimed on the plea that "in duty to himself"—a favourite phrase of his—he could not accept less. But I think his sense of duty was limited only by the fact that I had hardly another penny in the world. Under the circumstances he might have waived all remuneration. As he was firm, and as I had no time to haggle, I agreed to give him the money. Our bargain was only completed when Brande returned to the deck.

It was strange that on an island like that on which we were landing there should be a regular army of natives waiting to assist us with our baggage, and the saddled horses which were in readiness were out of place in a primeval wilderness. An Englishman came forward, and, saluting Brande, said all was ready for the start to the hills.

This explained the puzzle. An advance agent had made everything comfortable. For Brande, his sister, and Miss Metford the best appointed horses were selected. I, as physician to the chief, had one. The main body had to make the journey on foot, which they did by very easy stages, owing to the heat and the primitive track which formed the only road. Their journey was not very long—perhaps ten miles in a direct line.

Mounted as we were, it was often necessary to stoop to escape the dense masses of parasitic growth which hung in green festoons from every branch of the trees on either side. Under this thick shade all the riotous vegetation of the tropics had fought for life and struggled for light and air till the wealth of their luxuriant death had carpeted the underwood with a thick deposit of steaming foliage. As we ascended the height, every mile in distance brought changes in the botanical growths, which might have passed unnoticed by the ordinary observer or ignorant pioneer. All were noted and commented on by Brande, whose eye was still as keen as his brain had once been brilliant. His usual staid demeanour changed suddenly. He romped ahead of us like a schoolboy out for a holiday. Unlike a schoolboy, however, he was always seeking new items of knowledge and conveying them to us with unaffected pleasure. He was more like a master who had found new ground and new material for his class. Natalie gave herself up like him to this enjoyment of the moment. Edith Metford and I partly caught the glamour of their infectious good-humour. But with both of us it was tempered by the knowledge of what was in store.

When we arrived at our destination we dismounted, at Brande's request, and tied our horses to convenient branches. He went forward, and, pushing aside the underwood with both hands, motioned to us to follow him till he stopped on a ledge of rock which overtopped a hollow in the mountain. The gorge below was the most beautiful glade I ever looked upon.

It was a paradise of foliage. Here and there a fallen tree had formed a picturesque bridge over the mountain stream which meandered through it. Far down below there was a waterfall, where gorgeous tree-ferns rose in natural bowers, while others further still leant over the lotus-covered stream, their giant leaves trailing in the slow-moving current. Tangled masses of bracken rioted in wild abundance over a velvety green sod, overshadowed by waving magnolias. Through the trees bright-plumaged birds were flitting from branch to branch in songless flight, flashing their brilliant colours through the sunny leaves. In places the water splashed over moss-grown rocks into deep pools. Every drifting spray of cloud threw over the dell a new light, deepening the shadows under the great ferns.

It was here in this glorious fairyland; here upon this island, where before us no white foot had ever trod; whose nameless people represented the simplest types of human existence, that Herbert Brande was to put his devilish experiment to the proof. I marvelled that he should have selected so fair a spot for so terrible a purpose. But the papers which I found later amongst the man's effects on the *Esmeralda* explain much that was then incomprehensible to me.

Our camp was quickly formed, and our life was outwardly as happy as if we had been an ordinary company of tourists. I say outwardly, because, while we walked and climbed and collected specimens of botanical or geological interest, there remained that latent dread which always followed us, and dominated the most frivolous of our people, on all of whom a new solemnity had fallen. For myself, the fact that the hour of trial for my own experiment was daily drawing closer and more inevitable, was sufficient to account for my constant and extreme anxiety.

Brande joined none of our excursions. He was always at work in his improvised laboratory. The boxes of material which had been brought from the ship nearly filled it from floor to roof, and from the speed with which these were emptied, it was evident that their contents had been systematised before shipment. In place of the varied collection of substances there grew up within the room a cone of compound matter in which all were blended. This cone was smaller, Brande admitted, than what he had intended. The supply of subordinate fulminates, though several times greater than what was required, proved to be considerably short. But as he had allowed himself a large margin— everything being on a scale far exceeding the minimum which his calculations had pointed to as sufficient—this deficiency did not cause him more than a temporary annoyance. So he worked on.

When we had been three weeks on the island I found the suspense greater than I could bear. The crisis was at hand, and my heart failed me. I determined to make a last appeal to Natalie, to fly with me to the ship. Edith Metford would accompany us. The rest might take the risk to which they had consented.

I found Natalie standing on the high rock whence the most lovely view of the dell could be obtained, and as I approached her silently she was not aware of my presence until I laid my hand on her shoulder.

"Natalie," I said wistfully, for the girl's eyes were full of tears, "do you mind if I withdraw now from this enterprise, in which I cannot be of the slightest use, and of which I most heartily disapprove?"

"The Society would not allow you to withdraw. You cannot do so without its permission, and hope to live within a thousand miles of it," she answered gravely.

"I should not care to live within ten thousand miles of it. I should try to get and keep the earth's diameter between myself and it."

She looked up with an expression of such pain that my heart smote me. "How about me? I cannot live without you now," she said softly.

"Don't live without me. Come with me. Get rid of this infamous association of lunatics, whose object they themselves cannot really appreciate, and whose means are murder—"

But there she stopped me. "My brother could find me out at the uttermost ends of the earth if I forsook him, and you know I do not mean to forsake him. For yourself—do not try to desert. It would make no difference. Do not believe that any consideration would cause me willingly to give you a moment's pain, or that I should shrink from sacrificing myself to save you." With one of her small white hands she gently pressed my head towards her. Her lips touched my forehead, and she whispered: "Do not leave me. It will soon be over now. I—I—need you."

As I was returning dejected after my fruitless appeal to Natalie, I met Edith Metford, to whom I had unhappily mentioned my proposal for an escape.

"Is it arranged? When do we start?" she asked eagerly.

"It is not arranged, and we do not start," I answered in despair.

"You told me you would go with her or without her," she cried passionately. "It is shameful—unmanly."

"It is certainly both if I really said what you tell me. I was not myself at the moment, and my tongue must have slandered me. I stay to the end. But you will go. Captain Anderson will receive you—"

"How am I to be certain of that?"

"I paid him for your passage, and have his receipt."

"And you really think I would go and leave—leave—"

"Natalie? I think you would be perfectly justified."

At this the girl stamped her foot passionately on the ground and burst into tears. Nor would she permit any of the slight caresses I offered. I thought her old caprices were returning. She flung my arm rudely from her and left me bewildered.

XVII. "THIS EARTH SHALL DIE"

My memory does not serve me well in the scenes which immediately preceded the closing of the drama in which Brande was chief actor. It is doubtless the transcendental interest of the final situation which blunts my recollection of what occurred shortly before it. I did not abate one jot of my determination to fight my venture out unflinching, but my actions were probably more automatic than reasoned, as the time of our last encounter approached. On the whole, the fight had been a fair one. Brande had used his advantage over me for his own purpose as long as it remained with him. I used the advantage as soon as it passed to me for mine. The conditions had thus been equalised when, for the third and last time, I was to hear him address his Society.

This time the man was weak in health. His vitality was ebbing fast, but his marvellous inspiration was strong within him, and, supported by it, he battled manfully with the disease which I had manufactured for him. His lecture-room was the fairy glen; his canopy the heavens.

I cannot give the substance of this address, or any portion of it, verbatim as on former occasions, for I have not the manuscript. I doubt if Brande wrote out his last speech. Methodical as were his habits it is probable that his final words were not premeditated. They burst from him in a delirium that could hardly have been studied. His fine frenzy could not well have originated from considered sentences, although his language, regarded as mere oratory, was magnificent. It was appalling in the light through which I read it.

He stood alone upon the rock which overtopped the dell. We arranged ourselves in such groups as suited our inclinations, upon some rising ground below. The great trees waved overhead, low murmuring. The waterfall splashed drearily. Below, not a whisper was exchanged. Above, the man poured out his triumphant death-song in sonorous periods. Below, great fear was upon all. Above, the madman exulted wildly.

At first his voice was weak. As he went on it gained strength and depth. He alluded to his first address, in which he had hinted that the material Universe was not quite a success; to his second, in which he had boldly declared it was an absolute failure. This, his third declaration, was to tell us that the remedy as far as he, a mortal man, could apply it, was ready. The end was at hand. That night should see the consummation of his life-work. To-morrow's sun would rise—if it rose at all—on the earth restored to space.

A shiver passed perceptibly over the people, prepared as they were for this long foreseen announcement. Edith Metford, who stood by me on my left, slipped her hand into mine and pressed my fingers hard. Natalie Brande, on my right, did not move. Her eyes were dilated and fixed on the speaker. The old clairvoyant look was on her face. Her dark pupils were blinded save to their inward light. She was either unconscious or only partly conscious. Now that the hour had come, they who had believed their courage secure felt it wither. They, the people with us, begged for a little longer time to brace themselves for the great crisis—the plunge into an eternity from which there would be no resurrection, neither of matter nor of mind.

Brande heeded them not.

"This night," said he, with culminating enthusiasm, "the cloud-capped towers, the gorgeous palaces, the solemn temples, shall dissolve. To this great globe itself—this paltry speck of less account in space than a dew-drop in an ocean—and all its sorrow and pain, its trials and temptations, all the pathos and bathos of our tragic human farce, the end is near. The way has been hard, and the journey overlong, and the burden often beyond man's strength. But that long-drawn sorrow now shall cease. The tears will be wiped away. The burden will fall from weary shoulders. For the fulness of time has come. This earth shall die! And death is peace.

"I stand," he cried out in a strident voice, raising his arm aloft, "I may say, with one foot on sea and one on land, for I hold the elemental secret of them both. And I swear by the living god—Science incarnate—that the suffering of the centuries is over, that for this earth and all that it contains, from this night and for ever, *Time will be no more!*"

A great cry rose from the people. "Give us another day—only another day!"

But Brande made answer: "It is now too late."

"Too late!" the people wailed.

"Yes, too late. I warned you long ago. Are you not yet ready? In two hours the disintegrating agent will enter on its work. No human power could stop it now. Not if every particle of the material I have compounded were separated and scattered to the winds. Before I set my foot upon this rock I applied the key which will release its inherent energy. I myself am powerless."

"Powerless," sobbed the auditors.

"Powerless! And if I had ten thousand times the power which I have called forth from the universal element, I would use it towards the issue I have forecast."

Thereupon he turned away. Doom sounded in his words. The hand of Death laid clammy fingers on us. Edith Metford's strength failed at last. It had been sorely tested. She sank into my arms.

"Courage, true heart, our time has come," I whispered. "We start for the steamer at once. The horses are ready." My arrangements had been already made. My plan had been as carefully matured as any ever made by Brande himself.

"How many horses?"

"Three. One for you; another for Natalie; the third for myself. The rest must accept the fate they have selected."

The girl shuddered as she said, "But your interference with the formula? You are sure it will destroy the effect?"

"I am certain that the particular result on which Brande calculates will not take place. But short of that, he has still enough explosive matter stored to cause an earthquake. We are not safe within a radius of fifty miles. It will be a race against time."

"Natalie will not come."

"Not voluntarily. You must think of some plan. Your brain is quick. We have not a moment to lose. Ah, there she is! Speak to her."

Natalie was crossing the open ground which led from the glen to Brande's laboratory. She did not observe us till Edith called to her. Then she approached hastily and embraced her friend with visible emotion. Even to me she offered her cheek without reserve.

"Natalie," I said quickly, "there are three horses saddled and waiting in the palm grove. The *Esmeralda* is still lying in the harbour where we landed. You will come with us. Indeed, you have no choice. You must come if I have to carry you to your horse and tie you to the saddle. You will not force me to put that indignity upon you. To the horses, then! Come!"

For answer she called her brother loudly by his name. Brande immediately appeared at the door of his laboratory, and when he perceived from whom the call had come he joined us.

"Herbert," said Natalie, "our friend is deserting us. He must still cling to the thought that our purpose may fail, and he expects to escape on horseback from the fate of the earth. Reason with him yet a little further."

"There is no time to reason," I interrupted. "The horses are ready. This girl (pointing as I spoke to Edith Metford) takes one, I another, and you the third—whether your brother agrees or not."

"Surely you have not lost your reason? Have you forgotten the drop of water in the English Channel?" Brande said quietly.

"Brande," I answered, "the sooner you induce your sister to come with me the better; and the sooner you induce these maniac friends of yours to clear out the better, for your enterprise will fail."

"It is as certain as the law of gravitation. With my own hand I mixed the ingredients according to the formula."

"And," said I, "with my own hand I altered your formula."

Had Brande's heart stopped beating, his face could not have become more distorted and livid. He moved close to me, and, glaring into my eyes, hissed out:

"You altered my formula?"

"I did," I answered recklessly. "I multiplied your figures by ten where they struck me as insufficient."

"When?"

I strode closer still to him and looked him straight in the eyes while I spoke.

"That night in the Red Sea, when Edith Metford, by accident, mixed morphia in your medicine. The night I injected a subtle poison, which I picked up in India once, into your blood while you slept, thereby baffling some of the functions of your extraordinary brain. The night when in your sleep you stirred once, and had you stirred twice, I would have killed you, then and there, as ruthlessly as you would kill mankind now. The night I did kill your lieutenant, Rockingham, and throw his body overboard to the sharks."

Brande did not speak for a moment. Then he said in a gentle, uncomplaining voice:

"So it now devolves on Grey. The end will be the same. The Labrador expedition will succeed where I have failed." To Natalie: "You had better go. There will only be an explosion. The island will probably disappear. That will be all."

"Do you remain?" she asked.

"Yes. I perish with my failure."

"Then I perish with you. And you, Marcel, save yourself—you coward!"

I started as if struck in the face. Then I said to Edith: "Be careful to keep to the track. Take the bay horse. I saddled him for myself, but you can ride him safely. Lose no time, and ride hard for the coast."

"Arthur Marcel," she answered, so softly that the others did not hear, "your work in the world is not yet over. There is the Labrador expedition. Just now, when my strength failed, you whispered 'courage.' Be true to yourself! Half an hour is gone."

At length some glimmer of human feeling awoke in Brande. He said in a low, abstracted voice: "My life fittingly ends now. To keep you, Natalie, would only be a vulgar murder." The old will power seemed to come back to him. He looked into the girl's eyes, and said slowly and sternly: "Go! I command it."

Without another word he turned away from us. When he had disappeared into the laboratory, Natalie sighed, and said dreamily:

"I am ready. Let us go."

XVIII. THE FLIGHT

I led the girls hurriedly to the horses. When they were mounted on the ponies, I gave the bridle-reins of the bay horse—whose size and strength were necessary for my extra weight—to Edith Metford, and asked her to wait for me until I announced Brande's probable failure to the people, and advised a *sauve qui peut*.

Hard upon my warning there followed a strange metamorphosis in the crowd, who, after the passing weakness at the lecture, had fallen back into stoical indifference, or it may have been despair. The possibility of escape galvanized them into the desire for life. Cries of distress, and prayers for help, filled the air. Men and women rushed about like frightened sheep without concert or any sensible effort to escape, wasting in futile scrambles the short time remaining to them. For another half hour had now passed, and in sixty minutes the earthquake would take place.

"Follow us!" I shouted, as with my companions I rode slowly through the camp. "Keep the track to the sea. I shall have the steamer's boats ready for all who may reach the shore alive."

"The horses! Seize the horses!" rose in a loud shout, and the mob flung themselves upon us, as though three animals could carry all.

When I saw the rush, I called out: "Sit firm, Natalie; I am going to strike your horse." Saying which I struck the pony a sharp blow with my riding-whip crossways on the flank. It bounded like a deer, and then dashed forward down the rough pathway.

"Now you, Edith!" I struck her pony in the same way; but it only reared and nearly threw her. It could not get away. Already hands were upon both bridle-reins. There was no help for it. I pulled out my revolver and fired once, twice, and thrice—for I missed the second shot—and then the maddened animal sprang forward, released from the hands that held it.

It was now time to look to myself. I was in the midst of a dozen maniacs mad with fear. I kicked in my spurs desperately, and the bay lashed out his hind feet. One hoof struck young Halley on the forehead. He fell back dead, his skull in fragments. But the others refused to break the circle. Then I emptied my weapon on them, and my horse plunged through the opening, followed by despairing execrations. The moment I was clear, I returned my revolver to its case, and settled myself in the saddle, for, borne out of the proper path as I had been, there was a stiff bank to leap before I could regain the track to the shore. Owing to the darkness the horse refused to leap, and I nearly fell over his head. With a little scrambling I managed to get back into my seat, and then trotted along the bank for a hundred yards. At this point the bank disappeared, and there was nothing between me now and the open track to the sea.

Once upon the path, I put the bay to a gallop, and very soon overtook a man and a woman hurrying on. They were running hand in hand, the man a little in front dragging his companion on by force. It was plain to

me that the woman could not hold out much longer. The man, Claude
Lureau, hailed me as I passed.

"Help us, Marcel. Don't ride away from us."

"I cannot save both," I answered, pulling up.

"Then save Mademoiselle Veret. I'll take my chance."

This blunt speech moved me, the more especially as the man was
French. I could not allow him to point the way of duty to me—an
Englishman.

"Assist her up, then. Now, Mademoiselle, put your arms round me
and hold hard for your life. Lureau, you may hold my stirrup if you
agree to loose it when you tire."

"I will do so," he promised.

Hampered thus, I but slowly gained on Natalie and Edith, whose
ponies had galloped a mile before they could be stopped.

"Forward, forward!" I shouted when within hail. "Don't wait for me.
Ride on at top speed. Lash your ponies with the bridle-reins."

We were all moving on now at an easy canter, for I could not go fast
so long as Lureau held my stirrup, and the girls in front did not seem
anxious to leave me far behind. Besides, the tangled underwood and
overhanging creepers rendered hard riding both difficult and dangerous.
The ponies were hard held, but notwithstanding this my horse fell back
gradually in the race, and the hammering of the hoofs in front grew
fainter. The breath of the runner at my stirrup came in great sobs. He
was suffocating, but he struggled on a little longer. Then he threw up
his hand and gasped:

"I am done. Go on, Marcel. You deserve to escape. Don't desert
the girl."

"May God desert me if I do," I answered. "And do you keep on as
long as you can. You may reach the shore after all."

"Go on—save her!" he gasped, and then from sheer exhaustion fell
forward on his face.

"Sit still, Mademoiselle," I cried, pulling the French girl's arms round
me in time to prevent her from throwing herself purposely from the
horse. Then I drove in my spurs hard, and, being now released from
Lureau's grasp, I overtook the ponies.

For five minutes we all rode on abreast. And then the darkness began
to break, and a strange dawn glimmered over the tree-tops, although

the hour of midnight was still to come. A wild, red light, like that of a fiery sunset in a hazy summer evening, spread over the night sky. The quivering stars grew pale. Constellation after constellation, they were blotted out until the whole arc of heaven was a dull red glare. The horses were dismayed by this strange phenomenon, and dashed the froth from their foaming muzzles as they galloped now without stress of spur at their best speed. Birds that could not sing found voice, and chattered and shrieked as they dashed from tree to tree in aimless flight. Enormous bats hurtled in the air, blinded by the unusual light. From the dense undergrowth strange denizens of the woods, disturbed in their nightly prowl, leaped forth and scurried squealing between the galloping hoofs, reckless of anything save their own fear. Everything that was alive upon the island was in motion, and fear was the motor of them all.

So far, we saw no natives. Their absence did not surprise me, for I had no time for thought. It was explained later.

Edith Metford's pony soon became unmanageable in its fright. I unbuckled one spur and gave it to her, directing her to hold it in her hand, for of course she could not strap it to her boot, and drive it into the animal when he swerved. She took the spur, and as her pony, in one of his side leaps, nearly bounded off the path, she struck him hard on the ribs. He bolted and flew on far ahead of us.

The light grew stronger.

But that the rays were red, it would now have been as bright as day. We were chasing our shadows, so the light must be directly behind us. Mademoiselle Veret first noticed this, and drew my attention to it. I looked back, and my heart sank at the sight. In the terror it inspired, I regretted having burthened myself with the girl I had sworn to save.

The island was on fire!

"It is the end of the world," Mademoiselle Veret said with a shudder. She clung closer to me. I could feel her warm breath upon my cheek. The unmanly regret, which for a moment had touched me, passed.

The ponies now seemed to find out that their safety lay in galloping straight on, rather than in scared leaps from side to side. They stretched themselves like race horses, and gave my bay, with his double burthen, a strong lead. The pace became terrible considering the nature of the ground we covered.

At last the harbour came in view. But my horse, I knew, could not last another mile, and the shore was still distant two or three. I spurred him hard and drew nearly level with the ponies, so that my voice could be heard by both their riders.

"Ride on," I shouted, "and hail the steamer, so that there may be no delay when I come up. This horse is blown, and will not stand the pace. I am going to ease him. You will go on board at once, and send the boat back for us." Then I eased the bay, but in spite of this I immediately overtook Edith Metford, who had pulled up.

My reproaches she cut short by saying, "If that horse does the distance at all it will be by getting a lead all the way. And I am going to give it to him." So we started together.

Natalie was waiting for us a little further on. I spoke to her, but she did not answer. From the moment that Brande had commanded her to accompany us, her manner had remained absolutely passive. What I ordered, she obeyed. That was all. Instead of being alarmed by the horrors of the ride, she did not seem to be even interested. I had not leisure, however, to reflect on this. For the first time in the whole race she spoke to us.

"Would it not be better if Edith rode on?" she said. "I can take her place. It seems useless to sacrifice her. It does not matter to me. I cannot now be afraid."

"I am afraid; but I remain," Edith said resolutely.

The ground under us began to heave. Whole acres of it swayed disjointed. We were galloping on oscillating fragments, which trembled beneath us like floating logs under boys at play. To jump these cracks— sometimes an upward bank, sometimes a deep drop, in addition to the width of the seam, had to be taken—pumped out the failing horses, and the hope that was left to us disappeared utterly.

The glare of the red light behind waxed fiercer still, and a low rumbling as of distant thunder began to mutter round us. The air became difficult to breathe. It was no longer air, but a mephitic stench that choked us with disgusting fumes. Then a great shock shook the land, and right in front of us a seam opened that must have been fully fifteen feet in width. Natalie was the first to see it. She observed it too late to stop.

In the same mechanical way as she had acted before, she settled herself in the saddle, struck the pony with her hand, and raced him at the chasm. He cleared it with little to spare. Edith's took it next with less. Then my turn came. Before I could shake up my tired horse, Mademoiselle Veret said quickly:

"Monsieur has done enough. He will now permit me to alight. This time the horse cannot jump over with both."

"He shall jump over with both, Mademoiselle, or he shall jump in," I answered. "Don't look down when we are crossing."

The horse just got over, but he came to his knees, and we fell forward over his shoulder. The girl's head struck full on a slab of rock, and a faint moan was all that told me she was alive as I arose half stunned to my feet. My first thought was for the horse, for on him all depended. He was uninjured, apparently, but hardly able to stand from the shock and the stress of fatigue.

Edith Metford had dismounted and caught him; she was holding the bridle in her left hand, and winced as if in pain when I accidentally brushed against her right shoulder. I tied the horse to a young palm, and begged the girl to ride on. She obeyed me reluctantly. Natalie had to assist her to remount, so she must have been injured. When I saw her safely in her saddle, I ran back to Mademoiselle Veret.

The chasm was fast widening. From either side great fragments were breaking off and falling in with a roar of loose rocks crashing together, till far down the sound was dulled into a hollow boom. This ended in low guttural, which growled up from an abysmal depth. Mademoiselle Veret, or her dead body, lay now on the very edge of the seam, and I had to harden my heart before I could bring myself to venture close to it. But I had given my word, and there were no conditions in the promise when I made it.

I was spared the ordeal. Just as I stepped forward, the slab of rock on which the girl lay broke off in front of me, and, tipping up, overturned itself into the chasm. Far below I could see the shimmer of the girl's dress as her body went plunging down into that awful pit. And remembering her generous courage and offer of self-sacrifice, I felt tears rise in my eyes. But there was no time for tears.

I leaped on the bay, and got him into something approaching a gallop, shouting at the others to keep on, for they were now returning. When I came up with them, Edith Metford said with a shiver:

"The girl?"

"Is at the bottom of the pit. Ride on."

We gained the shore at last; and our presence there produced the explanation of the absence of the natives on the pathway to the sea. They were there before us. Lying prostrate on the beach in hundreds, they raised their bodies partly from the sands, like a resurrection of the already dead, and there then rang out upon the night air a sound such as my ears had never before heard in my life, such as, I pray God, they may never listen to again. I do not know what that dreadful death-wail meant in words, only that it touched the lowest depths of human horror. All along the beach that fearful chorus of the damned wailed forth, and echoed back from rock and cliff. The cry for mercy could not be mistaken—the supplication blended with despair. They were praying to us—their evil spirits, for this wrong had been wrought them by our advent, if not by ourselves.

I cannot dwell upon the scene. I could not describe it. I would not if I could.

The steamer was still in her berth; her head was pointed seawards. Loud orders rang over the water. The roar of the chain running out through the hawse-hole and the heavy splash could not be mistaken. Anderson had slipped his cable. Then the chime of the telegraph on the bridge was followed almost instantly by the first smashing stroke of the propeller.

The *Esmeralda* was under weigh!

XIX. THE CATASTROPHE

The *Esmeralda* was putting out to sea when I thought of a last expedient to draw the attention of her captain. Filling my revolver with cartridges which I had loose in my pockets, I fired all the chambers as fast as I could snap the trigger.

My signals were heard, and Anderson proved true to his bargain. He immediately reversed his engines, and, when he had backed in as close as he thought safe, sent a boat ashore for us. We got into it without any obstruction from the cowering natives, who only shrank from us in horror, now that their prayers had failed to move us. The moment our boat was made fast to the steamer's davit ropes and we were pulled out of the water, "full speed ahead" was rung from the bridge. We were raised to the deck while the vessel was getting up speed.

I crawled up the ladder to the bridge feebly, for I was becoming stiff from the bruises of the fall from my horse. Anderson received me coldly, and listened indifferently to my thanks. An agreement such as ours hardly prepared me for his loyalty.

"Oh, as to that," he interrupted, "when I make a bargain my word is my bond. On this occasion I am inclined to think the indenture will be a final one."

His bargain was a hard one, but, having made it, he abided faithfully by its conditions. He was honest, therefore, in his own way.

"How far can you get out in fifteen minutes?" I asked.

"We may make six or seven knots. But what is the good of that? There will be an earthquake on that island on a liberal scale—on such a scale that this ship would have very little chance in the wave that will follow us if we were fifty miles at sea."

"You have taken every precaution, of course—"

Anderson here looked at me contemptuously, and, with an air of sarcastic admiration, he said:

"You have guessed it at the first try. That is precisely what I have done."

"Pshaw! don't take offence at trifles at a time like this," I said testily. "If you knew as much about that earthquake as I do, you would be in no humour for bandying phrases."

"Might I ask how much you do know about it? You could not have foreseen the trouble more clearly if you had made it yourself."

"I did not make it myself, but I know the means which the man who did employed, and but for me that earthquake would have wrecked this earth."

Anderson made no direct answer to this, but he said earnestly:

"You will now go below, sir. You are done up. Roberts will take you to the doctor."

"I am not done up, and I mean to see it out," I retorted doggedly. My nervous system was completely unhinged, and a fit of stupid obstinacy came on me which rendered any interference with my actions intolerable.

"Then you cannot see it out upon my bridge," Anderson said. The determined tone in which he spoke only added to my impotent wrath.

"Very well, I will return to the deck, and if any of your men should attempt to interfere with me he will do so at his peril." With that, I slung my revolver round so as to have it ready to my hand. I was beside myself. My conduct was already bad enough, but I made it worse before I left the bridge.

"And if you, Anderson, disobey my orders—my orders, do you hear?—an explosion such as took place in the middle of the English channel shall take place in the middle of this ship."

"For God's sake leave the bridge. I want my wits about me, and I have no intention of earning another exhibition of your devilries."

"Then be careful not to trouble me again." Thus after having passed through much danger with a spirit not unbecoming—as I hope—an English gentleman, I acted, when the worst was passed, like a peevish schoolboy. I am ashamed of my conduct in this small matter, and trust it will pass without much notice in the narrative of events of greater moment.

On deck, Natalie Brande, Edith Metford, and Percival were standing together, their eyes fixed on the island. Edith's face was deathly white, even in the ruddy glow which was now over land and sea. When I saw her pallor, my evil temper passed away.

"It would be impossible for you to be quite well," I said to her anxiously; "but has anything happened since I left you? You are very pale."

"Oh no," she answered, "I'm all right; a little faint after that ride. I shall be better soon."

Natalie turned her weird eyes on me and said in the hollow voice we had heard once before—when she spoke to us on the island—"That is her way of telling you that your horse broke her right arm when she caught him for you. She held him, you remember, with her left hand. The doctor has set the limb. She will not suffer long."

"Heaven help us, this awful night," Edith cried. "How do you know that, Natalie?"

"I know much now, but I shall know more soon." After this she would not speak again.

With every pound of steam on that the *Esmeralda's* boilers would bear without bursting, we were now plunging through the great rollers of the Arafura Sea. Everything had indeed been done to put the vessel in trim. She was cleared for action, so to speak. And a gallant fight she made when the issue was knit. When the hour of midnight must be near at hand, I looked at my watch. It was one minute to twelve o'clock.

Thirty seconds more!

The stupendous corona of flame which hung over the island was pierced by long lines of smoke that stretched far above the glare and clutched with sooty fingers at the stars, now fitfully coming back to view at our distance. The rumbling of internal thunder waxed louder.

Fifteen seconds now!

Fearful peals rent the atmosphere. Vast tongues of flame protruded heavenward. The elements must be melting in that fervent heat. The blazing bowels of the earth were pouring forth.

Twelve, midnight!

A reverberation thundered out which shook the solid earth, and a roaring hell-breath of flame and smoke belched up so awful in its dread magnificence that every man who saw it and lived to tell his story might justly have claimed to have seen perdition. In that hurricane of incandescent matter the island was blotted out for ever from the map of this world.

Notwithstanding the speed of the *Esmeralda* she was a sloth when compared with the speed of the wave from such an earthquake. From the glare of the illumination to perfect darkness the contrast was sudden and extreme. But the blackness of the ocean was soon whitened by the snowy plumes of the avalanche of water which was now racing us, far astern as yet, but gaining fast. I, who had no business about the ship requiring my presence in any special part, decided to wait on deck and lash myself to the forward, which would be practically the lee-side of a deckhouse. Edith Metford we prevailed on to go below, that she might not run the risk of further injury to her fractured arm. As she left us she whispered to me, "So Natalie will be with you at the end, and I—" a sob stopped her. And it came into my mind at that moment that this girl had acted very nobly, and that I had hardly appreciated her and all that she had done for me.

Natalie refused to leave the deck. I lashed her securely beside me. Together we awaited the end. When the roar of the following wave came close, so close that the voices of the officers of the ship could be no longer heard, Natalie spoke. The hollow sound was no longer in her voice. Her own soft sweet tones had come back.

"Arthur," she asked, "is this the end?"

"I fear it is," I answered, speaking close to her ear so that she might hear.

"Then we have little time, and I have something which I must say, which you must promise me to remember when—when—I am no longer with you."

"You will be always with me while we live. I think I deserve that at last."

"Yes, you deserve that and more. I will be with you while I live, but that will not be for long."

I was about to interrupt her when she put her soft little hand upon my lips and said:

"Listen, there is very little time. It is all a mistake. I mean Herbert was wrong. He might as well have let me have my earthly span of happiness or folly—call it what you will."

"You see that now—thank God!"

"Yes, but I see it too late, I did not know it until—until I was dead. Hush!" Again I tried to interrupt her, for I thought her mind was wandering. "I died psychically with Herbert. That was when we first saw the light on the island. Since then I have lived mechanically, but it has only been life in so low a form that I do not now know what has happened between that time and this. And I could not now speak as I am speaking save by a will power which is costing me very dear. But it is the only voice you could hear. I do not therefore count the cost. My brother's brain so far overmatched my own that it first absorbed and finally destroyed my mental vitality. This influence removed, I am a rudderless ship at sea—bound to perish."

"May his torments endure for ever. May the nethermost pit of hell receive him!" I said with a groan of agony.

But Natalie said: "Hush! I might have lingered on a little longer, but I chose to concentrate the vital force which would have lasted me a few more senile years into the minutes necessary for this message from me to you—a message I could not have given you if he were not dead. And I am dying so that you may hear it. Dying! My God! I am already dead."

She seemed to struggle against some force that battled with her, and the roar of many waters was louder around us before she was able to speak again.

"Bend lower, Arthur; my strength is failing, and I have not yet said that for which I am here. Lower still.

"I said it is all a mistake—a hideous mistake. Existence as we know it is ephemeral. Suffering is ephemeral. There is nothing everlasting but love. There is nothing eternal but mind. Your mind is mine. Your love is mine. Your human life may belong to whomsoever you will it. It ought to belong to that brave girl below. I do not grudge it to her, for I have *you*. We two shall be together through the ages—for ever and for ever. Heart of my heart, you have striven manfully and well, and if you did not altogether succeed in saving my flesh from premature corruption, be satisfied in that you have my soul. Ah!"

She pressed her hands to her head as if in dreadful pain. When she spoke again her voice came in short gasps.

"My brain is reeling. I do not know what I am saying," she cried, distraught. "I do not know whether I am saying what is true or only what I imagine to be true. I know nothing but this. I was mesmerised. I have been so for two years. But for that I would have been happy in your love—for I was a woman before this hideous influence benumbed me. They told me it was only a fool's paradise that I missed. But I only know that I have missed it. Missed it—and the darkness of death is upon me."

She ceased to speak. A shudder convulsed her, and then her head sank gently on my shoulder.

At that moment the great wave broke over the vessel, whirling her helpless like a cork on the ripples of a mill pond; lashing her with mighty strokes; sweeping in giant cataracts from stern to stem; smashing, tearing everything; deluging her with hissing torrents; crushing her with avalanches of raging foam. Then the ocean tornado passed on and left the *Esmeralda* behind, with half the crew disabled and many lost, her decks a mass of wreckage, her masts gone. The crippled ship barely floated. When the last torrent of spray passed, and I was able to look to Natalie, her head had drooped down on her breast. I raised her face gently and looked into her wide open eyes.

She was dead.

XX. CONCLUSION

Taking up my girl's body in my arms, I stumbled over the wreck-encumbered deck, and bore it to the state-room she had occupied on the outward voyage. Percival was too busy attending to wounded sailors to be interrupted. His services, I knew, were useless now, but I wanted him to refute or corroborate a conviction which my own medical knowledge had forced upon me. The thought was so repellent, I clung to any hope which might lead to its dispersion. I waited alone with my dead.

Percival came after an hour, which seemed to me an eternity. He stammered out some incoherent words of sympathy as soon as he looked in my face. But this was not the purpose for which I had detached him from his pressing duties elsewhere. I made a gesture towards the dead girl. He attended to it immediately. I watched closely and took care that the light should be on his face, so that I might read his eyes rather than listen to his words.

"She has fainted!" he exclaimed, as he approached the rigid figure. I said nothing until he turned and faced me. Then I read his eyes. He said slowly: "You are aware, Marcel, that—that she is dead?"

"I am."

"That she has been dead—several hours?"

"I am."

"But let me think. It was only an hour—"

"No; do not think," I interrupted. "There are things in this voyage which will not bear to be thought of. I thank you for coming so soon. You will forgive me for troubling you when you have so much to do elsewhere. And now leave us alone. I mean, leave me alone."

He pressed my hand, and went away without a word. I am that man's friend.

They buried her at sea.

I was happily unconscious at the time, and so was spared that scene. Edith Metford, weak and suffering as she was, went through it all. She has told me nothing about it, save that it was done. More than that I could not bear. And I have borne much.

The voyage home was a dreary episode. There is little more to tell, and it must be told quickly. Percival was kind, but it distressed me to find that he now plainly regarded me as weak-minded from the stress of my trouble. Once, in the extremity of my misery, I began a relation of my adventures to him, for I wanted his help. The look upon his face was enough for me. I did not make the same mistake again.

To Anderson I made amends for my extravagant display of temper. He received me more kindly than I expected. I no longer thought of the money that had passed between us. And, to do him tardy justice, I do not think he thought of it either. At least he did not offer any of it back. His scruples, I presume, were conscientious. Indeed, I was no longer worth a man's enmity. Sympathy was now the only indignity that could be put upon me. And Anderson did not trespass in that direction. My misery was, I thought, complete. One note must still be struck in that long discord of despair.

We were steaming along the southern coast of Java. For many hours the rugged cliffs and giant rocks which fence the island against the onslaught of the Indian Ocean had passed before us as in review, and we—Edith Metford and I—sat on the deck silently, with many thoughts in common, but without the interchange of a spoken word. The stern, forbidding aspect of that iron coast increased the gloom which had settled on my brain. Its ramparts of lonely sea-drenched crags depressed me below the mental zero that was now habitual with me. The sun went down in a red glare, which moved me not. The short twilight passed quickly, but I noticed nothing. Then night came. The restless sea disappeared in darkness. The grand march past of the silent stars began. But I neither knew nor cared.

A soft whisper stirred me.

"Arthur, for God's sake rouse yourself! You are brooding a great deal too much. It will destroy you."

Listlessly I put my hand in hers, and clasped her fingers gently.

"Bear with me!" I pleaded.

"I will bear with you for ever. But you must fight on. You have not won yet."

"No, nor ever shall. I have fought my last fight. The victory may go to whosoever desires it."

On this she wept. I could not bear that she should suffer from my misery, and so, guarding carefully her injured arm, I drew her close to me. And then, out of the darkness of the night, far over the solitude of the sea, there came to us the sound of a voice. That voice was a woman's wail. The girl beside me shuddered and drew back. I did not ask her if she had heard. I knew she had heard.

We arose and stood apart without any explanation. From that moment a caress would have been a sacrilege. I did not hear that weird sound again, nor aught else for an hour or more save the bursting of the breakers on the crags of Java.

I kept no record of the commonplaces of our voyage thereafter. It only remains for me to say that I arrived in England broken in health and bankrupt in fortune. Brande left no money. His formula for the transmutation of metals is unintelligible to me. I can make no use of it.

Edith Metford remains my friend. To part utterly after what we have undergone together is beyond our strength. But between us there is a nameless shadow, reminiscent of that awful night in the Arafura Sea, when death came very near to us. And in my ears there is always the echo of that voice which I heard by the shores of Java when the misty borderland between life and death seemed clear.

My story is told. I cannot prove its truth, for there is much in it to which I am the only living witness. I cannot prove whether Herbert Brande was a scientific magician possessed of *all* the powers he claimed, or merely a mad physicist in charge of a new and terrible explosive; nor whether Edward Grey ever started for Labrador. The burthen of the proof of this last must be borne by others—unless it be left to Grey himself to show whether my evidence is false or true. If it be left to him, a few years will decide the issue.

I am content to wait.

THE STAR

H.G. WELLS

One of science fiction's most talented and influential writers, Herbert George Wells (1866–1946) explored end-of-the-world scenarios in several of his best-known stories, notably The Time Machine *(1895), which presents a vision of a far future world languishing in the light of a dying sun, and* The War of the Worlds *(1898), in which extraterrestrial invaders threaten the extinction of humankind. In this story, published in the Christmas 1897 issue of* The Graphic, *Wells speculates on the disastrous consequences of a rogue star passing through our solar system.*

It was on the first day of the New Year that the announcement was made, almost simultaneously from three observatories, that the motion of the planet Neptune, the outermost of all the planets that wheel about the sun, had become very erratic. Ogilvy had already called attention to a suspected retardation in its velocity in December. Such a piece of news was scarcely calculated to interest a world the greater portion of whose inhabitants were unaware of the existence of the planet Neptune, nor outside the astronomical profession did the subsequent discovery of a faint remote speck of light in the region of the perturbed planet cause any very great excitement. Scientific people, however, found the intelligence remarkable enough, even before it became known that the new body was rapidly growing larger and brighter, that its motion was quite different from the orderly progress of the planets, and that the deflection of Neptune and its satellite was becoming now of an unprecedented kind.

Few people without a training in science can realise the huge isolation of the solar system. The sun with its specks of planets, its dust of planetoids, and its impalpable comets, swims in a vacant immensity that almost defeats the imagination. Beyond the orbit of Neptune there is space, vacant so far as human observation has penetrated, without warmth or light or sound, blank emptiness, for twenty million times a million miles. That is the smallest estimate of the distance to be traversed before the very nearest of the stars is attained. And, saving a few comets more unsubstantial than the thinnest flame, no matter had ever to human knowledge crossed this gulf of space, until early in the twentieth century this strange wanderer appeared. A vast mass of matter it was, bulky, heavy, rushing without warning out of the black mystery of the sky into the radiance of the sun. By the second day it was clearly visible to any decent instrument, as a speck with a barely sensible diameter, in the constellation Leo near Regulus. In a little while an opera glass could attain it.

On the third day of the new year the newspaper readers of two hemispheres were made aware for the first time of the real importance of this unusual apparition in the heavens. "A Planetary Collision," one London paper headed the news, and proclaimed Duchaine's opinion that this strange new planet would probably collide with Neptune. The leader writers enlarged upon the topic; so that in most of the capitals of the world, on January 3rd, there was an expectation, however vague of some imminent phenomenon in the sky; and as the night followed the sunset round the globe, thousands of men turned their eyes skyward to see—the old familiar stars just as they had always been.

Until it was dawn in London and Pollux setting and the stars overhead grown pale. The Winter's dawn it was, a sickly filtering accumulation of daylight, and the light of gas and candles shone yellow in the windows to show where people were astir. But the yawning policeman saw the thing, the busy crowds in the markets stopped agape, workmen going to their work betimes, milkmen, the drivers of news-carts, dissipation going home jaded and pale, homeless wanderers, sentinels on their beats, and in the country, labourers trudging afield, poachers slinking home, all over the dusky quickening country it could be seen—and out at sea by seamen watching for the day—a great white star, come suddenly into the westward sky!

Brighter it was than any star in our skies; brighter than the evening star at its brightest. It still glowed out white and large, no mere twinkling spot of light, but a small round clear shining disc, an hour after the day had come. And where science has not reached, men stared and feared, telling one another of the wars and pestilences that are foreshadowed by these fiery signs in the Heavens. Sturdy Boers, dusky Hottentots, Gold Coast Negroes, Frenchmen, Spaniards, Portuguese, stood in the warmth of the sunrise watching the setting of this strange new star.

And in a hundred observatories there had been suppressed excitement, rising almost to shouting pitch, as the two remote bodies had rushed together; and a hurrying to and fro, to gather photographic apparatus and spectroscope, and this appliance and that, to record this novel astonishing sight, the destruction of a world. For it was a world, a sister planet of our earth, far greater than our earth indeed, that had so suddenly flashed into flaming death. Neptune it was, had been struck, fairly and squarely, by the strange planet from outer space and the heat of the concussion had incontinently turned two solid globes into one vast mass of incandescence. Round the world that day, two hours before the dawn, went the pallid great white star, fading only as it sank westward and the sun mounted above it. Everywhere men marvelled at it, but of all those who saw it none could have marvelled more than those sailors, habitual watchers of the stars, who far away at sea had heard nothing of its advent and saw it now rise like a pigmy moon and climb zenithward and hang overhead and sink westward with the passing of the night.

And when next it rose over Europe everywhere were crowds of watchers on hilly slopes, on house-roofs, in open spaces, staring eastward for the rising of the great new star. It rose with a white glow in front of it, like the glare of a white fire, and those who had seen it come into existence the night before cried out at the sight of it. "It is larger," they cried. "It is brighter!" And, indeed the moon a quarter full and sinking in the west was in its apparent size beyond comparison, but scarcely in all its breadth had it as much brightness now as the little circle of the strange new star.

"It is brighter!" cried the people clustering in the streets. But in the dim observatories the watchers held their breath and peered at one another. "It is nearer," they said. "Nearer!"

And voice after voice repeated, "It is nearer," and the clicking telegraph took that up, and it trembled along telephone wires, and in a thousand cities grimy compositors fingered the type. "It is nearer." Men writing in offices, struck with a strange realisation, flung down their pens, men talking in a thousand places suddenly came upon a grotesque possibility in those words, "It is nearer." It hurried along wakening streets, it was shouted down the frost-stilled ways of quiet villages; men who had read these things from the throbbing tape stood in yellow-lit doorways shouting the news to the passersby. "It is nearer." Pretty women, flushed and glittering, heard the news told jestingly between the dances, and feigned an intelligent interest they did not feel. "Nearer! Indeed. How curious! How very, very clever people must be to find out things like that!"

Lonely tramps faring through the wintry night murmured those words to comfort themselves—looking skyward. "It has need to be nearer, for the night's as cold as charity. Don't seem much warmth from it if it is nearer, all the same."

"What is a new star to me?" cried the weeping woman kneeling beside her dead.

The schoolboy, rising early for his examination work, puzzled it out for himself—with the great white star shining broad and bright through the frost-flowers of his window. "Centrifugal, centripetal," he said, with his chin on his fist. "Stop a planet in its flight, rob it of its centrifugal force, what then? Centripetal has it, and down it falls into the sun! And this—!

"Do we come in the way? I wonder—"

The light of that day went the way of its brethren, and with the later watches of the frosty darkness rose the strange star again. And it was now so bright that the waxing moon seemed but a pale yellow ghost of itself, hanging huge in the sunset. In a South African City a great man had married, and the streets were alight to welcome his return with his bride. "Even the skies have illuminated," said the flatterer. Under Capricorn, two negro lovers, daring the wild beasts and evil spirits, for love of one another, crouched together in a cane brake where the fire-flies hovered. "That is our star," they whispered, and felt strangely comforted by the sweet brilliance of its light.

The master mathematician sat in his private room and pushed the papers from him. His calculations were already finished. In a small white phial there still remained a little of the drug that had kept him awake and active for four long nights. Each day, serene, explicit, patient as ever, he had given his lecture to his students, and then had come back at once to this momentous calculation. His face was grave, a little drawn and hectic from his drugged activity. For some time he seemed lost in thought. Then he went to the window, and the blind went up with a click. Half way up the sky, over the clustering roofs, chimneys and steeples of the city, hung the star.

He looked at it as one might look into the eyes of a brave enemy. "You may kill me," he said after a silence. "But I can hold you—and all the universe for that matter—in the grip of this little brain. I would not change. Even now."

He looked at the little phial. "There will be no need of sleep again," he said. The next day at noon—punctual to the minute, he entered his lecture theatre, put his hat on the end of the table as his habit was, and carefully selected a large piece of chalk. It was a joke among his students that he could not lecture without that piece of chalk to fumble in his fingers, and once he had been stricken to impotence by their hiding his supply. He came and looked under his grey eyebrows at the rising tiers of young fresh faces, and spoke with his accustomed studied commonness of phrasing. "Circumstances have arisen—circumstances beyond my control," he said and paused, "which will debar me from completing the course I had designed. It would seem, gentlemen, if I may put the thing clearly and briefly, that—Man has lived in vain."

The students glanced at one another. Had they heard aright? Mad? Raised eyebrows and grinning lips there were, but one or two faces remained intent upon his calm grey-fringed face. "It will be interesting," he was saying, "to devote this morning to an exposition, so far as I can make it clear to you, of the calculations that have led me to this conclusion. Let us assume—"

He turned towards the blackboard, meditating a diagram in the way that was usual to him. "What was that about 'lived in vain?'" whispered one student to another. "Listen," said the other, nodding towards the lecturer.

And presently they began to understand.

That night the star rose later, for its proper eastward motion had carried it some way across Leo towards Virgo, and its brightness was so great that the sky became a luminous blue as it rose, and every star was hidden in its turn, save only Jupiter near the zenith, Capella, Aldebaran, Sirius and the pointers of the Bear. It was very white and beautiful. In many parts of the world that night a pallid halo encircled it about. It was perceptibly larger; in the clear refractive sky of the tropics it seemed as if it were nearly a quarter the size of the moon. The frost was still on the ground in England, but the world was as brightly lit as if it were midsummer moonlight. One could see to read quite ordinary print by that cold clear light, and in the cities the lamps burnt yellow and wan.

And everywhere the world was awake that night, and throughout Christendom a sombre murmur hung in the keen air over the countryside like the belling of bees in the heather, and this murmurous tumult grew to a clangour in the cities. It was the tolling of the bells in a million belfry towers and steeples, summoning the people to sleep no more, to sin no more, but to gather in their churches and pray. And overhead, growing larger and brighter as the earth rolled on its way and the night passed, rose the dazzling star.

And the streets and houses were alight in all the cities, the shipyards glared, and whatever roads led to high country were lit and crowded all night long. And in all the seas about the civilised lands, ships with throbbing engines, and ships with bellying sails, crowded with men and living creatures, were standing out to ocean and the north. For already the warning of the master mathematician had been telegraphed all over the world, and translated into a hundred tongues. The new planet and Neptune, locked in a fiery embrace, were whirling headlong, ever faster and faster towards the sun. Already every second this blazing mass flew a hundred miles, and every second its terrific velocity increased. As it flew now, indeed, it must pass a hundred million of miles wide of the earth and scarcely affect it. But near its destined path, as yet only slightly perturbed, spun the mighty planet Jupiter and his moons sweeping splendid round the sun. Every moment now the attraction between the fiery star and the greatest of the planets grew stronger. And the result of that attraction? Inevitably Jupiter would be deflected from its orbit into an elliptical path, and the burning star, swung by his attraction wide of its sunward rush, would "describe a curved path" and perhaps collide with, and certainly pass very close to, our earth. "Earthquakes, volcanic outbreaks, cyclones, sea waves, floods, and a steady rise in temperature to I know not what limit"—so prophesied the master mathematician.

And overhead, to carry out his words, lonely and cold and livid, blazed the star of the coming doom.

To many who stared at it that night until their eyes ached, it seemed that it was visibly approaching. And that night, too, the weather changed, and the frost that had gripped all Central Europe and France and England softened towards a thaw.

But you must not imagine because I have spoken of people praying through the night and people going aboard ships and people fleeing toward mountainous country that the whole world was already in a terror because of the star. As a matter of fact, use and wont still ruled the world, and save for the talk of idle moments and the splendour of the night, nine human beings out of ten were still busy at their common occupations. In all the cities the shops, save one here and there, opened and closed at their proper hours, the doctor and the undertaker plied their trades, the workers gathered in the factories, soldiers drilled, scholars studied, lovers sought one another, thieves lurked and fled, politicians planned their schemes. The presses of the newspapers roared through the night, and many a priest of this church and that would not open his holy building to further what he considered a foolish panic. The newspapers insisted on the lesson of the year 1000—for then, too, people had anticipated the end. The star was no star—mere gas—a comet; and were it a star it could not possibly strike the earth. There was no precedent for such a thing. Commonsense was sturdy everywhere, scornful, jesting, a little inclined to persecute the obdurate fearful. That night, at seven-fifteen by Greenwich time, the star would be at its nearest to Jupiter. Then the world would see the turn things would take. The master mathematician's grim warnings were treated by many as so much mere elaborate self-advertisement. Common sense at last, a little heated by argument, signified its unalterable convictions by going to bed. So, too, barbarism and savagery, already tired of the novelty, went about their nightly business, and save for a howling dog here and there, the beast world left the star unheeded.

And yet, when at last the watchers in the European States saw the star rise, an hour later it is true, but no larger than it had been the night before, there were still plenty awake to laugh at the master mathematician—to take the danger as if it had passed.

But hereafter the laughter ceased. The star grew—it grew with a terrible steadiness hour after hour, a little larger each hour, a little nearer the midnight zenith, and brighter and brighter, until it had turned night into a second day. Had it come straight to the earth instead of in a curved path, had it lost no velocity to Jupiter, it must have leapt the intervening gulf in a day, but as it was it took five days altogether to come by our planet. The next night it had become a third the size of the moon before it set to English eyes, and the thaw was assured. It rose over America near the size of the moon, but blinding white to look at, and *hot*; and a breath of hot wind blew now with its rising and gathering strength, and in Virginia, and Brazil, and down the St. Lawrence valley, it shone intermittently through a driving reek of thunder-clouds, flickering violet lightning, and hail unprecedented. In Manitoba was a thaw and devastating floods. And upon all the mountains of the earth the snow and ice began to melt that night, and all the rivers coming out of high country flowed thick and turbid, and soon—in their upper reaches—with swirling trees and the bodies of beasts and men. They rose steadily, steadily in the ghostly brilliance, and came trickling over their banks at last, behind the flying population of their valleys.

And along the coast of Argentina and up the South Atlantic the tides were higher than had ever been in the memory of man, and the storms drove the waters in many cases scores of miles inland, drowning whole cities. And so great grew the heat during the night that the rising of the sun was like the coming of a shadow. The earthquakes began and grew until all down America from the Arctic Circle to Cape Horn, hillsides were sliding, fissures were opening, and houses and walls crumbling to destruction. The whole side of Cotopaxi slipped out in one vast convulsion, and a tumult of lava poured out so high and broad and swift and liquid that in one day it reached the sea.

So the star, with the wan moon in its wake, marched across the Pacific, trailed the thunderstorms like the hem of a robe, and the growing tidal wave that toiled behind it, frothing and eager, poured over island and island and swept them clear of men. Until that wave came at last—in a blinding light and with the breath of a furnace, swift and terrible it came—a wall of water, fifty feet high, roaring hungrily, upon the long coasts of Asia, and swept inland across the plains of China. For a space the star, hotter now and larger and brighter than the sun in its strength, showed with pitiless brilliance the wide and populous country; towns and villages with their pagodas and trees, roads, wide cultivated fields, millions of sleepless people staring in helpless terror at the incandescent sky; and then, low and growing, came the murmur of the flood. And thus it was with millions of men that night—a flight nowhither, with limbs heavy with heat and breath fierce and scant, and the flood like a wall swift and white behind. And then death.

China was lit glowing white, but over Japan and Java and all the islands of Eastern Asia the great star was a ball of dull red fire because of the steam and smoke and ashes the volcanoes were spouting forth to salute its coming. Above was the lava, hot gases and ash, and below the seething floods, and the whole earth swayed and rumbled with the earthquake shocks. Soon the immemorial snows of Thibet and the Himalaya were melting and pouring down by ten million deepening converging channels upon the plains of Burmah and Hindostan. The tangled summits of the Indian jungles were aflame in a thousand places, and below the hurrying waters around the stems were dark objects that still struggled feebly and reflected the blood-red tongues of fire. And in a rudderless confusion a multitude of men and women fled down the broad river-ways to that one last hope of men—the open sea.

Larger grew the star, and larger, hotter, and brighter with a terrible swiftness now. The tropical ocean had lost its phosphorescence, and the whirling steam rose in ghostly wreaths from the black waves that plunged incessantly, speckled with storm-tossed ships.

And then came a wonder. It seemed to those who in Europe watched for the rising of the star that the world must have ceased its rotation. In a thousand open spaces of down and upland the people who had fled thither from the floods and the falling houses and sliding slopes of hill watched for that rising in vain. Hour followed hour through a terrible suspense, and the star rose not. Once again men set their eyes upon the old constellations they had counted lost to them forever. In England it was hot and clear overhead, though the ground quivered perpetually, but in the tropics, Sirius and Capella and Aldebaran showed through a veil of steam. And when at last the great star rose near ten hours late, the sun rose close upon it, and in the centre of its white heart was a disc of black.

Over Asia it was the star had begun to fall behind the movement of the sky, and then suddenly, as it hung over India, its light had been veiled. All the plain of India from the mouth of the Indus to the mouths of the Ganges was a shallow waste of shining water that night, out of which rose temples and palaces, mounds and hills, black with people. Every minaret was a clustering mass of people, who fell one by one into the turbid waters, as heat and terror overcame them. The whole land seemed a-wailing, and suddenly there swept a shadow across that furnace of despair, and a breath of cold wind, and a gathering of clouds, out of the cooling air. Men looking up, near blinded, at the star, saw that a black disc was creeping across the light. It was the moon, coming between the star and the earth. And even as men cried to God at this respite, out of the East with a strange inexplicable swiftness sprang the sun. And then star, sun and moon rushed together across the heavens.

So it was that presently, to the European watchers, star and sun rose close upon each other, drove headlong for a space and then slower, and at last came to rest, star and sun merged into one glare of flame at the zenith of the sky. The moon no longer eclipsed the star but was lost to sight in the brilliance of the sky. And though those who were still alive regarded it for the most part with that dull stupidity that hunger, fatigue, heat and despair engender, there were still men who could perceive the meaning of these signs. Star and earth had been at their nearest, had swung about one another, and the star had passed. Already it was receding, swifter and swifter, in the last stage of its headlong journey downward into the sun.

And then the clouds gathered, blotting out the vision of the sky, the thunder and lightning wove a garment round the world; all over the earth was such a downpour of rain as men had never before seen, and where the volcanoes flared red against the cloud canopy there descended torrents of mud. Everywhere the waters were pouring off the land, leaving mud-silted ruins, and the earth littered like a storm-worn beach with all that had floated, and the dead bodies of the men and brutes, its children. For days the water streamed off the land, sweeping away soil and trees and houses in the way, and piling huge dykes and scooping out Titanic gullies over the country side. Those were the days of darkness that followed the star and the heat. All through them, and for many weeks and months, the earthquakes continued.

But the star had passed, and men, hunger-driven and gathering courage only slowly, might creep back to their ruined cities, buried granaries, and sodden fields. Such few ships as had escaped the storms of that time came stunned and shattered and sounding their way cautiously through the new marks and shoals of once familiar ports. And as the storms subsided men perceived that everywhere the days were hotter than of yore, and the sun larger, and the moon, shrunk to a third of its former size, took now fourscore days between its new and new.

But of the new brotherhood that grew presently among men, of the saving of laws and books and machines, of the strange change that had come over Iceland and Greenland and the shores of Baffin's Bay, so that the sailors coming there presently found them green and gracious, and could scarce believe their eyes, this story does not tell. Nor of the movement of mankind now that the earth was hotter, northward and southward towards the poles of the earth. It concerns itself only with the coming and the passing of the Star.

The Martian astronomers—for there are astronomers on Mars, although they are very different beings from men—were naturally profoundly interested by these things. They saw them from their own standpoint of course. "Considering the mass and temperature of the missile that was flung through our solar system into the sun," one wrote, "it is astonishing what a little damage the earth, which it missed so narrowly, has sustained. All the familiar continental markings and the masses of the seas remain intact, and indeed the only difference seems to be a shrinkage of the white discoloration (supposed to be frozen water) round either pole." Which only shows how small the vastest of human catastrophes may seem, at a distance of a few million miles.

THE THAMES VALLEY CATASTROPHE

GRANT ALLEN

At the end of the nineteenth century, London was regarded as the pinnacle of the civilized world, and most people would have considered a threat to the city a threat to civilization itself. This story, by Canadian-born Grant Allen (1848–1899), appeared in the December 1897 issue of The Strand Magazine, *and is one of many written at the turn of the twentieth century to imagine the doom of London by an unforeseen catastrophe. That doom is averted in most stories—but not in all.*

It can scarcely be necessary for me to mention, I suppose, at this time of day, that I was one of the earliest and fullest observers of the sad series of events which finally brought about the transference of the seat of Government of these islands from London to Manchester. Nor need I allude here to the conspicuous position which my narrative naturally occupies in the Blue-book on the Thames Valley Catastrophe (vol. ii., part vii), ordered by Parliament in its preliminary Session under the new *régime* at Birmingham. But I think it also incumbent upon me, for the benefit of posterity, to supplement that necessarily dry and formal statement by a more circumstantial account of my personal adventures during the terrible period.

I am aware, of course, that my poor little story can possess little interest for our contemporaries, wearied out as they are with details of the disaster, and surfeited with tedious scientific discussions as to its origin and nature. But in after years, I venture to believe, when the crowning calamity of the nineteenth century has grown picturesque and, so to speak, ivy-clad, by reason of its remoteness (like the Great Plague or the Great Fire of London with ourselves), the world may possibly desire to hear how this unparalleled convulsion affected the feelings and fortunes of a single family in the middle rank of life, and in a part of London neither squalid nor fashionable.

It is such personal touches of human nature that give reality to history, which without them must become, as a great writer has finely said, nothing more than an old almanac. I shall not apologize, therefore, for being frankly egoistic and domestic in my reminiscences of that appalling day: for I know that those who desire to seek scientific information on the subject will look for it, not in vain, in the eight bulky volumes of the recent Blue-book. I shall concern myself here with the great event merely as it appeared to myself, a Government servant of the second grade, and in its relations to my own wife, my home, and my children.

On the morning of the 21st of August, in the memorable year of the calamity, I happened to be at Cookham, a pleasant and pretty village which then occupied the western bank of the Thames just below the spot where the Look-out Tower of the Earthquake and Eruption Department now dominates the whole wide plain of the Glassy Rock Desert. In place of the black lake of basalt which young people see nowadays winding its solid bays in and out among the grassy downs, most men still living can well remember a gracious and smiling valley, threaded in the midst by a beautiful river.

I had cycled down from London the evening before (thus forestalling my holiday), and had spent the night at a tolerable inn in the village. By a curious coincidence, the only other visitor at the little hotel that night was a fellow-cyclist, an American, George W. Ward by name, who had come over with his "wheel," as he called it, for six weeks in England, in order to investigate the geology of our southern counties for himself, and to compare it with that of the far western cretaceous system. I venture to describe this as a curious coincidence, because, as it happened, the mere accident of my meeting him gave me my first inkling of the very existence of that singular phenomenon of which we were all so soon to receive a startling example. I had never so much as heard before of fissure-eruptions; and if I had not heard of them from Ward that evening, I might not have recognised at sight the actuality when it first appeared, and therefore I might have been involved in the general disaster. In which case, of course, this unpretentious narrative would never have been written.

As we sat in the little parlour of the White Hart, however, over our evening pipe, it chanced that the American, who was a pleasant, conversable fellow, began talking to me of his reasons for visiting England. I was at that time a clerk in the General Post Office (of which I am now secretary), and was then no student of science; but his enthusiastic talk about his own country and its vastness amused and interested me. He had been employed for some years on the Geological Survey in the Western States, and he was deeply impressed by the solemnity and the colossal scale of everything American. "Mountains!" he said, when I spoke of Scotland; "why, for mountains, your Alps aren't in it,* and as for volcanoes, your Vesuviuses and Etnas just spit fire a bit at infrequent intervals; while ours do things on a scale worthy of a great country, I can tell you. Europe is a circumstance: America is a continent."

"But surely," I objected, "that was a pretty fair eruption that destroyed Pompeii!"

The American rose and surveyed me slowly. I can see him to this day, with his close-shaven face and his contemptuous smile at my European ignorance. "Well," he said, after a long and impressive pause, "the lava-flood that destroyed a few acres about the Bay of Naples was what we call a trickle: it came from a crater; and the crater it came from was nothing more than a small round vent-hole; the lava flowed down from it in a moderate stream over a limited area. But what do you say to the

---

* A slang phrase of the time, equivalent to our modern "Your Alps swob the show," or "fail to eventuate.

earth opening in a huge crack, forty or fifty miles long—say, as far as from here right away to London, or farther—and lava pouring out from the orifice, not in a little rivulet as at Etna or Vesuvius, but in a sea or inundation, which spread at once over a tract as big as England? That's something like volcanic action, isn't it? And that's the sort of thing we have out in Colorado."

"You are joking," I replied, "or bragging. You are trying to astonish me with the familiar spread eagle."

He smiled a quiet smile. "Not a bit of it," he answered. "What I tell you is at least as true as Gospel. The earth yawns in Montana. There are fissure-eruptions, as we call them, in the Western States, out of which the lava has welled like wine out of a broken skin—welled up in vast roaring floods, molten torrents of basalt, many miles across, and spread like water over whole plains and valleys."

"Not within historical times!" I exclaimed.

"I'm not so sure about that," he answered, musing. "I grant you, not within times which are historical right there—for Colorado is a very new country: but I incline to think some of the most recent fissure eruptions took place not later than when the Tudors reigned in England. The lava oozed out, red-hot—gushed out—was squeezed out—and spread instantly everywhere; it's so comparatively recent that the surface of the rock is still bare in many parts, unweathered sufficiently to support vegetation. I fancy the stream must have been ejected at a single burst, in a huge white-hot dome, and then flowed down on every side, filling up the valleys to a certain level, in and out among the hills, exactly as water might do. And some of these eruptions, I tell you, by measured survey, would have covered more ground than from Dover to Liverpool, and from York to Cornwall."

"Let us be thankful," I said, carelessly, "that such things don't happen in our own times."

He eyed me curiously. "Haven't happened, you mean," he answered. "We have no security that they mayn't happen again to-morrow. These fissure-eruptions, though not historically described for us, are common events in geological history—commoner and on a larger scale in America than elsewhere. Still, they have occurred in all lands and at various epochs; there is no reason at all why one shouldn't occur in England at present."

I laughed, and shook my head. I had the Englishman's firm conviction—so rudely shattered by the subsequent events, but then so universal—that nothing very unusual ever happened in England.

Next morning I rose early, bathed in Odney Weir (a picturesque pool close by), breakfasted with the American, and then wrote a hasty line to my wife, informing her that I should probably sleep that night at Oxford; for I was off on a few days' holiday, and I liked Ethel to know where a letter or telegram would reach me each day, as we were both a little anxious about the baby's teething. Even while I pen these words now, the grim humour of the situation comes back to me vividly. Thousands of fathers and mothers were anxious that morning about similar trifles, whose pettiness was brought home to them with an appalling shock in the all-embracing horror of that day's calamity.

About ten o'clock I inflated my tyres and got under way. I meant to ride towards Oxford by a leisurely and circuitous route, along the windings of the river, past Marlow and Henley; so I began by crossing Cookham Bridge, a wooden or iron structure, I scarcely remember which. It spanned the Thames close by the village: the curious will find its exact position marked in the maps of the period.

In the middle of the bridge, I paused and surveyed that charming prospect, which I was the last of living men perhaps to see as it then existed. Close by stood a weir; beside it, the stream divided into three separate branches, exquisitely backed up by the gentle green slopes of Hedsor and Cliveden. I could never pass that typical English view without a glance of admiration; this morning, I pulled up my bicycle for a moment, and cast my eye down stream with more than my usual enjoyment of the smooth blue water and the tall white poplars whose leaves showed their gleaming silver in the breeze beside it. I might have gazed at it too long—and one minute more would have sufficed for my destruction—had not a cry from the tow-path a little farther up attracted my attention.

It was a wild, despairing cry, like that of a man being overpowered and murdered.

I am confident this was my first intimation of danger. Two minutes before, it is true, I had heard a faint sound like distant rumbling of thunder; but nothing else. I am one of those who strenuously maintain that the catastrophe was not heralded by shocks of earthquake.*

I turned my eye up stream. For half a second I was utterly bewildered. Strange to say, I did not perceive at first the great flood of fire that was advancing towards me. I saw only the man who had shouted—a miserable, cowering, terror-stricken wretch, one of the abject creatures who used to earn a dubious livelihood in those days (when the river was a boulevard of pleasure) by towing boats up stream. But now, he was rushing wildly forward, with panic in his face; I could see he looked as if close pursued by some wild beast behind him. "A mad dog!" I said to myself at the outset; "or else a bull in the meadow!"

I glanced back to see what his pursuer might be; and then, in one second, the whole horror and terror of the catastrophe burst upon me. Its whole horror and terror, I say, but not yet its magnitude. I was aware at first just of a moving red wall, like dull, red-hot molten metal. Trying to recall at so safe a distance in time and space the feelings of the moment and the way in which they surged and succeeded one another, I think I can recollect that my earliest idea was no more than this: "He must run, or the moving wall will overtake him!" Next instant, a hot wave seemed to strike my face. It was just like the blast of heat that strikes one in a glasshouse when you stand in front of the boiling and seething glass in the furnace. At about the same point in time, I was aware, I believe, that the dull red wall was really a wall of fire. But it was cooled by contact with the air and the water. Even as I looked, however, a second wave from behind seemed to rush on and break: it overlaid and outran the first one. This second wave was white, not red—at white heat, I realized. Then, with a burst of recognition, I knew what it all meant. What Ward had spoken of last night—a fissure eruption!

I looked back. Ward was coming towards me on the bridge, mounted on his Columbia. Too speechless to utter one word, I pointed up stream with my hand He nodded and shouted back, in a singularly calm voice: "Yes; just what I told you. A fissure-eruption!"

They were the last words I heard him speak. Not that he appreciated the danger less than I did, though his manner was cool; but he was

---

*For an opposite opinion, see Dr. Haigh Wither's evidence in Vol. iii of the Blue-book.

wearing no clips to his trousers, and at that critical moment he caught his leg in his pedals. The accident disconcerted him; he dismounted hurriedly, and then, panic-stricken as I judged, abandoned his machine. He tried to run. The error was fatal. He tripped and fell. What became of him afterward I will mention later.

But for the moment I saw only the poor wretch on the tow-path. He was not a hundred yards off, just beyond the little bridge which led over the opening to a private boat-house. But as he rushed forwards and shrieked, the wall of fire overtook him. I do not think it quite caught him. It is hard at such moments to judge what really happens; but I believe I saw him shrivel like a moth in a flame a few seconds before the advancing wall of fire swept over the boat-house. I have seen an insect shrivel just so when flung into the midst of white-hot coals. He seemed to go off in gas, leaving a shower or powdery ash to represent his bones behind him. But of this I do not pretend to be positive; I will allow that my own agitation was far too profound to permit of my observing anything with accuracy.

How high was the wall at that time? This has been much debated. I should guess, thirty feet (though it rose afterwards to more than two hundred), and it advanced rather faster than a man could run down the centre of the valley. (Later on, its pace accelerated greatly with subsequent outbursts.) In frantic haste, I saw or felt that only one chance of safety lay before me: I must strike up hill by the field path to Hedsor.

I rode for very life, with grim death behind me. Once well across the bridge, and turning up the hill, I saw Ward on the parapet, with his arms flung up, trying wildly to save himself by leaping into the river. Next instant he shrivelled I think, as the beggar had shrivelled; and it is to this complete combustion before the lava flood reached them that I attribute the circumstance (so much commented upon in the scientific excavations among the ruins) that no cast of dead bodies, like those at Pompeii, have anywhere been found in the Thames Valley Desert. My own belief is that every human body was reduced to a gaseous condition by the terrific heat several seconds before the molten basalt reached it.

Even at the distance which I had now attained from the central mass, indeed, the heat was intolerable. Yet, strange to say, I saw few or no people flying as yet from the inundation. The fact is, the eruption came upon us so suddenly, so utterly without warning or premonitory symptoms (for I deny the earthquake shocks), that whole towns must have been destroyed before the inhabitants were aware that anything out of the common was happening. It is a sort of alleviation to the general horror to remember that a large proportion of the victims must have died without even knowing it; one second, they were laughing, talking, bargaining; the next, they were asphyxiated or reduced to ashes as you have seen a small fly disappear in an incandescent gas flame.

This, however, is what I learned afterward. At that moment, I was only aware of a frantic pace uphill, over a rough, stony road, and with my pedals working as I had never before worked them; while behind me, I saw purgatory let loose, striving hard to overtake me. I just knew that a sea of fire was filling the valley from end to end, and that its heat scorched my face as I urged on my bicycle in abject terror.

All this time, I will admit, my panic was purely personal. I was too much engaged in the engrossing sense of my own pressing danger to be vividly alive to the public catastrophe. I did not even think of Ethel and the children. But when I reached the hill by Hedsor Church—a neat, small building, whose shell still stands, though scorched and charred, by the edge of the desert—I was able to pause for half a minute to recover breath, and to look back upon the scene of the first disaster.

It was a terrible and yet I felt even then a beautiful sight—beautiful with the awful and unearthly beauty of a great forest fire, or a mighty conflagration in some crowded city. The whole river valley, up which I looked, was one sea of fire. Barriers of red-hot lava formed themselves for a moment now and again where the outer edge or vanguard of the inundation had cooled a little on the surface by exposure: and over these temporary dams, fresh cataracts of white-hot material poured themselves afresh into the valley beyond it. After a while, as the deeper portion of basalt was pushed out all was white alike. So glorious it looked in the morning sunshine that one could hardly realize the appalling reality of that sea of molten gold; one might almost have imagined a splendid triumph of the scene painter's art, did one not know that it was actually a river of fire, overwhelming, consuming, and destroying every object before it in its devastating progress.

I tried vaguely to discover the source of the disaster. Looking straight up stream, past Bourne End and Marlow, I descried with bleared and dazzled eyes a whiter mass than any, glowing fiercely in the daylight like an electric light, and filling up the narrow gorge of the river towards Hurley and Henley. I recollected at once that this portion of the valley was not usually visible from Hedsor Hill, and almost without thinking of it I instinctively guessed the reason why it had become so now: it was the centre of disturbance—the earth's crust just there had bulged upward slightly, till it cracked and gaped to emit the basalt.

Looking harder, I could make out (though it was like looking at the sun) that the glowing white dome-shaped mass, as of an electric light, was the molten lava as it gurgled from the mouth of the vast fissure. I say vast, because so it seemed to me, though, as everybody now knows, the actual gap where the earth opened measures no more than eight miles across, from a point near what was once Shiplake Ferry to the site of the old lime-kilns at Marlow. Yet when one saw the eruption actually taking place, the colossal scale of it was what most appalled one. A sea of fire, eight to twelve miles broad, in the familiar Thames Valley, impressed and terrified one a thousand times more than a sea of fire ten times as vast in the nameless wilds of Western America.

I could see dimly, too, that the flood spread in every direction from its central point, both up and down the river. To right and left, indeed, it was soon checked and hemmed in by the hills about Wargrave and Medmenham; but downward, it had filled the entire valley as far as Cookham and beyond; while upward, it spread in one vast glowing sheet towards Reading and the flats by the confluence of the Kennet. I did not then know, of course, that this gigantic natural dam or barrier was later on to fill up the whole low-lying level, and so block the course of the two rivers as to form those twin expanses of inland water, Lake Newbury and Lake Oxford. Tourists who now look down on still summer evenings where the ruins of Magdalen and of Merton may be dimly descried through the pale green depths, their broken masonry picturesquely overgrown with tangled water-weeds, can form but little idea of the terrible scene which that peaceful bank presented while the incandescent lava was pouring forth in a scorching white flood towards the doomed district. Merchants who crowd the busy quays of those mushroom cities which have sprung up with greater rapidity than

Chicago or Johannesburg on the indented shore where the new lakes abut upon the Berkshire Chalk Downs have half forgotten the horror of the intermediate time when the waters of the two rivers rose slowly, slowly, day after day, to choke their valleys and overwhelm some of the most glorious architecture in Britain. But though I did not know and could not then foresee the remoter effects of the great fire-flood in that direction, I saw enough to make my heart stand still within me. It was with difficulty that I grasped my bicycle, my hands trembled so fiercely. I realized that I was a spectator of the greatest calamity which had befallen a civilized land within the ken of history.

I looked southward along the valley in the direction of Maidenhead. As yet it did not occur to me that the catastrophe was anything more than a local flood, though even as such it would have been one of unexampled vastness. My imagination could hardly conceive that London itself was threatened. In those days one could not grasp the idea of the destruction of London. I only thought just at first, "It will go on towards Maidenhead!" Even as I thought it, I saw a fresh and fiercer gush of fire well out from the central gash, and flow still faster than ever down the centre of the valley, over the hardening layer already cooling on its edge by contact with the air and soil. This new outburst fell in a mad cataract over the end or van of the last, and instantly spread like water across the level expanse between the Clivden hills and the opposite range at Pinkneys. I realized with a throb that it was advancing towards Windsor. Then a wild fear thrilled through me. If Windsor, why not Staines and Chertsey and Hounslow? If Hounslow, why not London?

In a second I remembered Ethel and the children. Hitherto, the immediate danger of my own position alone had struck me. The fire was so near; the heat of it rose up in my face and daunted me. But now I felt I must make a wild dash to warn—not London—no, frankly, I forgot those millions; but Ethel and my little ones. In that thought, for the first moment, the real vastness of the catastrophe came home to me. The Thames Valley was doomed! I must ride for dear life if I wished to save my wife and children!

I mounted again, but found my shaking feet could hardly work the pedals. My legs were one jelly. With a frantic effort, I struck off inland in the direction of Burnham. I did not think my way out definitely; I hardly knew the topography of the district well enough to form any clear conception of what route I must take in order to keep to the hills and avoid the flood of fire that was deluging the lowlands. But by pure instinct, I believe, I set my face Londonwards along the ridge of the chalk downs. In three minutes I had lost sight of the burning flood, and was deep among green lanes and under shadowy beeches. The very contrast frightened me. I wondered if I was going mad. It was all so quiet. One could not believe that scarce five miles off from that devastating sheet of fire, birds were singing in the sky and men toiling in the fields as if nothing had happened.

Near Lambourne Wood I met a brother cyclist, just about to descend the hill. A curve in the road hid the valley from him I shouted aloud:—

"For Heaven's sake, don't go down! There is danger, danger!"

He smiled and looked back at me. "I can take any hill in England," he answered.

"It's not the hill," I burst out. "There has been an eruption—a fissure-eruption at Marlow—great floods of fire—and all the valley is filled with burning lava!"

He stared at me derisively. Then his expression changed of a sudden. I suppose he saw I was white-faced and horror-stricken. He drew away as if alarmed. "Go back to Colney Hatch!" he cried, pedalling faster and rode hastily down the hill, as if afraid of me. I have no doubt he must have ridden into the very midst of the flood, and been scorched by its advance, before he could check his machine on so sudden a slope.

Between Lambourne Wood and Burnham I did not see the fire-flood. I rode on at full speed among green fields and meadows. Here and there I passed a labouring man on the road. More than one looked up at me and commented on the oppressive heat, but none of them seemed to be aware of the fate that was overtaking their own homes close by, in the valley. I told one or two, but they laughed and gazed after me as if I were a madman. I grew sick of warning them. They took no heed of my words, but went on upon their way as if nothing out of the common were happening to England.

On the edge of the down, near Burnham, I caught sight of the valley again. Here, people were just awaking to what was taking place near them. Half the population was gathered on the slope, looking down with wonder on the flood of fire, which had now just turned the corner of the hills by Taplow. Silent terror was the prevailing type of expression. But when I told them I had seen the lava bursting forth from the earth in a white dome above Marlow, they laughed me to scorn; and when I assured them I was pushing forward in hot haste to London, they answered, "London! It won't never get as far as London!" That was the only place on the hills, as is now well known, where the flood was observed long enough beforehand to telegraph and warn the inhabitants of the great city; but nobody thought of doing it; and I must say, even if they had done so, there is not the slightest probability that the warning would have attracted the least attention in our ancient Metropolis. Men on the Stock Exchange would have made jests about the slump, and proceeded to buy and sell as usual.

I measured with my eye the level plain between Burnham and Slough, calculating roughly with myself whether I should have time to descend upon the well-known road from Maidenhead to London by Colnbrook and Hounslow. (I advise those who are unacquainted with the topography of this district before the eruption to follow out my route on a good map of the period.) But I recognised in a moment that this course would be impossible. At the rate that the flood had taken to progress from Cookham Bridge to Taplow, I felt sure it would be upon me before I reached Upton, or Ditton Park at the outside. It is true the speed of the advance might slacken somewhat as the lava cooled; and strange to say, so rapidly do realities come to be accepted in one's mind, that I caught myself thinking this thought in the most natural manner, as if I had all my life long been accustomed to the ways of fissure-eruptions. But on the other hand, the lava might well out faster and hotter than before, as I had already seen it do more than once; and I had no certainty even that it would not rise to the level of the hills on which I was standing. You who read this narrative nowadays take it for granted, of course, that the extent and height of the inundation was bound to be exactly what you know it to have been; we at the time could not guess how high it might rise and how large an area of the country it might overwhelm and devastate. Was it to stop at the Chilterns, or to go north to Birmingham, York, and Scotland?

Still, in my trembling anxiety to warn my wife and children, I debated with myself whether I should venture down into the valley, and hurry along the main road with a wild burst for London. I thought of Ethel, alone in our little home at Bayswater, and almost made up my mind to risk it. At that moment, I became aware that the road to London was already crowded with carriages, carts, and cycles, all dashing at a mad pace unanimously towards London. Suddenly a fresh wave turned the corner by Taplow and Maidenhead Bridge, and began to gain upon them visibly. It was an awful sight. I cannot pretend to describe it. The poor creatures on the road, men and animals alike, rushed wildly, despairingly on; the fire took them from behind, and, one by one, before the actual sea reached them, I saw them shrivel and melt away in the fierce white heat of the advancing inundation. I could not look at it any longer. I certainly could not descend and court instant death. I felt that my one chance was to strike across the downs, by Stoke Poges and Uxbridge, and then try the line of northern heights to London.

Oh, how fiercely I pedalled! At Farnham Royal (where again nobody seemed to be aware what had happened) a rural policeman tried to stop me for frantic riding. I tripped him up, and rode on. Experience had taught me it was no use telling those who had not seen it of the disaster. A little beyond, at the entrance to a fine park, a gatekeeper attempted to shut a gate in my face, exclaiming that the road was private. I saw it was the only practicable way without descending to the valley, and I made up my mind this was no time for trifling. I am a man of peace, but I lifted my fist and planted it between his eyes. Then, before he could recover from his astonishment, I had mounted again and ridden on across the park, while he ran after me in vain, screaming to the men in the pleasure-grounds to stop me. But I would not be stopped; and I emerged on the road once more at Stoke Poges.

Near Galley Hill, after a long and furious ride, I reached the descent to Uxbridge. Was it possible to descend? I glanced across, once more by pure instinct, for I had never visited the spot before, towards where I felt the Thames must run. A great white cloud hung over it. I saw what that cloud must mean: it was the steam of the river, where the lava sucked it up and made it seethe and boil suddenly. I had not noticed this white fleece of steam at Cookham, though I did not guess why till afterwards. In the narrow valley where the Thames ran between hills, the lava flowed over it all at once, bottling the steam beneath; and it is this imprisoned steam that gave rise in time to the subsequent series of appalling earthquakes, to supply forecasts of which is now the chief duty of the Seismologer Royal; whereas, in the open plain, the basalt advanced more gradually and in a thinner stream, and therefore turned the whole mass of water into white cloud as soon as it reached each bend of the river.

At the time, however, I had no leisure to think out all this. I only knew by such indirect signs that the flood was still advancing, and, therefore, that it would be impossible for me to proceed towards London by the direct route via Uxbridge and Hanwell. If I meant to reach town (as we called it familiarly), I must descend to the valley at once, pass through Uxbridge streets as fast as I could, make a dash across the plain, by what I afterwards knew to be Hillingdon (I saw it then as a nameless village), and aim at a house-crowned hill which I only learned later was Harrow, but which I felt sure would enable me to descend upon London by Hampstead or Highgate.

I am no strategist; but in a second, in that extremity, I picked out these points, feeling dimly sure they would lead me home to Ethel and the children.

The town of Uxbridge (whose place you can still find marked on many maps) lay in the valley of a small river, a confluent of the Thames. Up this valley it was certain that the lava-stream must flow; and, indeed, at the present day, the basin around is completely filled by one of the solidest and most forbidding masses of black basalt in the country. Still, I made up my mind to descend and cut across the low-lying ground towards Harrow. If I failed, I felt, after all, I was but one unit more in what I now began to realize as a prodigious national calamity.

I was just coasting down the hill, with Uxbridge lying snug and unconscious in the glen below me, when a slight and unimportant accident occurred which almost rendered impossible my further progress. It was past the middle of August; the hedges were being cut; and this particular lane, bordered by a high thorn fence, was strewn with the mangled branches of the may-bushes. At any other time, I should have remembered the danger and avoided them; that day, hurrying down hill for dear life and for Ethel, I forgot to notice them. The consequence was, I was pulled up suddenly by finding my front wheel deflated*; this untimely misfortune almost unmanned me. I

---

*The bicycles of that period were fitted with pneumatic tubes of india-rubber as tyres—a clumsy device, now long superseded.

dismounted and examined the tyre; it had received a bad puncture. I tried inflating again, in hopes the hole might be small enough to make that precaution sufficient. But it was quite useless. I found I must submit to stop and doctor up the puncture. Fortunately, I had the necessary apparatus in my wallet.

I think it was the weirdest episode of all that weird ride—this sense of stopping impatiently, while the fiery flood still surged on towards London, in order to go through all the fiddling and troublesome little details of mending a pneumatic tyre. The moment and the operation seemed so sadly out of harmony. A countryman passed by on a cart, obviously suspecting nothing; that was another point which added horror to the occasion—that so near the catastrophe, so very few people were even aware what was taking place beside them. Indeed, as is well known, I was one of the very few who saw the eruption during its course, and yet managed to escape from it. Elsewhere, those who tried to run before it, either to escape themselves or to warn others of the danger, were overtaken by the lava before they could reach a place of safety. I attribute this mainly to the fact that most of them continued along the high roads in the valley, or fled instinctively for shelter towards their homes, instead of making at once for the heights and the uplands.

The countryman stopped and looked at me.

"The more haste the less speed !" he said, with proverbial wisdom.

I glanced up at him, and hesitated. Should I warn him of his doom, or was it useless ? "Keep up on the hills," I said, at last. "An unspeakable calamity is happening in the valley. Flames of fire are flowing down it, as from a great burning mountain. You will be cut off by the eruption."

He stared at me blankly, and burst into a meaningless laugh. "Why, you're one of them Salvation Army fellows," he exclaimed, after a short pause. "You're trying to preach to me. I'm going to Uxbridge." And he continued down the hill towards certain destruction.

It was hours, I feel sure, before I had patched up that puncture, though I did it by the watch in four and a half minutes. As soon as I had blown out my tyre again I mounted once more, and rode at a breakneck pace to Uxbridge. I passed down the straggling main street of the suburban town, crying aloud as I went, "Run, run, to the downs! A flood of lava is rushing up the valley! To the hills, for your lives! All the Thames bank is blazing!" Nobody took the slightest heed; they stood still in the street for a minute with open mouths: then they returned to their customary occupations. A quarter of an hour later, there was no such place in the world as Uxbridge.

I followed the main road through the village which I have since identified as Hillingdon; then I diverged to the left, partly by roads and partly by field paths of whose exact course I am still uncertain, towards the hill at Harrow. When I reached the town, I did not strive to rouse the people, partly because my past experience had taught me the futility of the attempt, and partly because I rightly judged that they were safe from the inundation; for as it never quite covered the dome of St. Paul's, part of which still protrudes from the sea of basalt, it did not reach the level of the northern heights of London. I rode on through Harrow without one word to any body. I did not desire to be stopped or harassed as an escaped lunatic.

From Harrow I made my way tortuously along the rising ground, by the light of nature, through Wembley Park, to Willesden. At Willesden, for the first time, I found to a certainty that London was threatened. Great crowds of people in the profoundest excitement stood watching a dense cloud of smoke and steam that spread rapidly over the direction of Shepherd's Bush and Hammersmith. They were speculating as to its meaning, but laughed incredulously when I told them what it portended. A few minutes later, the smoke spread ominously towards Kensington and Paddington. That settled my fate. It was clearly impossible to descend into London; and indeed, the heat now began to be unendurable. It drove us all back, almost physically. I thought I must abandon all hope. I should never even know what had become of Ethel and the children.

My first impulse was to lie down and await the fire-flood. Yet the sense of the greatness of the catastrophe seemed somehow to blunt one's own private grief. I was beside myself with fear for my darlings; but I realized that I was but one among hundreds of thousands of fathers in the same position. What was happening at that moment in the great city of five million souls we did not know, we shall never know; but we may conjecture that the end was mercifully too swift to entail much needless suffering. All at once, a gleam of hope struck me. It was my father's birthday. Was it not just possible that Ethel might have taken the children up to Hampstead to wish their grandpa many happy returns of the day? With a wild determination not to give up all for lost, I turned my front wheel in the direction of Hampstead Hill, still skirting the high ground as far as possible. My heart was on fire within me. A restless anxiety urged me to ride my hardest. As all along the route, I was still just a minute or two in front of the catastrophe. People were beginning to be aware that something was taking place; more than once as I passed they asked me eagerly where the fire was. It was impossible for me to believe by this time that they knew nothing of an event in whose midst I seemed to have been living for months; how could I realize that all the things which had happened since I started from Cookham Bridge so long ago were really compressed into the space of a single morning?—nay, more, of an hour and a half only?

As I approached Windmill Hill, a terrible sinking seized me. I seemed to totter on the brink of a precipice. Could Ethel be safe? Should I ever again see little Bertie and the baby? I pedalled on as if automatically; for all life had gone out of me. I felt my hip-joint moving dry in its socket. I held my breath; my heart stood still. It was a ghastly moment.

At my father's door I drew up, and opened the garden gate. I hardly dared to go in. Though each second was precious, I paused and hesitated.

At last I turned the handle. I heard somebody within. My heart came up in my mouth. It was little Bertie's voice: "Do it again, Granpa; do it again; it amooses Bertie!"

I rushed into the room. "Bertie, Bertie!" I cried. "Is Mammy here?"

He flung himself upon me. "Mammy, Mammy, Daddy has comed home." I burst into tears. "And Baby?" I asked, trembling.

"Baby and Ethel are here, George," my father answered, staring at me. "Why, my boy, what's the matter?"

I flung myself into a chair and broke down. In that moment of relief, I felt that London was lost, but I had saved my wife and children.

I did not wait for explanations. A crawling four-wheeler was loitering by. I hailed it and hurried them in. My father wished to discuss the matter, but I cut him short. I gave the driver three pounds—all the gold I had with me. "Drive on!" I shouted, "drive on! Towards Hatfield—anywhere!"

He drove as he was bid. We spent that night, while Hampstead flared like a beacon, at an isolated farm-house on the high ground in Hertfordshire. For, of course, though the flood did not reach so high, it set fire to everything inflammable in its neighbourhood.

Next day, all the world knew the magnitude of the disaster. It can only be summed up in five emphatic words: There was no more London.

I have one other observation alone to make. I noticed at the time how, in my personal relief, I forgot for the moment that London was perishing. I even forgot that my house and property had perished. Exactly the opposite, it seemed to me, happened with most of those survivors who lost wives and children in the eruption. They moved about as in a dream, without a tear, without a complaint, helping others to provide for the needs of the homeless and houseless. The universality of the catastrophe made each man feel as though it were selfishness to attach too great an importance at such a crisis to his own personal losses. Nay, more; the burst of feverish activity and nervous excitement, I might even say enjoyment, which followed the horror, was traceable, I think, to this self-same cause. Even grave citizens felt they must do their best to dispel the universal gloom; and they plunged accordingly into around of dissipations which other nations thought both unseemly and un-English. It was one way of expressing the common emotion. We had all lost heart—and we flocked to the theatres to pluck up our courage. That, I believe, must be our national answer to M. Zola's strictures on our untimely levity. "This people," says the great French author, "which took its pleasures sadly while it was rich and prosperous, begins to dance and sing above the ashes of its capital—it makes merry by the open graves of its wives and children. What an enigma! What a puzzle! What chance of an Œdipus!"

A CORNER IN LIGHTNING

GEORGE GRIFFITH

At the time British writer George Griffith (1857–1906) wrote this tale about an entrepreneur who hopes to corner the electricity market, electricity was an invention whose harnessing and practical application were still being explored. In his day, Griffith was probably the second most popular writer of early science fiction after H.G. Wells. This cautionary tale first appeared in the March 1898 issue of Pearson's Magazine.

They had been dining for once in a way *tête-à-tête*, and she—that is to say, Mrs. Sidney Calvert, a bride of eighteen months' standing—was half-lying, half-sitting in the depths of a big, cosy, saddle-bag armchair on one side of a bright fire of mixed wood and coal that was burning in one of the most improved imitations of the mediæval fireplace. Her feet—very pretty little feet they were, too, and very daintily shod—were crossed, and poised on the heel of the right one at the corner of the black marble curb.

Dinner was over. The coffee service and the liqueur case were on the table, and Mr. Sidney Calvert, a well set-up young fellow of about thirty, with a handsome, good-humoured face which a close observer would have found curiously marred by a chilly glitter in the eyes and a hardness that was something more than firmness about the mouth, was walking up and down on the opposite side of the table smoking a cigarette.

Mrs. Calvert had just emptied her coffee cup, and as she put it down on a little three-legged console table by her side, she looked round at her husband and said:

"Really, Sid, I must say that I can't see why you should do it. Of course it's a very splendid scheme and all that sort of thing, but, surely you, one of the richest men in London, are rich enough to do without it. I'm sure it's wrong, too. What should we think if somebody managed to bottle up the atmosphere and made us pay for every breath we drew? Besides, there must surely be a good deal of risk in deliberately disturbing the economy of Nature in such a way. How are you going to get to the Pole, too, to put up your works?"

"Well," he said, stopping for a moment in his walk and looking thoughtfully at the lighted end of his cigarette, "in the first place, as to the geography, I must remind you that the Magnetic Pole is not the North Pole. It is in Boothia Land, British North America, some 1,500 miles south of the North Pole. Then, as to the risk, of course one can't do big things like this without taking a certain amount of it; but still, I think it will be mostly other people that will have to take it in this case.

"Their risk, you see, will come in when they find that cables and telephones and telegraphs won't work, and that no amount of steam-engine grinding can get up a respectable amount of electric light—when in short, all the electric plant of the world loses its value, and can't be set going without buying supplies from the Magnetic Polar Storage Company, or, in other words, from your humble servant and the few friends that he will be graciously pleased to let in on the ground floor. But that is a risk that they can easily overcome by just paying for it. Besides, there's no reason why we shouldn't improve the quality of the commodity. 'Our Extra Special Refined Lightning!' 'Our Triple Concentrated Essence of Electric Fluid' and 'Competent Thunder-Storms delivered at the Shortest Notice' would look very nice in advertisements, wouldn't they?"

"Don't you think that's rather a frivolous way of talking about a scheme which might end in ruining one of the most important industries in the world?" she said, laughing in spite of herself at the idea of delivering thunder-storms like pounds of butter or skeins of Berlin wool.

"Well, I'm afraid I can't argue that point with you because, you see, you will keep looking at me while you talk, and that isn't fair. Anyhow I'm equally sure that it would be quite impossible to run any business and make money out of it on the lines of the Sermon on the Mount. But, come, here's a convenient digression for both of us. That's the Professor, I expect."

"Shall I go?" she said, taking her feet off the fender.

"Certainly not, unless you wish to," he said; "or unless you think the scientific details are going to bore you."

"Oh, no, they won't do that," she said. "The Professor has such a perfectly charming way of putting them; and, besides, I want to know all that I can about it."

"Professor Kenyon, sir."

"Ah, good evening, Professor! So sorry you could not come to dinner." They both said this almost simultaneously as the man of science walked in.

"My wife and I were just discussing the ethics of this storage scheme when you came in," he went on. "Have you anything fresh to tell us about the practical aspects of it? I'm afraid she doesn't altogether approve of it, but as she is very anxious to hear all about it, I thought you wouldn't mind her making one of the audience."

"On the contrary, I shall be delighted," replied the Professor; "the more so as it will give me a sympathiser."

"I'm very glad to hear it," said Mrs. Calvert approvingly. "I think it will be a very wicked scheme if it succeeds, and a very foolish and expensive one if it fails."

"After which there is of course nothing mare to be said," laughed her husband, "except for the Professor to give his dispassionate opinion."

"Oh, it shall be dispassionate, I can assure you," he replied, noticing a little emphasis on the word. "The ethics of the matter are no business of mine, nor have I anything to do with its commercial bearings. You have asked me merely to look at technical possibilities and scientific probabilities, and of course I don't propose to go beyond these."

He took another sip at a cup of coffee that Mrs. Calvert had handed him, and went on:

"I've had a long talk with Markovitch this afternoon, and I must confess that I never met a more ingenious man or one who knew as much about magnetism and electricity as he does. His theory that they are the celestial and terrestrial manifestations of the same force, and that what is popularly called electric fluid is developed only at the stage where they become one, is itself quite a stroke of genius, or, at least, it will be if the theory stands the test of experience. His idea of locating the storage works over the Magnetic Pole of the earth is another, and I am bound to confess that, after a very careful examination of his plans and designs, I am distinctly of opinion that, subject to one or two reservations, he will be able to do what he contemplates."

"And the reservations what are they?" asked Culvert a trifle eagerly.

"The first is one that it is absolutely necessary to make with regard to all untried schemes, and especially to such a gigantic one as this. Nature, you know, has a way of playing most unexpected pranks with people who take liberties with her. Just at the last moment, when you are on the verge of success, something that you confidently expect to happen doesn't happen, and there you are left in the lurch. It is utterly impossible to foresee anything of this kind, but you must clearly understand that if such a thing did happen it would ruin the enterprise just when you have spent the greatest part of the money on it—that is to say, at the end and not at the beginning."

"All right," said Calvert, "we'll take that risk. Now, what's the other reservation?"

"I was going to say something about the immense cost, but that I presume you are prepared for."

Calvert nodded, and he went on:

"Well, that point being disposed of, it remains to be said that it may be very dangerous—I mean to those who live on the spot, and will be actually engaged in the work."

"Then, I hope you won't think of going near the place, Sid!" interrupted Mrs. Calvert, with a very pretty assumption of wifely authority.

"We'll see about that later, little woman. It's early days yet to get frightened about possibilities. Well, Professor, what was it you were going to say? Any more warnings?"

The Professor's manner stiffened a little as he replied:

"Yes, it is a warning, Mr. Calvert. The fact is I feel bound to tell you that you propose to interfere very seriously with the distribution of one of the subtlest and least-known forces of Nature, and that the consequences of such an interference might be most disastrous, not only for those engaged in the work, but even the whole hemisphere, and possibly the whole planet.

"On the other hand, I think it is only fair to say that nothing more than a temporary disturbance may take place. You may, for instance, give us a series of very violent thunderstorms, with very heavy rains; or you may abolish thunderstorms and rain altogether until you get to work. Both prospects are within the bounds of possibility, and, at the same time, neither may come to anything."

"Well, I think that quite good enough to gamble on, Professor," said Calvert, who was thoroughly fascinated by the grandeur and magnitude, to say nothing of the dazzling financial aspects of the scheme. "I am very much obliged to you for putting it so clearly and nicely. Unless something very unexpected happens, we shall get to work on it at once. Just fancy what a glorious thing it will be to play Jove to the nations of the earth, and dole out lightning to them at so much a flash!"

"Well, I don't want to be ill-natured," said Mrs. Calvert, "but I must say that I hope the unexpected will happen. I think the whole thing is very wrong to begin with, and I shouldn't be at all surprised if you blew us all up, or struck us all dead with lightning, or even brought on the Day of Judgment before its time. I think I shall go to Australia while you're doing it."

* * *

A little more than a year had passed since this after-dinner conversation in the dining-room of Mr. Sidney Calvert's London house. During that time the preparations for the great experiment had been swiftly but secretly carried out. Ship after ship loaded with machinery, fuel, and provisions, and carrying labourers and artificers to the number of some hundreds, had sailed away into the Atlantic, and had come back in ballast and with bare working crews on board of them. Mr. Calvert himself had disappeared and reappeared two or three times, and on his return he had neither admitted nor denied any of the various rumours which gradually got into circulation in the City and in the Press.

Some said that it was an expedition to the Pole, and that the machinery consisted partly of improved ice-breakers and newly-invented steam sledges, which were to attack the ice-hummocks after the fashion of battering rams, and so gradually smooth a road to the Pole. To these little details others added flying machines and navigable balloons. Others again declared that the object was to plough out the North-West passage and keep a waterway clear from Hudson's Bay to the Pacific all the year round, and yet others, somewhat less imaginative, pinned their faith to the founding of a great astronomical and meteorological observatory at the nearest possible point to the Pole, one of the objects of which was to be the determination of the true nature of the Aurora Borealis and the Zodiacal Light.

It was this last hypothesis that Mr. Calvert favoured as far as he could be said to favour any. There was a vagueness, and, at the same time, a distinction about a great scientific expedition which made it possible for him to give a sort of qualified countenance to the rumours without committing himself to anything, but so well had all his precautions been taken that not even a suspicion of the true object of the expedition to Boothia Land had got outside the little circle of those who were in his confidence.

So far everything had gone as Orloff Markovitch, the Russian Pole to whose extraordinary genius the inception and working out of the gigantic project were due, had expected and predicted. He himself was in supreme control of the unique and costly works which had grown up under his constant supervision on that lonely and desolate spot in the far North where the magnetic needle points straight down to the centre of the planet.

Professor Kenyon had paid a couple of visits with Calvert, once at the beginning of the work and once when it was nearing completion. So far not the slightest hitch or accident had occurred, and nothing abnormal had been noticed in connection with the earth's electrical phenomena save unusually frequent appearances of the Aurora Borealis, and a singular decrease in the deviation of the mariner's compass. Nevertheless, the Professor had firmly but politely refused to remain until the gigantic apparatus was set to work, and Calvert, too, had, with extreme reluctance, yielded to his wife's intreaties, and had come back to England about a month before the initial experiment was to be begun.

The twentieth of March, which was the day fixed for the commencement of operations, came and went, to Mrs. Calvert's intense relief, without anything out of the common happening. Though she knew that over a hundred thousand pounds of her husband's money had been sunk, she found it impossible not to feel a thrill of satisfaction in the hope that Markovitch had made his experiment and failed.

She knew that the great Calvert Company, which was practically himself, could very well afford it, and she would not have regretted the loss of three times the sum in exchange for the knowledge that Nature was to be allowed to dispose of her electrical forces as seemed good to her. As for her husband, he went about his business as usual, only displaying slight signs of suppressed excitement and anticipation now and then, as the weeks went by and nothing happened.

She had not carried out her threat of going to Australia. She had, however, escaped from the rigours of the English spring to a villa near Nice, where she was awaiting the arrival of her second baby, an event which she had found very useful in persuading her husband to stop away from the Magnetic Pole. Calvert himself was so busy with what might be called the home details of the scheme that lie had to spend the greater part of his time in London, and could only run over to Nice now and then.

It so happened that Miss Calvert put in an appearance a few days before she was expected, and therefore while her father was still in London. Her mother very naturally sent her maid with a telegram to inform him of the fact and ask him to come over at once. In about half-an-hour the maid came back with the form in her hand bringing a message from the telegraph office that, in consequence of some extraordinary accident, the wires had almost ceased to work properly and that no messages could be got through distinctly.

In the rapture of her new motherhood Kate Calvert had forgotten all about the great Storage Scheme, so she sent the maid back again with the request that the message should be sent off as soon as possible. Two hours later she sent again to ask if it had gone, and the reply came back that the wires had ceased working altogether and that no electrical communication by telegraph or telephone was for the present possible.

Then a terrible fear came to her. The experiment had been a success after all, and Markovitch's mysterious engines bad been all this time imperceptibly draining the earth of its electric fluid and storing it up in the vast accumulators which would only yield it back again at the bidding of the Trust which was controlled by her husband! Still she was a sensible little woman, and after the first shock she managed, for her baby's sake, to put the fear out of her mind, at any rate until her husband came. He would be with her in a day or two, and, perhaps, after all, it was only some strange but perfectly natural occurrence which Nature herself would set right in a few hours.

When it got dusk that night, and the electric lights were turned on, it was noticed that they gave an unusually dim and wavering light. The engines were worked to their highest power, and the lines were carefully examined. Nothing could be found wrong with them, but the lights refused to behave as usual, and the most extraordinary feature of the phenomenon was that exactly the same thing was happening in all the electrically lighted cities and towns in the northern hemisphere. By midnight, too, telegraphic and telephonic communication north of the Equator had practically ceased, and the electricians of Europe and America were at their wits' ends to discover any reason for this unheard of disaster, for such in sober truth it would be unless the apparently suspended force quickly resumed action on its own account. The next morning it was found that, so far as all the marvels of electrical science were concerned, the world had gone back a hundred years.

Then people began to awake to the magnitude of the catastrophe that had befallen the world. Civilised mankind had been suddenly deprived of the services of an obedient slave which it had come to look upon as indispensable.

But there was something even more serious than this to come. Observers in various parts of the hemisphere remembered that there hadn't been a thunder-storm anywhere for some weeks. Even the regions most frequently visited by them had had none. A most remarkable drought had also set in almost universally. A strange sickness, beginning with physical lassitude and depression of spirits which confounded the best medical science of the world was manifesting itself far and wide, and rapidly assuming the proportions of a gigantic epidemic.

In the physical world, too, metals were found to be afflicted with the same incomprehensible disease. Machinery of all sorts got "sick," to use a technical expression, and absolutely refused to act, and forges and foundries everywhere came to a standstill for the simple reason that metals seemed to have lost their best properties, and could no longer be utilised as they had been. Railway accidents and breakdowns on steamers, too, became matters of every day occurrence, for metals and driving wheels, piston rods and propeller shafts, had acquired an incomprehensible brittleness which only began to be understood when it was discovered that the electrical properties which iron and steel had formerly possessed had almost entirely disappeared.

So far Calvert had not wavered in his determination to make, as he thought, a colossal amount of money by his usurpation of one of the functions of Nature. To him the calamities which, it must be confessed, he had deliberately brought upon the world were only so many arguments for the ultimate success of the stupendous scheme. They were proof positive to the world, or at least they very soon would be, that the Calvert Storage Trust really did control the electricity of the Northern Hemisphere. From the Southern nothing had yet been heard beyond the news that the cables had ceased working.

Hence, as soon as he had demonstrated his power to restore matters to their normal condition, it was obvious that the world would have to pay his price under penalty of having the supply cut off again.

It was now getting towards the end of May. On the 1st of June, according to arrangement, Markovitch would stop his engines and permit the vast accumulation of electric fluid in his storage batteries to flow back into its accustomed channels. Then the Trust would issue its prospectus, setting forth the terms upon which it was prepared to permit the nations to enjoy that gift of Nature whose pricelessness the Trust had proved by demonstrating its own ability to corner it.

On the evening of May 25th Culvert was sitting in his sumptuous office in Victoria Street, writing by the light of a dozen wax candles in silver candelabra. He had just finished a letter to his wife, telling her to keep up her spirits and fear nothing; that in a few days the experiment would be over and everything restored to its former condition, shortly after which she would be the wife of a man who would soon be able to buy up all the other millionaires in the world.

As he put the letter into the envelope there was a knock at the door, and Professor Kenyon was announced. Culvert greeted him stiffly and coldly, for he more than half guessed the errand he had come on. There had been two or three heated discussions between them of late, and Culvert knew before the Professor opened his lips that he had come to tell him that he was about to fulfil a threat that he had made a few days before. And this the Professor did tell him in a few dry, quiet words.

"It's no use, Professor," he replied, " you know yourself that I am powerless, as powerless as you are. I have no means of communicating with Markovitch, and the work cannot be stopped until the appointed time."

"But you were warned, sir!" the Professor interrupted warmly. "You were warned, and when you saw the effects coming you might have stopped. I wish to goodness that I had had nothing to do with the infernal business, for infernal it really is. Who are you that you should usurp one of the functions of the Almighty, for it is nothing less than that? I have kept your criminal secret too long, and I will keep it no longer. You have made yourself the enemy of Society, and Society still has the power to deal with you—"

"My dear Professor, that's all nonsense, and you know it!" said Calvert, interrupting him with a contemptuous gesture: "If Society were to lock me up, it should do without electricity till I were free. If it hung one it would get none, except on Markovitch's terms, which would be higher than mine. So you can tell your story whenever you please. Meanwhile you'll excuse me if I remind you that I am rather busy."

Just as the Professor was about to take his leave the door opened and a boy brought in an envelope deeply edged with black. Calvert turned white to the lips and his hand trembled as he took it and opened it. It was in his wife's handwriting, and was dated five days before, as most of the journey had to be made on horseback. He read it through with fixed, staring eyes, then he crushed it into his pocket and strode towards the telephone. He rang the bell furiously, and then he started back with an oath on his lips, remembering that he had made it useless. The sound of the bell brought a clerk into the room immediately.

"Get me a hansom at once! " he almost shouted, and the clerk vanished.

"What is the matter? Where are you going?" asked the Professor.

"Matter? Read that!" he said, thrusting the crumpled letter into his hand. "My little girl is dead—dead of that accursed sickness which, as you justly say, I have brought on the world, and my wife is down with it, too, and may be dead by this time. That letter's five days old. My God, what have I done? What can I do? I'd give fifty thousand pounds to get a telegram to Markovitch. Curse him and his infernal scheme! If she dies I'll go to Boothia Land and kill him! Hullo! What's that? Lightning—by all that's holy—and thunder!"

As he spoke such a flash of lightning as had never split the skies of London before flared in a huge ragged stream of flame across the zenith, and a roar of thunder such as London's ears had never heard shook every house in the vast city to its foundation. Another and another followed in rapid succession, and all through the night and well into the next day there raged, as it was afterwards found, almost all over the whole Northern hemisphere, such a thunderstorm as had never been known in the world before and never would be again.

With it, too, came hurricanes and cyclones and deluges of rain; and when, after raging for nearly twenty-four hours, it at length ceased convulsing the atmosphere and growled itself away into silence, the first fact that came out of the chaos and desolation that it had left behind it was that the normal electrical conditions of the world had been restored—after which mankind set itself to repair the damage done by the cataclysm and went about its business in the usual way.

The epidemic vanished instantly and Mrs. Calvert did not die. Nearly six months later a white-haired wreck of a man crawled into her husband's office and said feebly:

"Don't you know me, Mr. Calvert? I'm Markovitch, or what there is left of him."

"Good heavens, so you are!" said Calvert. "What has happened to you? Sit down and tell me all about it."

"It is not a long story," said Markovitch, sitting down and beginning to speak in a thin, trembling voice. "It is not long, but it is very bad. Everything went well at first. All succeeded as I said it would and then, I think it was just four days before we should have stopped, it happened."

"What happened?"

"I don't know. We must have gone too far, or by some means an accidental discharge must have taken place. The whole works suddenly burst into white flame. Everything made of metal melted like tallow. Every man in the works died instantly, burnt, you know, to a cinder. I was four or five miles away, with some others, seal shooting. We were all struck down insensible. When I came to myself I found I was the only one alive. Yes, Mr. Culvert, I am the only man that has returned from Boothia alive. The works are gone. There are only some heaps of melted metal lying about on the ice. After that I don't know what happened. I must have gone mad. It was enough to make a man mad, you know. But some Indians and Eskimos, who used to trade with us, found me wandering about, so they told me, starving and out of my mind, and they took me to the coast. There I got better and then was picked up by a whaler and so I got home. That is all. It was very awful, wasn't it?"

Then his face fell forward into his trembling hands, and Culvert saw the tears trickling between his fingers. Then he reeled backward, and suddenly his body slipped gently out of the chair and on to the floor. When Culvert tried to pick him up he was dead. And so the secret of the Great Experiment, so far as the world at large was concerned, never got beyond the walls of Mr. Sidney Culvert's cosy dining-room after all.

WITHIN AN ACE OF THE END OF THE WORLD

ROBERT BARR

Originally subtitled "Being some account of the fearful disaster which overtook the inhabitants of this earth through scientific miscalculation in the year 1904," this tale by British writer Robert Barr (1849–1912) falls within the subgenre of stories in which doomsday is threatened by irresponsible science or experiments that get out of hand. Its earnest approach might have caused readers of it in the April 1900 issue of McClure's *to miss the humor of its depiction of a nitrogen-depleted earth whose populace is giddily intoxicated by an excess of oxygen.*

THE SCIENTIST'S SENSATION

The beginning of the end was probably the address delivered by Sir William Crookes to the British Association at Bristol, on September 7, 1898, although Herbert Bonsel, the young American experimenter, alleged afterward that his investigations were well on the way to their final success at the time sir William spoke.

All records being lost in the series of terrible conflagration which took place in 1904, it is now impossible to give any accurate statement regarding Sir William Crookes's remarkable paper; but it is known that his assertions attracted much attention at the time, and were the cause of editorial comment in almost every newspaper and scientific journal in the world.

The sixteen survivors out of the many millions who were alive at the beginning of 1904 were so much occupied in the preservation of their own lives, a task of almost insurmountable difficulty, that they have handed down to us, their descendants, an account of the six years beginning with 1898 which is, to say the least, extremely unsatisfactory to an exact writer.

Man, in that year, seems to have been a bread-eating animal, consuming, per head, something like six bushels of wheat per annum. Sir William appears to have pointed out to his associates that the limit of the earth's production of wheat had been reached, and he predicted universal starvation, did not science step in to the aid of a famine-stricken world.

Science, however, was prepared. What was needed to increase the wheat production of the world to something like double its then amount was nitrate of soda; but nitrate of soda did not exist in the quantity required —viz., some 12,000,000 tons annually. However, a supposedly unlimited supply of nitrogen existed in the atmosphere surrounding the earth, and from this storehouse science proposed to draw, so that the multitude might be fed.

Nitrogen in its free state in the air was useless as applied to wheat-growing, but it could be brought into solid masses for practical purposes by means of electricity generated by the waterfalls which are so abundant in many mountainous lands. The cost of nitrates made from the air by water-power approached $25 a ton, as compared with $130 a ton when steam was used. Visionary people had often been accused of occupying castles in the air, but now it was calmly proposed to feed future populations from granaries in the air. Naturally, as has been said, the project excited much comment, although it can hardly be asserted that it was taken seriously.

* * *

It is impossible at this time, because of the absence of exact data, to pass judgment on the conflicting claims of Sir William Crookes and Mr. Herbert Bonsel; but it is perhaps not too much to say that the actual beginning of disaster was the dinner given by the Marquis of Surrey to a number of wealthy men belonging to the city of London, at which Mr. Bonsel was the guest of the evening.

THE DINNER AT THE HOTEL CECIL

Early in April, 1900, a young man named Herbert Bonsel sailed for England from New York. He is said to have been a native of Coldwater, Michigan, and to have served some sort of apprenticeship in the workshops of Edison at Orange, New Jersey. It seems that he did not prosper there to his satisfaction, and after trying to interest New York people in his experiments, he returned to Coldwater, where he worked for some time in a carriage-building establishment. Bonsel's expertness with all kinds of machinery drew forth the commendation of his chief, and begot a friendship between them which ultimately led to Bonsel's divulging to the other at least part of his secret. The obstacle in the way of success was chiefly scarcity of money, for the experiments were costly in their nature. Bonsel's chief, whose name is not known, seems to have got together a small syndicate, which advanced a certain amount of capital, thus enabling the young man to try his fortune once more in New York. Again his efforts to enlist capital in New York were fruitless ; therefore, in April he sailed for England.

Bonsel's evil star being in the ascendant, he made the acquaintance of the wealthy Marquis of Surrey, who became much interested in the young man and his experiments. The Marquis bought out the Coldwater syndicate, returning the members tenfold the money they had invested, and took Bonsel to his estate in the country, where, with ample means now at his disposal, the youthful scientist pushed his investigations to success with marvelous rapidity. Nothing is known of him until December of that year, when the Marquis of Surrey gave a dinner in his honor at the Hotel Cecil, to which were invited twenty of the richest men in England. This festival became known as "The Millionaires' Dinner"; and although there was some curiosity excited regarding its purport, and several paragraphs appeared in the papers alluding to it, no surmise concerning it came anywhere near the truth.

The Marquis of Surrey presided, with Bonsel at his right and the Lord Mayor of London at his left. Even the magnates who sat at that table, accustomed as they were to the noted dinners in the City, agreed unanimously that they had never partaken of a better meal, when, to their amazement, the chairman asked them, at the close, how they had relished it.

A STRIKING AFTER-DINNER SPEECH

The Marquis of Surrey, before introducing the guest of the evening, said that, as they were all doubtless aware, this was not a social, but a commercial dinner. It was the intention, before the company separated, to invite subscriptions to a corporation which would have a larger capitalization than any limited liability concern that had ever before been floated. The young American at his right would explain the discoveries he had made and the inventions he had patented, which this newly formed corporation would exploit Thus introduced, Herbert Bonsel rose to his feet and said:

"Gentlemen, I was pleased to hear you admit that you liked the dinner which was spread before us to-night. I confess that I never tasted a better meal, but most of my life I have been poor, and therefore I am not so capable of passing an opinion on a banquet as any other here, having always been accustomed to plain fare. I have, therefore, to announce to you that all the viands you have tasted and all the liquors you have consumed were prepared by me in my laboratory. You have been dining simply on various forms of nitrogen, or on articles of which nitrogen is a constituent. The free nitrogen of the air has been changed to fixed nitrogen by means of electricity, and the other components of the food placed on the board have been extracted from various soils by the same means. The champagne and the burgundy are the product of the laboratory, and not of the wine-press, the soil used in their composition having been exported from the vine-bearing regions of France. More than a year ago, Sir William Crookes announced what the nitrogen free in the air might do for the people of this world. At the time I read his remarks I was engaged in the experiments that have now been completed. I trembled, fearing I was about to be forestalled; but up to this moment, so far as I know, there has been made no effort to put his theories into practical use. Sir William seemed to think it would be sufficient to use the nitrates extracted from the atmosphere for the purpose of fertilizing the ground. But this always appeared to me a most roundabout method. Why should we wait on slow-footed nature? If science is capable of wringing one constituent of our food from the air, why should it shrink from extracting the others from earth or water? In other words, why leave a job half finished? I knew of no reason; and, luckily, I succeeded in convincing our noble host that all food products may be speedily compounded in the laboratory, without waiting the progress of the tardy seasons. It is proposed, therefore, that a company be formed with a capital so large that it can control practically all the water-power available in the world. We will extract from earth, air, and water whatever we need, compound the products in our factories, and thus feed the whole world. The moment our plant is at work, the occupations of agriculturist, horticulturist, and stock-breeder are gone. There is little need to dwell on the profit that must accrue to such a company as the one now projected. All commercial enterprises that have hitherto existed, or even any combination of them, cannot be compared in wealth-producing power to the scheme we have now in hand. There is no man so poor but he must be our customer if he is to live, and none so rich that he can do without us."

THE GREAT FOOD CORPORATION (LIMITED)

After numerous questions and answers, the dinner party broke up, pledged to secrecy, and next day a special train took the twenty down to the Marquis of Surrey's country place, where they saw in operation the apparatus that transformed simple elements into palatable food. At the mansion of the Marquis was formed The Great Food Corporation (Limited), which was to have such an amazing effect upon the peoples of this earth. Although the company proved one of the most lucrative investments ever undertaken in England, still it did not succeed in maintaining the monopoly it had at first attempted. In many countries the patents did not hold, some governments refusing to sanction a monopoly on which life itself depended, others deciding that, although there were certain ingenious novelties in Bonsel's processes, still the general principles had been well known for years, and so the final patents were refused. Nevertheless, these decisions did not interfere as much as might have been expected with the prosperity of The

Great Food Producing Corporation (Limited). It had been first in the field, and its tremendous capitalization enabled it to crush opposition somewhat ruthlessly, aided by the advantage of having secured most of the available water-power of the world. For a time there was reckless speculation in food-manufacturing companies, and much money was lost in consequence. Agriculture was indeed killed, as Bonsel had predicted, but the farmers of Western America, in spite of the decline of soil-tilling, continued to furnish much of the world's food. They erected wind-mills, with which electricity was generated, and, drawing on the soil and the air, they manufactured nourishment almost as cheaply as the great water-power corporation itself. This went on in every part of the world where the Bonsel patents were held invalid. In a year or two every one became accustomed to the chemically compounded food, though a few old fogies kept writing to the newspapers proclaiming that the former manner of cultivation was better, and that they would never forsake the ancient wheaten loaf for its modern equivalent; yet nobody paid any attention to these conservatives, looking on them as harmless enthusiasts; and presently even they could not get the wheaten loaf of bygone days, as grain was no longer grown except as a curiosity in some botanist's garden.

REMARKABLE SCENE IN THE GUILDHALL

The first three years of the twentieth century were notable for the great increase of business confidence all over the world. A reign of universal prosperity seemed to have set in. Political questions appeared easier of solution. The anxieties that hitherto had oppressed the public mind, such as the ever-present poverty problem, provision for the old age of laborers, and so forth, lifted like a rising cloud, and disappeared. There were still the usual number of poor people; but, somehow, lack of wealth had lost its terror. It was true that the death-rate increased enormously; but nobody seemed to mind that. The episode at the Guildhall dinner in 1903 should have been sufficient to awaken the people, had an awakening been possible in the circumstances; but that amazing lesson, like others equally ominous, passed unheeded. When the Prime Minister who had succeeded Lord Salisbury was called upon to speak, he said:

"My Lord Mayor, Your Royal Highnesses, Your Excellencies, Your Graces, My Lords and Gentlemen: It has been the custom of Prime

Ministers from time immemorial to give at this annual banquet some indication of the trend of mind of the Government. I propose, with your kind permission, to deviate in slight measure from that ancient custom *(cheers)*. I think that hitherto we have all taken the functions of government rather more seriously than their merits demanded, and a festive occasion like this should not be marred by the introduction of debatable subjects *(renewed cheering)*. If, therefore, the band will be good enough to strike up that excellent tune, 'There will be a hot time in the old town to-night,' I shall have the pleasure of exhibiting to you a quick-step I have invented to the rhythm of that lively composition *(enthusiastic acclaim)*."

The Prime Minister, with the aid of some of the waiters, cleared away the dishes in front of him, stepped from the floor to his chair, and from the chair to the table, where, accompanied by the energetic playing of the band, he indulged in a break-down that would have done credit to any music-hall stage. All the applauding diners rose to their feet in the wildest excitement. His Royal Highness the Crown Prince of Alluria placed his hands on the shoulders of the Lord Mayor, the German Ambassador placed his hands on the shoulders of the Crown Prince, and so on down the table, until the distinguished guests formed a connected ring around the board on which the Prime Minister was dancing. Then all, imitating the quick-step, and keeping time with the music, began circling round the table, one after the other, shouting and hurrahing at the top of their voices. There were loud calls for the American Ambassador, a celebrated man, universally popular; and, the Prime Minister, reaching out a hand, helped him up on the table. Amidst vociferous cheering, he said that he took the selection of the tune as a special compliment to his countrymen, the American troops having recently entered a conquered city to its melodious strains. His Excellency hoped that this hilarious evening would cement still further the union of the English-speaking races, which in fact it really did, though not in the manner the honorable gentleman anticipated at the time of speaking. The company, headed by the band and the Prime Minister, then made their way to the street, marched up Cheapside, past St. Paul's, and along Fleet Street and the Strand, until they came to Westminster. Every one along the route joined the processional dance, and upward of 50,000 persons were assembled in the square next to

the Abbey and in the adjoining streets. The mob was exuberant in its
approval of the proceedings. The Prime Minister, waving his hands
toward the Houses of Parliament, cried, "Three cheers for the good
old House of Commons!" These being given with a tiger appended, a
workingman roared, "Three cheers for 'is Lordship and the old duffers
what sits with 'im in the 'Ouse of Lords." This was also cheered—until
the echoes reached the Mansion House.

The "Times" next morning, in a jocular leading article, congratulated
the people of England on the fact that at last politics were viewed in
the correct light. There had been, as the Prime Minister truly said,
too much solidity in the discussion of public affairs; but, linked with
song and dance, it was now possible for the ordinary man in the street
to take some interest in them, etc., etc. Foreign comment, as cabled
from various countries, was entirely sympathetic to the view taken of
the occurrence by all the English newspapers, which was that we had
entered a new era of jollity and good will.

A WARNING FROM OXFORD

I have now to speak of my great-grandfather, John Rule, who, at the
beginning of the twentieth century, was a science student at Balliol
College, Oxford, aged twenty-four. It is from the notes written by him
and the newspaper clippings which he preserved that I am enabled to
compile this imperfect account of the disaster of 1904 and the events
leading to it. I append, without alteration or comment, his letter to the
"Times," which appeared the day after that paper's flippant references
to the conduct of the Prime Minister and his colleagues:

> To The Editor of The 'Times':
> Sir,—The levity of the Prime Minister's recent conduct;
> the levity of your own leading article thereon; the levity
> of foreign reference to the deplorable episode, indicate
> but too clearly the crisis which mankind is called upon to
> face, and to face, alas, under conditions which make the
> averting of the greatest calamity well-nigh impossible.
> To put it plainly, every man, woman, and child on this
> earth, with the exception of eight persons in the United
> States and eight in England, are drunk—not with wine,

but with oxygen. *The numerous factories all over the world which are working night and day, making fixed nitrates from the air, are rapidly depleting the atmosphere of its nitrogen. When this disastrous manufacture was begun, 100 parts of air, roughly speaking, contained 76.9 parts of nitrogen and 23.1 parts of oxygen. At the beginning of this year, the atmosphere round Oxford was composed of nitrogen 53.218, oxygen 46.782. And here we have the explanation of the largely increased death-rate. Man is simply burning up. To-day the normal proportions of the two gases in the air is nearly reversed, standing nitrogen, 27.319, oxygen 72.681, a state of things simply appalling: due in a great measure to the insane folly of Russia, Germany, and France competing with each other in raising mountain ranges of food products as a reserve in case of war, just as the same fear of a conflict brought their armies to such enormous proportions a few years ago. The nitrogen factories must be destroyed instantly, if the people of this earth are to remain alive. If this is done, the atmosphere will gradually become nitrogenized once more. I invite the editor of the 'Times' to come to Oxford and live for a few days with us in our iron building, erected on Port Meadow, where a machine supplies us with nitrogen and keeps the atmosphere within the hut similar to that which once surrounded the earth. If he will direct the policy of the ' Times' from this spot, he may bring an insane people to their senses. Oxford yesterday bestowed a degree of D.C.L. on a man who walked the whole length of the High on his hands; so it will be seen that it is time something was done.*

I am, sir, yours, etc.,

JOHN RULE.
BALLIOL COLLEGE, OXFORD.

The "Times" in an editorial note said that the world had always been well provided with alarmists, and that their correspondent, Mr. Rule, was a good example of the class. That newspaper, it added, had been

for some time edited in Printing House Square, and it would continue
to be conducted in that quarter of London, despite the attractions of
the sheet-iron house near Oxford.

THE TWO NITROGEN COLONIES

The coterie in the iron house consisted of Rev. Mr. Hepburn, who was
a clergyman and tutor; two divinity students, two science students, and
three other undergraduates, all of whom had withdrawn from their
colleges, awaiting with anxiety the catastrophe they were powerless to
avert. Some years before, when the proposal to admit women to the
Oxford colleges was defeated, the Rev. Mr. Hepburn and John Rule
visited the United States to study the working of co-education in that
country. There Mr. Rule became acquainted with Miss Sadie Armour of
Vassar College on the Hudson, and the acquaintance speedily ripened
into friendship, with a promise of the closer relationship that was yet
to come. John and Sadie kept up a regular correspondence after his
return to Oxford, and naturally he wrote to her regarding his fears for
the future of mankind, should the diminution of the nitrogen in the air
continue. He told her of the precautions he and his seven comrades had
taken, and implored her to inaugurate a similar colony near Vassar. For
a long time the English Nitrogenists, as they were called, hoped to be
able to awaken the world to the danger that threatened; and by the time
they recognized that their efforts were futile, it was too late to attempt
the journey to America which had long been in John Rule's mind.

Parties of students were in the habit of coming to the iron house and
jeering at the inmates. Apprehending violence one day, the Rev. Mr.
Hepburn went outside to expostulate with them. He began seriously,
then paused, a comical smile lighting up his usually sedate face, and
finally broke out into roars of laughter, inviting those he had left to
come out and enjoy themselves. A moment later he began to turn
somersaults round the iron house, all the students outside hilariously
following his example, and screaming that he was a jolly good fellow.
John Rule and one of the most stalwart of the divinity students rushed
outside, captured the clergyman, and dragged him into the house by
main force, the whirling students being too much occupied with their
evolutions to notice the abduction. One of the students proposed that
the party should return to Carfax by hand-springs, and thus they all set

off, progressing like jumping-jacks across the meadow, the last human beings other than themselves that those within the iron house were to see for many a day. Rule and his companions had followed the example set by continental countries, and had, while there was yet time, accumulated a small mountain of food products inside and outside of their dwelling. The last letter Rule received from America informed him that the girls of Vassar had done likewise.

THE GREAT CATASTROPHE

The first intimation that the Nitrogenists had of impending doom was from the passage of a Great Western train running northward from Oxford. As they watched it, the engine suddenly burst into a brilliant flame, which was followed shortly by an explosion, and a moment later the wrecked train lay along the line blazing fiercely. As evening drew on, they saw that Oxford was on fire, even the stonework of the colleges seeming to burn as if it had been made of wax. Communication with the outside world ceased, and an ominous silence held the earth. They did not know then that London, New York, Paris, and many other cities had been consumed by fire; but they surmised as much. Curiously enough, the carbon dioxide evolved by these numerous and widespread conflagrations made the outside air more breathable, notwithstanding the poisonous nature of this mitigant of oxygenic energy. For days they watched for any sign of human life outside their own dwelling, but no one approached. As a matter of fact, all the inhabitants of the world were dead except themselves and the little colony in America, although it was long after that those left alive became aware of the full extent of the calamity that had befallen their fellows. Day by day they tested the outside air, and were overjoyed to note that it was gradually resuming its former quality. This process, however, was so slow that the young men became impatient, and endeavored to make their house movable, so that they might journey with it, like a snail, to Liverpool, for the one desire of each was to reach America and learn the fate of the Vassar girls. The moving of the house proved impracticable; and thus they were compelled to remain where they were until it became safe to venture into the outside air, which they did some time before it had reached its normal condition.

It seems to have been fortunate that they did so, for the difficulties they had to face might have proved insurmountable had they not been exhilarated by the excess of oxygen in the atmosphere. The diary which John Rule wrote showed that within the iron house his state of depression was extreme when he remembered that all communication between countries was cut off, and that the girl to whom he was betrothed was separated from him by 3,000 miles of ocean, whitened by no sail. After the eight set out, the whole tone of his notes changed, an optimism scarcely justified by the circumstances taking the place of his former dismay. It is not my purpose here to dwell on the appalling nature of the foot journey to Liverpool over a corpse-strewn land. They found, as they feared, that Liverpool also had been destroyed by fire, only a fringe of the river front escaping the general conflagration. So enthusiastic were the young men, according to my great-grandfather's notes, that on the journey to the seaport they had resolved to walk to America by way of Behring Straits, crossing the English Channel in a row-boat, should they find that the shipping at Liverpool was destroyed. This seems to indicate a state of oxygen intoxication hardly less intense than that which had caused the Prime Minister to dance on the table.

A VOYAGE TO A RUINED NEW YORK

They found the immense steamship *Teutonic* moored at the landing-stage, not apparently having had time to go to her dock when the universal catastrophe culminated. It is probable that the city was on fire when the steamer came in, and perhaps an attempt was made to board her, the ignorant people thinking to escape the fate that they felt overtaking them by putting out to sea. The landing-stage was packed with lifeless human beings, whole masses still standing up, so tightly were they wedged. Some stood transfixed with upright arms above their heads, and death seemed to have come to many in a form like suffocation. The eight at first resolved to take the *Teutonic* across the Atlantic, but her coal bunkers proved nearly empty, and they had no way of filling them. Not one of them knew anything of navigation, and Rule alone was acquainted with the rudiments of steam-engineering. They selected a small steam yacht, and loaded her with the coal that was left in the *Teutonic's* bunkers. Thus they started for the West, the Rev. Mr. Hepburn acting as captain and John Rule as engineer. It was fourteen days before they sighted the coast of Maine, having kept much too far north. They went ashore at the ruins of Portland; but embarked again, resolved to trust rather to their yacht than undertake a long land journey through an unknown and desolated country. They skirted the silent shores of America until they came to New York, and steamed down the bay. My great-grandfather describes the scene as somber in the extreme. The Statue of Liberty seemed to be all of the handiwork of man that remained intact. Brooklyn Bridge was not entirely consumed, and the collapsed remains hung from two pillars of fused stone, the ragged ends of the structure which once formed the roadway dragging in the water. The city itself presented a remarkable appearance. It was one conglomerate mass of gray-toned, semi-opaque glass, giving some indication of the intense heat that had been evolved in its destruction. The outlines of its principal thoroughfares were still faintly indicated, although the melting buildings had flowed into the streets like lava, partly obliterating them. Here and there a dome of glass showed where an abnormally high structure once stood, and thus the contour of the city bore a weird resemblance to its former self—the likeness that the grim outlines of a corpse over which a sheet has been thrown might bear to a living man. All along the shore lay the gaunt skeletons of half-fused steamships. The young men passed this dismal calcined graveyard in deep silence, keeping straight up the broad Hudson. No sign of life greeted them until they neared Poughkeepsie, when they saw, flying above a house situated on the top of a hill, that brilliant fluttering flag, the Stars and Stripes. Somehow its very motion in the wind gave promise that the vital spark had not been altogether extinguished in America. The great sadness which had oppressed the voyagers was lifted, and they burst forth into cheer after cheer. One of the young men rushed into the chart-room, and brought out the Union Jack, which was quickly hauled up to the mast-head, and the reverend captain pulled the cord that, for the first time during the voyage, let loose the roar of the steam whistle, rousing the echoes of the hills on either side of the noble stream. Instantly, on the veranda of the flag-covered house, was seen the glimmer of a white summer dress, then of another and another and another, until eight were counted.

AND FINALLY

The events that followed belong rather to the region of romance than
to a staid, sober narrative of fact like the present; indeed, the theme
has been a favorite one with poets and novelists, whose pens would
have been more able than mine to do justice to this international idyl.
America and England were indeed joined, as the American Ambassador
had predicted at the Guildhall, though at the time his words were
spoken lie had little idea of the nature and complete accord of that
union. While it cannot be denied that the unprecedented disaster
which obliterated human life in 1904 seemed to be a calamity, yet
it is possible to trace the design of a beneficent providence in this
wholesale destruction. The race which now inhabits the earth is one
that includes no savages and no war lords. Armies are unknown and
unthought of. There is no battleship on the face of the waters. It is
doubtful if universal peace could have been brought to the world short
of the annihilation of the jealous, cantankerous, quarrelsome peoples
who inhabited it previous to 1904. The Lord destroyed humanity once
by flood, and again by fire; but whether the race, as it enlarges, will
deteriorate after its second extinguishment, as it appears to have done
after its first, must remain for the future to determine.

THE LAST DAYS
OF EARTH

GEORGE C. WALLIS

Published in the July 1901 issue of The Harmsworth Magazine, *this story presents a vision of an earth millions of years in the future succumbing to the intense cold and darkness brought on by the death of its sun. British writer George C. Wallis (1871–1956) seems to suggest here that no matter how long humanity lives into the future, the noblest and ignoblest traits of human nature will endure.*

A man and a woman sat facing each other across a table in a large room. They were talking slowly, and eating—eating their last meal on earth. The end was near; the sun had ceased to warm, was but a red-hot cinder outwardly; and these two, to the best of their belief, were the last people left alive in a world-wilderness of ice and snow and unbearable cold.

The woman was beautiful—very fair and slight, but with the tinge of health upon her delicate skin and the fire of intellect in her eyes. The man was of medium height, broad-shouldered, with wide, bald head and resolute mien—a man of courage, dauntless purpose, strenuous life. Both were dressed in long robes of a thick, black material, held in at the waist by a girdle.

As they talked, their fingers were busy with a row of small white knobs let into the surface of the table, and marked with various signs. At the pressure of each knob a flap in the middle of the table opened, and a small glass vessel, with a dark, semi-liquid compound steaming in it, was pushed up. As these came, in obedience to the tapping of their fingers, the two ate their contents with the aid of tiny spoons. There was no other dining apparatus or dinner furniture upon the table, which stood upon a single but massive pedestal of grey metal.

The meal over, the glasses and spoons replaced, the table surface clean and clear, a silence fell between them. The man rested his elbows upon his knees and his chin upon his upturned palms. He did not look at his fair companion, but beyond her, at a complicated structure projecting from the wall. This was the Time Indicator, and gave, on its various discs, the year, the month, the day, the hour and the instant, all corrected to mean astronomical time and to the exact latitude and longitude of the place. He read the well-known symbols with defiant eyes. He saw that it was just a quarter to thirteen in the afternoon of Thursday, July 18th, 13,000,085 A.D. He reflected that the long association of the place with time-recording had been labour spent in vain. The room was in a great building on the site of ancient Greenwich. In fact, the last name given to the locality by its now dead and cold inhabitants had been Grenijia.

From the time machine, the man's gaze went round the room. He noted, with apparently keen interest, all the things that were so familiar to him—the severely plain walls, transparent on one side, but without window-frame or visible door in their continuity; the chilling prospect of a faintly-lit expanse of snow outside; the big telescope that moved in an airtight slide across the ceiling, and the little motor that controlled its motions; the electric radiators that heated the place, forming an almost unbroken dado around the walls; the globe of pail brilliance that hung in the middle of the room and assisted the twilight glimmer of the day; the neat library of books and photo-phono cylinders, and the tier of speaking machines beneath it; the bed in the further corner surrounded by yet more radiators; the two ventilating valves; the great dull disc of the Pictorial Telegraph; and the thermometer let into a vacant space of floor. On this last his glance rested for some time, and the woman's also. It registered the degrees from absolute zero, and stood at a figure equivalent to 42° Fahrenheit. From this tell-tale instrument the eyes of the two turned to each other, a common knowledge shining in each face. The man was the first to speak again.

"A whole degree, Celia, since yesterday. And the dynamos are giving out a current at a pressure of 6,000 volts. I can't run them at any higher efficiency. That means that any further fall of temperature will close the drama of this planet. Shall we go tonight?"

There was no quiver of fear nor hint of resentment in his voice, nor in the voice that answered him. Long ages of mental evolution had weeded all the petty vice and unreasoning passions out of the mind of man.

"I am ready any time, Alwyn. I do not like to go; I do not like the risk of going; but it's our last duty to the humanity behind us—and I must be with you to the end."

There was another silence between them; a silence in which the humming of the dynamos in the room below seemed to pervade the whole place, thrilling through everything with annoying audibility. Suddenly the man leaned forward, regarding his companion with a puzzled expression.

"Your eyelashes are damp, Celia. You are not crying? That is too archaic."

"I must plead guilty," she sad, banishing the sad look with an effort. "We are not yet so thoroughly adjusted to our surroundings as to be able to crush down every weak impulse. Wasn't it the day before yesterday that you said the sun had begun to cool about five million years too soon for man? But I will not give way again. Shall we start at once?"

"That is better; that sounds like Celia. Yes, if you wish, at once; but I had thought of taking a last look around the world—at least, as far as the telegraph system is in order. We have three hours' daylight yet."

For answer, Celia came and sat beside him on the couch facing the disc of the Pictorial Telegraph. His left hand clasped her right; both were cold. With his right hand he pulled over and held down a small lever under the disc—one of many, each bearing a distinctive name and numeral.

The side wall became opaque; the globe above ceased to be luminous. A moving scene grew out of the dullness of the disc, and a low, moaning sound stole into the room. They looked upon a telegraphically transmitted view of a place near which had once been Santiago, Chili. There were the ruins of an immense white city there now, high on the left of the picture. Down, on the right, far below the well-defined marks of six successive beach lines, a cold sea moan over an icy bar, and dashed in semi-frozen spray under the bluff of an overhanging glaciers edge.

Out to sea great bergs drifted slowly, and the distant horizon was pale with ice-blink from vast floes. The view had scarcely lasted a moment, when a great crack appeared on the top of the ice-front, and a huge fragment fell forward into the sea. It overturned on the bar, churning up a chaos of foam, and beginning to drift away. At the same instant came the deafening report of the breakage. There was no sign of life, neither of man nor beast, nor bird nor fish, in that cold scene. Polar bears and Arctic foxes, blubber-eating savages and hardy seals, had all long since passed away, even from the tropic zone.

Another lever pressed down, and the Rock of Gibraltar appeared on the disc. It rose vast and grim from the ice-arched waters of a shallow strait, with a vista of plain and mountain and glacier stretching behind it to the hazy distance—a vista of such intolerable whiteness that the two watchers put on green spectacles to look at it. On the flat top of the Rock—which ages ago had been leveled to make it an alighting station for the Continental aerial machines—rose, gaunt and frost-encrusted, the huge skeleton framework of one of the last flying conveyances used by man.

Another lever, and Colombo, Ceylon, glared lifeless on the disc. Another, and Nagasaki, Japan, the terminal front of a vast glacier, frowned out over black, ice-filling sea. Yet more levers, and yet more scenes; and everywhere ice and snow, and shallow, slowly-freezing seas, or countries here black and plantless, and there covered with glaciers from crumbling hills. No sign of life, save the vestiges of man's now-ended reign, and of his long fight with the relentless cold—here ruins, on the ice-free levels, of his Cities of Heat; here gigantic moats, excavated to retard the glaciers; here the skeletons of huge metallic floating palaces, jettisoned on some ice-bound coast; and everywhere that the ice had not overcome the tall masts of the Pictorial Telegraph, sending to the watchers at Greenwich, by reflected Marconi waves, a presentiment of each sight and sound impinging on the speculums and drums at their summits. And in every daylight scene, the pale ghost of a dim, red sun hung in a clear sky.

In the more northern and southern views, the magnetic lines were as brilliant as ever, but there were no views of the extreme Polar Regions. These were more inaccessible than in the remote past, for there cakes and patches of liquid and semi-solid air were slowly settling and spreading on land and sea.

Yet more levers, and yet more; and the two turned away from the disc; and the room grew light again.

"It appears just as we have seen it these last two years," said the man, "yet to-day the tragedy of it appals me as it has never done before. I did not think, after all the years of expectation and mental schooling, that it would seem like this at the last. I feel tempted to do as our parents did—to seek the safety of the Ultimate Silence."

"Not that, Alwyn—not that. From generation to generation this day has been foreseen and prepared for, and we promised, after we were chosen to remain, that we would not die until all the devices of our science failed. Let us go down and get ready to leave at once."

Celia's face had a glow upon it, a glow that Alwyn's caught.

"I only said 'tempted,' Celia. Were I alone, I do not think I should break my word. And I am also curious. And the old, strange desire for life has come to me. And you are here. Let me kiss you, Celia. That . . . at least is not archaic."

They walked hand-in-hand to a square space marked out on the floor in a corner of the room, and one of them pressed a button on the wall. The square sank with them, lowering them into a dimmer room, where the ceaseless humming of the dynamos became a throbbing roar. They saw, with eyes long used to faint light, the four great alternators spinning round the armatures; felt the fanning of the rapid revolutions upon their faces. By the side of each machine they saw the large, queer-shaped chemical engines that drove them, that were fed from dripping vats, and from many actions and re-actions supplied the power that stood between their owners and the cold that meant the end. Coal had long been exhausted, along with peat and wood and all inflammable oils and gases; no turbines could be worked from frozen streams and seas; no air wheels would revolve in an atmosphere but slightly stirred by a faded sun. The power in chemical actions and re-actions, in transmissions and compoundings of the elements, was the last great source of power left to man in the latter days.

After a brief glance round the room, they pressed another button, and the lift went down to a still lower floor. Here a small glow-lamp was turned on, and they stood before a sphere of bright red metal that filled the greater part of the room. They had not seen this many times in their lives. Its meaning was too forcible a reminder of a prevision for the time that had at last arrived.

The Red Sphere was made of a manufactured element, unknown except within the last million years, and so costly and troublesome to produce that only two Red Spheres had ever been built. It had been made 500 years before Alwyn and Celia were born. It was made for the purpose of affording the chosen survivors of humanity a means of escaping the earth when chemical power proved incapable of resisting the increasing cold. In the Red Sphere Alwyn and Celia intended to leave the earth, to plunge into space—not to seek warmth and light on any other member of the Solar System, for that would be useless—but to gain the neighbourhood of some yet young and fiery star. It was a terrible undertaking—as much more terrible than mere interplanetary voyages as the attempt of a savage to cross the Atlantic in his dugout after having learned to navigate his own narrow creek. It had been left undared until the last, when, however slight the chance of life in it, the earth could only offer instead the choice of soon and certain death.

"It appears just as it did the day I first saw it and was told its purpose," said Celia with a shudder she could not repress. "Are you sure, Alwyn, that it will carry us safely?—that you can follow out the Instructions?"

For generations the Red Sphere and all appertaining to it had been mentioned with a certain degree of awe.

"Don't trouble yourself on that point. The Instructions are simple. The necessary apparatus, and the ten years' supply of imperishable nutrient, are already inside and fixed. We have to subject the Red Metal to our 6,000 volt current for an hour, get inside, screw up the inlet, and cut ourselves adrift. The Red Metal, thus electrified, becomes, as you know, repulsive to gravitation, and will so continue for a year and a half. By that time, as we shall travel according to calculation, at twice the speed of light, we should be more than half-way to one of the nearer stars, and so become subject to its gravitation. With the earth in its present position, if we start a couple of hours, we should make F. 188, mag. 2, of the third order of the spectra. Our sun, according to the records, belonged to the same order. At least we know it has two planets.

"But if we fall right into F. 188, instead of just missing it, as we hope? Or if we miss, but so closely as to be fused by its heat? Or if we miss it too widey and are thrown back into space on a parabolic or hyperbolic orbit? Or if we should manage the happy medium and find there to be no life, nor any chance of life, upon the planets of that system? Or if there be life, but it be hostile to us?"

"Those are the inevitable dangers of our plunge, Celia. The balance of probabilities is in favour of either the first or second of those things befalling us. But that is not the same as absolute certainty, and the improbable *may* happen."

"Quite so, Alwyn; but—do you recollect if the Instructions make any reference to these possibilities?"

"To—? Yes. There is enough fulminate of sterarium packed in the Sphere to shiver it and us to fine dust in the thousandth part of a second—if we wish. We shall always have that resource. Now I'll attach the dynamo leads to the Sphere. Get your little items of personal property together and we shall be ready."

Celia went up to the lift again, and Alwyn, after fixing the connections to several small connections on the surface of the Sphere, followed her. They sat together in the darkening twilight of the dim room above, waiting for the first hour to pass. They spoke at intervals, and in fragmentary phrases.

"It will be cold while the Sphere is being prepared," said Alwyn.

"Yes, but we shall be together, dear, as we have been so long now. I remember how miserable I felt when I first knew my destiny; but when I learned that you were chosen to share it with me, I was glad. But you were not, Alwyn—you loved Amy."

"Yes."

"And you love her still, but you love me, too? Do you know why she was not chosen?"

"Yes; I love you Celia, though not so much as I loved Amy. They chose you instead of her, they said, because you had a stronger will and greater physical vigour. The slight curve we shall describe on rising will bring us over the Heat-house she and her other lover retired to after the Decision, and we shall perhaps see if they are really dead, as we believe. Amy, I remember, had an heretical turn of mind."

"If they are not dead, it is strange that they should not have answered our Marconi and telepathic messages after the first year—unless, of course, as you have so often suggested, they retired to the interior of the other Red Sphere. How strange that they should have been left there! If they have only enough food, they may live in it until old age intervenes, secure from all the rigours that approach, but what a tame end—what a prisonment!"

"Terrible. I could not endure the Red Sphere except as we shall endure it—travelling."

So the hour passed. They switched the electric current into the framework of the vehicle that was to bear them into space. All the radiators ceased to glow and all the lights went out, leaving them, in that lower room, in absolute darkness and intense cold. They sat huddled together against the wall, where they could feel the thrill of the humming dynamos, embracing each other, silent and resolute; waiting for the end of the cold hour. They could find few words to speak now, but their thoughts were busier.

They thought of the glorious, yet now futile past, with all its promises shattered, its ideals valueless, its hopes unfulfilled; and seemed to feel in themselves the concentration and culmination of the woes and fears of the ages. They saw, as in one long vista, the history of the millions of vanished years—"from earth's nebulous origins to its final ruin"; from its days of four hours to its days of twenty-six and a half; from its germinating specks of primal protoplasm to its last and greatest, and yet most evil creature, Man. They saw, in mental perspective, the uneven periods of human progress; the long stages of advance and retrogression, of failure and success. They saw the whole long struggle between the tendencies of Egoism and Altruism, and knew how these had merged at last into an automatic equilibration of Duty and Desire. They saw the climax of this equilibration, the Millennium of Man—and they knew how the inevitable decay had followed.

They saw how the knowledge of the sureness and nature of life's end had come to Man; slowly at first, and not influencing him much, but gaining ever more and more power as the time grew nearer and sympathy and intellect more far-sighted and acute; how, when the cold itself began, and the temperate zone grew frigid, and the tropic temperate, and Man was compelled to migrate, and his sources of heat and power failed one after the other, the knowledge of the end reacted on all forms of mental activity, throwing all thought and invention into one groove. They saw the whole course of the long fight; the ebb and flow of the struggle against the cold, in which, after each long period, it was seen that Man was the loser; how men armed with powers that to their ancestors would have made them seem as gods, had migrated to the other planets of the system, only to find that there, even on Mercury himself, the dying had made all life a fore-known lost battle; how many men, whole nations, had sought a premature refuge from the Fear in the Ultimate Silence called Death. They saw how all the old beliefs, down to the tiniest shreds of mysticism, had fallen from Man as a worn-out garment, leaving him spiritually naked to face the terrors of a relentless Cosmos; how, in the slow dissolving of the ideal Future, man's duties and thoughts were once more moulded with awe and reverence to the wishes of the past.

They saw the closing centuries of the struggle; the discovery of the Red Metal; the building of the Spheres that none dare venture to use, but which each succeeding and lessening generation handed down to the next as a sacred heritage only to be put to test in the last resort; they remembered, in their own childhood, the Conference of the Decision, when they two had been chosen, as the only pair of sufficient vigour and health and animal courage to accept the dread legacy and dare the dread adventure of seeking a fresh home in the outer vastness, so that haply the days of Man might not be ended; and they remembered, only two well, how the rest of humanity, retiring to their last few houses, had one and all pledged each other to seek the Silence and trouble the chilly earth no more. They knew how well that pledge had been kept, and in the darkness and silence of the room clutched each other closer and closer.

And at last they heard the Time Indicator in the uppermost room ring the peal of the completed hour, and knew that in their own lives they must act the final scene in the long life-tragedy of the earth.

Alwyn's hand reached out and touched the switch, and the glow-lamp sprang into radiance again. In silence he handed Celia into the

Sphere—which shone a deeper red now and coruscated strangely in the light—and then followed her, drawing the screw section in after him and making it secure. Within, the sphere was spacious and comfortable, and, save where thickly padded, transparent, even to the weak incandescence of the lamp. It was also pleasantly warm, for the Red Metal was impervious to heat. The man's hand went to the lever that worked through the shell and pushed aside the strong jaws of the spring clamp that held the sphere down; and as it went, he looked into the woman's eyes. He hesitated. There was a light in her eyes and his, a feeling in her heart and his, that neither had seen or experienced before.

"It's madness, Celia," he said, slowly. "It's not too late yet. The moment I pull this lever over the Sphere will tear its way through the building like an air-bubble through water, but until then it is not too late."

This was not a question in phrase, but it was in fact. Celia did not answer.

"Isn't it a miserable folly, this deference to the past? Don't we know perfectly well that death is as certain out there as here?" the man went on.

Then Celia answered: "Yes, Alwyn; Man, life everything, is a most miserable folly. But we have nothing to do with that; we can't help it. We don't know, until we try, what fortune may yet meet us. We should be untrue to our ancestors, cowards and recreants to ourselves, if we drew back now. Even in the face of the unconscious enmity of the whole Universe of Matter, let us remember that we are living and conscious yet."

As so often in the past, the woman was the man's strengthener in the time of need. Alwyn pulled over the lever, and cried, with antique impulsiveness:—

"Forgive me, Celia! We will not give in, not even against a hostile universe! She moves!—we go!"

There was a sudden shock that threw them staggering against each other for a moment; a rending, tearing, rolling crash of masonry and metal, and the Red Sphere rose through the falling ruins of the house and soared up into the night, slanting slightly to the west as it rose. One brief glimpse they had of the dials of the Time Indicator falling across a gap of the ruin; and their eyes were busy with the white face of the earth beneath and the clear brilliance of the starry dome above.

They were still clinging to each other, when they both caught sight of a small dark object approaching them from beneath. It came, apparently, from a black spot on the chill whiteness of the landscape to the west of their abandoned home, and it was traveling faster than themselves.

They gazed down at it with sudden interest, that, as they gazed, turned into acute apprehension, and then to a numb horror.

"The other Sphere!"

"Amy and her lover!"

While they spoke it grew definitely larger, and they saw that a collision was unavoidable. By what caprice of fate it had so fallen out that the helpless paths of the two Red Spheres should thus come to coincide in point of space and time, they could not imagine. The idea of leaving the earth might, by magnetic sympathy, have occurred to both couples about the same time, but the rest of the unlucky coincidence was inexplicable. They turned from looking at the second Sphere and sought each other's eyes and hands, saying much by look and pressure that words could not convey.

"They did not mean to keep the pledge of the Decision," said Alwyn. "The desire for life must have come to them as it came to me to-day, and Amy must have remembered the Instructions. I can understand them coming up faster than us, because their Sphere was in a sheet-metal shed in the open, and so would start with less opposition and greater initial velocity. But it is strange that their path should be so nearly ours. It can only be a matter of minutes, at the rate they are gaining, before the end comes to all of us It will be before we get through the atmosphere and gather our full speed. And it will be the end of Humanity's troubled dream . . . And Amy is in that . . .

The thought of possible malice, impulsive or premeditated, on the part of the occupants of the second Red Sphere, never entered into the mind of those of the first.

"The responsibility of action rests upon us," said Celia. "They evidently cannot see us, against the background of the black sky. They are coming up swiftly, dear."

"It will have to be that: there is no other way. Better one than both," said the man.

"Be what, Alwyn?"

"The fulminate of sterarium."

"It will not injure them?"

"No; not if we fire the fuse within—about—three minutes. It must seem hard to you, Celia, to know that my hand will send you to the Silence so that Amy may have the last desperate chance of life. Somehow, these last few hours, I have felt the ancient emotions surging back."

The hand that clasped his gave a gentle pressure.

"And I, too, Alwyn; but their reign will be brief. I would rather die with you now than live without you. I am ready. Do not be too late with the fulminate, Alwyn."

They swayed together; their arms were about each other; their lips met in the last kiss. While their faces were yet very near, Alwyn's disengaged right hand touched a tiny white button that was embedded in the padding of the interior.

There was an instantaneous flash of light and roar of sound, and the man and the woman in the second sphere were startled by the sudden glare and concussion of it, as their metal shell drove upward through the cloud of elemental dust that was all that remained of the first Red Sphere and its occupants.

The silence and clear darkness that had been round them a moment before, had returned when they recovered their balance; and in that silence and clear darkness, the man and woman who had not been chosen passed out into the abyss of the Beyond, ignorant of the cause and meaning of that strange explosion in the air, and knew that they were alone in Space, bound they knew not whither.

THE END OF THE WORLD

SIMON NEWCOMB

An astronomer and mathematician by profession, Canadian writer Simon Newcomb (1835–1909) takes his cue in this tale from Robert Duncan Milne's "Into the Sun," with his depiction of the havoc wrought on earth when a celestial body plunges into our sun. This story appeared in the May 1903 issue of McClure's *and is unusual for its upbeat suggestion that the end of life as we know it portends the beginning of something new and potentially vital to an evolutionarily stagnant world.*

M ars is signaling a dark star"
 The world to which this news was flashed from the Central Observatory on the Himalayas had long been dull and stagnant. Almost every scientific discovery had been made thousands of years before; and the inventions for their application had been so perfected that it seemed as if no real improvement could be made in them. Methods of conducting human affairs had been brought into such good shape that

everything went on as by machinery. Successive Defenders of the Peace of the World had built up a code of international law so complete that every question at issue between nations was settled by its principles. The only history of great interest was that of a savage time, lying far back in the mists of antiquity, when men fought and killed each other in war. The daily newspapers chronicled little but births, marriages, deaths, and the weather reports. They would not publish what was not worth talking about, and a subscriber often found at his door a paper containing little more than the simple announcement, on an otherwise blank page— "Nothing worthy of note had happened since our last issue." Only one language was spoken the world over, and all generations dined in blue coats with gilt buttons, and wore white neckties with red borders. Even China, the most distant nation of all, had fallen into line several thousand years before, and lived like the rest of the world.

To find a time of real excitement it was necessary to go back 3,000 years, when messages had first been successfully interchanged with the inhabitants of Mars. To send a signal which they could see required a square mile of concentrated light as bright as the sun, and experiments extending through thousands of years had been necessary before this result could be brought about by any manageable apparatus. Signals from the plains of Siberia had been made nightly during two or three oppositions of the planet, without any answer being received. Then the world was electrified by hearing that return signals could be seen flashing in such a way that no doubt could exist about them. Their interpretation required more study than was ever expended by our archaeologists on a Moabite inscription. When success was at last reached, it became evident by a careful comparison of the records that the people of Mars were more successful watchers of the stars than we were ourselves. It was found that a row of four lights diminishing in intensity from one end to the other, pointing in one direction, meant that a new star was showing itself in that direction. Some object of this sort had been seen every two or three years, from the earliest historical times, but in recent times a star had often been signaled from Mars before even the sensitive photographic plates and keen eyes of our Himalayan astronomers had discerned it.

Ordinary comets were plentiful enough. More than 25,000 had been recorded, and the number was still increasing every year. But dark stars were so rare that not one had appeared for three centuries, and only about twenty had been recorded in astronomical history. They differed from comets in not belonging to the solar system, but coming from far distant regions among the stars, and in being comparatively dark in color, with very short tails, or perhaps none at all. They were found to be dark bodies whose origin and destination were alike unknown, each pursuing its own way through the immeasurable abysses of space. It had been found that a certain arrangement of five lights in the form of a cross on the planet meant that one of these bodies was flying through or past our system, and the head of the cross showed the direction in which it was to be looked for.

After a dozen generations of men had passed away without seeing a body of this kind, it goes without saying that the news from Mars of a coming dark star excited universal interest. Where was it? What does it mean? What is a dark star? The Himalayan astronomers were nearly buried under telegrams asking these and other questions without numbers. They could only reply that they had not yet succeeded in finding the object, but that the constellation to which the signal pointed was the head of the Dragon.

There was no likelihood that the object was yet visible, even through powerful telescopes, but this did not prevent the family telescope being brought out in every dwelling in the world, in order to scour the heavens for the new star. For some time it evaded the scrutiny even of the Himalayan astronomers. When a week had passed and it had not been sighted, men began to ask whether it could be possible that the telescopes of another another planet were as much better than ours as their failure would seem to indicate. The conviction began to gain ground that the signal had been misinterpreted and that there was no dark star or anything else unusual coming. But when interest in the subject had about died away, it was suddenly renewed by the announcement that the object had been photographed very near where the signals had indicated it. It was about half-way between the head of the Dragon and the constellation Lyra, moving very slowly toward the East and South.

The problem now was to determine the orbit of the new star, and for this purpose the astronomers began to make the most accurate observations possible. Owing to the slowness of the motion, several days, perhaps two weeks, would be required. While waiting for more news curiosity was excited by a new announcement:

"Mars appears to be in a state of extraordinary exictment. The five signal lights which have been seen from time to time ever since the dark star appeared are flashing in a way never before recorded. We cannot imagine what it means."

Our world could only ask: "What can it mean?" and wait patiently.

The astronomers were much puzzled about the orbit, and a month passed before they could reach a decision on the subject. Then Himalaya sent out an announcement more startling than any that had preceded it:

"The dark star has no orbit. It is falling straight toward the sun with a speed that has already reached 30 kilometers a second, and which is continually increasing as it falls. It will reach the sun in about 210 days."

The first man to see the possibilities suggested by this announcement was the Professor of Physics. Although all the scientific discoveries had probably been made, a single great physical laboratory had been established in which experiments were conducted with a faint hope of something new being learned. The laboratory was placed near the southern end of a peninsula, the site of one of the greatest cities of the ancient world, known as Neeork, the ruins of which, buried ages before by an earthquake, we known to extend over many square miles. To the north now stood the city of Hattan, the mighty city of the world, whose well-paved streets, massive buildings, public institutions, and lofty towers extended a day's journey to the north and west, whose wealth was fabulous, and whose sights every man in the world wanted to see at least once in his lifetime. Most of the investigations to which the laboratory was devoted had to be carried on where the temperature was the same from one year's end to another. To bring about this result an immense vault hundreds of yards in extent had been excavated at a depth of more than a hundred feet under the ground. Here was stored what one might suppose to be every piece of apparatus that human ingenuity had invented for making physical researches, and every instrument that men could make use of.

Of course the Professor of Physics, like all the rest of the world, heard that a dark star was going to fall into the sun. His proceedings after this announcement would have excited curiosity had it not been that the thoughts of men were too much occupied with the celestial visitor to notice his doings. He proceeded to supplement his immense stock of physical apparatus by a kind of supplies never before known to form the outfit of a laboratory. These consisted of flour, fresh wheat, edibles of every kind, and a supply of seeds of almost every plant known to Botany. The few people who noticed what he was doing gave the subject no attention, supposing that he was merely extending his experiments into the vegetable kingdom. Having got his suppliers all stored away, he called his assistants around him.

"I have something to say to you, and the first condition that I impose is that it must be kept an absolute secret. Those who are not willing to pledge themselves to secrecy will please retire."

None retired.

"Will you all hold up your rights hands in evidence of your adherence to the pledge which I extract from you?"

All did so.

"Now let me tell you what none but ourselves must hear. You all know that from the beginning of recorded history stars supposed to be new from time to time blazed out in the heavens. The scientific men know that these stars were not really new. They were simply commonplace stars which, through the action of some cause that no one has yet brought to light, suddenly increased their heat and light thousands of times. Then, in the course of a few months, they faded away into their former insignificance, of rather, perhaps, turned into nebulae.

"We have also known that dark bodies many times larger than the earth are flying through space like the stars themselves. Now, my theory is that if one of those objects chances to strike a star it bursts through its outer envelope and sets free the enormous fires pent up within, which burst forth in all their fury.

"Next December one of these objects is going to fall into our sun. Now I do not want to frighten you unnecessarily, but I think we may as well look this matter in the face. If my theory is correct, the light and heat of the sun will be suddenly increased thousands of times. Should this result follow, can there be any doubt as to the consequences? The whole surface of the earth will be exposed to a radiation as intense as that in the focus of a burning glass, which, you all know, will not only set fire to wood, but melt iron and crumble stone. The flood of heat will destroy all the works of man and every living being that exists upon the earth. The polar regions alone will be exempt from the radiation, because the sun will not be shining on them at the time of collision. But they will be visited by such a flood of hot air and steam that their fate can hardly be different from that of the rest of the world.

"Under such circumstances I do not know what to do. For the present I shall merely hope that my theory is all wrong. At the same time I invite you to be in readiness to bring your wives and families here at the critical moment, so that we can all take refuge in our vaults. If nothing occurs, well and good. Nobody need know what we have planned. It s not likely that we shall feel it worth while to live if the rest of the world is destroyed. But we cannot decide that question until we face it. Keep in readiness and say nothing, that is all I have to advise for the present.

During the month that followed the Professor was very much perplexed as to whether he should make his fears known. Against doing this was the consideration that the world could not help itself, and it had better go on to the last moment in ignorance of what was coming. Physicians make it a point of honour not to inform their patient that he has a fatal illness, why should the race be apprised of its inevitable doom? The mental suffering endured in the mean time would be useless, no matter whether they were saved or lost. Why make them suffer to no purpose?

But, in spite of this reticence on his part, the world was much concerned, especially by the signals from Mars. These, instead of ceasing as always before, after one or two nights, now flashed out incessantly night after night. The Martians must be trying to tell us something of unprecedented importance. What could it be? The Professor of Physics was loudly called upon to know if there was not really some danger from the dark comet falling into the sun. The calls became so pressing that he was forced to make some sort of reply.

"While it is impossible to state with certainty the effect that will be produced by the fall of the dark star into the sun, it is only right to say that it may possibly be followed by an increase in the sun's radiation, which will have reached its height in tow or three days, and may continue abnormally great for some weeks. It will therefore be prudent to guard against the possible consequences of an increase in the sun's heat. The roofs of houses, and all combustible objects exposed to the sun's rays, should, as far as possible, be protected by a non-combustible covering. Food and clothing liable to be injured by the heat should be protected by being stored in cellars."

The Professor of Logic in the University of Hattan put all the data bearing on the subject into equations which he proceeded to solve, and then announced his judgment on the view of the Professor of Physics.

"'Ten thousand years of recorded experience has led to the conclusion that the sun is one of the most stable bodies in the universe. During all the years through which meteorological records have extended there has not been a change of a single degree in the annual amount of heat radiated to the earth. In favor of the view that a sudden change will be produced by any cause whatever we have only a doubtful physical theory, sustained by no experience whatever. It is, therefore, not logical to be frightened by the prediction of the Professor of Physics, especially when he is himself in doubt about the correctness of his own view. Yet, in view of the magnitude of the interests involved, the prudence of the suggestion made by the Professor cannot be questioned. No harm can be done by taking every possible precaution."

A torrent of dispatches now poured down upon the Professor of Physics from every part of the world wanting to know whether his mathematical theory of the case was really well grounded. After all, was not the Professor of Logic right, and was it not unreasonable to suppose that an order of things which had continued, probably, for millions of years should be so suddenly changed? He could only reply that his theory had never been verified in any known case. He was glad to find his view in doubt. The main fact on which it was based—that the new stars which blazed up every few years were not new, but old stars which had suddenly burst out from inscrutable cause—he purposely kept in the background.

While this discussion was going on, the terrible object which was darting toward out sun remained for some time invisible in every telescope but the great one of the Himalayas. In a few weeks, however, growing brighter as it came nearer the sun, it could be seen in smaller and smaller telescopes, and at last was clearly made out by every watcher of the heavens. Two months before its occurrence the time of the catastrophe was predicted to a minute by the Himalayan astronomers. It would be in the afternoon of December 12th, after

the sun had set in Europe, and while it was still shining on all but
the northeastern portion of the American continent and on most of
the Pacific Ocean. The sun would have set to regions as far east as
Labrador, and would be about an hour high on the middle portions
of the Atlantic coast. The star was followed night after night with
constantly increasing concern. As each evening approached, men
indulged in a vain hope that the black star might prove a phantom—
some ghost of the sky which would disappear never again to be seen.
But this impression was always dispelled when night came on, and the
telescope was pointed. The idea of an illusion vanished entirely when
the object became visible to the naked eye, and was seen night after
night without any telescope at all.

Every night it was very little brighter than the night before. Yet
there was nothing in the object itself that would excite alarm. Even
in the most superstitious age of the world people might never have
noticed it, or, if they had, would only have wondered how the
star happened to be there when it had not before been seen. Now,
however, the very slowness of the increase inflicted a slow torture
upon the whole human race, like that experienced by a Chinese
prisoner whose shaved head is made to feel the slow dropping of
water. What is hardly noticeable at first gets father and farther beyond
the limit of endurance. The slowness with which the light of the star
increased only lengthened the torture. Men could scarcely pursue
their daily vocations. Notes went to protest on a scale that threatened
universal bankruptcy. When December approached it was seen
that the fall toward the sun was becoming more rapid, and that the
increase in brightness was going on at a greater and still greater rate.
Formerly the star had been seen only at night. Now the weird object,
constantly growing larger, could be seen in full daylight, like some
dragon in the sky.

As December approached the thoughts and sentiments of remote
ancestors, which had been absent for untold ages, were revived in the
minds of men. They had long worshipped the invisible, beneficent,
and all-pervading Power which informed the universe and breathed
into its atoms the breath of life. Now this power became a remorseless
Judge, about to punish the men of the present for the sins of ancestors
during all time.

December forced its way in, and now the days were counted. Eleven days—ten—to-morrow nine only will elapse before the fate of the world will be decided. It required nerve to face the star; men shut their eyes to it, as if the unseen were nonexistent. Those who dared to point the telescope saw it look as large as the moon to the naked eye. But the mild and serene aspect of our satellite was not there—only a fierce glow, as that of the eye of a beast of prey.

Seven days—six days—five days—fiercer glowed the eye which in waking hours belonged to a being breathing naught but vengeance. Even in sleep men still in imagination saw the eye and felt such terrors as might be inspired by the chase of malignant and pitiless demons of the bottomless pit. They lived over again the lives of their ancestors who had been chased by wild beasts.

Three days—two days—reason began to leave its seat. The insane rushed madly about, but the guardians of the peace heeded them not. In the streets men glared into each other's eyes, but not one word was necessary to express the thought.

The last day dawns: tonight—what? Calm and still was the morning; mildly as ever shone the sun, all unconscious of the enemy ready to strike him. His unconcern seemed to calm the minds f men, as if he meant to assure them that nothing was to happen. They plucked up courage to look with eye and telescope. The sun, unmoved as ever, advanced toward the West, the hours were counted—now the minutes.

At every telescope, some watcher found the nerve to see what would happen. Every minute the malignant eye grew brighter and glared more fiercely; every minute it could be seen nearer the sun. A shudder spread over the whole city of Hattan as the object seemed to touch the sun's disc. A moment of relief followed when it disappeared without giving any sign. Perhaps, under the fervent heat of the sun, the star had dissolved into the air. But this hope was speedily dashed by its reappearance as a black spot on the sun, slowly passing along its face. Those who considered the case now knew that we were mainly looking at the object as seen between us and the sun, and that it had not yet fallen into the latter. For a moment there was a vague hope that the computations of the astronomers had, for the first time in history, led them astray, and that the black object would continue its course over the sun, to leave it again like the planet Mercury or Venus during a transit. But this illusion was dispelled when the dark object disappeared in a moment and its place was taken by an effulgence of such intensity that, notwithstanding the darkness of the glass through which the sun was being viewed, the eyes of the lookers on were dazzled with the brightness.

No telescope was necessary to see what followed. Looking with the naked eye through a dark-glass a spot many times brighter than the rest of the sun was seen where the black object had just disappeared. Every minute it grew larger and brighter. In half an hour this effulgence, continually increasing and expanding, was seen to project away from the sun like a fan or the tail of a comet. An unearthly glow spread over the whole landscape, in the light of which pebbles glistened like diamonds. By the time the sun had set to the Eastern States its size seemed to be doubled and its brightness to have increased fourfold. Before it set on the Pacific coast the light and heat became so intense that every one had to seek the shade.

The setting of the sun afforded a respite for the night. But no sooner had it grown dark than a portentous result was seen in the heavens. It happened that Mars, in opposition, had just risen in the East, while Venus, as the evening star, was seen in the West. These objects both glowed—Venus like an electric light, Mars like a burning coal. Every one knew the cause. Shining by the reflected light of the sun, their brightness increased in the same proportion as the sunlight. It was like seeing a landscape by the light of some invisible conflagration. Its very suggestivenesss added a new terror. The beholders could imagine what results were being produced on other continents by the rapidly increasing conflagration, and awaited in calm despair the result when our central luminary should again come around to our longitude.

The earth, continuing its revolution, exposed the oceans and continents in succession to the burning rays. When the sun set at San Francisco the heat was still not unbearable. But from Asia and Europe came the most portentous news through the period of what, for them, was day, while on the American continent it was night. In China and India, men could only remain out of doors a few minutes at a time. In the afternoon all had to flee from the heat and take refuge in their houses.

Yet worse was the case in Europe. For a time detailed dispatches came from London. The telegraph offices had been removed to the cellars of the buildings in which they were located, and men were trying to store everything combustible where the sun's rays could not reach it. Every fire-engine in the city was called out to sprinkle the roofs of houses with. Notwithstanding these precautions, at eleven o'clock a roof in Cheapside took fire, and soon after fires broke out here and there in nearly every quarter. By noon the whole city seemed to be in flames, the firemen fighting heat above them and around them. It would soon become impossible for a human being to live in the streets.

A few minutes later came the news that sudden relief had been experienced. A violent gale came in from the Atlantic, bringing with it a torrent of rain, which, for the time being, extinguished the flames. But a new horror was now added. The wind increased to a hurricane of unexampled force. Houses were everywhere blown down and roofs were flying in mid-air, exposing everything in the interior to the flood of water.

About 3 P.M. it was announced that the sun, having dissolved the clouds with its fervent heat, had again shone forth hotter than ever, and that the telegraph offices would soon have to be abandoned. Not another word was heard from the European side until night. Then it was announced that the heat had again been followed by a torrent of rain, and that the sun, having set, another respite had been obtained. The damage done was incalculable and the loss of life frightful, yet hope would have survived had it not been for might be expected on the morrow.

The American continent, forewarned, undertook the most vigorous defense possible. Before the sun rose every fire-engine in Hattan was in place ready for action. Everything combustible in the city was covered with woolen cloth and sprinkled with water. The possibility of doing something occupied all minds, and after the sun rose men fought the heat with the courage of despair. Fiercely though the sun poured down its flood of fire, an engine was ready to extinguish the flames wherever they burst forth. As in Europe they were soon aided by floods of rain. Thus passed the day, while the sun shed a fiercer heat with every passing hour.

The scene while the sun was setting filled all minds with despair. The size of our luminary was multiplied so many times that it was an hour after the lower edge touched the horizon before the upper edge had set. When it finally disappeared the place of twilight was taken by a lurid illumination of the whole heavens, which still left the evening brighter than an ordinary day. Cosmic flames millions of miles in extent, rising from the sun, still appeared above the horizon from time to time. Even at midnight a sort of aurora, tenfold brighter than any that had ever been recorded, seemed to spread over the sky in rising sheets of fiery vapor, which disappeared at the zenith. The trained eye of the Professor of Physics watched the scene from the iron door of his vault. He knew the cause. The exploded sun was sending forth its ions with a velocity almost comparable with that of light to every part of the solar system. In the midst of the illumination the planet Mars could still be seen glowing with supernatural brightness, but no word came from the Himalayan Observatory as to any signals it might be sending to us. Communication from other continents had entirely ceased, and the inhabitants of the whole American continent awaited the coming of what they knew must be the last day.

After midnight, although the ions were flying thicker than ever, a supernatural light seemed to spread over the landscape. The very contrast to what was expected to come in the morning added to the depression and terror. If any vain hope was entertained that the sun might, during its course over the Pacific Ocean and Asia, abate some of its fiery stream, it was dispelled when, shortly after three o'clock, the first sign of the approaching luminary was seen in the East. Still thicker the ions flew, as a bright radiance, far exceeding that of the evening before, heralded the approach of what had always been considered the great luminary, but now was the great engine of destruction. Brighter and brighter grew the eastern horizon until, long before the actual sun blazed above it, the eye could no longer endure the dazzling blaze. When, an hour later, the sun itself appeared, its rays struck the continent like a fiery flood. As they advanced from the Atlantic to the Pacific everything combustible which they struck burst into flame, stones were crumbled by the heat, towers and steeples fell as if shaken by an earthquake. Men had to take refuge in caves or cellars beneath any covering which could protect them from the fierce heat. Old and young, rich and poor, male and female crowded together in the confusion of despair. The great magnates of commerce and industry, whose names were everywhere familiar as household words, on whose wealth and power all the millions that inhabited the continent had looked with envy or admiration, were now huddled with their liveried servants beneath the ruins of falling houses, in the cellars of their own homes, in the vaults of their banks, or under any shelter which could protect them from the burning of a thousand suns.

The Professor of Physics, with his assistants, could only look through a crevice in the covering of his vault and see the fiery radiance which was coming from the East. When the covering grew so hot that he felt refuge must soon be taken in the lowest vaults, the sun was suddenly cut off by a rising cloud of blackness coming in from the Atlantic. The whole ocean was boiling like a pot, and the rising steam carried over the land by a gale produced by the expansion of the air over the ocean. Moving with inconceivable velocity, the gale passed over the continent, sweeping before it every vestige of human work that stood in its path. Even the stones of the buildings, cracked and pulverized by the heat, were now blown through the air like dust, and, churned with the rain, buried the land under a torrent of mud. The lightning played incessantly everywhere, and, if it did not destroy every living being exposed to it, it was only because no living beings survived where it struck. Constantly thickening and darkening clouds poured down their storm of rain upon the ruins. But no relief was thus afforded to the mass of cringing humanity which remained protected in vaults and cellars. The falling flood was boiling hot, scalding to death every one upon whom it fell. It poured through cracks and crevices, flooding cellars, saturating the ruins of buildings, and if a living being remained it scalded him to death.

The Professor and his official family were, for the time being, saved from destruction by the construction of their subterranean chambers. The heat and the wind had effaced every structure at the mouth of the cave, and driven them into the lowest recess of their vaults. Against the iron doors which welled them in, the flood pressed like the water against the compartments of a ship riven in two by a collision. The doors burned the hand that touched them, but the boiling water leaked through only in small streams.

The few survivors of the human race here huddled together could only envy their more fortunate fellow-men who, in the sleep of death, had escaped such an imprisonment as they now suffered. Had the question of continuing to survive been put to a vote, all would have answered in the negative. Hope was gone, and speedy death was the best that could be prayed for. Only the conscience which had been implanted in the race through long ages prohibited their taking their own lives. They had provisions for two years, and might, therefore, survive during that period, if the supply of air and oxygen should hold out. For producing the latter both material and apparatus existed in the vaults. The reflection that such was the case was painful rather than pleasurable. While they did not have the nerve to let themselves be smothered to death, they felt that the devices for prolonging their lives, to which instinct compelled them to resort, could only be the means of continuing their torture. Electric light they have in abundance, but by day or night nothing could be done. They were in the regions of eternal night, except when they chose to turn on the current. From time to time one or another, moved more by the necessity of doing something than by any real object, examined the doors of the cave to see what changes might have taken lace in the pressure of the water against them. Long after the latter had ceased to trickle through the cracks the doors continued hot, but as time passed—they could not say whether days, weeks, or months—they found the doors growing cooler.

They at length ventured to open them. A sea of mud, knee-deep, but not quite at a scalding temperature, was found in the passages outside of them. Through this they were at length able to wade, and in time made their way to the open air. Emerging, it was impossible to say whether it was day or night. The illumination was brighter than anything ever known in the brightest day, yet no sun could be seen in the sky. The latter seemed filled with a nebulous mass of light, through and over which the clouds of ions were still streaming like waves of fire. The temperature was barely endurable, but it was not worse than the stifling closeness of their subterranean abode.

The first effect of the outer air was to produce an impression of waking from a dream. But a glance over the landscape dispelled this impression in a moment. What they saw must be reality, though awful by conception. Vainly their eyes looked for the great city. No city, not even a ruin was there. They longed in vain for human help; not an animated being was in sight. Every vestige of the work of Nature was gone. On three sides were what seemed great rivers of slime, while, toward the North, the region which had swarmed with the life and activity of the great world-center was a flat surface of dried clay, black

sand, or steaming mud, in which not even an insect crawled. In the
thick and vaporous air not a bird warbled its note. To return to their
dungeons was like a prisoner returning his cell. Farther they must go
in search for some familiar object or some sign of humanity. Is there
no telegraph to send a word of news? No railway on which a train may
run? No plow with which the furrow may be turned? No field in which
wheat can be sown? These questions were asked in silence; had they
been asked aloud not even an echo would have answered. When the
Professor had stored seeds and provisions in his vaults it was with the
thought that, if the worst should happen, he and his companions might
repopulate the earth. But now every such prospect dissolved away.

As their strength ebbed, a holy calm spread over the souls of all.
The Professor found words:

"Such is the course of evolution. The sun, which for millions of
years gave light and heat to our system and supported life on the earth,
was about to sink into exhaustion and become a cold and inert mass.
Its energy could not be revived, except by such a catastrophe as has
occurred. The sun is restored to what it was before there was any earth
upon which it could shed its rays, and will in time be ready to run its
course anew. In order that a race may be renewed it must die like an
individual. Untold ages must once more elapse while life is reappearing
on earth and developing in higher forms. But to the Power which
directs and controls the whole process the ages of humanity are but as
days, and it will await in sublime patience the evolution of a new earth
and a new order of animated nature, perhaps as far superior to that we
have witnessed as ours was to that which preceded it."

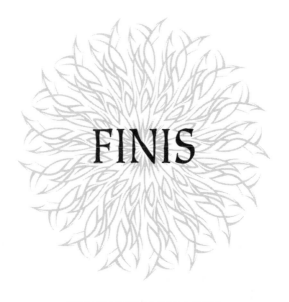

FINIS

FRANK LILLIE POLLOCK

This story offers an inventive variation on the theme of the Earth doomed by a celestial threat: a sun central to our universe but so remote from our solar system that its intense rays haven't reached us—yet. It appeared in the June 1906 issue of the American pulp fiction magazine Argosy. *Author Frank Lillie Pollock (1876–1957) imagines a harrowing scenario in which our planet's surface roasts like a rotisserie as it rotates through the new sun's rays.*

I 'm getting tired," complained Davis, lounging in the window of the Physics Building, "and sleepy. It's after eleven o'clock. This makes the fourth night I've sat up to see your new star, and it'll be the last. Why, the thing was billed to appear three weeks ago."

"Are *you* tired, Miss Wardour?" asked Eastwood, and the girl glanced up with a quick flush and a negative murmur.

Eastwood made the reflection anew that she certainly was painfully shy. She was almost as plain as she was shy, though her hair had an unusual beauty of its own, fine as silk and colored like palest flame.

Probably she had brains; Eastwood had seen her reading some extremely "deep" books, but she seemed to have no amusements, few interests. She worked daily at the Art Students' League, and boarded where he did, and he had thus come to ask her with the Davises to watch for the new star from the laboratory windows on the Heights.

"Do you really think that it's worth while to wait any longer, Professor?" inquired Mrs. Davis, concealing a yawn.

Eastwood was somewhat annoyed by the continued failure of the star to show itself and he hated to be called "professor," being only an assistant professor of physics.

"I don't know," he answered somewhat curtly. "This is the twelfth night that I have waited for it. Of course, it would have been a mathematical miracle if astronomers should have solved such a problem exactly, though they've been figuring on it for a quarter of a century."

The new Physics Building of Columbia University was about twelve stories high. The physics laboratory occupied the ninth and tenth floors, with the astronomical rooms above it, an arrangement which would have been impossible before the invention of the oil vibration cushion, which practically isolated the instrument rooms from the earth.

Eastwood had arranged a small telescope at the window, and below them spread the illuminated map of Greater New York, sending up a faintly musical roar. All the streets were crowded, as they had been every night since the fifth of the month, when the great new star, or sun, was expected to into view.

* * *

Some error had been made in the calculations, though, as Eastwood said, astronomers had been figuring on them for twenty-five years.

It was, in fact, nearly forty years since Professor Adolphe Bernier first announced his theory of a limited universe at the International Congress of Sciences in Paris, where it was counted as little more than a masterpiece of imagination.

Professor Bernier did not believe that the universe was infinite. Somewhere, he argued, the universe must have a center, which is the pivot for its revolution.

The moon revolves around the earth, the planetary system revolves about the sun, the solar system revolves about one of the fixed stars, and this whole system in turn undoubtedly revolves around some more distant point. But this sort of progression must definitely stop somewhere.

Somewhere there must be a central sun, a vast incandescent body which does not move at all. And as a sun is always larger and hotter than its satellites, therefore the body at the center of the universe must be of an immensity and temperature beyond anything known or imagined.

It was objected that this hypothetical body should then be large enough to be visible from the earth, and Professor Bernier replied that some day it undoubtedly would be visible. Its light simply had not yet had time to reach the earth.

The passage of light from the nearest of the fixed stars is a matter of three years, and there must be many stars so distant that their rays have not yet reached us. The great central sun must be so inconceivably remote that perhaps hundreds, perhaps thousands of years would elapse before its light should burst upon the solar system.

All this was contemptuously classed as "newspaper science" till the extraordinary mathematical revival a little after the middle of the twentieth century afforded the means of verifying it.

Following the new theorems discovered by Professor Burnside, of Princeton, and elaborated by Dr. Taneka, of Tokyo, astronomers succeeded in calculating the arc of the sun's movements through space, and its ratio to the orbit of its satellites. With this as a basis, it was possible to follow the widening circles, the consecutive systems of the heavenly bodies and their rotations.

The theory of Professor Bernier was justified. It was demonstrated that there really was a gigantic mass of incandescent matter, which, whether the central point of the universe or not, appeared to be without motion.

The weight and distance of this new sun were approximately calculated, and, the speed of light being known, it was an easy matter to reckon when its rays would reach the earth.

It was then estimated that the approaching rays would arrive at the earth in twenty-six years, and that was twenty-six years ago. Three weeks had passed since the date when the new heavenly body was expected to become visible, and it had not yet appeared.

Popular interest had risen to a high pitch, stimulated by innumerable newspaper and magazine articles, and the streets were nightly thronged with excited crowds armed with opera-glasses and star maps, while at every corner a telescope man had planted his tripod instrument at a nickel a look.

Similar scenes were taking place in every civilized city on the globe.

It was generally supposed that the new luminary would appear in size about midway between Venus and the moon. Better informed persons expected something like the sun, and a syndicate of capitalists quietly leased large areas of the coast of Greenland in anticipation of a great rise in temperature and a northward movement in population.

Even the business situation was appreciably affected by the public uncertainty and excitement. There was a decline in stocks, and a minor religious sect boldly prophesied the end of the world.

"I've had enough of this," said Davis, looking at his watch again. "Are you ready to go, Grace? By the way, isn't it getting warmer?"

It had been a sharp February day, but the temperature was certainly rising. Water was dripping from the roofs, and from the icicles that fringed the window ledges, as if a warm wave had suddenly arrived.

"What's that light?" suddenly asked Alice Wardour, who was lingering by the open window.

"It must be moonrise," said Eastwood, though the illumination of the horizon was almost like daybreak.

Davis abandoned his intention of leaving, and they watched the east grow pale and flushed till at last a brilliant white disc heaved itself above the horizon.

It resembled the full moon, but as if trebled in luster, and the streets grew almost as light as by day.

"Good heavens, that must be the new star, after all!" said Davis in an awed voice.

"No, it's only the moon. This is the hour and minute for her rising," answered Eastwood, who had grasped the cause of the phenomenon.

"But the new sun must have appeared on the other side of the earth. Its light is what makes the moon so brilliant. It will rise here just as the sun does, no telling how soon. It must be brighter than was expected—and maybe hotter," he added with a vague uneasiness.

"Isn't it getting warm in here?" said Mrs. Davis, loosening her jacket. "Couldn't you turn off some of the steam heat?"

Eastwood turned it all off, for in spite of the open window, the room was really growing uncomfortably close. But the warmth appeared to come from without; it was like a warm spring evening, and the icicles were breaking loose from the cornices.

* * *

For half an hour they leaned from the windows with but desultory conversation, and below them the streets were black with people and whitened with upturned faces. The brilliant moon rose higher, and the mildness of the night sensibly increased.

It was after midnight when Eastwood first noticed the reddish flush tinging the clouds low in the east, and he pointed it out to his companions.

"That must be it at last," he exclaimed, with a thrill of vibrating excitement at what he was going to see, a cosmic event unprecedented in intensity.

The brightness waxed rapidly.

"By Jove, see it redden!" Davis ejaculated. "It's getting lighter than day—and hot! Whew!"

The whole eastern sky glowed with a deepening pink that extended half round the horizon. Sparrows chirped from the roofs, and it looked as if the disc of the unknown star might at any moment be expected to lift above the Atlantic, but it delayed long.

The heavens continued to burn with myriad hues, gathering at last to a fiery furnace glow on the skyline.

Mrs. Davis suddenly screamed. An American flag blowing freely from its staff on the roof of the tall building had all at once burst into flame.

Low in the east lay a long streak of intense fire which broadened as they squinted with watering eyes. It was as if the edge of the world had been heated to whiteness.

The brilliant moon faded to a feathery white film in the glare. There was a confused outcry from the observatory overhead, and a crash of something being broken, and as the strange new sunlight fell through the window the onlookers leaped back as if a blast furnace had been opened before them.

The glass cracked and fell inward. Something like the sun, but magnified fifty times in size and hotness, was rising out of the sea. An iron instrument-table by the window began to smoke with an acrid smell of varnish.

"What the devil is this, Eastwood?" shouted David accusingly.

From the streets rose a sudden, enormous wail of fright and pain, the outcry of a million throats at once, and the roar of a stampede followed. The pavements were choked with struggling, panic-stricken people in the fierce glare, and above the din arose the clanging rush of fire engines and trucks.

Smoke began to rise from several points below Central Park, and two or three church chimes pealed crazily.

The observers from overhead came running down the stairs with a thunderous trampling, for the elevator mad had deserted his post.

"Here, we've got to get out of this," shouted Davis, seizing his wife by the arm and hustling her toward the door. "This place'll be on fire directly."

"Hold on. You can't go down into that crush on the street," Eastwood cried, trying to prevent him.

But Davis broke away and raced down the stairs, half carrying his terrified wife. Eastwood got his back against the door in time to prevent Alice from following them.

"There's nothing in this building that will burn, Miss Wardour," he said as calmly as he could. "We had better stay here for the present. It would be sure death to get involved in that stampede below. Just listen to it."

The crowds on the street seemed to sway to and fro in contending waves, and the cries, curses, and screams came up in a savage chorus.

The heat was already almost blistering to the skin, though they carefully avoided the direct rays, and instruments of glass in the laboratory cracked loudly one by one.

A vast cloud of dark smoke began to rise from the harbor, where the shipping must have caught fire, and something exploded with a terrific report. A few minutes later half a dozen fires broke out in the lower part of the city, rolling up volumes of smoke that faded to a thin mist in the dazzling light.

The great new sun was now fully above the horizon, and the whole east seemed ablaze. The stampede in the streets had quieted all at once, for the survivors had taken refuge in the nearest houses, and the pavements were black with motionless forms of men and women.

"I'll do whatever you say," said Alice, who was deadly pale, but remarkably collected. Even at that moment Eastwood was struck by the splendor of her ethereally brilliant hair that burned like pale flame above her pallid face. "But we can't stay here, can we?"

"No," replied Eastwood, trying to collect his faculties in the face of this catastrophic revolution of nature. "We'd better go to the basement, I think."

In the basement were deep vaults used for the storage of delicate instruments, and these would afford shelter for a time at least. It occurred to him as he spoke that perhaps temporary safety was the best that any living thing on earth could hope for.

But he led the way down the well staircase. They had gone down six or seven flights when a gloom seemed to grow upon the air, with a welcome relief.

It seemed almost cool, and the sky had clouded heavily, with the appearance of polished and heated silver.

A deep but distant roaring arose and grew from the southeast, and they stopped on the second landing to look from the window.

* * *

A vast black mass seemed to fill the space between sea and sky, and it was sweeping toward the city, probably from the harbor, Eastwood thought, at a speed that made it visibly grow as they watched it.

"A cyclone—and a waterspout!" muttered Eastwood, appalled.

He might have foreseen it from the sudden, excessive evaporation and the heating of the air. The gigantic black pillar drove toward them swaying and reeling, and a gale came with it, and a wall of impenetrable mist behind.

As Eastwood watched its progress he saw its cloudy bulk illumined momentarily by a dozen lightning-like flashes, and a moment later, above its roar, came the tremendous detonations of heavy cannon.

The forts and warships were firing shells to break the waterspout, but the shots seemed to produce no effect. It was the city's last and useless attempt at resistance. A moment later forts and ships alike must have been engulfed.

"Hurry! This building will collapse!" Eastwood shouted.

They rushed down another flight, and heard the crash with which the monster broke over the city. A deluge of water, like the emptying of a reservoir, thundered upon the street, and the water was steaming hot as it fell.

There was a rending crash of falling walls, and in another instant the Physics Building seemed to be twisted around by a powerful hand. The walls blew out, and the whole structure sank in a chaotic mass.

But the tough steel frame was practically unwreckable, and, in fact, the upper portion was simply bent down upon the lower stories, peeling off most of the shell of masonry and stucco.

Eastwood was stunned as he was hurled to the floor, but when he came to himself he was still upon the landing, which was tilted at an alarming angle. A tangled mass of steel rods and beams hung a yard over his head, and a huge steel girder had plunged down perpendicularly from above, smashing everything in its way.

Wreckage choked the well of the staircase, a mass of plaster, bricks, and shattered furniture surrounded him, and he could look out in almost every direction through the rent iron skeleton.

A yard away Alice was sitting up, mechanically wiping the mud and water from her face, and apparently uninjured. Tepid water was pouring through the interstices of the wreck in torrents, though it did not appear to be raining.

A steady, powerful gale had followed the whirlwind, and it brought a little coolness with it. Eastwood inquired perfunctorily of Alice if she were hurt, without being able to feel any degree of interest in the matter. His faculty of sympathy seemed paralyzed.

"I don't know. I thought—I thought that we were all dead!" the girl murmured in a sort of daze. "What was it? Is it all over?"

"I think it's only beginning," Eastwood answered dully.

The gale had brought up more clouds and the skies were thickly overcast, but shining white-hot. Presently the rain came down in almost scalding floods and as it fell upon the hissing streets it steamed again into the air.

In three minutes all the world was choked with hot vapor, and from the roar and splash the streets seemed to be running rivers.

The downpour seemed too violent to endure, and after an hour it did cease, while the city reeked with mist. Through the whirling fog Eastwood caught glimpses of ruined buildings, vast heaps of debris, all the wreckage of the greatest city of the twentieth century.

Then the torrents fell again, like a cataract, as if the waters of the earth were shuttlecocking between sea and heaven. With a jarring tremor of the ground a landslide went down into the Hudson.

The atmosphere was like a vapor bath, choking and sickening. The physical agony of respiration aroused Alice from a sort of stupor, and she cried out pitifully that she would die.

The strong wind drove the hot spray and steam through the shattered building till it seemed impossible that human lungs could extract life from the semi-liquid that had replaced the air, but the two lived.

After hours of this parboiling the rain slackened, and, as the clouds parted, Eastwood caught a glimpse of a familiar form halfway up the heavens. It was the sun, the old sun, looking small and watery.

But the intense and brightness told that the enormous body still blazed behind the clouds. The rain seemed to have ceased definitely, and the hard, shining whiteness of the sky grew rapidly hotter.

The heat of the air increased to an oven-like degrees; the mists were dissipated, the clouds licked up, and the earth seemed to dry itself almost immediately. The heat from the two suns beat down simultaneously till it became a monstrous terror, unendurable.

An odor of smoke began to permeate the air; there was a dazzling shimmer over the streets, and great clouds of mist arose from the bay, but these appeared to evaporate before they could darken the sky.

The piled wreck of the building sheltered the two refugees from the direct rays of the new sun, now almost overhead, but not from the penetrating heat of the air. But the body will endure almost anything, short of tearing asunder, for a time at least; it is the finer mechanism of the nerves that suffers most.

★ ★ ★

Alice lay face down among the bricks, gasping and moaning. The blood hammered in Eastwood's brain, and the strangest mirages flickered before his eyes.

Alternately he lapsed into heavy stupors, and awoke to the agony of the day. In his lucid moments he reflected that this could not last long, and tried to remember what degree of heat would cause death.

Within an hour after the drenching rains he was feverishly thirsty, and the skin felt as if peeling from his whole body.

This fever and horror lasted until he forgot he had ever known another state; but at last the west reddened, and the flaming sun went down. It left the familiar planet high in the heavens, and there was no darkness until the usual hour, though there was a slight lowering of the temperature.

But when night did come it brought life-giving coolness, and though the heat was still intense it seemed temperate by comparison. More than all, the kindly darkness seemed to set a limit to the cataclysmic disorders of the day.

"Ouf! This is heavenly," said Eastwood, drawing long breaths and feeling mind and body revived in the gloom.

"It won't last long," replied Alice, and her voice sounded extraordinarily calm through the darkness. "The heat will come again when the new sun rises in a few hours."

"We might find some better place in the meanwhile—a deep cellar; or we might get into the subway," Eastwood suggested.

"It would be no use. Don't you understand? I have been thinking it all out. After this, the new sun will always shine, and we could not endure it even another day. The wave of heat is passing round the world as it revolves, and in a few hours the whole earth will be a burnt-up ball. Very likely we are the only people left alive in New York, or perhaps in America."

She seemed to have taken the intellectual initiative, and spoke with an assumption of authority that amazed him.

"But there must be others," said Eastwood, after thinking for a moment. "Other people have found sheltered places, or miners, or men underground."

"They would have been drowned by the rain. At any rate, there will be none left alive by tomorrow night.

"Think of it," she went dreamily on, "for a thousand years this wave of fire has been rushing toward us, while life has been going on so happily in the world, so unconscious that the world was doomed all the time. And now this is the end of life."

"I don't know," Eastwood said slowly. "It may be the end of all human life, but there may be some forms that will survive—some microorganisms perhaps capable of resisting high temperatures, if nothing higher. The seed of life will be left at any rate, and that is everything. Evolution will begin all over again, producing new types to suit the changed conditions. I only wish I could see what creatures will be here in a few thousand years.

"But I can't realize it at all—this thing!" he cried passionately, after a pause. "Is it real? Or have we all gone mad? It seems too much like a bad dream."

The rain crashed down again as he spoke, and the earth steamed though not with dense reek of the day. For hours the waters roared and splashed against the earth in hot billows till the streets were foaming yellow rivers, damned by the wreck of fallen buildings.

There was a continual rumble as earth and rock slid into the East River, and at last the Brooklyn Bridge collapsed with a thunderous crash and splash that made all Manhattan vibrate. A gigantic billow like a tidal wave swept up the river from its fall.

The downpour slackened and ceased soon after the moon began to shed an obscured but brilliant light through the clouds.

Presently the east commenced to grow luminous, and this time there could be no doubt as to what was coming.

Alice crept closer to the man as the gray light rose upon the watery air.

"Kiss me!" she whispered suddenly, throwing her arms around his neck. He could feel her trembling. "Say you love me; hold me in your arms. There is only an hour."

"Don't be afraid. Try to face it bravely," stammered Eastwood.

"I don't fear it—not death. But I have nevere lived. I have always been timid and wretched and afraid—afraid to speak—and I've almost wished for suffering and misery or anything rather than to be stupid and dumb and dead, the way I've always been.

"I've never dared to tell anyone what I was, what I wanted. I've been afraid all my life, but I'm not afraid now. I have never lived; I have never been happy; and now we must die together!"

It seemed to Eastwood the cry of the perishing world. He held her in his arms and kissed her wet, tremulous face that was strained to his.

* * *

The twilight was gone before they knew it. The sky was blue already, with crimson flakes mounting to the zenith, and the heat was growing once more intense.

"This is the end, Alice," said Eastwood, and his voice trembled.

She looked at him, here eyes shining with an unearthly softness and brilliancy, and turned her face to the east.

There, in crimson and orange, flamed the last dawn that human eyes would ever see.

THE SCARLET PLAGUE

JACK LONDON

In his popular tales of adventure—notably the classic novels The Call of the Wild *(1903) and* White Fang *(1906)—Jack London (1876–1916) often contrasted the civilized and the savage life. Likewise in this post-apocalyptic tale, first published in the June 1912 issue of* The London Magazine, *in which London reflects on how rapidly civilization and society might revert to primitivism in the wake of a devastating pandemic.*

I

The way led along upon what had once been the embankment of a railroad. But no train had run upon it for many years. The forest on either side swelled up the slopes of the embankment and crested across it in a green wave of trees and bushes. The trail was as narrow as a man's body, and was no more than a wild-animal runway. Occasionally, a piece of rusty iron, showing through the forest-mould, advertised that the rail and the ties still remained. In one place, a ten-inch tree, bursting through at a connection, had lifted the end of a rail clearly into view. The tie had evidently followed the rail, held to it by the spike long enough for its bed to be filled with gravel and rotten leaves, so that now the crumbling, rotten timber thrust itself up at a curious slant. Old as the road was, it was manifest that it had been of the mono-rail type.

An old man and a boy travelled along this runway. They moved slowly, for the old man was very old, a touch of palsy made his movements tremulous, and he leaned heavily upon his staff. A rude skull-cap of goat-skin protected his head from the sun. From beneath this fell a scant fringe of stained and dirty-white hair. A visor, ingeniously made from a large leaf, shielded his eyes, and from under this he peered at the way of his feet on the trail. His beard, which should have been snow-white but which showed the same weather-wear and camp-stain as his hair, fell nearly to his waist in a great tangled mass. About his chest and shoulders hung a single, mangy garment of goat-skin. His arms and legs, withered and skinny, betokened extreme age, as well as did their sunburn and scars and scratches betoken long years of exposure to the elements.

The boy, who led the way, checking the eagerness of his muscles to the slow progress of the elder, likewise wore a single garment—a ragged-edged piece of bear-skin, with a hole in the middle through which he had thrust his head. He could not have been more than twelve years old. Tucked coquettishly over one ear was the freshly severed tail of a pig. In one hand he carried a medium-sized bow and an arrow. On his back was a quiverful of arrows. From a sheath hanging about his neck on a thong, projected the battered handle of a hunting knife. He was as brown as a berry, and walked softly, with almost a catlike tread. In marked contrast with his sunburned skin were his eyes—blue, deep blue, but keen and sharp as a pair of gimlets. They seemed to bore into aft about him in a way that was habitual. As he went along he smelled things, as well, his distended, quivering nostrils carrying to his brain an endless series of messages from the outside world. Also, his hearing was acute, and had been so trained that it operated automatically. Without conscious effort, he heard all the slight sounds in the apparent quiet—heard, and differentiated, and classified these sounds—whether they were of the wind rustling the leaves, of the humming of bees and gnats, of the distant rumble of the sea that drifted to him only in lulls, or of the gopher, just under his foot, shoving a pouchful of earth into the entrance of his hole.

Suddenly he became alertly tense. Sound, sight, and odor had given him a simultaneous warning. His hand went back to the old man, touching him, and the pair stood still. Ahead, at one side of the top of the embankment, arose a crackling sound, and the boy's gaze was fixed on the tops of the agitated bushes. Then a large bear, a grizzly, crashed into view, and likewise stopped abruptly, at sight of the humans. He did not like them, and growled querulously. Slowly the boy fitted the arrow to the bow, and slowly he pulled the bowstring taut. But he never removed his eyes from the bear. The old man peered from under his green leaf at the danger, and stood as quietly as the boy. For a few seconds this mutual scrutinizing went on; then, the bear betraying a growing irritability, the boy, with a movement of his head, indicated that the old man must step aside from the trail and go down the embankment. The boy followed, going backward, still holding the bow taut and ready. They waited till a crashing among the bushes from the opposite side of the embankment told them the bear had gone on. The boy grinned as he led back to the trail.

"A big un, Granser," he chuckled.

The old man shook his head.

"They get thicker every day," he complained in a thin, undependable falsetto. "Who'd have thought I'd live to see the time when a man would be afraid of his life on the way to the Cliff House. When I was a boy, Edwin, men and women and little babies used to come out here from San Francisco by tens of thousands on a nice day. And there weren't any bears then. No, sir. They used to pay money to look at them in cages, they were that rare."

"What is money, Granser?"

Before the old man could answer, the boy recollected and triumphantly shoved his hand into a pouch under his bear-skin and pulled forth a battered and tarnished silver dollar. The old man's eyes glistened, as he held the coin close to them.

"I can't see," he muttered. "You look and see if you can make out the date, Edwin."

The boy laughed.

"You're a great Granser," he cried delightedly, "always making believe them little marks mean something."

The old man manifested an accustomed chagrin as he brought the coin back again close to his own eyes.

"2012," he shrilled, and then fell to cackling grotesquely. "That was the year Morgan the Fifth was appointed President of the United States by the Board of Magnates. It must have been one of the last coins minted, for the Scarlet Death came in 2013. Lord! Lord!—think of it! Sixty years ago, and I am the only person alive to-day that lived in those times. Where did you find it, Edwin?"

The boy, who had been regarding him with the tolerant curiousness one accords to the prattlings of the feeble-minded, answered promptly.

"I got it off of Hoo-Hoo. He found it when we was herdin' goats down near San José last spring. Hoo-Hoo said it was *money*. Ain't you hungry, Granser?"

The ancient caught his staff in a tighter grip and urged along the trail, his old eyes shining greedily.

"I hope Har-Lip 's found a crab. . . or two," he mumbled. "They're good eating, crabs, mighty good eating when you've no more teeth and you've got grandsons that love their old grandsire and make a point of catching crabs for him. When I was a boy—"

But Edwin, suddenly stopped by what he saw, was drawing the bowstring on a fitted arrow. He had paused on the brink of a crevasse in the embankment. An ancient culvert had here washed out, and the stream, no longer confined, had cut a passage through the fill. On the opposite side, the end of a rail projected and overhung. It showed rustily through the creeping vines which overran it. Beyond, crouching by a bush, a rabbit looked across at him in trembling hesitancy. Fully fifty feet was the distance, but the arrow flashed true; and the transfixed rabbit, crying out in sudden fright and hurt, struggled painfully away into the brush. The boy himself was a flash of brown skin and flying fur as he bounded down the steep wall of the gap and up the other side. His lean muscles were springs of steel that released into graceful and efficient action. A hundred feet beyond, in a tangle of bushes, he overtook the wounded creature, knocked its head on a convenient tree-trunk, and turned it over to Granser to carry.

"Rabbit is good, very good," the ancient quavered, "but when it comes to a toothsome delicacy I prefer crab. When I was a boy—"

"Why do you say so much that ain't got no sense?" Edwin impatiently interrupted the other's threatened garrulousness.

The boy did not exactly utter these words, but something that remotely resembled them and that was more guttural and explosive and economical of qualifying phrases. His speech showed distant kinship with that of the old man, and the latter's speech was approximately an English that had gone through a bath of corrupt usage.

"What I want to know," Edwin continued, "is why you call crab 'toothsome delicacy?' Crab is crab, ain't it? No one I never heard calls it such funny things."

The old man sighed but did not answer, and they moved on in silence. The surf grew suddenly louder, as they emerged from the forest upon a stretch of sand dunes bordering the sea. A few goats were browsing among the sandy hillocks, and a skin-clad boy, aided by a wolfish-looking dog that was only faintly reminiscent of a collie, was watching them. Mingled with the roar of the surf was a continuous, deep-throated barking or bellowing, which came from a cluster of jagged rocks a hundred yards out from shore. Here huge sea-lions hauled themselves up to lie in the sun or battle with one another. In the immediate foreground arose the smoke of a fire, tended by a third savage-looking boy. Crouched near him were several wolfish dogs similar to the one that guarded the goats.

The old man accelerated his pace, sniffing eagerly as he neared the fire.

"Mussels! " he muttered ecstatically. "Mussels! And ain't that a crab, Hoo-Hoo? Ain't that a crab? My, my, you boys are good to your old grandsire."

Hoo-Hoo, who was apparently of the same age as Edwin, grinned.

"All you want, Granser. I got four."

The old man's palsied eagerness was pitiful. Sitting down in the sand as quickly as his stiff limbs would let him, he poked a large rock-mussel from out of the coals. The heat had forced its shells apart, and the meat, salmon-colored, was thoroughly cooked. Between thumb and forefinger, in trembling haste, he caught the morsel and carried it to his mouth. But it was too hot, and the next moment was violently ejected.

The old man spluttered with the pain, and tears ran out of his eyes and down his cheeks.

The boys were true savages, possessing only the cruel humor of the savage. To them the incident was excruciatingly funny, and they burst into loud laughter. Hoo-Hoo danced up and down, while Edwin rolled gleefully on the ground. The boy with the goats came running to join in the fun.

"Set 'em to cool, Edwin, set 'em to cool," the old man besought, in the midst of his grief, making no attempt to wipe away the tears that still flowed from his eyes. "And cool a crab, Edwin, too. You know your grandsire likes crabs."

From the coals arose a great sizzling, which proceeded from the many mussels bursting open their shells and exuding their moisture. They were large shellfish, running from three to six inches in length. The boys raked them out with sticks and placed them on a large piece of driftwood to cool.

"When I was a boy, we did not laugh at our elders; we respected them."

The boys took no notice, and Granser continued to babble an incoherent flow of complaint and censure. But this time he was more careful, and did not burn his mouth. All began to eat, using nothing but their hands and making loud mouth-noises and lip-smackings. The third boy, who was called Hare-Lip, slyly deposited a pinch of sand on a mussel the ancient was carrying to his mouth; and when the grit of it bit into the old fellow's mucous membrane and gums, the laughter was again uproarious. He was unaware that a joke had been played on him, and spluttered and spat until Edwin, relenting, gave him a gourd of fresh water with which to wash out his mouth.

"Where's them crabs, Hoo-Hoo?" Edwin demanded. "Granser's set upon having a snack."

Again Granser's eyes burned with greediness as a large crab was handed to him. It was a shell with legs and all complete, but the meat had long since departed. With shaky fingers and babblings of anticipation, the old man broke off a leg and found it filled with emptiness.

"The crabs, Hoo-Hoo?" he wailed. "The crabs?"

"I was fooling Granser. They ain't no crabs! I never found one."

The boys were overwhelmed with delight at sight of the tears of senile disappointment that dribbled down the old man's cheeks. Then, unnoticed, Hoo-Hoo replaced the empty shell with a fresh-cooked crab. Already dismembered, from the cracked legs the white meat sent forth a small cloud of savory steam. This attracted the old man's nostrils, and he looked down in amazement.

The change of his mood to one of joy was immediate. He snuffled and muttered and mumbled, making almost a croon of delight, as he began to eat. Of this the boys took little notice, for it was an accustomed spectacle. Nor did they notice his occasional exclamations and utterances of phrases which meant nothing to them, as, for instance, when he smacked his lips and champed his gums while muttering: "Mayonnaise! Just think—mayonnaise! And it's sixty years since the last was ever made! Two generations and never a smell of it! Why, in those days it was served in every restaurant with crab."

When he could eat no more, the old man sighed, wiped his hands on his naked legs, and gazed out over the sea. With the content of a full stomach, he waxed reminiscent.

"To think of it! I've seen this beach alive with men, women, and children on a pleasant Sunday. And there weren't any bears to eat them up, either. And right up there on the cliff was a big restaurant where you could get anything you wanted to eat. Four million people lived in San Francisco then. And now, in the whole city and county there aren't forty all told. And out there on the sea were ships and ships always to be seen, going in for the Golden Gate or coming out. And airships in the air—dirigibles and flying machines. They could travel two hundred miles an hour. The mail contracts with the New York and San Francisco Limited demanded that for the minimum. There was a chap, a Frenchman, I forget his name, who succeeded in making three hundred; but the thing was risky, too risky for conservative persons. But he was on the right clew, and he would have managed it if it hadn't been for the Great Plague. When I was a boy, there were men alive who remembered the coming of the first aeroplanes, and now I have lived to see the last of them, and that sixty years ago."

The old man babbled on, unheeded by the boys, who were long accustomed to his garrulousness, and whose vocabularies, besides, lacked the greater portion of the words he used. It was noticeable that in these rambling soliloquies his English seemed to recrudesce into better construction and phraseology. But when he talked directly with the boys it lapsed, largely, into their own uncouth and simpler forms.

"But there weren't many crabs in those days," the old man wandered on. "They were fished out, and they were great delicacies. The open season was only a month long, too. And now crabs are accessible the whole year around. Think of it—catching all the crabs you want, any time you want, in the surf of the Cliff House beach! "

A sudden commotion among the goats brought the boys to their feet. The dogs about the fire rushed to join their snarling fellow who guarded the goats, while the goats themselves stampeded in the direction of their human protectors. A half dozen forms, lean and gray, glided about on the sand hillocks and faced the bristling dogs. Edwin arched an arrow that fell short. But Hare-Lip, with a sling such as David carried into battle against Goliath, hurled a stone through the air that whistled from the speed of its flight. It fell squarely among the wolves and caused them to slink away toward the dark depths of the eucalyptus forest.

The boys laughed and lay down again in the sand, while Granser sighed ponderously. He had eaten too much, and, with hands clasped on his paunch, the fingers interlaced, he resumed his maunderings.

" 'The fleeting systems lapse like foam,' " he mumbled what was evidently a quotation. "That's it—foam, and fleeting. All man's toil upon the planet was just so much foam. He domesticated the serviceable animals, destroyed the hostile ones, and cleared the land of its wild vegetation. And then he passed, and the flood of primordial life rolled back again, sweeping his handiwork away—the weeds and the forest inundated his fields, the beasts of prey swept over his flocks, and now there are wolves on the Cliff House beach." He was appalled by the thought. "Where four million people disported themselves, the wild wolves roam to-day, and the savage progeny of our loins, with prehistoric weapons, defend themselves against the fanged despoilers. Think of it! And all because of the Scarlet Death—"

The adjective had caught Hare-Lip's ear.

"He's always saying that," he said to Edwin. "What is *scarlet*? "

" 'The scarlet of the maples can shake me like the cry of bugles going by,' " the old man quoted.

"It's red," Edwin answered the question. "And you don't know it because you come from the Chauffeur Tribe. They never did know nothing, none of them. Scarlet is red—I know that."

"Red is red, ain't it?" Hare-Lip grumbled. "Then what's the good of gettin' cocky and calling it scarlet?"

"Granser, what for do you always say so much what nobody knows?" he asked. "Scarlet ain't anything, but red is red. Why don't you say red, then?"

"Red is not the right word," was the reply. "The plague was scarlet. The whole face and body turned scarlet in an hour's time. Don't I know? Didn't I see enough of it? And I am telling you it was scarlet because—well, because it *was* scarlet. There is no other word for it."

"Red is good enough for me," Hare-Lip muttered obstinately. "My dad calls red red, and he ought to know. He says everybody died of the Red Death."

"Your dad is a common fellow, descended from a common fellow," Granser retorted heatedly. "Don't I know the beginnings of the Chauffeurs? Your grandsire was a chauffeur, a servant, and without education. He worked for other persons. But your grandmother was of good stock, only the children did not take after her. Don't I remember when I first met them, catching fish at Lake Temescal?"

"What is *education*?" Edwin asked.

"Calling red scarlet," Hare-Lip sneered, then returned to the attack on Granser. "My dad told me, an' he got it from his dad afore he croaked, that your wife was a Santa Rosan, an' that she was sure no account. He said she was a *hash-slinger* before the Red Death, though I don't know what a *hash-slinger* is. You can tell me, Edwin."

But Edwin shook his head in token of ignorance.

"It is true, she was a waitress," Granser acknowledged. "But she was a good woman, and your mother was her daughter. Women were very scarce in the days after the Plague. She was the only wife I could find, even if she was a *hash-slinger*, as your father calls it. But it is not nice to talk about our progenitors that way."

"Dad says that the wife of the first Chauffeur was a *lady*—"

"What's a *lady*?" Hoo-Hoo demanded.

"A *lady*'s a Chauffeur squaw," was the quick reply of Hare-Lip.

"The first Chauffeur was Bill, a common fellow, as I said before," the old man expounded; "but his wife was a lady, a great lady. Before

the Scarlet Death she was the wife of Van Worden. He was President
of the Board of Industrial Magnates, and was one of the dozen men
who ruled America. He was worth one billion, eight hundred millions
of dollars—coins like you have there in your pouch, Edwin. And then
came the Scarlet Death, and his wife became the wife of Bill, the first
Chauffeur. He used to beat her, too. I have seen it myself."

Hoo-Hoo, lying on his stomach and idly digging his toes in the sand,
cried out and investigated, first, his toe-nail, and next, the small hole he
had dug. The other two boys joined him, excavating the sand rapidly
with their hands till there lay three skeletons exposed. Two were of
adults, the third being that of a part-grown child. The old man hudged
along on the ground and peered at the find.

"Plague victims," he announced. "That's the way they died
everywhere in the last days. This must have been a family, running
away from the contagion and perishing here on the Cliff House beach.
They—what are you doing, Edwin?"

This question was asked in sudden dismay, as Edwin, using the back
of his hunting knife, began to knock out the teeth from the jaws of
one of the skulls.

"Going to string 'em," was the response.

The three boys were now hard at it; and quite a knocking and
hammering arose, in which Granser babbled on unnoticed.

"You are true savages. Already has begun the custom of wearing
human teeth. In another generation you will be perforating your noses
and ears and wearing ornaments of bone and shell. I know. The human
race is doomed to sink back farther and farther into the primitive night
ere again it begins its bloody climb upward to civilization. When we
increase and feel the lack of room, we will proceed to kill one another.
And then I suppose you will wear human scalp-locks at your waist,
as well—as you, Edwin, who are the gentlest of my grandsons, have
already begun with that vile pigtail. Throw it away, Edwin, boy; throw
it away."

"What a gabble the old geezer makes," Hare-Lip remarked, when,
the teeth all extracted, they began an attempt at equal division.

They were very quick and abrupt in their actions, and their speech,
in moments of hot discussion over the allotment of the choicer
teeth, was truly a gabble. They spoke in monosyllables and short

jerky sentences that was more a gibberish than a language. And yet, through it ran hints of grammatical construction, and appeared vestiges of the conjugation of some superior culture. Even the speech of Granser was so corrupt that were it put down literally it would be almost so much nonsense to the reader. This, however, was when he talked with the boys. When he got into the full swing of babbling to himself, it slowly purged itself into pure English. The sentences grew longer and were enunciated with a rhythm and ease that was reminiscent of the lecture platform.

"Tell us about the Red Death, Granser," Hare-Lip demanded, when the teeth affair had been satisfactorily concluded.

"The Scarlet Death," Edwin corrected.

"An' don't work all that funny lingo on us," Hare-Lip went on. "Talk sensible, Granser, like a Santa Rosan ought to talk. Other Santa Rosans don't talk like you."

II

The old man showed pleasure in being thus called upon. He cleared his throat and began.

"Twenty or thirty years ago my story was in great demand. But in these days nobody seems interested—"

"There you go!" Hare-Lip cried hotly. "Cut out the funny stuff and talk sensible. What's *interested*? You talk like a baby that don't know how."

"Let him alone," Edwin urged, "or he'll get mad and won't talk at all. Skip the funny places. We'll catch on to some of what he tells us."

"Let her go, Granser," Hoo-Hoo encouraged; for the old man was already maundering about the disrespect for elders and the reversion to cruelty of all humans that fell from high culture to primitive conditions.

The tale began.

"There were very many people in the world in those days. San Francisco alone held four millions—"

"What is millions?" Edwin interrupted.

Granser looked at him kindly.

"I know you cannot count beyond ten, so I will tell you. Hold up your two hands. On both of them you have altogether ten fingers and thumbs. Very well. I now take this grain of sand—you hold it, Hoo-Hoo." He dropped the grain of sand into the lad's palm and went on.

"Now that grain of sand stands for the ten fingers of Edwin. I add another grain. That's ten more fingers. And I add another, and another, and another, until I have added as many grains as Edwin has fingers and thumbs. That makes what I call one hundred. Remember that word—one hundred. Now I put this pebble in Hare-Lip's hand. It stands for ten grains of sand, or ten tens of fingers, or one hundred fingers. I put in ten pebbles. They stand for a thousand fingers. I take a mussel-shell, and it stands for ten pebbles, or one hundred grains of sand, or one thousand fingers. . . ."

And so on, laboriously, and with much reiteration, he strove to build up in their minds a crude conception of numbers. As the quantities increased, he had the boys holding different magnitudes in each of their hands. For still higher sums, he laid the symbols on the log of driftwood; and for symbols he was hard put, being compelled to use the teeth from the skulls for millions, and the crab-shells for billions. It was here that he stopped, for the boys were showing signs of becoming tired.

"There were four million people in San Francisco—four teeth."

The boys' eyes ranged along from the teeth and from hand to hand, down through the pebbles and sand-grains to Edwin's fingers. And back again they ranged along the ascending series in the effort to grasp such inconceivable numbers.

"That was a lot of folks, Granser," Edwin at last hazarded.

"Like sand on the beach here, like sand on the beach, each grain of sand a man, or woman, or child. Yes, my boy, all those people lived right here in San Francisco. And at one time or another all those people came out on this very beach—more people than there are grains of sand. More—more—more. And San Francisco was a noble city. And across the bay—where we camped last year, even more people lived, clear from Point Richmond, on the level ground and on the hills, all the way around to San Leandro—one great city of seven million people.—Seven teeth . . . there, that's it, seven millions."

Again the boys' eyes ranged up and down from Edwin's fingers to the teeth on the log.

"The world was full of people. The census of 2010 gave eight billions for the whole world—eight crab-shells, yes, eight billions. It was not like to-day. Mankind knew a great deal more about getting food. And the more food there was, the more people there were. In the year 1800, there were one hundred and seventy millions in Europe alone. One hundred years later—a grain of sand, Hoo-Hoo—one hundred years later, at 1900, there were five hundred millions in Europe—five grains of sand, Hoo-Hoo, and this one tooth. This shows how easy was the getting of food, and how men increased. And in the year 2000 there were fifteen hundred millions in Europe. And it was the same all over the rest of the world. Eight crab-shells there, yes, eight billion people were alive on the earth when the Scarlet Death began.

"I was a young man when the Plague came—twenty-seven years old; and I lived on the other side of San Francisco Bay, in Berkeley. You remember those great stone houses, Edwin, when we came down the hills from Contra Costa? That was where I lived, in those stone houses. I was a professor of English literature."

Much of this was over the heads of the boys, but they strove to comprehend dimly this tale of the past.

"What was them stone houses for?" Hare-Lip queried.

"You remember when your dad taught you to swim?" The boy nodded. "Well, in the University of California—that is the name we had for the houses—we taught young men and women how to think, just as I have taught you now, by sand and pebbles and shells, to know how many people lived in those days. There was very much to teach. The young men and women we taught were called students. We had large rooms in which we taught. I talked to them, forty or fifty at a time, just as I am talking to you now. I told them about the books other men had written before their time, and even, sometimes, in their time—"

"Was that all you did?—just talk, talk, talk?" Hoo-Hoo demanded. "Who hunted your meat for you? and milked the goats? and caught the fish?"

"A sensible question, Hoo-Hoo, a sensible question. As I have told you, in those days food-getting was easy. We were very wise. A few men got the food for many men. The other men did other things. As you say, I talked. I talked all the time, and for this food was given me—much food, fine food, beautiful food, food that I have not tasted in sixty years and shall never taste again. I sometimes think the most wonderful achievement of our tremendous civilization was food—its inconceivable abundance, its infinite variety, its marvellous delicacy.

O my grandsons, life was life in those days, when we had such wonderful things to eat."

This was beyond the boys, and they let it slip by, words and thoughts, as a mere senile wandering in the narrative.

"Our food-getters were called *freemen*. This was a joke. We of the ruling classes owned all the land, all the machines, everything. These food-getters were our slaves. We took almost all the food they got, and left them a little so that they might eat, and work, and get us more food—"

"I'd have gone into the forest and got food for myself," Hare-Lip announced; "and if any man tried to take it away from me, I'd have killed him."

The old man laughed.

"Did I not tell you that we of the ruling class owned all the land, all the forest, everything? Any food-getter who would not get food for us, him we punished or compelled to starve to death. And very few did that. They preferred to get food for us, and make clothes for us, and prepare and administer to us a thousand—a mussel-shell, Hoo-Hoo—a thousand satisfactions and delights. And I was Professor Smith in those days—Professor James Howard Smith. And my lecture courses were very popular—that is, very many of the young men and women liked to hear me talk about the books other men had written.

"And I was very happy, and I had beautiful things to eat. And my hands were soft, because I did no work with them, and my body was clean all over and dressed in the softest garments—" He surveyed his mangy goat-skin with disgust. "We did not wear such things in those days. Even the slaves had better garments. And we were most clean. We washed our faces and hands often every day. You boys never wash unless you fall into the water or go swimming."

"Neither do you Granser," Hoo-Hoo retorted.

"I know, I know, I am a filthy old man, but times have changed. Nobody washes these days, there are no conveniences. It is sixty years since I have seen a piece of soap. "You do not know what soap is, and I shall not tell you, for I am telling the story of the Scarlet Death. You know what sickness is. We called it a disease. Very many of the diseases came from what we called germs. Remember that word—germs. A germ is a very small thing. It is like a woodtick, such as you find on the dogs in the spring of the year when they run in the forest. Only the germ is very small. It is so small that you cannot see it—"

Hoo-Hoo began to laugh.

"You're a queer un, Granser, talking about things you can't see. If you can't see 'em, how do you know they are? That's what I want to know. How do you know anything you can't see?"

"A good question, a very good question, Hoo-Hoo. But we did see—some of them. We had what we called microscopes and ultramicroscopes, and we put them to our eyes and looked through them, so that we saw things larger than they really were, and many things we could not see without the microscopes at all. Our best ultramicroscopes could make a germ look forty thousand times larger. A mussel-shell is a thousand fingers like Edwin's. Take forty mussel-shells, and by as many times larger was the germ when we looked at it through a microscope. And after that, we had other ways, by using what we called moving pictures, of making the forty-thousand-times germ many, many thousand times larger still. And thus we saw all these things which our eyes of themselves could not see. Take a grain of sand. Break it into ten pieces. Take one piece and break it into ten. Break one of those pieces into ten, and one of those into ten, and one of those into ten, and one of those into ten, and do it all day, and maybe, by sunset, you will have a piece as small as one of the germs."

The boys were openly incredulous. Hare-Lip sniffed and sneered and Hoo-Hoo snickered, until Edwin nudged them to be silent.

"The woodtick sucks the blood of the dog, but the germ, being so very small, goes right into the blood of the body, and there it has many children. In those days there would be as many as a billion—a crab-shell, please—as many as that crab-shell in one man's body. We called germs micro-organisms. When a few million, or a billion, of them were in a man, in all the blood of a man, he was sick. These germs were a disease. There were many different kinds of them—more different kinds than there are grains of sand on this beach. We knew only a few of the kinds. The micro-organic world was an invisible world, a world we could not see, and we knew very little about it. Yet we did know something. There was the *bacillus anthracis*; there was the *micrococcus*; there was the *Bacterium termo*, and the *Bacterium lactis*—that's what turns the goat milk sour even to this day, Hare-Lip; and there were *Schizomycetes* without end. And there were many others. . ."

Here the old man launched into a disquisition on germs and their natures, using words and phrases of such extraordinary length and meaninglessness, that the boys grinned at one another and looked out over the deserted ocean till they forgot the old man was babbling on.

"But the Scarlet Death, Granser," Edwin at last suggested.

Granser recollected himself, and with a start tore himself away from the rostrum of the lecture-hall, where, to another world audience, he had been expounding the latest theory, sixty years gone, of germs and germ-diseases.

"Yes, yes, Edwin; I had forgotten. Sometimes the memory of the past is very strong upon me, and I forget that I am a dirty old man, clad in goat-skin, wandering with my savage grandsons who are goatherds in the primeval wilderness. 'The fleeting systems lapse like foam,' and so lapsed our glorious, colossal civilization. I am Granser, a tired old man. I belong to the tribe of Santa Rosans. I married into that tribe. My sons and daughters married into the Chauffeurs, the Sacramentos, and the Palo-Altos. You, Hare-Lip, are of the Chauffeurs. You, Edwin, are of the Sacramentos. And you, Hoo-Hoo, are of the Palo-Altos. Your tribe takes its name from a town that was near the seat of another great institution of learning. It was called Stanford University. Yes, I remember now. It is perfectly clear. I was telling you of the Scarlet Death. Where was I in my story?"

"You was telling about germs, the things you can't see but which make men sick," Edwin prompted.

"Yes, that's where I was. A man did not notice at first when only a few of these germs got into his body. But each germ broke in half and became two germs, and they kept doing this very rapidly so that in a short time there were many millions of them in the body. Then the man was sick. He had a disease, and the disease was named after the kind of a germ that was in him. It might be measles, it might be influenza, it might be yellow fever; it might be any of thousands and thousands of kinds of diseases.

"Now this is the strange thing about these germs. There were always new ones coming to live in men's bodies. Long and long and long ago, when there were only a few men in the world, there were few diseases. But as men increased and lived closely together in great cities and civilizations, new diseases arose, new kinds of germs entered their bodies. Thus were countless millions and billions of human beings killed. And the more thickly men packed together, the more terrible were the new diseases that came to be. Long before my time, in the middle ages, there was the Black Plague that swept across Europe. It swept across Europe many times. There was tuberculosis, that entered into men wherever they were thickly packed. A hundred years before my time there was the bubonic plague. And in Africa was the sleeping sickness. The bacteriologists fought all these sicknesses and destroyed them, just as you boys fight the wolves away from your goats, or squash the mosquitoes that light on you. The bacteriologists—"

"But, Granser, what is a what-you-call-it?" Edwin interrupted.

"You, Edwin, are a goatherd. Your task is to watch the goats. You know a great deal about goats. A bacteriologist watches germs. That's his task, and he knows a great deal about them. So, as I was saying, the bacteriologists fought with the germs and destroyed them—sometimes. There was leprosy, a horrible disease. A hundred years before I was born, the bacteriologists discovered the germ of leprosy. They knew all about it. They made pictures of it. I have seen those pictures. But they never found a way to kill it. But in 1984, there was the Pantoblast Plague, a disease that broke out in a country called Brazil and that killed millions of people. But the bacteriologists found it out, and found the way to kill it, so that the Pantoblast Plague went no farther. They made what they called a serum, which they put into a man's body and which killed the pantoblast germs without killing the man. And in 1910, there was Pellagra, and also the hookworm. These were easily killed by the bacteriologists. But in 1947 there arose a new disease that had never been seen before. It got into the bodies of babies of only ten months old or less, and it made them unable to move their hands and feet, or to eat, or anything; and the bacteriologists were eleven years in discovering how to kill that particular germ and save the babies.

"In spite of all these diseases, and of all the new ones that continued to arise, there were more and more men in the world. This was because it was easy to get food. The easier it was to get food, the more men there were; the more men there were, the more thickly were they packed together on the earth; and the more thickly they were packed, the more new kinds of germs became diseases. There were warnings. Soldervetzsky, as early as 1929, told the bacteriologists that they had no guaranty against some new disease, a thousand times more deadly than any they knew, arising and killing by the hundreds of millions and even by the billion. You see, the micro-organic world remained a mystery to the end. They knew there was such a world, and that from time to time armies of new germs emerged from it to kill men. And that was all they knew about it. For all they knew, in that invisible micro-organic world there might be as many different kinds of germs as there are grains of sand on this beach. And also, in that same invisible world it might well be that new kinds of germs came to be. It might be there that life originated—the 'abysmal fecundity,' Soldervetzsky called it, applying the words of other men who had written before him. . . ."

It was at this point that Hare-Lip rose to his feet, an expression of huge contempt on his face.

"Granser," he announced, "you make me sick with your gabble. Why don't you tell about the Red Death? If you ain't going to, say so, an' we'll start back for camp."

The old man looked at him and silently began to cry. The weak tears of age rolled down his cheeks and all the feebleness of his eighty-seven years showed in his grief-stricken countenance.

"Sit down," Edwin counselled soothingly. "Granser's all right. He's just gettin' to the Scarlet Death, ain't you, Granser? He's just goin' to tell us about it right now. Sit down, Hare-Lip. Go ahead, Granser."

III

The old man wiped the tears away on his grimy knuckles and took up the tale in a tremulous, piping voice that soon strengthened as he got the swing of the narrative.

"It was in the summer of 2013 that the Plague came. I was twenty-seven years old, and well do I remember it. Wireless despatches—"

Hare-Lip spat loudly his disgust, and Granser hastened to make amends.

"We talked through the air in those days, thousands and thousands of miles. And the word came of a strange disease that had broken out in New York. There were seventeen millions of people living then in that noblest city of America. Nobody thought anything about the news.

It was only a small thing. There had been only a few deaths. It seemed, though, that they had died very quickly, and that one of the first signs of the disease was the turning red of the face and all the body. Within twenty-four hours came the report of the first case in Chicago. And on the same day, it was made public that London, the greatest city in the world, next to Chicago, had been secretly fighting the plague for two weeks and censoring the news despatches—that is, not permitting the word to go forth to the rest of the world that London had the plague.

"It looked serious, but we in California, like everywhere else, were not alarmed. We were sure that the bacteriologists would find a way to overcome this new germ, just as they had overcome other germs in the past. But the trouble was the astonishing quickness with which this germ destroyed human beings, and the fact that it inevitably killed any human body it entered. No one ever recovered. There was the old Asiatic cholera, when you might eat dinner with a well man in the evening, and the next morning, if you got up early enough, you would see him being hauled by your window in the death-cart. But this new plague was quicker than that—much quicker. From the moment of the first signs of it, a man would be dead in an hour. Some lasted for several hours. Many died within ten or fifteen minutes of the appearance of the first signs.

"The heart began to beat faster and the heat of the body to increase. Then came the scarlet rash, spreading like wildfire over the face and body. Most persons never noticed the increase in heat and heart-beat, and the first they knew was when the scarlet rash came out. Usually, they had convulsions at the time of the appearance of the rash. But these convulsions did not last long and were not very severe. If one lived through them, he became perfectly quiet, and only did he feel a numbness swiftly creeping up his body from the feet. The heels became numb first, then the legs, and hips, and when the numbness reached as high as his heart he died. They did not rave or sleep. Their minds always remained cool and calm up to the moment their heart numbed and stopped. And another strange thing was the rapidity of decomposition. No sooner was a person dead than the body seemed to fall to pieces, to fly apart, to melt away even as you looked at it. That was one of the reasons the plague spread so rapidly. All the billions of germs in a corpse were so immediately released.

"And it was because of all this that the bacteriologists had so little chance in fighting the germs. They were killed in their laboratories even as they studied the germ of the Scarlet Death. They were heroes. As fast as they perished, others stepped forth and took their places.

It was in London that they first isolated it. The news was telegraphed everywhere. Trask was the name of the man who succeeded in this, but within thirty hours he was dead. Then came the struggle in all the laboratories to find something that would kill the plague germs. All drugs failed. You see, the problem was to get a drug, or serum, that would kill the germs in the body and not kill the body. They tried to fight it with other germs, to put into the body of a sick man germs that were the enemies of the plague germs—"

"And you can't see these germ-things, Granser," Hare-Lip objected, "and here you gabble, gabble, gabble about them as if they was anything, when they're nothing at all. Anything you can't see, ain't, that's what. Fighting things that ain't with things that ain't! They must have been all fools in them days. That's why they croaked. I ain't goin' to believe in such rot, I tell you that."

Granser promptly began to weep, while Edwin hotly took up his defence.

"Look here, Hare-Lip, you believe in lots of things you can't see."

Hare-Lip shook his head.

"You believe in dead men walking about. You never seen one dead man walk about."

"I tell you I seen 'em, last winter, when I was wolf-hunting with dad."

"Well, you always spit when you cross running water," Edwin challenged.

"That's to keep off bad luck," was Hare-Lip's defence.

"You believe in bad luck?"

"Sure."

"An' you ain't never seen bad luck," Edwin concluded triumphantly. "You're just as bad as Granser and his germs. You believe in what you don't see. Go on, Granser."

Hare-Lip, crushed by this metaphysical defeat, remained silent, and the old man went on. Often and often, though this narrative must not be clogged by the details, was Granser's tale interrupted while the boys squabbled among themselves. Also, among themselves they kept up a constant, low-voiced exchange of explanation and conjecture, as they strove to follow the old man into his unknown and vanished world.

"The Scarlet Death broke out in San Francisco. The first death came on a Monday morning. By Thursday they were dying like flies in Oakland and San Francisco. They died everywhere—in their beds, at their work, walking along the street. It was on Tuesday that I saw my first death—Miss Collbran, one of my students, sitting right there before my eyes, in my lecture-room. I noticed her face while I was talking. It had suddenly turned scarlet. I ceased speaking and could only look at her, for the first fear of the plague was already on all of us and we knew that it had come. The young women screamed and ran out of the room. So did the young men run out, all but two. Miss Collbran's convulsions were very mild and lasted less than a minute. One of the young men fetched her a glass of water. She drank only a little of it, and cried out:

" 'My feet! All sensation has left them.'

"After a minute she said, 'I have no feet. I am unaware that I have any feet. And my knees are cold. I can scarcely feel that I have knees.'

"She lay on the floor, a bundle of notebooks under her head. And we could do nothing. The coldness and the numbness crept up past her hips to her heart, and when it reached her heart she was dead. In fifteen minutes, by the clock—I timed it—she was dead, there, in my own classroom, dead. And she was a very beautiful, strong, healthy young woman. And from the first sign of the plague to her death only fifteen minutes elapsed. That will show you how swift was the Scarlet Death.

"Yet in those few minutes I remained with the dying woman in my classroom, the alarm had spread over the university; and the students, by thousands, all of them, had deserted the lecture-room and laboratories. When I emerged, on my way to make report to the President of the Faculty, I found the university deserted. Across the campus were several stragglers hurrying for their homes. Two of them were running.

"President Hoag, I found in his office, all alone, looking very old and very gray, with a multitude of wrinkles in his face that I had never seen before. At the sight of me, he pulled himself to his feet and tottered away to the inner office, banging the door after him and locking it. You see, he knew I had been exposed, and he was afraid.

He shouted to me through the door to go away. I shall never forget my feelings as I walked down the silent corridors and out across that deserted campus. I was not afraid. I had been exposed, and I looked upon myself as already dead. It was not that, but a feeling of awful depression that impressed me. Everything had stopped. It was like the end of the world to me—my world. I had been born within sight and sound of the university. It had been my predestined career. My father had been a professor there before me, and his father before him. For a century and a half had this university, like a splendid machine, been running steadily on. And now, in an instant, it had stopped. It was like seeing the sacred flame die down on some thrice-sacred altar. I was shocked, unutterably shocked.

"When I arrived home, my housekeeper screamed as I entered, and fled away. And when I rang, I found the housemaid had likewise fled. I investigated. In the kitchen I found the cook on the point of departure. But she screamed, too, and in her haste dropped a suitcase of her personal belongings and ran out of the house and across the grounds, still screaming. I can hear her scream to this day. You see, we did not act in this way when ordinary diseases smote us. We were always calm over such things, and sent for the doctors and nurses who knew just what to do. But this was different. It struck so suddenly, and killed so swiftly, and never missed a stroke. When the scarlet rash appeared on a person's face, that person was marked by death. There was never a known case of a recovery.

"I was alone in my big house. As I have told you often before, in those days we could talk with one another over wires or through the air. The telephone bell rang, and I found my brother talking to me. He told me that he was not coming home for fear of catching the plague from me, and that he had taken our two sisters to stop at Professor Bacon's home. He advised me to remain where I was, and wait to find out whether or not I had caught the plague.

"To all of this I agreed, staying in my house and for the first time in my life attempting to cook. And the plague did not come out on me. By means of the telephone I could talk with whomsoever I pleased and get the news. Also, there were the newspapers, and I ordered all of them to be thrown up to my door so that I could know what was happening with the rest of the world.

"New York City and Chicago were in chaos. And what happened with them was happening in all the large cities. A third of the New York police were dead. Their chief was also dead, likewise the mayor. All law and order had ceased. The bodies were lying in the streets un-buried. All railroads and vessels carrying food and such things into the great city had ceased runnings and mobs of the hungry poor were pillaging the stores and warehouses. Murder and robbery and drunkenness were everywhere. Already the people had fled from the city by millions—at first the rich, in their private motor-cars and dirigibles, and then the great mass of the population, on foot, carrying the plague with them, themselves starving and pillaging the farmers and all the towns and villages on the way.

"The man who sent this news, the wireless operator, was alone with his instrument on the top of a lofty building. The people remaining in the city—he estimated them at several hundred thousand—had gone mad from fear and drink, and on all sides of him great fires were raging. He was a hero, that man who staid by his post—an obscure newspaperman, most likely.

"For twenty-four hours, he said, no transatlantic airships had arrived, and no more messages were coming from England. He did state, though, that a message from Berlin—that's in Germany—announced that Hoffmeyer, a bacteriologist of the Metchnikoff School, had discovered the serum for the plague. That was the last word, to this day, that we of America ever received from Europe. If Hoffmeyer discovered the serum, it was too late, or otherwise, long ere this, explorers from Europe would have come looking for us. We can only conclude that what happened in America happened in Europe, and that, at the best, some several score may have survived the Scarlet Death on that whole continent.

"For one day longer the despatches continued to come from New York. Then they, too, ceased. The man who had sent them, perched in his lofty building, had either died of the plague or been consumed in the great conflagrations he had described as raging around him. And what had occurred in New York had been duplicated in all the other cities. It was the same in San Francisco, and Oakland, and Berkeley. By Thursday the people were dying so rapidly that their corpses could not be handled, and dead bodies lay everywhere. Thursday night the panic outrush for the country began. Imagine, my grandsons, people, thicker than the salmon-run you have seen on the Sacramento river, pouring out of the cities by millions, madly over the country, in vain attempt to escape the ubiquitous death. You see, they carried the germs with them. Even the airships of the rich, fleeing for mountain and desert fastnesses, carried the germs.

"Hundreds of these airships escaped to Hawaii, and not only did they bring the plague with them, but they found the plague already there before them. This we learned, by the despatches, until all order in San Francisco vanished, and there were no operators left at their posts to receive or send. It was amazing, astounding, this loss of communication with the world. It was exactly as if the world had ceased, been blotted out. For sixty years that world has no longer existed for me. I know there must be such places as New York, Europe, Asia, and Africa; but not one word has been heard of them—not in sixty years. With the coming of the Scarlet Death the world fell apart, absolutely, irretrievably. Ten thousand years of culture and civilization passed in the twinkling of an eye, 'lapsed like foam.'

"I was telling about the airships of the rich. They carried the plague with them and no matter where they fled, they died. I never encountered but one survivor of any of them—Mungerson. He was afterwards a Santa Rosan, and he married my eldest daughter. He came into the tribe eight years after the plague. He was then nineteen years old, and he was compelled to wait twelve years more before he could marry. You see, there were no unmarried women, and some of the older daughters of the Santa Rosans were already bespoken. So he was forced to wait until my Mary had grown to sixteen years. It was his son, Gimp-Leg, who was killed last year by the mountain lion.

"Mungerson was eleven years old at the time of the plague. His father was one of the Industrial Magnates, a very wealthy, powerful man. It was on his airship, the Condor, that they were fleeing, with all the family, for the wilds of British Columbia, which is far to the north of here. But there was some accident, and they were wrecked near Mount Shasta. You have heard of that mountain. It is far to the north. The plague broke out amongst them, and this boy of eleven was the only survivor. For eight years he was alone, wandering over a deserted land and looking vainly for his own kind. And at last, travelling south, he picked up with us, the Santa Rosans.

"But I am ahead of my story. When the great exodus from the cities around San Francisco Bay began, and while the telephones were still working, I talked with my brother. I told him this flight from the cities was insanity, that there were no symptoms of the plague in me, and that the thing for us to do was to isolate ourselves and our relatives in some safe place. We decided on the Chemistry Building, at the university, and we planned to lay in a supply of provisions, and by force of arms to prevent any other persons from forcing their presence upon us after we had retired to our refuge.

"All this being arranged, my brother begged me to stay in my own house for at least twenty-four hours more, on the chance of the plague developing in me. To this I agreed, and he promised to come for me next day. We talked on over the details of the provisioning and the defending of the Chemistry Building until the telephone died. It died in the midst of our conversation. That evening there were no electric lights, and I was alone in my house in the darkness. No more newspapers were being printed, so I had no knowledge of what was taking place outside. I heard sounds of rioting and of pistol shots, and from my windows I could see the glare of the sky of some conflagration in the direction of Oakland. It was a night of terror. I did not sleep a wink. A man—why and how I do not know—was killed on the sidewalk in front of the house. I heard the rapid reports of an automatic pistol, and a few minutes later the wounded wretch crawled up to my door, moaning and crying out for help. Arming myself with two automatics, I went to him. By the light of a match I ascertained that while he was dying of the bullet wounds, at the same time the plague was on him. I fled indoors, whence I heard him moan and cry out for half an hour longer.

"In the morning, my brother came to me. I had gathered into a handbag what things of value I purposed taking, but when I saw his face I knew that he would never accompany me to the Chemistry Building. The plague was on him. He intended shaking my hand, but I went back hurriedly before him.

" 'Look at yourself in the mirror,' I commanded.

"He did so, and at sight of his scarlet face, the color deepening as he looked at it, he sank down nervelessly in a chair.

" 'My God!' he said. 'I've got it. Don't come near me. I am a dead man.'

"Then the convulsions seized him. He was two hours in dying, and he was conscious to the last, complaining about the coldness and loss of sensation in his feet, his calves, his thighs, until at last it was his heart and he was dead.

"That was the way the Scarlet Death slew. I caught up my handbag and fled. The sights in the streets were terrible. One stumbled on bodies everywhere. Some were not yet dead. And even as you looked, you saw men sink down with the death fastened upon them. There were numerous fires burning in Berkeley, while Oakland and San Francisco were apparently being swept by vast conflagrations. The smoke of the burning filled the heavens, so that the midday was as a gloomy twilight, and, in the shifts of wind, sometimes the sun shone through dimly, a dull red orb. Truly, my grandsons, it was like the last days of the end of the world.

"There were numerous stalled motor cars, showing that the gasoline and the engine supplies of the garages had given out. I remember one such car. A man and a woman lay back dead in the seats, and on the pavement near it were two more women and a child. Strange and terrible sights there were on every hand. People slipped by silently, furtively, like ghosts—white-faced women carrying infants in their arms; fathers leading children by the hand; singly, and in couples, and in families—all fleeing out of the city of death. Some carried supplies of food, others blankets and valuables, and there were many who carried nothing.

"There was a grocery store—a place where food was sold. The man to whom it belonged—I knew him well—a quiet, sober, but stupid and obstinate fellow, was defending it. The windows and doors had been broken in, but he, inside, hiding behind a counter, was discharging his pistol at a number of men on the sidewalk who were breaking in. In the entrance were several bodies—of men, I decided, whom he had killed earlier in the day. Even as I looked on from a distance, I saw one of the robbers break the windows of the adjoining store, a place where shoes were sold, and deliberately set fire to it. I did not go to the groceryman's assistance. The time for such acts had already passed. Civilization was crumbling, and it was each for himself."

IV

"I went away hastily, down a cross-street, and at the first corner I saw
another tragedy. Two men of the working class had caught a man and
a woman with two children, and were robbing them. I knew the man
by sight, though I had never been introduced to him. He was a poet
whose verses I had long admired. Yet I did not go to his help, for at the
moment I came upon the scene there was a pistol shot, and I saw him
sinking to the ground. The woman screamed, and she was felled with
a fist-blow by one of the brutes. I cried out threateningly, whereupon
they discharged their pistols at me and I ran away around the corner.
Here I was blocked by an advancing conflagration. The buildings on
both sides were burning, and the street was filled with smoke and
flame. From somewhere in that murk came a woman's voice calling
shrilly for help. But I did not go to her. A man's heart turned to iron
amid such scenes, and one heard all too many appeals for help.

"Returning to the corner, I found the two robbers were gone. The
poet and his wife lay dead on the pavement. It was a shocking sight.
The two children had vanished—whither I could not tell. And I knew,
now, why it was that the fleeing persons I encountered slipped along
so furtively and with such white faces. In the midst of our civilization,
down in our slums and labor-ghettos, we had bred a race of barbarians,
of savages; and now, in the time of our calamity, they turned upon us
like the wild beasts they were and destroyed us. And they destroyed
themselves as well. They inflamed themselves with strong drink and
committed a thousand atrocities, quarreling and killing one another in
the general madness. One group of workingmen I saw, of the better
sort, who had banded together, and, with their women and children
in their midst, the sick and aged in litters and being carried, and with a
number of horses pulling a truck-load of provisions, they were fighting
their way out of the city. They made a fine spectacle as they came
down the street through the drifting smoke, though they nearly shot
me when I first appeared in their path. As they went by, one of their
leaders shouted out to me in apologetic explanation. He said they were
killing the robbers and looters on sight, and that they had thus banded
together as the only-means by which to escape the prowlers.

"It was here that I saw for the first time what I was soon to
see so often. One of the marching men had suddenly shown the

unmistakable mark of the plague. Immediately those about him drew away, and he, without a remonstrance, stepped out of his place to let them pass on. A woman, most probably his wife, attempted to follow him. She was leading a little boy by the hand. But the husband commanded her sternly to go on, while others laid hands on her and restrained her from following him. This I saw, and I saw the man also, with his scarlet blaze of face, step into a doorway on the opposite side of the street. I heard the report of his pistol, and saw him sink lifeless to the ground.

"After being turned aside twice again by advancing fires, I succeeded in getting through to the university. On the edge of the campus I came upon a party of university folk who were going in the direction of the Chemistry Building. They were all family men, and their families were with them, including the nurses and the servants. Professor Badminton greeted me, I had difficulty in recognizing him. Somewhere he had gone through flames, and his beard was singed off. About his head was a bloody bandage, and his clothes were filthy. He told me he had prowlers, and that his brother had been killed the previous night, in the defence of their dwelling.

"Midway across the campus, he pointed suddenly to Mrs. Swinton's face. The unmistakable scarlet was there. Immediately all the other women set up a screaming and began to run away from her. Her two children were with a nurse, and these also ran with the women. But her husband, Doctor Swinton, remained with her.

" 'Go on, Smith,' he told me. 'Keep an eye on the children. As for me, I shall stay with my wife. I know she is as already dead, but I can't leave her. Afterwards, if I escape, I shall come to the Chemistry Building, and do you watch for me and let me in.'

"I left him bending over his wife and soothing her last moments, while I ran to overtake the party. We were the last to be admitted to the Chemistry Building. After that, with our automatic rifles we maintained our isolation. By our plans, we had arranged for a company of sixty to be in this refuge. Instead, every one of the number originally planned had added relatives and friends and whole families until there were over four hundred souls. But the Chemistry Building was large, and, standing by itself, was in no danger of being burned by the great fires that raged everywhere in the city.

"A large quantity of provisions had been gathered, and a food committee took charge of it, issuing rations daily to the various families and groups that arranged themselves into messes. A number of committees were appointed, and we developed a very efficient organization. I was on the committee of defence, though for the first day no prowlers came near. We could see them in the distance, however, and by the smoke of their fires knew that several camps of them were occupying the far edge of the campus. Drunkenness was rife, and often we heard them singing ribald songs or insanely shouting. While the world crashed to ruin about them and all the air was filled with the smoke of its burning, these low creatures gave rein to their bestiality and fought and drank and died. And after all, what did it matter? Everybody died anyway, the good and the bad, the efficients and the weaklings, those that loved to live and those that scorned to live. They passed. Everything passed.

"When twenty-four hours had gone by and no signs of the plague were apparent, we congratulated ourselves and set about digging a well. You have seen the great iron pipes which in those days carried water to all the city-dwellers. We feared that the fires in the city would burst the pipes and empty the reservoirs. So we tore up the cement floor of the central court of the Chemistry Building and dug a well. There were many young men, undergraduates, with us, and we worked night and day on the well. And our fears were confirmed. Three hours before we reached water, the pipes went dry.

"A second twenty-four hours passed, and still the plague did not appear among us. We thought we were saved. But we did not know what I afterwards decided to be true, namely, that the period of the incubation of the plague germs in a human's body was a matter of a number of days. It slew so swiftly when once it manifested itself, that we were led to believe that the period of incubation was equally swift. So, when two days had left us unscathed, we were elated with the idea that we were free of the contagion.

"But the third day disillusioned us. I can never forget the night preceding it. I had charge of the night guards from eight to twelve, and from the roof of the building I watched the passing of all man's glorious works. So terrible were the local conflagrations that all the sky was lighted up. One could read the finest print in the red glare. All the world seemed wrapped in flames. San Francisco spouted smoke and fire from a score of vast conflagrations that were like so many active volcanoes. Oakland, San Leandro, Haywards—all were burning; and to the northward, clear to Point Richmond, other fires were at work. It was an awe-inspiring spectacle. Civilization, my grandsons, civilization was passing in a sheet of flame and a breath of death. At ten o'clock that night, the great powder magazines at Point Pinole exploded in rapid succession. So terrific were the concussions that the strong building rocked as in an earthquake, while every pane of glass was broken. It was then that I left the roof and went down the long corridors, from room to room, quieting the alarmed women and telling them what had happened.

"An hour later, at a window on the ground floor, I heard pandemonium break out in the camps of the prowlers. There were cries and screams, and shots from many pistols. As we afterward conjectured, this fight had been precipitated by an attempt on the part of those that were well to drive out those that were sick. At any rate, a number of the plague-stricken prowlers escaped across the campus and drifted against our doors. We warned them back, but they cursed us and discharged a fusillade from their pistols. Professor Merryweather, at one of the windows, was instantly killed, the bullet striking him squarely between the eyes. We opened fire in turn, and all the prowlers fled away with the exception of three. One was a woman. The plague was on them and they were reckless. Like foul fiends, there in the red glare from the skies, with faces blazing, they continued to curse us and fire at us. One of the men I shot with my own hand. After that the other man and the woman, still cursing us, lay down under our windows, where we were compelled to watch them die of the plague.

"The situation was critical. The explosions of the powder magazines had broken all the windows of the Chemistry Building, so that we were exposed to the germs from the corpses. The sanitary committee was called upon to act, and it responded nobly. Two men were required to go out and remove the corpses, and this meant the probable sacrifice of their own lives, for, having performed the task, they were not to be permitted to re-enter the building. One of the professors, who was a bachelor, and one of the undergraduates volunteered. They bade good-bye to us and went forth. They were heroes. They gave up their lives that four hundred others might live. After they had performed their work, they stood for a moment, at a distance, looking at us wistfully. Then they waved their hands in farewell and went away slowly across the campus toward the burning city.

"And yet it was all useless. The next morning the first one of us was smitten with the plague—a little nurse-girl in the family of Professor Stout. It was no time for weak-kneed, sentimental policies. On the chance that she might be the only one, we thrust her forth from the building and commanded her to be gone. She went away slowly across the campus, wringing her hands and crying pitifully. We felt like brutes, but what were we to do? There were four hundred of us, and individuals had to be sacrificed.

"In one of the laboratories three families had domiciled themselves, and that afternoon we found among them no less than four corpses and seven cases of the plague in all its different stages.

"Then it was that the horror began. Leaving the dead lie, we forced the living ones to segregate themselves in another room. The plague began to break out among the rest of us, and as fast as the symptoms appeared, we sent the stricken ones to these segregated rooms. We compelled them to walk there by themselves, so as to avoid laying hands on them. It was heartrending. But still the plague raged among us, and room after room was filled with the dead and dying. And so we who were yet clean retreated to the next floor and to the next, before this sea of the dead, that, room by room and floor by floor, inundated the building.

"The place became a charnel house, and in the middle of the night the survivors fled forth, taking nothing with them except arms and ammunition and a heavy store of tinned foods. We camped on the opposite side of the campus from the prowlers, and, while some stood guard, others of us volunteered to scout into the city in quest of horses, motor cars, carts, and wagons, or anything that would carry our provisions and enable us to emulate the banded workingmen I had seen fighting their way out to the open country.

"I was one of these scouts; and Doctor Hoyle, remembering that his motor car had been left behind in his home garage, told me to look for it. We scouted in pairs, and Dombey, a young undergraduate, accompanied me. We had to cross half a mile of the residence portion of the city to get to Doctor Hoyle's home. Here the buildings stood apart, in the midst of trees and grassy lawns, and here the fires had played freaks, burning whole blocks, skipping blocks and often skipping a single house in a block. And here, too, the prowlers were still at their work. We carried our automatic pistols openly in our hands, and looked desperate enough, forsooth, to keep them from attacking us. But at Doctor Hoyle's house the thing happened. Untouched by fire, even as we came to it the smoke of flames burst forth.

"The miscreant who had set fire to it staggered down the steps and out along the driveway. Sticking out of his coat pockets were bottles of whiskey, and he was very drunk. My first impulse was to shoot him, and I have never ceased regretting that I did not. Staggering and maundering to himself, with bloodshot eyes, and a raw and bleeding slash down one side of his bewhiskered face, he was altogether the most nauseating specimen of degradation and filth I had ever encountered. I did not shoot him, and he leaned against a tree on the lawn to let us go by. It was the most absolute, wanton act. Just as we were opposite him, he suddenly drew a pistol and shot Dombey through the head. The next instant I shot him. But it was too late. Dombey expired without a groan, immediately. I doubt if he even knew what had happened to him.

"Leaving the two corpses, I hurried on past the burning house to the garage, and there found Doctor Hoyle's motor car. The tanks were filled with gasoline, and it was ready for use. And it was in this car that I threaded the streets of the ruined city and came back to the survivors on the campus. The other scouts returned, but none had been so fortunate. Professor Fairmead had found a Shetland pony, but the poor creature, tied in a stable and abandoned for days, was so weak from want of food and water that it could carry no burden at all. Some of the men were for turning it loose, but I insisted that we should lead it along with us, so that, if we got out of food, we would have it to eat.

"There were forty-seven of us when we started, many being women and children. The President of the Faculty, an old man to begin with, and now hopelessly broken by the awful appenings of the past week, rode in the motor car with several young children and the aged mother of Professor Fairmead. Wathope, a young professor of English, who had a grievous bullet-wound in his leg, drove the car. The rest of us walked, Professor Fairmead leading the pony.

"It was what should have been a bright summer day, but the smoke from the burning world filled the sky, through which the sun shone murkily, a dull and lifeless orb, blood-red and ominous. But we had grown accustomed to that blood-red sun. With the smoke it was different. It bit into our nostrils and eyes, and there was not one of us whose eyes were not bloodshot. We directed our course to the southeast through the endless miles of suburban residences, travelling along where the first swells of low hills rose from the flat of the central city. It was by this way, only, that we could expect to gain the country.

"Our progress was painfully slow. The women and children could not walk fast. They did not dream of walking, my grandsons, in the way all people walk to-day. In truth, none of us knew how to walk. It was not until after the plague that I learned really to walk. So it was that the pace of the slowest was the pace of all, for we dared not separate on account of the prowlers. There were not so many now of these human beasts of prey. The plague had already well diminished their numbers, but enough still lived to be a constant menace to us. Many of the beautiful residences were untouched by fire, yet smoking ruins were everywhere. The prowlers, too, seemed to have got over their insensate desire to burn, and it was more rarely that we saw houses freshly on fire.

"Several of us scouted among the private garages in search of motor cars and gasoline. But in this we were unsuccessful. The first great flights from the cities had swept all such utilities away. Calgan, a fine young man, was lost in this work. He was shot by prowlers while crossing a lawn. Yet this was our only casualty, though, once, a drunken brute deliberately opened fire on all of us. Luckily, he fired wildly, and we shot him before he had done any hurt.

"At Fruitvale, still in the heart of the magnificent residence section of the city, the plague again smote us. Professor Fairmead was the victim. Making signs to us that his mother was not to know, he turned aside into the grounds of a beautiful mansion. He sat down forlornly on the steps of the front veranda, and I, having lingered, waved him a last farewell. That night, several miles beyond Fruitvale and still in the city, we made camp. And that night we shifted camp twice to get away from our dead. In the morning there were thirty of us. I shall never forget the President of the Faculty. During the morning's march his wife, who was walking, betrayed the fatal symptoms, and when she drew aside to let us go on, he insisted on leaving the motor car and remaining with her. There was quite a discussion about this, but in the end we gave in. It was just as well, for we knew not which ones of us, if any, might ultimately escape.

"That night, the second of our march, we camped beyond Haywards in the first stretches of country. And in the morning there were eleven of us that lived. Also, during the night, Wathope, the professor with the wounded leg, deserted us in the motor car. He took with him his sister and his mother and most of our tinned provisions. It was that day, in the afternoon, while resting by the wayside, that I saw the last airship I shall ever see. The smoke was much thinner here in the country, and I first sighted the ship drifting and veering helplessly at an elevation of two thousand feet. What had happened I could not conjecture, but even as we looked we saw her bow dip down lower and lower. Then the bulkheads of the various gas-chambers must have burst, for, quite perpendicular, she fell like a plummet to the earth. And from that day to this I have not seen another airship. Often and often, during the next few years, I scanned the sky for them, hoping against hope that somewhere in the world civilization had survived. But it was not to be. What happened with us in California must have happened with everybody everywhere.

"Another day, and at Niles there were three of us. Beyond Niles, in the middle of the highway, we found Wathope. The motor car had broken down, and there, on the rugs which they had spread on the ground, lay the bodies of his sister, his mother, and himself.

"Wearied by the unusual exercise of continual walking, that night I slept heavily. In the morning I was alone in the world. Canfield and Parsons, my last companions, were dead of the plague. Of the four hundred that sought shelter in the Chemistry Building, and of the forty-seven that began the march, I alone remained—I and the Shetland pony. Why this should be so there is no explaining. I did not catch the plague, that is all. I was immune. I was merely the one lucky man in a million—just as every survivor was one in a million, or, rather, in several millions, for the proportion was at least that."

V

"For two days I sheltered in a pleasant grove where there had been no deaths. In those two days, while badly depressed and believing that my turn would come at any moment, nevertheless I rested and recuperated. So did the pony. And on the third day, putting what small store of tinned provisions I possessed on the pony's back, I started on across a very lonely land. Not a live man, woman, or child, did I encounter, though the dead were everywhere. Food, however, was abundant. The land then was not as it is now. It was all cleared of trees and brush, and it was cultivated. The food for millions of mouths was growing, ripening, and going to waste. From the fields and orchards I gathered vegetables, fruits, and berries. Around the deserted farmhouses I got eggs and caught chickens. And frequently I found supplies of tinned provisions in the store-rooms.

"A strange thing was what was taking place with all the domestic animals. Everywhere they were going wild and preying on one another. The chickens and ducks were the first to be destroyed, while the pigs were the first to go wild, followed by the cats. Nor were the dogs long in adapting themselves to the changed conditions. There was a veritable plague of dogs. They devoured the corpses, barked and howled during the nights, and in the daytime slunk about in the distance. As the time went by, I noticed a change in their behavior. At first they were apart from one another, very suspicious and very prone to fight. But after a not very long while they began to come together and run in packs. The dog, you see, always was a social animal, and this was true before ever he came to be domesticated by man. In the last days of the world before the plague, there were many many very different kinds of dogs—dogs without hair and dogs with warm fur, dogs so small that they would make scarcely a mouthful for other dogs that were as large as mountain lions. Well, all the small dogs, and the weak types, were killed by their fellows. Also, the very large ones were not adapted for the wild life and bred out. As a result, the many different kinds of dogs disappeared, and there remained, running in packs, the medium-sized wolfish dogs that you know to-day."

"But the cats don't run in packs, Granser," Hoo-Hoo objected.

"The cat was never a social animal. As one writer in the nineteenth century said, the cat walks by himself. He always walked by himself, from before the time he was tamed by man, down through the long ages of domestication, to to-day when once more he is wild.

"The horses also went wild, and all the fine breeds we had degenerated into the small mustang horse you know to-day. The cows likewise went wild, as did the pigeons and the sheep. And that a few of the chickens survived you know yourself. But the wild chicken of to-day is suite a different thing from the chickens we had in those days.

"But I must go on with my story. I travelled through a deserted land. As the time went by I began to yearn more and more for human beings. But I never found one, and I grew lonelier and lonelier. I crossed Livermore Valley and the mountains between it and the great valley of the San Joaquin. You have never seen that valley, but it is very large and it is the home of the wild horse. There are great droves there, thousands and tens of thousands. I revisited it thirty years after, so I know. You think there are lots of wild horses down here in the coast valleys, but they are as nothing compared with those of the San Joaquin. Strange to say, the cows, when they went wild, went back into the lower mountains. Evidently they were better able to protect themselves there.

"In the country districts the ghouls and prowlers had been less in evidence, for I found many villages and towns untouched by fire. But they were filled by the pestilential dead, and I passed by without exploring them. It was near Lathrop that, out of my loneliness, I picked up a pair of collie dogs that were so newly free that they were urgently willing to return to their allegiance to man. These collies accompanied me for many years, and the strains of them are in those very dogs there that you boys have to-day. But in sixty years the collie strain has worked out. These brutes are more like domesticated wolves than anything else."

Hare-Lip rose to his feet, glanced to see that the goats were safe, and looked at the sun's position in the afternoon sky, advertising impatience at the prolixity of the old man's tale. Urged to hurry by Edwin, Granser went on.

"There is little more to tell. With my two dogs and my pony, and riding a horse I had managed to capture, I crossed the San Joaquin and went on to a wonderful valley in the Sierras called Yosemite. In the great hotel there I found a prodigious supply of tinned provisions. The pasture was abundant, as was the game, and the river that ran through the valley was full of trout. I remained there three years in an utter loneliness that none but a man who has once been highly civilized can understand. Then I could stand it no more. I felt that I was going crazy. Like the dog, I was a social animal and I needed my kind. I reasoned that since I had survived the plague, there was a possibility that others had survived. Also, I reasoned that after three years the plague germs must all be gone and the land be clean again.

"With my horse and dogs and pony, I set out. Again I crossed the San Joaquin Valley, the mountains beyond, and came down into Livermore Valley. The change in those three years was amazing. All the land had been splendidly tilled, and now I could scarcely recognize it, such was the sea of rank vegetation that had overrun the agricultural handiwork of man. You see, the wheat, the vegetables, and orchard trees had always been cared for and nursed by man, so that they were soft and tender. The weeds and wild bushes and such things, on the contrary, had always been fought by man, so that they were tough and resistant. As a result, when the hand of man was removed, the wild vegetation smothered and destroyed practically all the domesticated vegetation. The coyotes were greatly increased, and it was at this time that I first encountered wolves, straying in twos and threes and small packs down from the regions where they had always persisted.

"It was at Lake Temescal, not far from the one-time city of Oakland, that I came upon the first live human beings. Oh, my grandsons, how can I describe to you my emotion, when, astride my horse and dropping down the hillside to the lake, I saw the smoke of a campfire rising through the trees. Almost did my heart stop beating. I felt that I was going crazy. Then I heard the cry of a babe—a human babe. And dogs barked, and my dogs answered. I did not know but what I was the one human alive in the whole world. It could not be true that here were others—smoke, and the cry of a babe.

"Emerging on the lake, there, before my eyes, not a hundred yards away, I saw a man, a large man. He was standing on an outjutting rock and fishing. I was overcome. I stopped my horse. I tried to call out but could not. I waved my hand. It seemed to me that the man looked at me, but he did not appear to wave. Then I laid my head on my arms there in the saddle. I was afraid to look again, for I knew it was an hallucination, and I knew that if I looked the man would be gone. And so precious was the hallucination, that I wanted it to persist yet a little while. I knew, too, that as long as I did not look it would persist.

"Thus I remained, until I heard my dogs snarling, and a man's voice. What do you think the voice said? I will tell you. It said: *'Where in hell did you come from?'*

"Those were the words, the exact words. That was what your other grandfather said to me, Hare-Lip, when he greeted me there on the shore of Lake Temescal fifty-seven years ago. And they were the most ineffable words I have ever heard. I opened my eyes, and there he stood before me, a large, dark, hairy man, heavy-jawed, slant-browed, fierce-eyed. How I got off my horse I do not know. But it seemed that the next I knew I was clasping his hand with both of mine and crying. I would have embraced him, but he was ever a narrow-minded, suspicious man, and he drew away from me. Yet did I cling to his hand and cry."

Granser's voice faltered and broke at the recollection, and the weak tears streamed down his cheeks while the boys looked on and giggled.

"Yet did I cry," he continued, "and desire to embrace him, though the Chauffeur was a brute, a perfect brute—the most abhorrent man I have ever known. His name was. . . strange, how I have forgotten his name. Everybody called him Chauffeur—it was the name of his occupation, and it stuck. That is how, to this day, the tribe he founded is called the Chauffeur Tribe.

"He was a violent, unjust man. Why the plague germs spared him I can never understand. It would seem, in spite of our old metaphysical notions about absolute justice, that there is no justice in the universe. Why did he live?—an iniquitous, moral monster, a blot on the face of nature, a cruel, relentless, bestial cheat as well. All he could talk about was motor cars, machinery, gasoline, and garages—and especially, and with huge delight, of his mean pilferings and sordid swindlings of the persons who had employed him in the days before the coming of the plague. And yet he was spared, while hundreds of millions, yea, billions, of better men were destroyed.

"I went on with him to his camp, and there I saw her, Vesta, the one woman. It was glorious and . . . pitiful. There she was, Vesta Van Warden, the young wife of John Van Warden, clad in rags, with marred and scarred and toil-calloused hands, bending over the campfire and doing scullion work—she, Vesta, who had been born to the purple of the greatest baronage of wealth the world had ever known. John Van Warden, her husband, worth one billion, eight hundred millions and President of the Board of Industrial Magnates, had been the ruler of America. Also, sitting on the International Board of Control, he had been one of the seven men who ruled the world. And she herself had come of equally noble stock. Her father, Philip Saxon, had been President of the Board of Industrial Magnates up to the time of his death. This office was in process of becoming hereditary, and had Philip Saxon had a son that son would have succeeded him. But his only child was Vesta, the perfect flower of generations of the highest culture this planet has ever produced. It was not until the engagement between Vesta and Van Warden took place, that Saxon indicated the latter as his successor. It was, I am sure, a political marriage. I have reason to believe that Vesta never really loved her husband in the mad passionate way of which the poets used to sing. It was more like the marriages that obtained among crowned heads in the days before they were displaced by the Magnates.

"And there she was, boiling fish-chowder in a soot-covered pot, her glorious eyes inflamed by the acrid smoke of the open fire. Hers was a sad story. She was the one survivor in a million, as I had been, as the Chauffeur had been. On a crowning eminence of the Alameda Hills, overlooking San Francisco Bay, Van Warden had built a vast summer palace. It was surrounded by a park of a thousand acres. When the plague broke out, Van Warden sent her there. Armed guards patrolled the boundaries of the park, and nothing entered in the way of provisions or even mail matter that was not first fumigated. And yet did the plague enter, killing the guards at their posts, the servants at their tasks, sweeping away the whole army of retainers—or, at least, all of them who did not flee to die elsewhere. So it was that Vesta found herself the sole living person in the palace that had become a charnel house.

"Now the Chauffeur had been one of the servants that ran away. Returning, two months afterward, he discovered Vesta in a little summer pavilion where there had been no deaths and where she had established herself. He was a brute. She was afraid, and she ran away and hid among the trees. That night, on foot, she fled into the mountains—she, whose tender feet and delicate body had never known the bruise of stones nor the scratch of briars. He followed, and that night he caught her. He struck her. Do you understand? He beat her with those terrible fists of his and made her his slave. It was she who had to gather the firewood, build the fires, cook, and do all the degrading camp-labor—she, who had never performed a menial act in her life. These things he compelled her to do, while he, a proper savage, elected to lie around camp and look on. He did nothing, absolutely nothing, except on occasion to hunt meat or catch fish."

"Good for Chauffeur," Hare-Lip commented in an undertone to the other boys. "I remember him before he died. He was a corker. But he did things, and he made things go. You know, Dad married his daughter, an' you ought to see the way he knocked the spots outa Dad. The Chauffeur was a son-of-a-gun. He made us kids stand around. Even when he was croaking he reached out for me, once, an' laid my head open with that long stick he kept always beside him."

Hare-Lip rubbed his bullet head reminiscently, and the boys returned to the old man, who was maundering ecstatically about Vesta, the squaw of the founder of the Chauffeur Tribe.

"And so I say to you that you cannot understand the awfulness of the situation. The Chauffeur was a servant, understand, a servant. And he cringed, with bowed head, to such as she. She was a lord of life, both by birth and by marriage. The destinies of millions, such as he, she carried in the hollow of her pink-white hand. And, in the days before the plague, the slightest contact with such as he would have been pollution. Oh, I have seen it. Once, I remember, there was Mrs. Goldwin, wife of one of the great magnates. It was on a landing stage, just as she was embarking in her private dirigible, that she dropped her parasol. A servant picked it up and made the mistake of handing it to her—to her, one of the greatest royal ladies of the land! She shrank back, as though he were a leper, and indicated her secretary to receive it. Also, she ordered her secretary to ascertain the creature's name and to see that he was immediately discharged from service. And such a woman was Vesta Van Warden. And her the Chauffeur beat and made his slave.

"—Bill—that was it; Bill, the Chauffeur. That was his name. He was a wretched, primitive man, wholly devoid of the finer instincts and chivalrous promptings of a cultured soul. No, there is no absolute justice, for to him fell that wonder of womanhood, Vesta Van Warden. The grievousness of this you will never understand, my grandsons; for you are yourselves primitive little savages, unaware of aught else but savagery. Why should Vesta not have been mine? I was a man of culture and refinement, a professor in a great university. Even so, in the time before the plague, such was her exalted position, she would not have deigned to know that I existed. Mark, then, the abysmal degradation to which she fell at the hands of the Chauffeur. Nothing less than the destruction of all mankind had made it possible that I should know her, look in her eyes, converse with her, touch her hand—ay, and love her and know that her feelings toward me were very kindly. I have reason to believe that she, even she, would have loved me, there being no other man in the world except the Chauffeur. Why, when it destroyed eight billions of souls, did not the plague destroy just one more man, and that man the Chauffeur?

"Once, when the Chauffeur was away fishing, she begged me to kill him. With tears in her eyes she begged me to kill him. But he was a strong and violent man, and I was afraid. Afterwards, I talked with him. I offered him my horse, my pony, my dogs, all that I possessed, if he would give Vesta to me. And he grinned in my face and shook his head. He was very insulting. He said that in the old days he had been a servant, had been dirt under the feet of men like me and of women like Vesta, and that now he had the greatest lady in the land to be servant to him and cook his food and nurse his brats. 'You had your day before the plague,' he said; 'but this is my day, and a damned good day it is. I wouldn't trade back to the old times for anything.' Such words he spoke, but they are not his words. He was a vulgar, low-minded man, and vile oaths fell continually from his lips.

"Also, he told me that if he caught me making eyes at his woman he'd wring my neck and give her a beating as well. What was I to do? I was afraid. He was a brute. That first night, when I discovered the camp, Vesta and I had great talk about the things of our vanished world. We talked of art, and books, and poetry; and the Chauffeur listened and grinned and sneered. He was bored and angered by our way of speech which he did not comprehend, and finally he spoke up and said: 'And this is Vesta Van Warden, one-time wife of Van Warden the Magnate—a high and stuck-up beauty, who is now my squaw. Eh,

Professor Smith, times is changed, times is changed. Here, you, woman, take off my moccasins, and lively about it. I want Professor Smith to see how well I have you trained.'

"I saw her clench her teeth, and the flame of revolt rise in her face. He drew back his gnarled fist to strike, and I was afraid, and sick at heart. I could do nothing to prevail against him. So I got up to go, and not be witness to such indignity. But the Chauffeur laughed and threatened me with a beating if I did not stay and behold. And I sat there, perforce, by the campfire on the shore of Lake Temescal, and saw Vesta, Vesta Van Warden, kneel and remove the moccasins of that grinning, hairy, apelike human brute.

"—Oh, you do not understand, my grandsons. You have never known anything else, and you do not understand.

" 'Halter-broke and bridle-wise,' the Chauffeur gloated, while she performed that dreadful, menial task. 'A trifle balky at times, Professor, a trifle balky; but a clout alongside the jaw makes her as meek and gentle as a lamb.'

"And another time he said: 'We've got to start all over and replenish the earth and multiply. You're handicapped, Professor. You ain't got no wife, and we're up against a regular Garden-of-Eden proposition. But I ain't proud. I'll tell you what, Professor.' He pointed at their little infant, barely a year old. 'There's your wife, though you'll have to wait till she grows up. It's rich, ain't it? We're all equals here, and I'm the biggest toad in the splash. But I ain't stuck up—not I. I do you the honor, Professor Smith, the very great honor of betrothing to you my and Vesta Van Warden's daughter. Ain't it cussed bad that Van Warden ain't here to see?' "

VI

"I lived three weeks of infinite torment there in the Chauffeur's camp. And then, one day, tiring of me, or of what to him was my bad effect on Vesta, he told me that the year before, wandering through the Contra Costa Hills to the Straits of Carquinez, across the Straits he had seen a smoke. This meant that there were still other human beings, and that for three weeks he had kept this inestimably precious information from me. I departed at once, with my dogs and horses, and journeyed across the Contra Costa Hills to the Straits. I saw no smoke on the other side, but at Port Costa discovered a small steel barge on which I was able to embark my animals. Old canvas which I found served me for a sail, and a southerly breeze fanned me across the Straits and up to the ruins of Vallejo. Here, on the outskirts of the city, I found evidences of a recently occupied camp. Many clam-shells showed me why these humans had come to the shores of the Bay. This was the Santa Rosa Tribe, and I followed its track along the old railroad right of way across the salt marshes to Sonoma Valley. Here, at the old brickyard at Glen Ellen, I came upon the camp. There were eighteen souls all told. Two were old men, one of whom was Jones, a banker. The other was Harrison, a retired pawnbroker, who had taken for wife the matron of the State Hospital for the Insane at Napa. Of all the persons of the city of Napa, and of all the other towns and villages in that rich and populous valley, she had been the only-survivor. Next, there were the three young men—Cardiff and Hale, who had been farmers, and Wainwright, a common day-laborer. All three had found wives. To Hale, a crude, illiterate farmer, had fallen Isadore, the greatest prize, next to Vesta, of the women who came through the plague. She was one of the world's most noted singers, and the plague had caught her at San Francisco. She has talked with me for hours at a time, telling me of her adventures, until, at last, rescued by Hale in the Mendocino Forest Reserve, there had remained nothing for her to do but become his wife. But Hale was a good fellow, in spite of his illiteracy. He had a keen sense of justice and right-dealing, and she was far happier with him than was Vesta with the Chauffeur.

"The wives of Cardiff and Wainwright were ordinary women, accustomed to toil with strong constitutions—just the type for the wild new life which they were compelled to live. In addition were two adult idiots from the feeble-minded home at Eldredge, and five or six young children and infants born after the formation of the Santa Rosa Tribe. Also, there was Bertha. She was a good woman, Hare-Lip, in spite of the sneers of your father. Her I took for wife. She was the mother of your father, Edwin, and of yours, Hoo-Hoo. And it was our daughter, Vera, who married your father, Hare-Lip—your father, Sandow, who was the oldest son of Vesta Van Warden and the Chauffeur.

"And so it was that I became the nineteenth member of the Santa Rosa Tribe. There were only two outsiders added after me. One was

Mungerson, descended from the Magnates, who wandered alone
in the wilds of Northern California for eight years before he came
south and joined us. He it was who waited twelve years more before
he married my daughter, Mary. The other was Johnson, the man
who founded the Utah Tribe. That was where he came from, Utah,
a country that lies very far away from here, across the great deserts,
to the east. It was not until twenty-seven years after the plague that
Johnson reached California. In all that Utah region he reported but
three survivors, himself one, and all men. For many years these three
men lived and hunted together, until, at last, desperate, fearing that
with them the human race would perish utterly from the planet, they
headed westward on the possibility of finding women survivors in
California. Johnson alone came through the great desert, where his two
companions died. He was forty-six years old when he joined us, and
he married the fourth daughter of Isadore and Hale, and his eldest son
married your aunt, Hare-Lip, who was the third daughter of Vesta and
the Chauffeur. Johnson was a strong man, with a will of his own. And it
was because of this that he seceded from the Santa Rosans and formed
the Utah Tribe at San Jose. It is a small tribe—there are only nine in it;
but, though he is dead, such was his influence and the strength of his
breed, that it will grow into a strong tribe and play a leading part in the
recivilization of the planet.

"There are only two other tribes that we know of—the Los
Angelitos and the Carmelitos. The latter started from one man and
woman. He was called Lopez, and he was descended from the ancient
Mexicans and was very black. He was a cowherd in the ranges beyond
Carmel, and his wife was a maidservant in the great Del Monte
Hotel. It was seven years before we first got in touch with the Los
Angelitos. They have a good country down there, but it is too warm.
I estimate the present population of the world at between three
hundred and fifty and four hundred—provided, of course, that there
are no scattered little tribes elsewhere in the world. If there be such,
we have not heard from them. Since Johnson crossed the desert from
Utah, no word nor sign has come from the East or anywhere else.
The great world which I knew in my boyhood and early manhood is
gone. It has ceased to be. I am the last man who was alive in the days
of the plague and who knows the wonders of that far-off time. We,

who mastered the planet—its earth, and sea, and sky—and who were as very gods, now live in primitive savagery along the water courses of this California country.

"But we are increasing rapidly—your sister, Hare-Lip, already has four children. We are increasing rapidly and making ready for a new climb toward civilization. In time, pressure of population will compel us to spread out, and a hundred generations from now we may expect our descendants to start across the Sierras, oozing slowly along, generation by generation, over the great continent to the colonization of the East—a new Aryan drift around the world.

"But it will be slow, very slow; we have so far to climb. We fell so hopelessly far. If only one physicist or one chemist had survived! But it was not to be, and we have forgotten everything. The Chauffeur started working in iron. He made the forge which we use to this day.

But he was a lazy man, and when he died he took with him all he knew of metals and machinery. What was I to know of such things? I was a classical scholar, not a chemist. The other men who survived were not educated. Only two things did the Chauffeur accomplish—the brewing of strong drink and the growing of tobacco. It was while he was drunk, once, that he killed Vesta. I firmly believe that he killed Vesta in a fit of drunken cruelty though he always maintained that she fell into the lake and was drowned.

"And, my grandsons, let me warn you against the medicine-men. They call themselves *doctors*, travestying what was once a noble profession, but in reality they are medicine-men, devil-devil men, and they make for superstition and darkness. They are cheats and liars. But so debased and degraded are we, that we believe their lies. They, too, will increase in numbers as we increase, and they will strive to rule us. Yet are they liars and charlatans. Look at young Cross-Eyes, posing as a doctor, selling charms against sickness, giving good hunting, exchanging promises of fair weather for good meat and skins, sending the death-stick, performing a thousand abominations. Yet I say to you, that when he says he can do these things, he lies. I, Professor Smith, Professor James Howard Smith, say that he lies. I have told him so to his teeth. Why has he not sent me the death-stick? Because he knows that with me it is without avail. But you, Hare-Lip, so deeply are you sunk in black superstition that did you awake this night and find the death-stick beside you, you would surely die. And you would die, not because of any virtues in the stick, but because you are a savage with the dark and clouded mind of a savage.

"The doctors must be destroyed, and all that was lost must be discovered over again. Wherefore, earnestly, I repeat unto you certain things which you must remember and tell to your children after you. You must tell them that when water is made hot by fire, there resides in it a wonderful thing called steam, which is stronger than ten thousand men and which can do all man's work for him. There are other very useful things. In the lightning flash resides a similarly strong servant of man, which was of old his slave and which some day will be his slave again.

"Quite a different thing is the alphabet. It is what enables me to know the meaning of fine markings, whereas you boys know only rude picture-writing. In that dry cave on Telegraph Hill, where you see me often go when the tribe is down by the sea, I have stored many books. In them is great wisdom. Also, with them, I have placed a key to the alphabet, so that one who knows picture-writing may also know print. Some day men will read again; and then, if no accident has befallen my cave, they will know that Professor James Howard Smith once lived and saved for them the knowledge of the ancients.

"There is another little device that men inevitably will rediscover. It is called gunpowder. It was what enabled us to kill surely and at long distances. Certain things which are found in the ground, when combined in the right proportions, will make this gunpowder. What these things are, I have forgotten, or else I never knew. But I wish I did know. Then would I make powder, and then would I certainly kill Cross-Eyes and rid the land of superstition—"

"After I am man-grown I am going to give Cross-Eyes all the goats, and meat, and skins I can get, so that he'll teach me to be a doctor," Hoo-Hoo asserted. "And when I know, I'll make everybody else sit up and take notice. They'll get down in the dirt to me, you bet."

The old man nodded his head solemnly, and murmured:

"Strange it is to hear the vestiges and remnants of the complicated Aryan speech falling from the lips of a filthy little skin-clad savage. All the world is topsy-turvy. And it has been topsy-turvy ever since the plague."

"You won't make me sit up," Hare-Lip boasted to the would-be medicine-man. "If I paid you for a sending of the death-stick and it didn't work, I'd bust in your head—understand, you Hoo-Hoo, you?"

"I'm going to get Granser to remember this here gunpowder stuff," Edwin said softly, "and then I'll have you all on the run. You, Hare-Lip, will do my fighting for me and get my meat for me, and you, Hoo-Hoo, will send the death-stick for me and make everybody afraid. And if I catch Hare-Lip trying to bust your head, Hoo-Hoo, I'll fix him with that same gunpowder. Granser ain't such a fool as you think, and I'm going to listen to him and some day I'll be boss over the whole bunch of you."

The old man shook his head sadly, and said:

"The gunpowder will come. Nothing can stop it—the same old story over and over. Man will increase, and men will fight. The gunpowder will enable men to kill millions of men, and in this way only, by fire and blood, will a new civilization, in some remote day, be evolved. And of what profit will it be? Just as the old civilization passed, so will the new. It may take fifty thousand years to build, but it will pass. All things pass. Only remain cosmic force and matter, ever in flux, ever acting and reacting and realizing the eternal types—the priest, the soldier, and the king. Out of the mouths of babes comes the wisdom of all the ages. Some will fight, some will rule, some will pray; and all the rest will toil and suffer sore while on their bleeding carcasses is reared again, and yet again, without end, the amazing beauty and surpassing wonder of the civilized state. It were just as well that I destroyed those cave-stored books—whether they remain or perish, all their old truths will be discovered, their old lies lived and handed down. What is the profit—"

Hare-Lip leaped to his feet, giving a quick glance at the pasturing goats and the afternoon sun.

"Gee!" he muttered to Edwin, "The old geezer gets more long-winded every day. Let's pull for camp."

While the other two, aided by the dogs, assembled the goats and started them for the trail through the forest, Edwin stayed by the old man and guided him in the same direction. When they reached the old right of way, Edwin stopped suddenly and looked back. Hare-Lip and Hoo-Hoo and the dogs and the goats passed on. Edwin was looking at a small herd of wild horses which had come down on the hard sand. There were at least twenty of them, young colts and yearlings and mares, led by a beautiful stallion which stood in the foam at the edge of the surf, with arched neck and bright wild eyes, sniffing the salt air from off the sea.

"What is it?" Granser queried.

"Horses," was the answer. "First time I ever seen 'em on the beach. It's the mountain lions getting thicker and thicker and driving 'em down."

The low sun shot red shafts of light, fan-shaped, up from a cloud-tumbled horizon. And close at hand, in the white waste of shore-lashed waters, the sea-lions, bellowing their old primeval chant, hauled up out of the sea on the black rocks and fought and loved.

"Come on, Granser," Edwin prompted. And old man and boy, skin-clad and barbaric, turned and went along the right of way into the forest in the wake of the goats.

THE LAST SUNSET

EDWIN A. START

In "Finis," Frank Lillie Pollock contemplated the last sunrise viewed on a rapidly incinerating earth. This story, first published in the March 1907 issue of the popular fiction magazine The Red Book, *presents the opposite: the last sunset seen on earth as a rapidly cooling sun winks out of existence. Author Edwin A. Start seemed to know that even a catastrophe of this magnitude could be softened with a bit of romance.*

I t was a chill gray day, with leaden skies and ice still lying hard and cold in the city streets. The cold was not that of a sharp but sunlit winter, such as bygone generations had known, but the terrible glooming chill of a world struggling against the want of that radiance that for millions of years had sustained its life.

Hamilton, fur-wrapped and stamping his feet, entered his club and sought a quiet corner where an open fire blazed upon the hearth under a supply of artificial oxygen. He took up the latest number of the

Twentieth Century Review and opened it at an article on "The End of the World." It was not an assertion of any new theory but the summing up, from a conscientious sense of a painful public duty, of conditions long understood and now approaching fulfilment:

> *Eighty years ago an eminent American astronomer,*
> *realizing from the examination of carefully collected*
> *data that climatic conditions were changing throughout*
> *the world, advanced the hypothesis that chemical*
> *changes were taking place in the sun by which it was*
> *losing its heat . . . Since that time careful observations*
> *followed up continuously by astronomers, together with*
> *the rapid change in atmosphere and climate recorded*
> *by the meteorological bureaus have confirmed what at*
> *first was merely an hypothesis. Professor Gammell's*
> *epoch-making book, published ten years ago, brought*
> *speculation into harmony with fact and more recently*
> *Lemoine in France, Baur in Germany, Kinemoto in Japan,*
> *and Lassiter in our own country have, by coincident and*
> *cooperative observations, proved the rate of fall in the*
> *sun's temperature and its rapid acceleration, so that now*
> *it is established that the final dissolution of the sun as an*
> *agent of light and heat will occur on the tenth of June in*
> *the present year.* * * * * *The eminent authorities already*
> *cited tell us that during the whole of the present century*
> *there has been a steady increase in the severity of weather*
> *conditions and the present generation well knows at*
> *what cost and by what elaboration of scientific agencies*
> *life is sustained and the activity of the race maintained.*
> *Indeed it would appear that the tremendous development*
> *of applied science which began in the latter half of the*
> *nineteenth century and the great accumulations of wealth*
> *which marked that and the succeeding half century were*
> *intended but as preparations for the herculean struggle of*
> *the human race against a fate that it could not control or*
> *prevent* * * * * *The loss of radiant energy has been gradual*
> *and some will remain until the last, when chemical and*

> *physical forces, long preparing will produce an immediate*
> *result, and the sun's active career in the universe will be*
> *brought to an abrupt close.*

There was much more, but Hamilton dropped the magazine and settled back in his chair. Why should he read more of the story of the world's tragedy that he already knew so well? He had read widely and intelligently in the literatures of the nineteenth and twentieth centuries; he had watched the transformation of the world from year to year and knew its every stage; and he had followed closely the course of the latest scientific thought upon the subject.

The world knew itself very well in that year of the Christian era. The accumulated knowledge of centuries of science had been focused rapidly on great problems during the last fifty years and many physical, chemical and meteorological developments had proved or disproved old hypotheses and determined the elements of definite knowledge. Much that was hidden from the fathers had become the common knowledge of the sons. One ancient mystery still lay behind the veil, only guessed at dimly as in long ages past—the mystery of the future that lies beyond the mortal life men know. Science, pseudo-science, mysticism, all sought to penetrate the veil, but all fell back unsatisfied as they had for ages. And now, how much men would give to know the secret, for this they did know, that their world was doomed. The sun, giver of life; the sun, worshiped by millions in ages past; the sun that Akbar had chosen as the type of the omnipotent and eternal God, the universal father; the sun that had inspired poets, that had seemed to be permanent, that men had been unable to bear the temporary hiding of for many days—the sun was dying.

Ever since the appearance of Professor Gammell's notable work, "The Doom of the World," there had been a general acceptance of its conclusions, the product of the severest scientific reasoning, based on well-established facts and *formulae*. Its startling predictions, bringing close home the fate which two other preceding generations had believed to be only a remote possibility for future ages, caused a temporary paralysis of activities, and then the buoyancy of humanity reasserted itself and sought in an intensifying of the game of life relief from the anticipation of evil.

Even now the full consequences of this mighty change were imperfectly realized. What might follow the darkness, who could tell? It was possible, nay, was it not probable, that the change in the sun would be followed by its physical dissolution. Its particles might float out into the great seas of star dust. Then the force that controlled the earth in its orbit would be lost and the darkened planet would drift off, a hopeless derelict in the infinite reaches of space.

And now the fatal day that was to be the beginning of the end had come, and by the accurate prevision of its men of science the world realized its significance. Monthly, weekly, and of late daily, dense masses of vapor had settled closer and closer about the earth. Day by day the expiring sun had thrown dimmer rays, rising like a weakling in the morning, sinking in the west like a tired man at night.

Decade by decade the increasing severity of the seasons had destroyed the weak and made life a strenuous battle for the strong, until there survived only a picked race mentally and physically. But as each age has its degenerates, so this had a large and growing class of those who had been able to maintain the struggle up to a certain point, when they, too, had given way in mind or body, failing to find in the products of man's science adequate substitutes for the vital principles of the universe. So they, in turn, became the wards and hangers-on of society. Now this remnant—the strong and brave, the weak and inefficient—was doomed to extinction. The earth would become a dead planet, for without the sun it must move through absolute darkness in absolute cold.

Amid the many changes of the last fifty years had been the decline and extinction of greater industries, and the rise of new ones as science, taxed to its utmost, sought to meet the changing needs of men. Life had assumed a somber tone. In the face of annihilation men ceased to jest. But the mad race for wealth and power inaugurated so long became a consuming passion. Men who had hoped and dreamed of other things were swept along by the current. The changing physical conditions compelled the maintenance of highly artificial means of life, unless man was to elapse from achievement, give up his conquests, and revert to the condition of the Esquimaux. The rare natural life that had formerly spread over all the world outside of the Arctic regions survived only in spared and scanty remnants in one two favored corners, and life in the country and out of doors that had delighted and maintained the sanity of preceding ages had passed into ancient history.

Hamilton was one of the vigorous spirits who, while he swam with the current of his time, retained the normal aspirations of better days of earth. With all the strength of his manhood he longed for the freer, more natural existence denied the world. He had sought power and won it, only to find it a shadow in the void. Wealth had come to him without bringing satisfaction. A man, capable of the fullness of life at forty years of age, he looked across empty and lonely years, asking the question that for ages had tormented men: "Is this the end? Then of what use is the struggle, the toil, the pain."

How acute this question became when the race faced early extinction, so far as life is concerned. Yet the mind of this man, thoroughly trained though it was in the logic of the ages, found no answer to his question, any more than had the myriads who had preceded him in the inquiry. But the human heart of him, in the flood tide of his manhood, strong and insistent, refused to recognize the sentence. He would have given all the prizes that he had won for a breath of the airs that still pulsed, fragrant with abounding life, through the literature of a hundred years ago, for the woods, the living things, the rich warm sunlight, flooding an earth that smiled in gladness. Now, when final darkness was so near, when it seemed that, do the best men might with the appliances that science had given, the time would only be counted by weeks when they must all lay down their burdens on the threshold of futurity, everything in the life about him seemed unreal. His keenly awakened sensibilities saw in the past, of which he had read and heard from the elders, the true reality; in the present, a phantom life, with no beginning and no end for all its effort; and in the future only an unanswered question. Against the maddening grip that the assurance of continuous night and deadly cold took upon hope and effort, every instinct revolted.

For some men the sources of life are physical. Give them good surroundings, homes, prosperity, and their lives are colored accordingly. Reverse the conditions and you change the man. It is just as it is with the plants. Some must have provided in the soil where they grow the elements that enable them to be strong and flourish. Without this they give way to noxious weeds. But there arc some that reach out and gather in the sources of life from the generous air and ask few favors of fate. So some men draw from the spirit and for them there is no death no any defeat.

Robert Hamilton was one of these. He had faced many difficulties in his active life and had not flinched. Now he faced a crisis against which no effort of his could be of any avail, yet from the depths of his heart rang a cry that was not of defeat, nor grief, nor terror—a fierce in its intensity, for something more real than power, more permanent than wealth, stronger than death—hope and assurance of immortality.

Elsewhere on that fatal afternoon men gathered in groups, shunning solitude. Hamilton was one of the few who dared to meet himself face to face in this crucial hour. And in response to his need there was unveiled from somewhere in memory's deep recesses a picture from his boyhood—a golden sunset on a summer sea. It seemed to him now, as he saw it against the background of the present, that the world was flooded with radiance and that in it was life, life, life. Instinctively he stretched out his arms as if reaching out to some means of salvation. He remembered, however, that even then, thirty years ago, his grandfather had said that it was far different from the wonderful visions of his own youth, when rich color flooded the east at dawn and the west at evening fall. But the sunset was only a background, the light, the color, for Hamilton's memory picture, for its central figure was a girl, his playmate with the deep blue eyes and wind-tossed hair. Why was it the girl who came to him now and not the woman who in all the years since then had been his friend, wise of counsel, considerate of his faults, never failing him in his joys or sorrows, his triumphs or adversities? Why, except to carry him back across the years, to teach him to read the meaning of his life.

It was a natural consequence of the tense life of the time that marriage filled a less and less place in men's lives as the years went on and they became more absorbed in the game. What use to make hopes when the end was so near? Love had become an old-world tale. In most men, the sentiments preserved in books from happier, more hopeful days called forth only an impersonal curiosity, but in Hamilton's heart, as he followed through successive pictures that passed before his vision—the child, the girl, the woman, new life quickened the ashes of the dead years and blazed up into a passion that was like pain for something lost out of the past. But with this pain was exultation at the new realization of himself and his possibilities.

What would she say to him today, this woman, noblest of all he knew, who had retained through all the difficult years the sweetness of her thoughtless girlhood and had added to it the dignity and strength of a regnant womanhood?

In attempting to answer that question he accused himself of selfishness. How much had he thought of her, her desires, her hopes, in the years that he had gone to her with his ambitions and his problems? What had he given to her of the tenderness, the thoughtfulness, the sympathy that women love? He had exacted so much from her unfailing friendship; had he ever given an adequate return?

It was not Hamilton's way to leave a doubt of himself to vex him. It must have immediate solution. This quality had made him in large measure the man he was. Now, in this hour of self-revealment, thoughtless selfishness and ambition fell away. Artificial standards, methods and aims were laid aside like outworn garments. In his own sight he stood as simply as a man of the elder world in the face of the great realities and heard within his heart the primal call of the man for his mate—that call stronger than death, as old as the race, potent alike for good and evil—and because in frank nakedness of soul he had called upon the spirit for the way of life he knew that the answer had been found and that he need question no farther.

At the flash of this revelation his heart, here in the face of a dying world, leaped like a boy's when it gives glad welcome to the hopes and mysteries of life, when difficulty and danger are forgotten or unknown, and the measure of joy is hope. What the fulfilment would be he knew not; he only knew that they could pass into the shadows hand in hand, and that would be enough.

Up in the house on the hill in the library where they had passed many hours he knew she would await him tonight. There together, man and woman, they would watch this final sunset as the boy and girl had watched that earlier, brighter one so many years ago.

He drew on his furs and passed down the steps into the street. Those who saw him wondered at the radiance of his face and the buoyant quickness of his step.

"Robert Hamilton looks as if he had a corner in sunlight," said one.

"Faith, it's but a little thing to corner this day," was the grim and hopeless reply.

In the great auditorium were gathering for a mad revel those who dared not remember and could not forget. Hamilton shrugged his shoulders in disgust as he passed. A little farther on he met a man about his own age but of thin and stooping figure.

"You'll join us at the observatory, Hamilton?" he asked. "You know something of these things and this is a great event in the history of science."

"After which there will be no history. No, Lassiter, I thank you for the invitation, but I have entered upon an investigation at seems to me of more importance at is time."

The eminent astronomer looked inquiringly over his glasses. "You make me curious," he said. "What subject can transcend this unparalleled event?"

"Myself," replied Hamilton, smiling with courteous directness.

He passed on his way while the man of science mused, "These men of power and material possessions are self-absorbed beyond all belief. I really thought better of Hamilton."

So Professor Lassiter went to his profitless observations, never dreaming that the other was the one who had stepped out of a narrow circle into the realm of a larger life.

Again Hamilton paused to greet a friend whose manner of social greeting changed to intense seriousness as his eyes swept the cheerless street in the dim half light. "How is it all to end?" he said.

"God knows," replied Hamilton, "but I know," and he squared his shoulders instinctively, "we can meet whatever comes he old brave way of strong men, not like those cowards down yonder," and he pointed to Auditorium Hall. "Or the members of the suicide clubs," he added.

"The suicide clubs seem to have a certain excuse for being now. They claim that they are simply bringing the organization of society into harmony with natural forces."

Hamilton laughed. "What is the use hurrying nature's interesting work? I shall wait and see it through to the end." And he strode on while his friend wondered at his easy tone and untroubled look.

A sad faced man, smooth shaven, with clear-cut features, greeted Hamilton gravely a block farther on.

"I have been seeking for something that I can say to my people. I should give them a message of faith but my own is sorely shaken."

"Has religion, too, failed?" said Hamilton. "Then are we indeed adrift on a chartless sea."

The minister bowed his head. "I think it is I who have failed," he said. "I am unequal to the demands of God's service."

Hamilton laid his hand kindly on the other's shoulder. The light in his eye drew the minister's gaze and held it. "We are two strong men," he said. "We have no right to doubt or fear. Speak to your people tonight as you never spoke before of faith and hope and love and the life of the spirit. We are vital spirits, not mere material things. The history of sixty centuries of human civilization, of love and hope and effort, has not been wrought out for nothing."

"You give me new courage," said the other. "You should have been the minister, not I."

"No, not at all," and Hamilton made a deprecatory movement. "I have had my own battle; I have climbed out of the pit; and I know that we are all much in need of help. That is all."

And the minister in his turn followed Hamilton with his eyes, saying to himself, "Ah, Robert Hamilton, Robert Hamilton, would there were more men like you."

* * *

Just beyond the bustle and turmoil of the city, on a slope that looked out across the western sea, stood a house that retained in structure and surroundings, as much as was possible, the atmosphere of the earlier years of the century. On its western side, opening upon a terrace, was the library, with its book-lined walls, its fireplace, and a wide window looking out into the west.

In the glow of the firelight a woman, who was good to look upon, sat thinking, and the reflections of her thoughts found expression from time to time upon her face. Because she was a woman her thoughts swept rapidly from the general with which they began to the particular and the personal, and then to their immediate object. The sun, the earth, the day and its significance—and then all things were lost in the question, would Robert come tonight? He had come so often when he needed her; would he come now? For at last, after years of unquestioning friendship, the woman's heart made its demand, insistent, hardly to be denied. If she must go out into the eternal darkness, she would not fear if she could go with her hand in his. And if he came—what then? He would come in the old friendly way—and she did not feel equal to that tonight. She wanted more, more—all the strength and tenderness of manly loving that had been the glory and pride of women in all the ages past. The passionate heart that had been kept within its bounds these many years could be restrained no longer. She had waited so long, so long, and now her heart claimed him for the faith and trust and loyal sympathy that had been given to him all these years, with no thought of any return.

Ah, what had she given him, this man of men, this leader whose commands men were accustomed to obey, whose face and bearing women loved to look upon? What could she have done for him? asked self-depreciation. And even while doubt and fear pleaded the question her stronger, truer consciousness gave the answer. She knew that she had filled a place in his busy life that no other had filled or could fill. She knew that she had shared his trials and his triumphs, that when he had come to the rough places of his career he had looked to her for sympathy; for counsel, for strength.

But did this kind of partnership ever permanently satisfy a woman who was true to the highest ideals of her womanhood?

Her heart claimed him as its own. Why, it went back to their childhood. Once, she remembered, back down the long years, she sat with Robert on the rocks beside the sea at the close of a long summer day, and the waves were tipped with rosy light as the sun went down in the west. What bright days those were! Since then life had brought many sorrows and there had been many times when it would have been little worth but for this strong, loyal friend, whose manhood fully kept the promise of his gallant hearted boyhood. What could they not do together, with all the world before them.

A sudden shock at this thought her relentlessly out of dreamland world—what was the world now, and its inhabitants, ship-wrecked in space!

But what need they fear, having other? She could make him forget the hours, forget everything but her, and when the end came they could go out into infinite spaces fearlessly, for where there is love there is life and hope.

She had thought of sending for him to come tonight, but she wished him to come because he wished to, because he must. She knew how many calls there would be for him this night and if he came to her now she would know—

She rose and paced back and forth through the long room, looking out of window at the dreary landscape, where even now darkness was gathering, with sun still two hours high. She put hands before her face to shut out the picture and turned away. Again her thoughts rested on what she had suddenly acknowledged to be life's greatest fact. The hours she had spent with Hamilton in d gone by, his grave and gentle courtesy, which mingled no suspicion of the lover—why should she expect that because woman's heart had found itself, he would come to her in any other way than he h in the past years? And to this was always the one persistent reply of woman's intuition, "He loves me. I know it, and he will know it."

Sitting once more before the fireplace her head thrown back upon the cushions, her eyes closed, she dreamed the day dreams that have been woman's for countless years, untroubled now by any shadow of the future.

There Hamilton found her, the firelight playing like a caress about her face. At the sight of her there rose within him longing, deep and tender and passionate with a kind of wonder at his own blindness these many years. All that was petty, all that was passing and non-essential, even the dying world itself slipped from his consciousness—and feeling thus and being man he resolutely held himself in check, speaking of the occurrences of the day in the simplest and most matter of fact way he knew, fencing with himself for time against his hurrying, crowding thoughts, this new impatience that possessed him. He spoke of many things—of the events of the hour, of the gathering of the wise men at the observatory, of the general cessation of activities in the town, of the courage and fear exhibited by different men at the crisis, of the latest social happening, of his work, of a dozen little things-conscious all the time that these things interested neither her nor him at that moment; that it was very futile this playing with words, when there lay upon his lips the wonderful refrain of the ages-old poem of the race.

He was conscious, too, of a certain expectancy in her, of a new, indescribable, invisible something that drew him as the magnet draws the iron. She had been carrying on her part of the conversation with a woman's easy composure, yet she was strangely restless, this calm, self-contained woman he had known so long and well. This was scarcely apparent in her outward manner, but he felt it by that subtle comprehension that comes between those who have been drawn close together sympathy. At length his commonplaces refused to come and she would not help. Silence fell between them, and through its stillness they approached each other in spirit more than they could through words. He stood looking down at her as her hands slowly clasped and unclasped. She sat, her head bent a little forward, gazing into the fire. He noted, with new appreciation, the poise of her ad, the rich masses of her hair. After a few minutes she slowly raised her head. Her face was a little pale but a flush like the rosy light of an old-fashioned dawn spread over it as she put out her hand to and said simply:

"I am glad you came tonight, Robert. I wondered if you would. I knew you would be so much in demand." There was little in the mere words, but voice and look, as she spoke, quickened the man's heart and seemed to open wide to him the gates of perfect peace.

He held her hand in a strong and silent grasp, gazing down at the sweet face with that wonderful look upon it that a woman wears but once in a lifetime, and then for the man she has chosen out of all the world. To their new consciousness words were little needed, for that moment was one of perfect mutual recognition that needed no ratification of speech. Finally he broke the silence, speaking low and evenly at first, as one who holds himself in close control:

"I could not have gone elsewhere tonight. My life, my hope was here. I think it has been here all these years, but," and his voice broke, "I never knew, dear heart, I never knew."

"I knew," she smiled up at him, "long ago, but you were too much absorbed—"

"Yes," the man broke in impatiently, "I have been chasing the shadows when the substance of life lay close at hand."

Gently, tenderly, as if it were a consecration, he bent down and kissed her forehead. As he straightened she rose swiftly and stood before him in all the splendor of her womanhood, a smile trembling

softly on her lips, her eyes flashing straight into his own, and in them
the light that was never on land or sea. He held her at arm's length
for a minute, then with a low exclamation, "My God, how many lost
years!" he drew her to him.

Her face was raised to his, their lips met, and took long tribute
for the wasted years. For these two there was no past of struggle or
denial, no future of disaster or death. To them, as eternal night was
closing upon the world it was as when primeval man and woman
came together in the dawn of life and hope, when the morning stars
sang together.

"Do you remember" he said a little later, "long years ago; when
my grandfather was still alive and you and I, boy and girl, with him
watched the sunset from the rocks looking out across the sea? It came
back to me this afternoon, and then I came on down the long reaches
of memory, realizing for the first time, because for the first time I
stopped to think, how much you have been to me all these years, and
in that realization I found that I loved you more than fame or power or
wealth or life, that with you alone I could face the terrors of the future,
that in you alone I could find its hope. I learned then that in such love
lie the immortal years."

Her head upon his shoulder drew closer. "I am glad that you
remembered that, too. We have unconsciously shared even our dreams
today. Sometimes I think I have always loved you, but I awaited your
sovereign pleasure, as a woman must."

So they talked together, as men and women have since human
life began, with great silences between that had no need of words.
As the hour of sunset approached, the chimes in the city rang out
their requiem for the closing day, the passing light, the dying sun.
Then they stood together by the great window that looked out into
the west.

Dense vapory clouds hung low here and there, casting black and
ominous shadows, like birds of prey hovering over a battle field. From
the city rose a mournful tumult of sound. In the observatory not
far away astronomers watched the event, bringing to bear upon it
knowledge that was of no avail, making observations that would be
lost with all the other works of men. In that quiet intense group the
scientific spirit of the ages reached its apotheosis.

In their clubs men of millions, who had controlled the destiny of half the world and traded with those who controlled the other half, looked on with cynical gibes, with fear, sometimes with prayer, or with a business-like acceptance of an unquestioned fact. In many places men and women gathered to find in dance and song and wine Lethean relief from present doubt and fear. Lesser and franker cowards grovelled on the earth and wept in abject despair and terror.

In the great cathedral where the ancient Church still maintained its pomp and circumstance, the celebration of mass as for the passing of a soul had begun and gorgeously vested prelates maintained the dignity of an order centuries old. In other churches gathered small congregations of those whom principle or fear had brought together for an hour of prayer.

So the world faced its last sunset, each in his way, with the courage of the stoic, with forced gaiety, with prayers or curses or cries of grief and pain; but around these two upon the heights lay deep and brooding silence.

Slowly the clock on the mantle ticked off the minutes. Away in the west, fading and slowly sinking to the dim horizon line, a dull red spot hung low in the heavens. Dense clouds that it had not the power to illumine drifted heavily across the sky and sank nearer and nearer to the earth. Once they obscured the sun and a cry arose from the distant mob, who thought that the end had come, in truth. How mankind clung to this wasted relic of the universal light! But the heavy drift passed by and again the red disk appeared in view. The two at the window, their arms about each other, looked on silent and fascinated. For tens of thousands of years this sun had been the one reliable thing in all the universe, the type of permanence, the determinant of time, the source of light and life unfailing, and now—

Before the sun reached the line there was a sudden flare, as if some explosive action had taken place. It died out and then, like the rise of a conflagration, a brilliant glare swept outward into space, throwing a broad light upon the gloomy sky and illuminating, for an instant, the watching earth. The Master of Light in his last agony threw this challenge in the face of death. Slowly this also faded into darkness and a sound swept by like the rush of mighty wings. The day was done. Cold, through the heavy atmosphere, shone out, one by one, the glittering stars.

Within, the firelight flickered slowly and uncertainly. Below, the puny lights of the town struggled against the darkness that would never more be lifted. The chimes in the cathedral tower were to tolling a dirge. Out along the coast the waves the ocean, lost to sight in the impenetrable blackness, boomed upon the ice-bound rocks with weary iteration. Somewhere in the vast spaces a star shot down among its silent mates and vanished. The two by the window turned away, but they looked into each other's eyes they knew that for them the morning had ready dawned.

THE MACHINE STOPS

E.M. FORSTER

Best known as the author of A Passage to India, A Room with a View, *and other literary novels, E.M. Forster (1879–1970) wrote several works of fantasy and science fiction, including this dystopian tale of a future where humans have begun to worship the machines that they themselves created. First published in the November 1909 issue of the* Oxford and Cambridge Review, *this story offers a vision of a world where humans have become overdependent on technology, and a rumination on the fate of human civilization when the machine stops.*

I. THE AIR-SHIP

Imagine, if you can, a small room, hexagonal in shape, like the cell of a bee. It is lighted neither by window nor by lamp, yet it is filled with a soft radiance. There are no apertures for ventilation, yet the air is fresh. There are no musical instruments, and yet, at the moment that my meditation opens, this room is throbbing with melodious sounds.

An arm-chair is in the centre, by its side a reading-desk—that is all the furniture. And in the arm-chair there sits a swaddled lump of flesh—a woman, about five feet high, with a face as white as a fungus. It is to her that the little room belongs.

An electric bell rang.

The woman touched a switch and the music was silent.

"I suppose I must see who it is," she thought, and set her chair in motion. The chair, like the music, was worked by machinery and it rolled her to the other side of the room where the bell still rang importunately.

"Who is it?" she called. Her voice was irritable, for she had been interrupted often since the music began. She knew several thousand people, in certain directions human intercourse had advanced enormously.

But when she listened into the receiver, her white face wrinkled into smiles, and she said:

"Very well. Let us talk, I will isolate myself. I do not expect anything important will happen for the next five minutes—for I can give you fully five minutes, Kuno. Then I must deliver my lecture on 'Music during the Australian Period.' "

She touched the isolation knob, so that no one else could speak to her. Then she touched the lighting apparatus, and the little room was plunged into darkness.

"Be quick!" She called, her irritation returning. "Be quick, Kuno; here I am in the dark wasting my time."

But it was fully fifteen seconds before the round plate that she held in her hands began to glow. A faint blue light shot across it, darkening to purple, and presently she could see the image of her son, who lived on the other side of the earth, and he could see her.

"Kuno, how slow you are."

He smiled gravely.

"I really believe you enjoy dawdling."

"I have called you before, mother, but you were always busy or isolated. I have something particular to say."

"What is it, dearest boy? Be quick. Why could you not send it by pneumatic post?"

"Because I prefer saying such a thing. I want—"

"Well?"

"I want you to come and see me."

Vashti watched his face in the blue plate.

"But I can see you!" she exclaimed. "What more do you want?"

"I want to see you not through the Machine," said Kuno. "I want to speak to you not through the wearisome Machine."

"Oh, hush!" said his mother, vaguely shocked. "You mustn't say anything against the Machine."

"Why not?"

"One mustn't."

"You talk as if a god had made the Machine," cried the other. "I believe that you pray to it when you are unhappy. Men made it, do not forget that. Great men, but men. The Machine is much, but it is not everything. I see something like you in this plate, but I do not see you. I hear something like you through this telephone, but I do not hear you. That is why I want you to come. Pay me a visit, so that we can meet face to face, and talk about the hopes that are in my mind."

She replied that she could scarcely spare the time for a visit.

"The air-ship barely takes two days to fly between me and you."

"I dislike air-ships."

"Why?"

"I dislike seeing the horrible brown earth, and the sea, and the stars when it is dark. I get no ideas in an air-ship."

"I do not get them anywhere else."

"What kind of ideas can the air give you?"

He paused for an instant.

"Do you not know four big stars that form an oblong, and three stars close together in the middle of the oblong, and hanging from these stars, three other stars?"

"No, I do not. I dislike the stars. But did they give you an idea? How interesting; tell me."

"I had an idea that they were like a man."

"I do not understand."

"The four big stars are the man's shoulders and his knees. The three stars in the middle are like the belts that men wore once, and the three stars hanging are like a sword."

"A sword?"

"Men carried swords about with them, to kill animals and other men."

"It does not strike me as a very good idea, but it is certainly original. When did it come to you first?"

"In the air-ship—" He broke off, and she fancied that he looked sad. She could not be sure, for the Machine did not transmit nuances of expression. It only gave a general idea of people—an idea that was good enough for all practical purposes, Vashti thought. The imponderable bloom, declared by a discredited philosophy to be the actual essence of intercourse, was rightly ignored by the Machine, just as the imponderable bloom of the grape was ignored by the manufacturers of artificial fruit. Something "good enough" had long since been accepted by our race.

"The truth is," he continued, "that I want to see these stars again. They are curious stars. I want to see them not from the air-ship, but from the surface of the earth, as our ancestors did, thousands of years ago. I want to visit the surface of the earth."

She was shocked again.

"Mother, you must come, if only to explain to me what is the harm of visiting the surface of the earth."

"No harm," she replied, controlling herself. "But no advantage. The surface of the earth is only dust and mud, no life remains on it, and you would need a respirator, or the cold of the outer air would kill you. One dies immediately in the outer air."

"I know; of course I shall take all precautions."

"And besides——"

"Well?"

She considered, and chose her words with care. Her son had a queer temper, and she wished to dissuade him from the expedition.

"It is contrary to the spirit of the age," she asserted.

"Do you mean by that, contrary to the Machine?"

"In a sense, but——"

His image is the blue plate faded.

"Kuno!"

He had isolated himself.

For a moment Vashti felt lonely.

Then she generated the light, and the sight of her room, flooded with radiance and studded with electric buttons, revived her. There were buttons and switches everywhere—buttons to call for food for music, for clothing. There was the hot-bath button, by pressure of which a basin of (imitation) marble rose out of the floor, filled to the brim with a warm deodorized liquid. There was the cold-bath button. There was the button that produced literature. And there were of course the buttons by which she communicated with her friends. The room, though it contained nothing, was in touch with all that she cared for in the world.

Vashti's next move was to turn off the isolation-switch, and all the accumulations of the last three minutes burst upon her. The room was filled with the noise of bells, and speaking-tubes. What was the new food like? Could she recommend it? Has she had any ideas lately? Might one tell her one's own ideas? Would she make an engagement to visit the public nurseries at an early date?—say this day month.

To most of these questions she replied with irritation—a growing quality in that accelerated age. She said that the new food was horrible. That she could not visit the public nurseries through press of engagements. That she had no ideas of her own but had just been told one—that four stars and three in the middle were like a man: she doubted there was much in it. Then she switched off her correspondents, for it was time to deliver her lecture on Australian music.

The clumsy system of public gatherings had been long since abandoned; neither Vashti nor her audience stirred from their rooms. Seated in her armchair she spoke, while they in their armchairs heard her, fairly well, and saw her, fairly well. She opened with a humorous account of music in the pre-Mongolian epoch, and went on to describe the great outburst of song that followed the Chinese conquest. Remote and primæval as were the methods of I-San-So and the Brisbane school, she yet felt (she said) that study of them might repay the musicians of today: they had freshness; they had, above all, ideas.

Her lecture, which lasted ten minutes, was well received, and at its conclusion she and many of her audience listened to a lecture on the sea; there were ideas to be got from the sea; the speaker had donned a respirator and visited it lately. Then she fed, talked to many friends, had a bath, talked again, and summoned her bed.

The bed was not to her liking. It was too large, and she had a feeling for a small bed. Complaint was useless, for beds were of the same dimension all over the world, and to have had an alternative size would have involved vast alterations in the Machine. Vashti isolated herself—it was necessary, for neither day nor night existed under the ground-and reviewed all that had happened since she had summoned the bed last. Ideas? Scarcely any. Events—was Kuno's invitation an event?

By her side, on the little reading-desk, was a survival from the ages of litter—one book. This was the Book of the Machine. In it were instructions against every possible contingency. If she was hot or cold or dyspeptic or at a loss for a word, she went to the book, and it told her which button to press. The Central Committee published it. In accordance with a growing habit, it was richly bound.

Sitting up in the bed, she took it reverently in her hands. She glanced round the glowing room as if some one might be watching her. Then, half ashamed, half joyful, she murmured "O Machine! O Machine!" and raised the volume to her lips. Thrice she kissed it, thrice inclined her head, thrice she felt the delirium of acquiescence. Her ritual performed, she turned to page 1367, which gave the times of the departure of the air-ships from the island in the southern hemisphere, under whose soil she lived, to the island in the northern hemisphere, whereunder lived her son.

She thought, "I have not the time."

She made the room dark and slept; she awoke and made the room light; she ate and exchanged ideas with her friends, and listened to music and attended lectures; she make the room dark and slept. Above her, beneath her, and around her, the Machine hummed eternally; she did not notice the noise, for she had been born with it in her ears. The earth, carrying her, hummed as it sped through silence, turning her now to the invisible sun, now to the invisible stars. She awoke and made the room light.

"Kuno!"

"I will not talk to you." he answered, "until you come."

"Have you been on the surface of the earth since we spoke last?"

His image faded.

Again she consulted the book. She became very nervous and lay back in her chair palpitating. Think of her as without teeth or hair. Presently she directed the chair to the wall, and pressed an unfamiliar button.

The wall swung apart slowly. Through the opening she saw a tunnel that curved slightly, so that its goal was not visible. Should she go to see her son, here was the beginning of the journey.

Of course she knew all about the communication-system. There was nothing mysterious in it. She would summon a car and it would fly with her down the tunnel until it reached the lift that communicated with the air-ship station: the system had been in use for many, many years, long before the universal establishment of the Machine. And of course she had studied the civilisation that had immediately preceded her own—the civilization that had mistaken the functions of the system, and had used it for bringing people to things, instead of for bringing things to people. Those funny old days, when men went for change of air instead of changing the air in their rooms! And yet—she was frightened of the tunnel: she had not seen it since her last child was born. It curved—but not quite as she remembered; it was brilliant-but not quite as brilliant as a lecturer had suggested. Vashti was seized with the terrors of direct experience. She shrank back into the room, and the wall closed up again.

"Kuno," she said, "I cannot come to see you. I am not well."

Immediately an enormous apparatus fell on to her out of the ceiling, a thermometer was automatically laid upon her heart. She lay powerless. Cool pads soothed her forehead. Kuno had telegraphed to her doctor.

So the human passions still blundered up and down in the Machine. Vashti drank the medicine that the doctor projected into her mouth, and the machinery retired into the ceiling. The voice of Kuno was heard asking how she felt.

"Better." Then with irritation: "But why do you not come to me instead?"

"Because I cannot leave this place."

"Why?"

"Because, any moment, something tremendous many happen."

"Have you been on the surface of the earth yet?"

"Not yet."

"Then what is it?"

"I will not tell you through the Machine."

She resumed her life.

But she thought of Kuno as a baby, his birth, his removal to the public nurseries, her own visit to him there, his visits to her-visits which stopped when the Machine had assigned him a room on the other side of the earth. "Parents, duties of," said the Book of the Machine," cease at the moment of birth. P.422327483." True, but there was something special about Kuno—indeed there had been something special about all her children—and, after all, she must brave the journey if he desired it. And "something tremendous might happen." What did that mean? The nonsense of a youthful man, no doubt, but she must go. Again she pressed the unfamiliar button, again the wall swung back, and she saw the tunnel that curves out of sight. Clasping the Book, she rose, tottered on to the platform, and summoned the car. Her room closed behind her: the journey to the northern hemisphere had begun.

Of course it was perfectly easy. The car approached and in it she found arm-chairs exactly like her own. When she signaled, it stopped, and she tottered into the lift. One other passenger was in the lift, the first fellow creature she had seen face to face for months. Few travelled in these days, for, thanks to the advance of science, the earth was exactly alike all over. Rapid intercourse, from which the previous civilization had hoped so much, had ended by defeating itself. What was the good of going to Peking when it was just like Shrewsbury? Why return to Shrewsbury when it would all be like Peking? Men seldom moved their bodies; all unrest was concentrated in the soul.

The air-ship service was a relic form the former age. It was kept up, because it was easier to keep it up than to stop it or to diminish it, but it now far exceeded the wants of the population. Vessel after vessel would rise form the vomitories of Rye or of Christchurch (I use the antique names), would sail into the crowded sky, and would draw up at the wharves of the south—empty. So nicely adjusted was the system, so independent of meteorology, that the sky, whether calm or cloudy, resembled a vast kaleidoscope whereon the same patterns periodically recurred. The ship on which Vashti sailed started now at sunset, now at dawn. But always, as it passed above Rheims, it would neighbour the ship that served between Helsingfors and the Brazils, and, every third time it surmounted the Alps, the fleet of Palermo would cross its track behind. Night and day, wind and storm, tide and earthquake, impeded man no longer. He had harnessed Leviathan.

All the old literature, with its praise of Nature, and its fear of Nature, rang false as the prattle of a child.

Yet as Vashti saw the vast flank of the ship, stained with exposure to the outer air, her horror of direct experience returned. It was not quite like the air-ship in the cinematophote. For one thing it smelt—not strongly or unpleasantly, but it did smell, and with her eyes shut she should have known that a new thing was close to her. Then she had to walk to it from the lift, had to submit to glances form the other passengers. The man in front dropped his Book—no great matter, but it disquieted them all. In the rooms, if the Book was dropped, the floor raised it mechanically, but the gangway to the air-ship was not so prepared, and the sacred volume lay motionless. They stopped—the thing was unforeseen—and the man, instead of picking up his property, felt the muscles of his arm to see how they had failed him. Then some one actually said with direct utterance: "We shall be late"—and they trooped on board, Vashti treading on the pages as she did so.

Inside, her anxiety increased. The arrangements were old-fashioned and rough. There was even a female attendant, to whom she would have to announce her wants during the voyage. Of course a revolving platform ran the length of the boat, but she was expected to walk from it to her cabin. Some cabins were better than others, and she did not get the best. She thought the attendant had been unfair, and spasms of rage shook her. The glass valves had closed, she could not go back. She saw, at the end of the vestibule, the lift in which she had ascended going quietly up and down, empty. Beneath those corridors of shining tiles were rooms, tier below tier, reaching far into the earth, and in each room there sat a human being, eating, or sleeping, or producing ideas. And buried deep in the hive was her own room. Vashti was afraid.

"O Machine! O Machine!" she murmured, and caressed her Book, and was comforted.

Then the sides of the vestibule seemed to melt together, as do the passages that we see in dreams, the lift vanished , the Book that had been dropped slid to the left and vanished, polished tiles rushed by like a stream of water, there was a slight jar, and the air-ship, issuing from its tunnel, soared above the waters of a tropical ocean.

It was night. For a moment she saw the coast of Sumatra edged by the phosphorescence of waves, and crowned by lighthouses, still sending forth their disregarded beams. These also vanished, and only the stars distracted her. They were not motionless, but swayed to and fro above her head, thronging out of one skylight into another, as if the universe and not the air-ship was careening. And, as often happens on clear nights, they seemed now to be in perspective, now on a plane; now piled tier beyond tier into the infinite heavens, now concealing infinity, a roof limiting for ever the visions of men. In either case they seemed intolerable. "Are we to travel in the dark?" called the passengers angrily, and the attendant, who had been careless, generated the light, and pulled down the blinds of pliable metal. When the air-ships had been built, the desire to look direct at things still lingered in the world. Hence the extraordinary number of skylights and windows, and the proportionate discomfort to those who were civilized and refined. Even in Vashti's cabin one star peeped through a flaw in the blind, and after a few hours' uneasy slumber, she was disturbed by an unfamiliar glow, which was the dawn.

Quick as the ship had sped westwards, the earth had rolled eastwards quicker still, and had dragged back Vashti and her companions towards the sun. Science could prolong the night, but only for a little, and those high hopes of neutralizing the earth's diurnal revolution had passed, together with hopes that were possibly higher. To "keep pace with the sun," or even to outstrip it, had been the aim of the civilization preceding this. Racing aeroplanes had been built for the purpose, capable of enormous speed, and steered by the greatest intellects of the epoch. Round the globe they went, round and round, westward, westward, round and round, amidst humanity's applause. In vain. The globe went eastward quicker still, horrible accidents occurred, and the Committee of the Machine, at the time rising into prominence, declared the pursuit illegal, unmechanical, and punishable by Homelessness.

Of Homelessness more will be said later.

Doubtless the Committee was right. Yet the attempt to "defeat the sun" aroused the last common interest that our race experienced about the heavenly bodies, or indeed about anything. It was the last time that men were compacted by thinking of a power outside the world. The sun had conquered, yet it was the end of his spiritual dominion.

Dawn, midday, twilight, the zodiacal path, touched neither men's lives not their hearts, and science retreated into the ground, to concentrate herself upon problems that she was certain of solving.

So when Vashti found her cabin invaded by a rosy finger of light, she was annoyed, and tried to adjust the blind. But the blind flew up altogether, and she saw through the skylight small pink clouds, swaying against a background of blue, and as the sun crept higher, its radiance entered direct, brimming down the wall, like a golden sea. It rose and fell with the air-ship's motion, just as waves rise and fall, but it advanced steadily, as a tide advances. Unless she was careful, it would strike her face. A spasm of horror shook her and she rang for the attendant. The attendant too was horrified, but she could do nothing; it was not her place to mend the blind. She could only suggest that the lady should change her cabin, which she accordingly prepared to do.

People were almost exactly alike all over the world, but the attendant of the air-ship, perhaps owing to her exceptional duties, had grown a little out of the common. She had often to address passengers with direct speech, and this had given her a certain roughness and originality of manner. When Vashti served away form the sunbeams with a cry, she behaved barbarically—she put out her hand to steady her.

"How dare you!" exclaimed the passenger. "You forget yourself!"

The woman was confused, and apologized for not having let her fall. People never touched one another. The custom had become obsolete, owing to the Machine.

"Where are we now?" asked Vashti haughtily.

"We are over Asia," said the attendant, anxious to be polite.

"Asia?"

"You must excuse my common way of speaking. I have got into the habit of calling places over which I pass by their unmechanical names."

"Oh, I remember Asia. The Mongols came from it."

"Beneath us, in the open air, stood a city that was once called Simla."

"Have you ever heard of the Mongols and of the Brisbane school?"

"No."

"Brisbane also stood in the open air."

"Those mountains to the right—let me show you them." She pushed back a metal blind. The main chain of the Himalayas was revealed.

"They were once called the Roof of the World, those mountains."

"You must remember that, before the dawn of civilization, they seemed to be an impenetrable wall that touched the stars. It was supposed that no one but the gods could exist above their summits. How we have advanced, thanks to the Machine!"

"How we have advanced, thanks to the Machine!" said Vashti.

"How we have advanced, thanks to the Machine!" echoed the passenger who had dropped his Book the night before, and who was standing in the passage.

"And that white stuff in the cracks?—what is it?"

"I have forgotten its name."

"Cover the window, please. These mountains give me no ideas."

The northern aspect of the Himalayas was in deep shadow: on the Indian slope the sun had just prevailed. The forests had been destroyed during the literature epoch for the purpose of making newspaper-pulp, but the snows were awakening to their morning glory, and clouds still hung on the breasts of Kinchinjunga. In the plain were seen the ruins of cities, with diminished rivers creeping by their walls, and by the sides of these were sometimes the signs of vomitories, marking the cities of to day. Over the whole prospect air-ships rushed, crossing the inter-crossing with incredible *aplomb*, and rising nonchalantly when they desired to escape the perturbations of the lower atmosphere and to traverse the Roof of the World.

"We have indeed advance, thanks to the Machine," repeated the attendant, and his the Himalayas behind a metal blind.

The day dragged wearily forward. The passengers sat each in his cabin, avoiding one another with an almost physical repulsion and longing to be once more under the surface of the earth. There were eight or ten of them, mostly young males, sent out from the public nurseries to inhabit the rooms of those who had died in various parts of the earth. The man who had dropped his Book was on the homeward journey. He had been sent to Sumatra for the purpose of propagating the race. Vashti alone was travelling by her private will.

At midday she took a second glance at the earth. The air-ship was crossing another range of mountains, but she could see little, owing to clouds. Masses of black rock hovered below her, and merged indistinctly into grey. Their shapes were fantastic; one of them resembled a prostrate man.

"No ideas here," murmured Vashti, and hid the Caucasus behind a metal blind.

In the evening she looked again. They were crossing a golden sea, in which lay many small islands and one peninsula. She repeated, "No ideas here," and hid Greece behind a metal blind.

II. THE MENDING APPARATUS

By a vestibule, by a lift, by a tubular railway, by a platform, by a sliding door—by reversing all the steps of her departure did Vashti arrive at her son's room, which exactly resembled her own. She might well declare that the visit was superfluous. The buttons, the knobs, the reading-desk with the Book, the temperature, the atmosphere, the illumination—all were exactly the same. And if Kuno himself, flesh of her flesh, stood close beside her at last, what profit was there in that? She was too well-bred to shake him by the hand.

Averting her eyes, she spoke as follows:

"Here I am. I have had the most terrible journey and greatly retarded the development of my soul. It is not worth it, Kuno, it is not worth it. My time is too precious. The sunlight almost touched me, and I have met with the rudest people. I can only stop a few minutes. Say what you want to say, and then I must return."

"I have been threatened with Homelessness," said Kuno.

She looked at him now.

"I have been threatened with Homelessness, and I could not tell you such a thing through the Machine."

Homelessness means death. The victim is exposed to the air, which kills him.

"I have been outside since I spoke to you last. The tremendous thing has happened, and they have discovered me."

"But why shouldn't you go outside?" she exclaimed, "It is perfectly legal, perfectly mechanical, to visit the surface of the earth. I have lately been to a lecture on the sea; there is no objection to that; one simply summons a respirator and gets an Egression-permit. It is not the kind of thing that spiritually-minded people do, and I begged you not to do it, but there is no legal objection to it."

"I did not get an Egression-permit."

"Then how did you get out?"

"I found out a way of my own."

The phrase conveyed no meaning to her, and he had to repeat it.

"A way of your own?" she whispered. "But that would be wrong."

"Why?"

The question shocked her beyond measure.

"You are beginning to worship the Machine," he said coldly. "You think it irreligious of me to have found out a way of my own. It was just what the Committee thought, when they threatened me with Homelessness."

At this she grew angry. "I worship nothing!" she cried. "I am most advanced. I don't think you irreligious, for there is no such thing as religion left. All the fear and the superstition that existed once have been destroyed by the Machine. I only meant that to find out a way of your own was—Besides, there is no new way out."

"So it is always supposed."

"Except through the vomitories, for which one must have an Egression-permit, it is impossible to get out. The Book says so."

"Well, the Book's wrong, for I have been out on my feet."

For Kuno was possessed of a certain physical strength.

By these days it was a demerit to be muscular. Each infant was examined at birth, and all who promised undue strength were destroyed. Humanitarians may protest, but it would have been no true kindness to let an athlete live; he would never have been happy in that state of life to which the Machine had called him; he would have yearned for trees to climb, rivers to bathe in, meadows and hills against which he might measure his body. Man must be adapted to his surroundings, must he not? In the dawn of the world our weakly must be exposed on Mount Taygetus, in its twilight our strong will suffer euthanasia, that the Machine may progress, that the Machine may progress, that the Machine may progress eternally.

"You know that we have lost the sense of space. We say "space is annihilated," but we have annihilated not space, but the sense thereof. We have lost a part of ourselves. I determined to recover it, and I began by walking up and down the platform of the railway outside my room. Up and down, until I was tired, and so did recapture the meaning of 'Near' and 'Far.' 'Near' is a place to which I can get quickly *on my feet*, not a place to which the train or the air-ship will take me quickly. 'Far' is a place to which I cannot get quickly on my feet; the vomitory is 'far,' though I could be there in thirty-eight seconds by summoning the train. Man is the measure. That was my first lesson. Man's feet are the measure for distance, his hands are the measure for ownership, his body is the measure for all that is lovable and desirable and strong. Then I went further: it was then that I called to you for the first time, and you would not come.

"This city, as you know, is built deep beneath the surface of the earth, with only the vomitories protruding. Having paced the platform outside my own room, I took the lift to the next platform and paced that also, and so with each in turn, until I came to the topmost, above which begins the earth. All the platforms were exactly alike, and all that I gained by visiting them was to develop my sense of space and my muscles. I think I should have been content with this—it is not a little thing—but as I walked and brooded, it occurred to me that our cities had been built in the days when men still breathed the outer air, and that there had been ventilation shafts for the workmen. I could think of nothing but these ventilation shafts. Had they been destroyed by all the food-tubes and medicine-tubes and music- tubes that the Machine has evolved lately? Or did traces of them remain? One thing was certain. If I came upon them anywhere, it would be in the railway-tunnels of the topmost storey. Everywhere else, all space was accounted for.

"I am telling my story quickly, but don't think that I was not a coward or that your answers never depressed me. It is not the proper thing, it is not mechanical, it is not decent to walk along a railway-tunnel. I did not fear that I might tread upon a live rail and be killed. I feared something far more intangible—doing what was not contemplated by the Machine. Then I said to myself, 'Man is the measure,' and I went, and after many visits I found an opening.

"The tunnels, of course, were lighted. Everything is light, artificial light; darkness is the exception. So when I saw a black gap in the tiles, I knew that it was an exception, and rejoiced. I put in my arm—I could put in no more at first—and waved it round and round in ecstasy. I loosened another tile, and put in my head, and shouted into the darkness: 'I am coming, I shall do it yet,' and my voice reverberated down endless passages. I seemed to hear the spirits of those dead workmen who had returned each evening to the starlight and to their wives, and all the generations who had lived in the open air called back to me, 'You will do it yet, you are coming.'"

He paused, and, absurd as he was, his last words moved her. For Kuno had lately asked to be a father, and his request had been refused by the Committee. His was not a type that the Machine desired to hand on.

"Then a train passed. It brushed by me, but I thrust my head and arms into the hole. I had done enough for one day, so I crawled back to the platform, went down in the lift, and summoned my bed. Ah what dreams! And again I called you, and again you refused."

She shook her head and said:

"Don't. Don't talk of these terrible things. You make me miserable. You are throwing civilization away."

"But I had got back the sense of space and a man cannot rest then. I determined to get in at the hole and climb the shaft. And so I exercised my arms. Day after day I went through ridiculous movements, until my flesh ached, and I could hang by my hands and hold the pillow of my bed outstretched for many minutes. Then I summoned a respirator, and started.

"It was easy at first. The mortar had somehow rotted, and I soon pushed some more tiles in, and clambered after them into the darkness, and the spirits of the dead comforted me. I don't know what I mean by that. I just say what I felt. I felt, for the first time, that a protest had been lodged against corruption, and that even as the dead were comforting me, so I was comforting the unborn. I felt that humanity existed, and that it existed without clothes. How can I possibly explain this? It was naked, humanity seemed naked, and all these tubes and buttons and machineries neither came into the world with us, nor will they follow us out, nor do they matter supremely while we are here. Had I been strong, I would have torn off every garment I had, and gone out into the outer air unswaddled. But this is not for me, nor perhaps for my generation. I climbed with my respirator and my hygienic clothes and my dietetic tabloids! Better thus than not at all.

"There was a ladder, made of some primæval metal. The light from the railway fell upon its lowest rungs, and I saw that it led straight upwards out of the rubble at the bottom of the shaft. Perhaps our ancestors ran up and down it a dozen times daily, in their building.

As I climbed, the rough edges cut through my gloves so that my hands bled. The light helped me for a little, and then came darkness and, worse still, silence which pierced my ears like a sword. The Machine hums! Did you know that? Its hum penetrates our blood, and may even guide our thoughts. Who knows! I was getting beyond its power. Then I thought: 'This silence means that I am doing wrong.' But I heard voices in the silence, and again they strengthened me." He laughed. "I had need of them. The next moment I cracked my head against something."

She sighed.

"I had reached one of those pneumatic stoppers that defend us from the outer air. You may have noticed them no the air- ship. Pitch dark, my feet on the rungs of an invisible ladder, my hands cut; I cannot explain how I lived through this part, but the voices till comforted me, and I felt for fastenings. The stopper, I suppose, was about eight feet across. I passed my hand over it as far as I could reach. It was perfectly smooth. I felt it almost to the centre. Not quite to the centre, for my arm was too short. Then the voice said: "Jump. It is worth it. There may be a handle in the centre, and you may catch hold of it and so come to us your own way. And if there is no handle, so that you may fall and are dashed to pieces—it is still worth it: you will still come to us your own way." So I jumped. There was a handle, and—"

He paused. Tears gathered in his mother's eyes. She knew that he was fated. If he did not die today he would die tomorrow. There was not room for such a person in the world. And with her pity disgust mingled. She was ashamed at having borne such a son, she who had always been so respectable and so full of ideas. Was he really the little boy to whom she had taught the use of his stops and buttons, and to whom she had given his first lessons in the Book? The very hair that disfigured his lip showed that he was reverting to some savage type. On atavism the Machine can have no mercy.

"There was a handle, and I did catch it. I hung tranced over the darkness and heard the hum of these workings as the last whisper in a dying dream. All the things I had cared about and all the people I had spoken to through tubes appeared infinitely little. Meanwhile the handle revolved. My weight had set something in motion and I span slowly, and then——

"I cannot describe it. I was lying with my face to the sunshine. Blood poured from my nose and ears and I heard a tremendous roaring. The stopper, with me clinging to it, had simply been blown out of the earth, and the air that we make down here was escaping through the vent into the air above. It burst up like a fountain. I crawled back to it—for the upper air hurts—and, as it were, I took great sips from the edge. My respirator had flown goodness knows here, my clothes were torn. I just lay with my lips close to the hole, and I sipped until the bleeding stopped. You can imagine nothing so curious. This hollow in the grass—I will speak of it in a minute—the sun shining into it, not brilliantly but through marbled clouds—the peace, the nonchalance, the sense of space, and, brushing my cheek, the roaring fountain of our artificial air! Soon I spied my respirator, bobbing up and down in the current high above my head, and higher still were many air-ships. But no one ever looks out of air-ships, and in any case they could not have picked me up. There I was, stranded. The sun shone a little way down the shaft, and revealed the topmost rung of the ladder, but it was hopeless trying to reach it. I should either have been tossed up again by the escape, or else have fallen in, and died. I could only lie on the grass, sipping and sipping, and from time to time glancing around me.

"I knew that I was in Wessex, for I had taken care to go to a lecture on the subject before starting. Wessex lies above the room in which we are talking now. It was once an important state. Its kings held all the southern coast form the Andredswald to Cornwall, while the Wansdyke protected them on the north, running over the high ground. The lecturer was only concerned with the rise of Wessex, so I do not know how long it remained an international power, nor would the knowledge have assisted me. To tell the truth I could do nothing but laugh, during this part. There was I, with a pneumatic stopper by my side and a respirator bobbing over my head, imprisoned, all three of us, in a grass-grown hollow that was edged with fern."

Then he grew grave again.

"Lucky for me that it was a hollow. For the air began to fall back into it and to fill it as water fills a bowl. I could crawl about. Presently I stood. I breathed a mixture, in which the air that hurts predominated whenever I tried to climb the sides. This was not so bad. I had not lost my tabloids and remained ridiculously cheerful, and as for the Machine,

I forgot about it altogether. My one aim now was to get to the top, where the ferns were, and to view whatever objects lay beyond.

"I rushed the slope. The new air was still too bitter for me and I came rolling back, after a momentary vision of something grey. The sun grew very feeble, and I remembered that he was in Scorpio—I had been to a lecture on that too. If the sun is in Scorpio, and you are in Wessex, it means that you must be as quick as you can, or it will get too dark. (This is the first bit of useful information I have ever got from a lecture, and I expect it will be the last.) It made me try frantically to breathe the new air, and to advance as far as I dared out of my pond. The hollow filled so slowly. At times I thought that the fountain played with less vigour. My respirator seemed to dance nearer the earth; the roar was decreasing."

He broke off.

"I don't think this is interesting you. The rest will interest you even less. There are no ideas in it, and I wish that I had not troubled you to come. We are too different, mother."

She told him to continue.

"It was evening before I climbed the bank. The sun had very nearly slipped out of the sky by this time, and I could not get a good view. You, who have just crossed the Roof of the World, will not want to hear an account of the little hills that I saw—low colourless hills. But to me they were living and the turf that covered them was a skin, under which their muscles rippled, and I felt that those hills had called with incalculable force to men in the past, and that men had loved them. Now they sleep—perhaps for ever. They commune with humanity in dreams. Happy the man, happy the woman, who awakes the hills of Wessex. For though they sleep, they will never die."

His voice rose passionately.

"Cannot you see, cannot all you lecturers see, that it is we that are dying, and that down here the only thing that really lives in the Machine? We created the Machine, to do our will, but we cannot make it do our will now. It has robbed us of the sense of space and of the sense of touch, it has blurred every human relation and narrowed down love to a carnal act, it has paralysed our bodies and our wills, and now it compels us to worship it. The Machine develops— but not on our lies. The Machine proceeds—but not to our goal. We only exist as the blood corpuscles that course through its arteries, and if it could work without us, it would let us die. Oh, I have no remedy— or, at least, only one—to tell men again and again that I have seen the hills of Wessex as Ælfrid saw them when he overthrew the Danes.

"So the sun set. I forgot to mention that a belt of mist lay between my hill and other hills, and that it was the colour of pearl."

He broke off for the second time.

"Go on," said his mother wearily.

He shook his head.

"Go on. Nothing that you say can distress me now. I am hardened."

"I had meant to tell you the rest, but I cannot: I know that I cannot: good-bye."

Vashti stood irresolute. All her nerves were tingling with his blasphemies. But she was also inquisitive.

"This is unfair," she complained. "You have called me across the world to hear our story, and hear it I will. Tell me—as briefly as possible, for this is a disastrous waste of time—tell me how you returned to civilization."

"Oh—that!" he said, starting. "You would like to hear about civilization. Certainly. Had I got to where my respirator fell down?"

"No—but I understand everything now. You put on your respirator, and managed to walk along the surface of the earth to a vomitory, and there your conduct was reported to the Central Committee."

"By no means."

He passed his hand over his forehead, as if dispelling some strong impression. Then, resuming his narrative, he warmed to it again.

"My respirator fell about sunset. I had mentioned that the fountain seemed feebler, had I not?"

"Yes."

"About sunset, it let the respirator fall. As I said, I had entirely forgotten about the Machine, and I paid no great attention at the time, being occupied with other things. I had my pool of air, into which I could dip when the outer keenness became intolerable, and which would possibly remain for days, provided that no wind sprang up to disperse it. Not until it was too late did I realize what the stoppage of the escape implied. You see—the gap in the tunnel had been mended; the Mending Apparatus; the Mending Apparatus, was after me.

"One other warning I had, but I neglected it. The sky at night was clearer than it had been in the day, and the moon, which was about half the sky behind the sun, shone into the dell at moments quite brightly. I was in my usual place—on the boundary between the two atmospheres—when I thought I saw something dark move across the bottom of the dell, and vanish into the shaft. In my folly, I ran down. I bent over and listened, and I thought I heard a faint scraping noise in the depths.

"At this—but it was too late—I took alarm. I determined to put on my respirator and to walk right out of the dell. But my respirator had gone. I knew exactly where it had fallen—between the stopper and the aperture—and I could even feel the mark that it had made in the turf. It had gone, and I realized that something evil was at work, and I had better escape to the other air, and, if I must die, die running towards the cloud that had been the colour of a pearl. I never started. Out of the shaft—it is too horrible. A worm, a long white worm, had crawled out of the shaft and gliding over the moonlit grass.

"I screamed. I did everything that I should not have done, I stamped upon the creature instead of flying from it, and it at once curled round the ankle. Then we fought. The worm let me run all over the dell, but edged up my leg as I ran. 'Help!' I cried. (That part is too awful. It belongs to the part that you will never know.) 'Help!' I cried. (Why cannot we suffer in silence?) 'Help!' I cried. When my feet were wound together, I fell, I was dragged away from the dear ferns and the living hills, and past the great metal stopper (I can tell you this part), and I thought it might save me again if I caught hold of the handle. It also was enwrapped, it also. Oh, the whole dell was full of the things. They were searching it in all directions, they were denuding it, and the white snouts of others peeped out of the hole, ready if needed. Everything that could be moved they brought—brushwood, bundles of fern, everything, and down we all went intertwined into hell. The last things that I saw, ere the stopper closed after us, were certain stars, and I felt that a man of my sort lived in the sky. For I did fight, I fought till the very end, and it was only my head hitting against the ladder that quieted me. I woke up in this room. The worms had vanished. I was surrounded by artificial air, artificial light, artificial peace, and my friends were calling to me

down speaking-tubes to know whether I had come across any new
ideas lately."

Here his story ended. Discussion of it was impossible, and Vashti
turned to go.

"It will end in Homelessness," she said quietly.

"I wish it would," retorted Kuno.

"The Machine has been most merciful."

"I prefer the mercy of God."

"By that superstitious phrase, do you mean that you could live in the
outer air?"

"Yes."

"Have you ever seen, round the vomitories, the bones of those who
were extruded after the Great Rebellion?"

"Yes."

"They were left where they perished for our edification. A few
crawled away, but they perished, too—who can doubt it? And so with
the Homeless of our own day. The surface of the earth supports life
no longer."

"Indeed."

"Ferns and a little grass may survive, but all higher forms have
perished. Has any air-ship detected them?"

"No."

"Has any lecturer dealt with them?"

"No."

"Then why this obstinacy?"

"Because I have seen them," he exploded.

"Seen *what*?"

"Because I have seen her in the twilight—because she came to my
help when I called—because she, too, was entangled by the worms,
and, luckier than I, was killed by one of them piercing her throat."

He was mad. Vashti departed, nor, in the troubles that followed, did
she ever see his face again.

III. THE HOMELESS

During the years that followed Kuno's escapade, two important
developments took place in the Machine. On the surface they were
revolutionary, but in either case men's minds had been prepared

beforehand, and they did but express tendencies that were latent already.

The first of these was the abolition of respirators.

Advanced thinkers, like Vashti, had always held it foolish to visit the surface of the earth. Air-ships might be necessary, but what was the good of going out for mere curiosity and crawling along for a mile or two in a terrestrial motor? The habit was vulgar and perhaps faintly improper: it was unproductive of ideas, and had no connection with the habits that really mattered. So respirators were abolished, and with them, of course, the terrestrial motors, and except for a few lecturers, who complained that they were debarred access to their subject-matter, the development was accepted quietly. Those who still wanted to know what the earth was like had after all only to listen to some gramophone, or to look into some cinematophote. And even the lecturers acquiesced when they found that a lecture on the sea was none the less stimulating when compiled out of other lectures that had already been delivered on the same subject. "Beware of first-hand ideas!" exclaimed one of the most advanced of them. "First-hand ideas do not really exist. They are but the physical impressions produced by love and fear, and on this gross foundation who could erect a philosophy? Let your ideas be second-hand, and if possible tenth-hand, for then they will be far removed from that disturbing element—direct observation. Do not learn anything about this subject of mine—the French Revolution. Learn instead what I think that Enicharmon thought Urizen thought Gutch thought Ho-Yung thought Chi-Bo-Sing thought Lafcadio Hearn thought Carlyle thought Mirabeau said about the French Revolution. Through the medium of these ten great minds, the blood that was shed at Paris and the windows that were broken at Versailles will be clarified to an idea which you may employ most profitably in your daily lives. But be sure that the intermediates are many and varied, for in history one authority exists to counteract another. Urizen must counteract the scepticism of Ho-Yung and Enicharmon, I must myself counteract the impetuosity of Gutch. You who listen to me are in a better position to judge about the French Revolution than I am. Your descendants will be even in a better position than you, for they will learn what you think I think, and yet another intermediate will be added to the chain. And in time"—his voice rose—"there will come a generation that had got beyond facts, beyond impressions, a generation absolutely colourless, a generation

'seraphically free
From taint of personality,'

which will see the French Revolution not as it happened, nor as they would like it to have happened, but as it would have happened, had it taken place in the days of the Machine."

Tremendous applause greeted this lecture, which did but voice a feeling already latent in the minds of men—a feeling that terrestrial facts must be ignored, and that the abolition of respirators was a positive gain. It was even suggested that air-ships should be abolished too. This was not done, because air-ships had somehow worked themselves into the Machine's system. But year by year they were used less, and mentioned less by thoughtful men.

The second great development was the re-establishment of religion.

This, too, had been voiced in the celebrated lecture. No one could mistake the reverent tone in which the peroration had concluded, and it awakened a responsive echo in the heart of each. Those who had long worshipped silently, now began to talk. They described the strange feeling of peace that came over them when they handled the Book of the Machine, the pleasure that it was to repeat certain numerals out of it, however little meaning those numerals conveyed to the outward ear, the ecstasy of touching a button, however unimportant, or of ringing an electric bell, however superfluously.

"The Machine," they exclaimed, "feeds us and clothes us and houses us; through it we speak to one another, through it we see one another, in it we have our being. The Machine is the friend of ideas and the enemy of superstition: the Machine is omnipotent, eternal; blessed is the Machine." And before long this allocution was printed on the first page of the Book, and in subsequent editions the ritual swelled into a complicated system of praise and prayer. The word "religion" was sedulously avoided, and in theory the Machine was still the creation and the implement of man. but in practice all, save a few retrogrades, worshipped it as divine. Nor was it worshipped in unity. One believer would be chiefly impressed by the blue optic plates, through which he

saw other believers; another by the mending apparatus, which sinful
Kuno had compared to worms; another by the lifts, another by the
Book. And each would pray to this or to that, and ask it to intercede
for him with the Machine as a whole. Persecution—that also was
present. It did not break out, for reasons that will be set forward shortly.
But it was latent, and all who did not accept the minimum known as
"undenominational Mechanism" lived in danger of Homelessness,
which means death, as we know.

To attribute these two great developments to the Central Committee,
is to take a very narrow view of civilization. The Central Committee
announced the developments, it is true, but they were no more the cause
of them than were the kings of the imperialistic period the cause of war.
Rather did they yield to some invincible pressure, which came no one
knew whither, and which, when gratified, was succeeded by some new
pressure equally invincible. To such a state of affairs it is convenient to
give the name of progress. No one confessed the Machine was out of
hand. Year by year it was served with increased efficiency and decreased
intelligence. The better a man knew his own duties upon it, the less he
understood the duties of his neighbour, and in all the world there was not
one who understood the monster as a whole. Those master brains had
perished. They had left full directions, it is true, and their successors had
each of them mastered a portion of those directions. But Humanity, in its
desire for comfort, had over-reached itself. It had exploited the riches of
nature too far. Quietly and complacently, it was sinking into decadence,
and progress had come to mean the progress of the Machine.

As for Vashti, her life went peacefully forward until the final disaster.
She made her room dark and slept; she awoke and made the room
light. She lectured and attended lectures. She exchanged ideas with
her innumerable friends and believed she was growing more spiritual.
At times a friend was granted Euthanasia, and left his or her room for
the Homelessness that is beyond all human conception. Vashti did not
much mind. After an unsuccessful lecture, she would sometimes ask for
Euthanasia herself. But the death-rate was not permitted to exceed the
birth-rate, and the Machine had hitherto refused it to her.

The troubles began quietly, long before she was conscious of them.

One day she was astonished at receiving a message from her
son. They never communicated, having nothing in common, and

she had only heard indirectly that he was still alive, and had been transferred from the northern hemisphere, where he had behaved so mischievously, to the southern—indeed, to a room not far from her own.

"Does he want me to visit him?" she thought. "Never again, never. And I have not the time."

No, it was madness of another kind.

He refused to visualize his face upon the blue plate, and speaking out of the darkness with solemnity said:

"The Machine stops."

"What do you say?"

"The Machine is stopping, I know it, I know the signs."

She burst into a peal of laughter. He heard her and was angry, and they spoke no more.

"Can you imagine anything more absurd?" she cried to a friend. "A man who was my son believes that the Machine is stopping. It would be impious if it was not mad."

"The Machine is stopping?" her friend replied. "What does that mean? The phrase conveys nothing to me."

"Nor to me."

"He does not refer, I suppose, to the trouble there has been lately with the music?"

"Oh no, of course not. Let us talk about music."

"Have you complained to the authorities?"

"Yes, and they say it wants mending, and referred me to the Committee of the Mending Apparatus. I complained of those curious gasping sighs that disfigure the symphonies of the Brisbane school. They sound like some one in pain. The Committee of the Mending Apparatus say that it shall be remedied shortly."

Obscurely worried, she resumed her life. For one thing, the defect in the music irritated her. For another thing, she could not forget Kuno's speech. If he had known that the music was out of repair—he could not know it, for he detested music—if he had known that it was wrong, "the Machine stops" was exactly the venomous sort of remark he would have made. Of course he had made it at a venture, but the coincidence annoyed her, and she spoke with some petulance to the Committee of the Mending Apparatus.

They replied, as before, that the defect would be set right shortly.

"Shortly! At once!" she retorted. "Why should I be worried by imperfect music? Things are always put right at once. If you do not mend it at once, I shall complain to the Central Committee."

"No personal complaints are received by the Central Committee," the Committee of the Mending Apparatus replied.

"Through whom am I to make my complaint, then?"

"Through us."

"I complain then."

"Your complaint shall be forwarded in its turn."

"Have others complained?"

This question was unmechanical, and the Committee of the Mending Apparatus refused to answer it.

"It is too bad!" she exclaimed to another of her friends.

"There never was such an unfortunate woman as myself. I can never be sure of my music now. It gets worse and worse each time I summon it."

"What is it?"

"I do not know whether it is inside my head, or inside the wall."

"Complain, in either case."

"I have complained, and my complaint will be forwarded in its turn to the Central Committee."

Time passed, and they resented the defects no longer. The defects had not been remedied, but the human tissues in that latter day had become so subservient, that they readily adapted themselves to every caprice of the Machine. The sigh at the crises of the Brisbane symphony no longer irritated Vashti; she accepted it as part of the melody. The jarring noise, whether in the head or in the wall, was no longer resented by her friend. And so with the mouldy artificial fruit, so with the bath water that began to stink, so with the defective rhymes that the poetry machine had taken to emit. All were bitterly complained of at first, and then acquiesced in and forgotten. Things went from bad to worse unchallenged.

It was otherwise with the failure of the sleeping apparatus. That was a more serious stoppage. There came a day when over the whole world—in Sumatra, in Wessex, in the innumerable cities of Courland and Brazil—the beds, when summoned by their tired owners, failed to appear. It may seem a ludicrous matter, but from it we may date the collapse of humanity. The Committee responsible for the failure was assailed by complainants, whom it referred, as usual, to the Committee of the Mending Apparatus, who in its turn assured them that their complaints would be forwarded to the Central Committee. But the discontent grew, for mankind was not yet sufficiently adaptable to do without sleeping.

"Some one is meddling with the Machine—" they began.

"Some one is trying to make himself king, to reintroduce the personal element."

"Punish that man with Homelessness."

"To the rescue! Avenge the Machine! Avenge the Machine!"

"War! Kill the man!"

But the Committee of the Mending Apparatus now came forward, and allayed the panic with well-chosen words. It confessed that the Mending Apparatus was itself in need of repair.

The effect of this frank confession was admirable.

"Of course," said a famous lecturer—he of the French Revolution, who gilded each new decay with splendour—"of course we shall not press our complaints now. The Mending Apparatus has treated us so well in the past that we all sympathize with it, and will wait patiently for its recovery. In its own good time it will resume its duties. Meanwhile let us do without our beds, our tabloids, our other little wants. Such, I feel sure, would be the wish of the Machine."

Thousands of miles away his audience applauded. The Machine still linked them. Under the seas, beneath the roots of the mountains, ran the wires through which they saw and heard, the enormous eyes and ears that were their heritage, and the hum of many workings clothed their thoughts in one garment of subserviency. Only the old and the sick remained ungrateful, for it was rumoured that Euthanasia, too, was out of order, and that pain had reappeared among men.

It became difficult to read. A blight entered the atmosphere and dulled its luminosity. At times Vashti could scarcely see across her room. The air, too, was foul. Loud were the complaints, impotent the remedies, heroic the tone of the lecturer as he cried: "Courage! courage! What matter so long as the Machine goes on? To it the darkness and the light are one." And though things improved again after a time, the old brilliancy was never recaptured, and humanity never recovered from its entrance into twilight. There was an hysterical talk of "measures," of "provisional dictatorship," and the inhabitants of Sumatra were asked to familiarize themselves with the workings of the central power station, the said power station being situated in France. But for the most part panic reigned, and men spent their strength praying to their Books, tangible proofs of the Machine"s omnipotence. There were gradations of terror—at times came rumours of hope—the Mending Apparatus was almost mended-the enemies of the Machine had been got under—new "nerve-centres" were evolving which would do the work even more magnificently than before. But there came a day when, without the slightest warning, without any previous hint of feebleness, the entire communication-system broke down, all over the world, and the world, as they understood it, ended.

Vashti was lecturing at the time and her earlier remarks had been punctuated with applause. As she proceeded the audience became silent, and at the conclusion there was no sound. Somewhat displeased, she called to a friend who was a specialist in sympathy. No sound: doubtless the friend was sleeping. And so with the next friend whom she tried to summon, and so with the next, until she remembered Kuno's cryptic remark, "The Machine stops."

The phrase still conveyed nothing. If Eternity was stopping it would of course be set going shortly.

For example, there was still a little light and air—the atmosphere had improved a few hours previously. There was still the Book, and while there was the Book there was security.

Then she broke down, for with the cessation of activity came an unexpected terror—silence.

She had never known silence, and the coming of it nearly killed her—it did kill many thousands of people outright. Ever since her birth she had been surrounded by the steady hum. It was to the ear what artificial air was to the lungs, and agonizing pains shot across her head. And scarcely knowing what she did, she stumbled forward and pressed the unfamiliar button, the one that opened the door of her cell.

Now the door of the cell worked on a simple hinge of its own. It was not connected with the central power station, dying far away in France. It opened, rousing immoderate hopes in Vashti, for she thought that the Machine had been mended. It opened, and she saw the dim tunnel that curved far away towards freedom. One look, and then she shrank back. For the tunnel was full of people—she was almost the last in that city to have taken alarm.

People at any time repelled her, and these were nightmares from her worst dreams. People were crawling about, people were screaming, whimpering, gasping for breath, touching each other, vanishing in the dark, and ever and anon being pushed off the platform on to the live rail. Some were fighting round the electric bells, trying to summon trains which could not be summoned. Others were yelling for Euthanasia or for respirators, or blaspheming the Machine. Others stood at the doors of their cells fearing, like herself, either to stop in them or to leave them. And behind all the uproar was silence—the silence which is the voice of the earth and of the generations who have gone.

No—it was worse than solitude. She closed the door again and sat down to wait for the end. The disintegration went on, accompanied by horrible cracks and rumbling. The valves that restrained the Medical Apparatus must have weakened, for it ruptured and hung hideously from the ceiling. The floor heaved and fell and flung her from the chair. A tube oozed towards her serpent fashion. And at last the final horror approached—light began to ebb, and she knew that civilization"s long day was closing.

She whirled around, praying to be saved from this, at any rate, kissing the Book, pressing button after button. The uproar outside was increasing, and even penetrated the wall. Slowly the brilliancy of her cell was dimmed, the reflections faded from the metal switches. Now she could not see the reading-stand, now not the Book, though she held it in her hand. Light followed the flight of sound, air was following light, and the original void returned to the cavern from which it has so long been excluded. Vashti continued to whirl, like the devotees of an earlier religion, screaming, praying, striking at the buttons with bleeding hands.

It was thus that she opened her prison and escaped—escaped in the spirit: at least so it seems to me, ere my meditation closes. That she escapes in the body—I cannot perceive that. She struck, by chance, the switch that released the door, and the rush of foul air on her skin, the loud throbbing whispers in her ears, told her that she was facing the tunnel again, and that tremendous platform on which she had seen men fighting. They were not fighting now. Only the whispers remained, and the little whimpering groans. They were dying by hundreds out in the dark.

She burst into tears.

Tears answered her.

They wept for humanity, those two, not for themselves. They could not bear that this should be the end. Ere silence was completed their hearts were opened, and they knew what had been important on the earth. Man, the flower of all flesh, the noblest of all creatures visible, man who had once made god in his image, and had mirrored his strength on the constellations, beautiful naked man was dying, strangled in the garments that he had woven. Century after century had he toiled, and here was his reward. Truly the garment had seemed heavenly at first, shot with colours of culture, sewn with the threads of self-denial. And heavenly it had been so long as man could shed it at will and live by the essence that is his soul, and the essence, equally divine, that is his body. The sin against the body—it was for that they wept in chief; the centuries of wrong against the muscles and the nerves, and those five portals by which we can alone apprehend—glozing it over with talk of evolution, until the body was white pap, the home of ideas as colourless, last sloshy stirrings of a spirit that had grasped the stars.

"Where are you?" she sobbed.

His voice in the darkness said, "Here."

Is there any hope, Kuno?"

"None for us."

"Where are you?"

She crawled over the bodies of the dead. His blood spurted over her hands.

"Quicker," he gasped, "I am dying—but we touch, we talk, not through the Machine."

He kissed her.

"We have come back to our own. We die, but we have recaptured life, as it was in Wessex, when Ælfrid overthrew the Danes. We know what they know outside, they who dwelt in the cloud that is the colour of a pearl."

"But Kuno, is it true ? Are there still men on the surface of the earth ? Is this—tunnel, this poisoned darkness— really not the end?"

He replied:

"I have seen them, spoken to them, loved them. They are hiding in the midst and the ferns until our civilization stops. Today they are the Homeless—tomorrow —"

"Oh, tomorrow—some fool will start the Machine again, tomorrow."

"Never," said Kuno, "never. Humanity has learnt its lesson."

As he spoke, the whole city was broken like a honeycomb. An airship had sailed in through the vomitory into a ruined wharf. It crashed downwards, exploding as it went, rending gallery after gallery with its wings of steel. For a moment they saw the nations of the dead, and, before they joined them, scraps of the untainted sky.

THE POISON BELT

ARTHUR CONAN DOYLE

After Sherlock Holmes, the greatest literary invention of Sir Arthur Conan Doyle (1859–1930) was surely scientist-adventurer Professor George E. Challenger, hero of five stories written between 1912 and 1929. The Poison Belt *was first serialized in the March through July 1913 issues of* The Strand Magazine, *and it reconvenes several characters from Professor Challenger's first adventure in the series* The Lost World *(1912). This short novel presents a unique celestial threat to earth in the form of a toxic cloud advancing toward the planet through the cosmic ether.*

I. THE BLURRING OF THE LINES

It is imperative that now at once, while these stupendous events are still clear in my mind, I should set them down with that exactness of detail which time may blur. But even as I do so, I am overwhelmed by the wonder of the fact that it should be our little group of the "Lost World"—Professor Challenger, Professor

Summerlee, Lord John Roxton, and myself—who have passed through this amazing experience.

When, some years ago, I chronicled in the *Daily Gazette* our epoch-making journey in South America, I little thought that it should ever fall to my lot to tell an even stranger personal experience, one which is unique in all human annals and must stand out in the records of history as a great peak among the humble foothills which surround it. The event itself will always be marvellous, but the circumstances that we four were together at the time of this extraordinary episode came about in a most natural and, indeed, inevitable fashion. I will explain the events which led up to it as shortly and as clearly as I can, though I am well aware that the fuller the detail upon such a subject the more welcome it will be to the reader, for the public curiosity has been and still is insatiable.

It was upon Friday, the twenty-seventh of August—a date forever memorable in the history of the world—that I went down to the office of my paper and asked for three days' leave of absence from Mr. McArdle, who still presided over our news department. The good old Scotchman shook his head, scratched his dwindling fringe of ruddy fluff, and finally put his reluctance into words.

"I was thinking, Mr. Malone, that we could employ you to advantage these days. I was thinking there was a story that you are the only man that could handle as it should be handled."

"I am sorry for that," said I, trying to hide my disappointment. "Of course if I am needed, there is an end of the matter. But the engagement was important and intimate. If I could be spared—"

"Well, I don't see that you can."

It was bitter, but I had to put the best face I could upon it. After all, it was my own fault, for I should have known by this time that a journalist has no right to make plans of his own.

"Then I'll think no more of it," said I with as much cheerfulness as I could assume at so short a notice. "What was it that you wanted me to do?"

"Well, it was just to interview that deevil of a man down at Rotherfield."

"You don't mean Professor Challenger?" I cried.

"Aye, it's just him that I do mean. He ran young Alec Simpson of the *Courier* a mile down the high road last week by the collar of his coat and the slack of his breeches. You'll have read of it, likely, in the police report. Our boys would as soon interview a loose alligator in the Zoo. But you could do it, I'm thinking—an old friend like you."

"Why," said I, greatly relieved, "this makes it all easy. It so happens that it was to visit Professor Challenger at Rotherfield that I was asking for leave of absence. The fact is, that it is the anniversary of our main adventure on the plateau three years ago, and he has asked our whole party down to his house to see him and celebrate the occasion."

"Capital!" cried McArdle, rubbing his hands and beaming through his glasses. "Then you will be able to get his opeenions out of him. In any other man I would say it was all moonshine, but the fellow has made good once, and who knows but he may again!"

"Get what out of him?" I asked. "What has he been doing?"

"Haven't you seen his letter on 'Scientific Possibeelities' in to-day's *Times*?"

"No."

McArdle dived down and picked a copy from the floor.

"Read it aloud," said he, indicating a column with his finger. "I'd be glad to hear it again, for I am not sure now that I have the man's meaning clear in my head."

This was the letter which I read to the news editor of the *Gazette*:—

"SCIENTIFIC POSSIBILITIES

"Sir,—I have read with amusement, not wholly unmixed with some less complimentary emotion, the complacent and wholly fatuous letter of James Wilson MacPhail which has lately appeared in your columns upon the subject of the blurring of Fraunhofer's lines in the spectra both of the planets and of the fixed stars. He dismisses the matter as of no significance. To a wider intelligence it may well seem of very great possible importance—so great as to involve the ultimate welfare of every man, woman, and child upon this planet. I can hardly hope, by the use of scientific language, to convey any sense of my meaning to those ineffectual people who gather their ideas from the columns of a daily newspaper. I will endeavour, therefore, to condescend to their limitation and to indicate the situation by the use of a homely analogy which will be within the limits of the intelligence of your readers."

"Man, he's a wonder—a living wonder!" said McArdle, shaking his head reflectively. "He'd put up the feathers of a sucking-dove and set up a riot in a Quakers' meeting. No wonder he has made London too hot for him. It's a peety, Mr. Malone, for it's a grand brain! We'll let's have the analogy."

"We will suppose," I read, "that a small bundle of connected corks was launched in a sluggish current upon a voyage across the Atlantic. The corks drift slowly on from day to day with the same conditions all round them. If the corks were sentient we could imagine that they would consider these conditions to be permanent and assured. But we, with our superior knowledge, know that many things might happen to surprise the corks. They might possibly float up against a ship, or a sleeping whale, or become entangled in seaweed. In any case, their voyage would probably end by their being thrown up on the rocky coast of Labrador. But what could they know of all this while they drifted so gently day by day in what they thought was a limitless and homogeneous ocean?

"Your readers will possibly comprehend that the Atlantic, in this parable, stands for the mighty ocean of ether through which we drift and that the bunch of corks represents the little and obscure planetary system to which we belong. A third-rate sun, with its rag-tag and bobtail of insignificant satellites, we float under the same daily conditions towards some unknown end, some squalid catastrophe which will overwhelm us at the ultimate confines of space,

where we are swept over an etheric Niagara or
dashed upon some unthinkable Labrador. I see no
room here for the shallow and ignorant optimism
of your correspondent, Mr. James Wilson MacPhail,
but many reasons why we should watch with a very
close and interested attention every indication of
change in those cosmic surroundings upon which
our own ultimate fate may depend."

"Man, he'd have made a grand meenister," said McArdle. "It just
booms like an organ. Let's get doun to what it is that's troubling him."

"The general blurring and shifting of Fraunhofer's
lines of the spectrum point, in my opinion, to a
widespread cosmic change of a subtle and singular
character. Light from a planet is the reflected light
of the sun. Light from a star is a self-produced light.
But the spectra both from planets and stars have,
in this instance, all undergone the same change. Is
it, then, a change in those planets and stars? To me
such an idea is inconceivable. What common change
could simultaneously come upon them all? Is it a
change in our own atmosphere? It is possible, but in
the highest degree improbable, since we see no signs
of it around us, and chemical analysis has failed to
reveal it. What, then, is the third possibility? That
it may be a change in the conducting medium, in
that infinitely fine ether which extends from star to
star and pervades the whole universe. Deep in that
ocean we are floating upon a slow current. Might
that current not drift us into belts of ether which
are novel and have properties of which we have
never conceived? There is a change somewhere.
This cosmic disturbance of the spectrum proves
it. It may be a good change. It may be an evil one.
It may be a neutral one. We do not know. Shallow
observers may treat the matter as one which can be

disregarded, but one who like myself is possessed
of the deeper intelligence of the true philosopher
will understand that the possibilities of the universe
are incalculable and that the wisest man is he who
holds himself ready for the unexpected. To take an
obvious example, who would undertake to say that
the mysterious and universal outbreak of illness,
recorded in your columns this very morning as
having broken out among the indigenous races
of Sumatra, has no connection with some cosmic
change to which they may respond more quickly
than the more complex peoples of Europe? I throw
out the idea for what it is worth. To assert it is, in
the present stage, as unprofitable as to deny it, but
it is an unimaginative numskull who is too dense to
perceive that it is well within the bounds of scientific
possibility.
"Yours faithfully,
    "GEORGE EDWARD CHALLENGER
        "THE BRIARS, ROTHERFIELD"

"It's a fine, steemulating letter," said McArdle thoughtfully, fitting
a cigarette into the long glass tube which he used as a holder. "What's
your opeenion of it, Mr. Malone?"

I had to confess my total and humiliating ignorance of the subject
at issue. What, for example, were Fraunhofer's lines? McArdle had just
been studying the matter with the aid of our tame scientist at the office,
and he picked from his desk two of those many-coloured spectral bands
which bear a general resemblance to the hat-ribbons of some young
and ambitious cricket club. He pointed out to me that there were
certain black lines which formed crossbars upon the series of brilliant
colours extending from the red at one end through gradations of
orange, yellow, green, blue, and indigo to the violet at the other.

"Those dark bands are Fraunhofer's lines," said he. "The colours are
just light itself. Every light, if you can split it up with a prism, gives the
same colours. They tell us nothing. It is the lines that count, because
they vary according to what it may be that produces the light. It is these

lines that have been blurred instead of clear this last week, and all the astronomers have been quarreling over the reason. Here's a photograph of the blurred lines for our issue to-morrow. The public have taken no interest in the matter up to now, but this letter of Challenger's in the *Times* will make them wake up, I'm thinking."

"And this about Sumatra?"

"Well, it's a long cry from a blurred line in a spectrum to a sick nigger in Sumatra. And yet the chiel has shown us once before that he knows what he's talking about. There is some queer illness down yonder, that's beyond all doubt, and to-day there's a cable just come in from Singapore that the lighthouses are out of action in the Straits of Sunda, and two ships on the beach in consequence. Anyhow, it's good enough for you to interview Challenger upon. If you get anything definite, let us have a column by Monday."

I was coming out from the news editor's room, turning over my new mission in my mind, when I heard my name called from the waiting-room below. It was a telegraph-boy with a wire which had been forwarded from my lodgings at Streatham. The message was from the very man we had been discussing, and ran thus:—

> Malone, 17, Hill Street, Streatham.—
> Bring oxygen.—CHALLENGER."

"Bring oxygen!" The Professor, as I remembered him, had an elephantine sense of humour capable of the most clumsy and unwieldly gambollings. Was this one of those jokes which used to reduce him to uproarious laughter, when his eyes would disappear and he was all gaping mouth and wagging beard, supremely indifferent to the gravity of all around him? I turned the words over, but could make nothing even remotely jocose out of them. Then surely it was a concise order—though a very strange one. He was the last man in the world whose deliberate command I should care to disobey. Possibly some chemical experiment was afoot; possibly— Well, it was no business of mine to speculate upon why he wanted it. I must get it. There was nearly an hour before I should catch the train at Victoria. I took a taxi, and having ascertained the address from the telephone book, I made for the Oxygen Tube Supply Company in Oxford Street.

As I alighted on the pavement at my destination, two youths emerged from the door of the establishment carrying an iron cylinder, which, with some trouble, they hoisted into a waiting motor-car. An elderly man was at their heels scolding and directing in a creaky, sardonic voice. He turned towards me. There was no mistaking those austere features and that goatee beard. It was my old cross-grained companion, Professor Summerlee.

"What!" he cried. "Don't tell me that *you* have had one of these preposterous telegrams for oxygen?"

I exhibited it.

"Well, well! I have had one too, and, as you see, very much against the grain, I have acted upon it. Our good friend is as impossible as ever. The need for oxygen could not have been so urgent that he must desert the usual means of supply and encroach upon the time of those who are really busier than himself. Why could he not order it direct?"

I could only suggest that he probably wanted it at once.

"Or thought he did, which is quite another matter. But it is superfluous now for you to purchase any, since I have this considerable supply."

"Still, for some reason he seems to wish that I should bring oxygen too. It will be safer to do exactly what he tells me."

Accordingly, in spite of many grumbles and remonstrances from Summerlee, I ordered an additional tube, which was placed with the other in his motor-car, for he had offered me a lift to Victoria.

I turned away to pay off my taxi, the driver of which was very cantankerous and abusive over his fare. As I came back to Professor Summerlee, he was having a furious altercation with the men who had carried down the oxygen, his little white goat's beard jerking with indignation. One of the fellows called him, I remember, "a silly old bleached cockatoo," which so enraged his chauffeur that he bounded out of his seat to take the part of his insulted master, and it was all we could do to prevent a riot in the street.

These little things may seem trivial to relate, and passed as mere incidents at the time. It is only now, as I look back, that I see their relation to the whole story which I have to unfold.

The chauffeur must, as it seemed to me, have been a novice or else have lost his nerve in this disturbance, for he drove vilely on the way to the station. Twice we nearly had collisions with other equally erratic vehicles, and I remember remarking to Summerlee that the standard of driving in London had very much declined. Once we brushed the very edge of a great crowd which was watching a fight at the corner of the Mall. The people, who were much excited, raised cries of anger at the clumsy driving, and one fellow sprang upon the step and waved a stick above our heads. I pushed him off, but we were glad when we had got clear of them and safe out of the park. These little events, coming one after the other, left me very jangled in my nerves, and I could see from my companion's petulant manner that his own patience had got to a low ebb.

But our good humour was restored when we saw Lord John Roxton waiting for us upon the platform, his tall, thin figure clad in a yellow tweed shooting-suit. His keen face, with those unforgettable eyes, so fierce and yet so humorous, flushed with pleasure at the sight of us. His ruddy hair was shot with grey, and the furrows upon his brow had been cut a little deeper by Time's chisel, but in all else he was the Lord John who had been our good comrade in the past.

"Hullo, Herr Professor! Hullo, young fellah!" he shouted as he came toward us.

He roared with amusement when he saw the oxygen cylinders upon the porter's trolly behind us. "So you've got them too!" he cried. "Mine is in the van. Whatever can the old dear be after?"

"Have you seen his letter in the *Times*?" I asked.

"What was it?"

"Stuff and nonsense!" said Summerlee harshly.

"Well, it's at the bottom of this oxygen business, or I am mistaken," said I.

"Stuff and nonsense!" cried Summerlee again with quite unnecessary violence. We had all got into a first-class smoker, and he had already lit the short and charred old briar pipe which seemed to singe the end of his long, aggressive nose.

"Friend Challenger is a clever man," said he with great vehemence. "No one can deny it. It's a fool that denies it. Look at his hat. There's a sixty-ounce brain inside it—a big engine, running smooth, and turning out clean work. Show me the engine-house and I'll tell you the size of the engine. But he is a born charlatan—you've heard me tell him so to his face—a born charlatan, with a kind of dramatic trick

of jumping into the limelight. Things are quiet, so friend Challenger
sees a chance to set the public talking about him. You don't imagine
that he seriously believes all this nonsense about a change in the ether
and a danger to the human race? Was ever such a cock-and-bull story
in this life?"

He sat like an old white raven, croaking and shaking with sardonic
laughter.

A wave of anger passed through me as I listened to Summerlee. It
was disgraceful that he should speak thus of the leader who had been
the source of all our fame and given us such an experience as no men
have ever enjoyed. I had opened my mouth to utter some hot retort,
when Lord John got before me.

"You had a scrap once before with old man Challenger," said he
sternly, "and you were down and out inside ten seconds. It seems to me,
Professor Summerlee, he's beyond your class, and the best you can do
with him is to walk wide and leave him alone."

"Besides," said I, "he has been a good friend to every one of us.
Whatever his faults may be, he is as straight as a line, and I don't believe
he ever speaks evil of his comrades behind their backs."

"Well said, young fellah my lad," said Lord John Roxton. Then, with
a kindly smile, he slapped Professor Summerlee upon his shoulder.
"Come, Herr Professor, we're not going to quarrel at this time of day.
We've seen too much together. But keep off the grass when you get
near Challenger, for this young fellah and I have a bit of a weakness for
the old dear."

But Summerlee was in no humour for compromise. His face was
screwed up in rigid disapproval, and thick curls of angry smoke rolled
up from his pipe.

"As to you, Lord John Roxton," he creaked, "your opinion upon a
matter of science is of as much value in my eyes as my views upon a
new type of shot-gun would be in yours. I have my own judgment, sir,
and I use it in my own way. Because it has misled me once, is that any
reason why I should accept without criticism anything, however far-
fetched, which this man may care to put forward? Are we to have a Pope
of science, with infallible decrees laid down *ex cathedrâ*, and accepted
without question by the poor humble public? I tell you, sir, that I have a
brain of my own and that I should feel myself to be a snob and a slave if

I did not use it. If it pleases you to believe this rigmarole about ether and Fraunhofer's lines upon the spectrum, do so by all means, but do not ask one who is older and wiser than yourself to share in your folly. Is it not evident that if the ether were affected to the degree which he maintains, and if it were obnoxious to human health, the result of it would already be apparent upon ourselves?" Here he laughed with uproarious triumph over his own argument. "Yes, sir, we should already be very far from our normal selves, and instead of sitting quietly discussing scientific problems in a railway train we should be showing actual symptoms of the poison which was working within us. Where do we see any signs of this poisonous cosmic disturbance? Answer me that, sir! Answer me that! Come, come, no evasion! I pin you to an answer!"

I felt more and more angry. There was something very irritating and aggressive in Summerlee's demeanour.

"I think that if you knew more about the facts you might be less positive in your opinion," said I.

Summerlee took his pipe from his mouth and fixed me with a stony stare.

"Pray what do you mean, sir, by that somewhat impertinent observation?"

"I mean that when I was leaving the office the news editor told me that a telegram had come in confirming the general illness of the Sumatra natives, and adding that the lights had not been lit in the Straits of Sunda."

"Really, there should be some limits to human folly!" cried Summerlee in a positive fury. "Is it possible that you do not realize that ether, if for a moment we adopt Challenger's preposterous supposition, is a universal substance which is the same here as at the other side of the world? Do you for an instant suppose that there is an English ether and a Sumatran ether? Perhaps you imagine that the ether of Kent is in some way superior to the ether of Surrey, through which this train is now bearing us. There really are no bounds to the credulity and ignorance of the average layman. Is it conceivable that the ether in Sumatra should be so deadly as to cause total insensibility at the very time when the ether here has had no appreciable effect upon us whatever? Personally, I can truly say that I never felt stronger in body or better balanced in mind in my life."

"That may be. I don't profess to be a scientific man," said I, "though I have heard somewhere that the science of one generation is usually the fallacy of the next. But it does not take much common sense to see that, as we seem to know so little about ether, it might be affected by some local conditions in various parts of the world and might show an effect over there which would only develop later with us."

"With 'might' and 'may' you can prove anything," cried Summerlee furiously. "Pigs may fly. Yes, sir, pigs *may* fly—but they don't. It is not worth arguing with you. Challenger has filled you with his nonsense and you are both incapable of reason. I had as soon lay arguments before those railway cushions."

"I must say, Professor Summerlee, that your manners do not seem to have improved since I last had the pleasure of meeting you," said Lord John severely.

"You lordlings are not accustomed to hear the truth," Summerlee answered with a bitter smile. "It comes as a bit of a shock, does it not, when someone makes you realize that your title leaves you none the less a very ignorant man?"

"Upon my word, sir," said Lord John, very stern and rigid, "if you were a younger man you would not dare to speak to me in so offensive a fashion."

Summerlee thrust out his chin, with its little wagging tuft of goatee beard.

"I would have you know, sir, that, young or old, there has never been a time in my life when I was afraid to speak my mind to an ignorant coxcomb—yes, sir, an ignorant coxcomb, if you had as many titles as slaves could invent and fools could adopt."

For a moment Lord John's eyes blazed, and then, with a tremendous effort, he mastered his anger and leaned back in his seat with arms folded and a bitter smile upon his face. To me all this was dreadful and deplorable. Like a wave, the memory of the past swept over me, the good comradeship, the happy, adventurous days—all that we had suffered and worked for and won. That it should have come to this—to insults and abuse! Suddenly I was sobbing—sobbing in loud, gulping, uncontrollable sobs which refused to be concealed. My companions looked at me in surprise. I covered my face with my hands.

"It's all right," said I. "Only—only it *is* such a pity!"

"You're ill, young fellah, that's what's amiss with you," said Lord John. "I thought you were queer from the first."

"Your habits, sir, have not mended in these three years," said Summerlee, shaking his head. "I also did not fail to observe your strange manner the moment we met. You need not waste your sympathy, Lord John. These tears are purely alcoholic. The man has been drinking. By the way, Lord John, I called you a coxcomb just now, which was perhaps unduly severe. But the word reminds me of a small accomplishment, trivial but amusing, which I used to possess. You know me as the austere man of science. Can you believe that I once had a well-deserved reputation in several nurseries as a farmyard imitator? Perhaps I can help you to pass the time in a pleasant way. Would it amuse you to hear me crow like a cock?"

"No, sir," said Lord John, who was still greatly offended, "it would *not* amuse me."

"My imitation of the clucking hen who had just laid an egg was also considered rather above the average. Might I venture?"

"No, sir, no—certainly not."

But in spite of this earnest prohibition, Professor Summerlee laid down his pipe and for the rest of our journey he entertained—or failed to entertain—us by a succession of bird and animal cries which seemed so absurd that my tears were suddenly changed into boisterous laughter, which must have become quite hysterical as I sat opposite this grave Professor and saw him—or rather heard him—in the character of the uproarious rooster or the puppy whose tail had been trodden upon. Once Lord John passed across his newspaper, upon the margin of which he had written in pencil, "Poor devil! Mad as a hatter." No doubt it was very eccentric, and yet the performance struck me as extraordinarily clever and amusing.

Whilst this was going on, Lord John leaned forward and told me some interminable story about a buffalo and an Indian rajah which seemed to me to have neither beginning nor end. Professor Summerlee had just begun to chirrup like a canary, and Lord John to get to the climax of his story, when the train drew up at Jarvis Brook, which had been given us as the station for Rotherfield.

And there was Challenger to meet us. His appearance was glorious. Not all the turkey-cocks in creation could match the slow, high-stepping

dignity with which he paraded his own railway station and the
benignant smile of condescending encouragement with which he
regarded everybody around him. If he had changed in anything since
the days of old, it was that his points had become accentuated. The
huge head and broad sweep of forehead, with its plastered lock of black
hair, seemed even greater than before. His black beard poured forward
in a more impressive cascade, and his clear grey eyes, with their insolent
and sardonic eyelids, were even more masterful than of yore.

He gave me the amused hand-shake and encouraging smile which
the head master bestows upon the small boy, and, having greeted the
others and helped to collect their bags and their cylinders of oxygen,
he stowed us and them away in a large motor-car which was driven by
the same impassive Austin, the man of few words, whom I had seen in
the character of butler upon the occasion of my first eventful visit to
the Professor. Our journey led us up a winding hill through beautiful
country. I sat in front with the chauffeur, but behind me my three
comrades seemed to me to be all talking together. Lord John was still
struggling with his buffalo story, so far as I could make out, while once
again I heard, as of old, the deep rumble of Challenger and the insistent
accents of Summerlee as their brains locked in high and fierce scientific
debate. Suddenly Austin slanted his mahogany face toward me without
taking his eyes from his steering-wheel.

"I'm under notice," said he.

"Dear me!" said I.

Everything seemed strange to-day. Everyone said queer, unexpected
things. It was like a dream.

"It's forty-seven times," said Austin reflectively.

"When do you go?" I asked, for want of some better observation.
"I don't go," said Austin.

The conversation seemed to have ended there, but presently he came
back to it.

"If I was to go, who would look after 'im?" He jerked his head toward
his master. "Who would 'e get to serve 'im?"

"Someone else," I suggested lamely.

"Not 'e. No one would stay a week. If I was to go, that 'ouse would
run down like a watch with the mainspring out. I'm telling you because
you're 'is friend, and you ought to know. If I was to take 'im at 'is

word—but there, I wouldn't have the 'eart. 'E and the missus would be like two babes left out in a bundle. I'm just everything. And then 'e goes and gives me notice."

"Why would no one stay?" I asked.

"Well, they wouldn't make allowances, same as I do. 'E's a very clever man, the master—so clever that 'e's clean balmy sometimes. I've seen 'im right off 'is onion, and no error. Well, look what 'e did this morning."

"What did he do?"

Austin bent over to me.

"'E bit the 'ousekeeper," said he in a hoarse whisper.

"Bit her?"

"Yes, sir. Bit 'er on the leg. I saw 'er with my own eyes startin' a marathon from the 'all-door."

"Good gracious!"

"So you'd say, sir, if you could see some of the goings on. 'E don't make friends with the neighbors. There's some of them thinks that when 'e was up among those monsters you wrote about, it was just "Ome, Sweet 'Ome' for the master, and 'e was never in fitter company. That's what *they* say. But I've served 'im ten years, and I'm fond of 'im, and, mind you, 'e's a great man, when all's said an' done, and it's an honor to serve 'im. But 'e does try one cruel at times. Now look at that, sir. That ain't what you might call old-fashioned 'ospitality, is it now? Just you read it for yourself."

The car on its lowest speed had ground its way up a steep, curving ascent. At the corner a notice-board peered over a well-clipped hedge. As Austin said, it was not difficult to read, for the words were few and arresting:—

WARNING.

———

Visitors, Pressmen, and Mendicants
Are not encouraged.

G.E. CHALLENGER

"No, it's not what you might call 'earty," said Austin, shaking his head and glancing up at the deplorable placard. "It wouldn't look well in a Christmas card. I beg your pardon, sir, for I haven't spoke as much as this for many a long year, but to-day my feelings seem to 'ave got the better of me. 'E can sack me till 'e's blue in the face, but I ain't going, and that's flat. I'm 'is man and 'e's my master, and so it will be, I expect, to the end of the chapter."

We had passed between the white posts of a gate and up a curving drive, lined with rhododendron bushes. Beyond stood a low brick house, picked out with white woodwork, very comfortable and pretty. Mrs. Challenger, a small, dainty, smiling figure, stood in the open doorway to welcome us.

"Well, my dear," said Challenger, bustling out of the car, "here are our visitors. It is something new for us to have visitors, is it not? No love lost between us and our neighbors, is there? If they could get rat poison into our baker's cart, I expect it would be there."

"It's dreadful—dreadful!" cried the lady, between laughter and tears. "George is always quarreling with everyone. We haven't a friend on the countryside."

"It enables me to concentrate my attention upon my incomparable wife," said Challenger, passing his short, thick arm round her waist. Picture a gorilla and a gazelle, and you have the pair of them. "Come, come, these gentlemen are tired from the journey, and luncheon should be ready. Has Sarah returned?"

The lady shook her head ruefully, and the Professor laughed loudly and stroked his beard in his masterful fashion.

"Austin," he cried, "when you have put up the car you will kindly help your mistress to lay the lunch. Now, gentlemen, will you please step into my study, for there are one or two very urgent things which I am anxious to say to you."

II. THE TIDE OF DEATH

As we crossed the hall the telephone-bell rang, and we were the involuntary auditors of Professor Challenger's end of the ensuing dialogue. I say "we," but no one within a hundred yards could have failed to hear the booming of that monstrous voice, which reverberated through the house. His answers lingered in my mind.

"Yes, yes, of course, it is I. . . . Yes, certainly, *the* Professor Challenger, the famous Professor, who else? . . . Of course, every word of it, otherwise I should not have written it. . . . I shouldn't be surprised. . . . There is every indication of it. . . . Within a day or so at the furthest. . . . Well, I can't help that, can I? . . . Very unpleasant, no doubt, but I rather fancy it will affect more important people than you. There is no use whining about it. . . . No, I couldn't possibly. You must take your chance. . . That's enough, sir. Nonsense! I have something more important to do than to listen to such twaddle."

He shut off with a crash and led us upstairs into a large airy apartment which formed his study. On the great mahogany desk seven or eight unopened telegrams were lying.

"Really," he said as he gathered them up, "I begin to think that it would save my correspondents' money if I were to adopt a telegraphic address. Possibly 'Noah, Rotherfield,' would be the most appropriate."

As usual when he made an obscure joke, he leaned against the desk and bellowed in a paroxysm of laughter, his hands shaking so that he could hardly open the envelopes.

"Noah! Noah!" he gasped, with a face of beetroot, while Lord John and I smiled in sympathy and Summerlee, like a dyspeptic goat, wagged his head in sardonic disagreement. Finally Challenger, still rumbling and exploding, began to open his telegrams. The three of us stood in the bow window and occupied ourselves in admiring the magnificent view.

It was certainly worth looking at. The road in its gentle curves had really brought us to a considerable elevation—seven hundred feet, as we afterwards discovered. Challenger's house was on the very edge of the hill, and from its southern face, in which was the study window, one looked across the vast stretch of the weald to where the gentle curves of the South Downs formed an undulating horizon. In a cleft of the hills a haze of smoke marked the position of Lewes. Immediately at our feet there lay a rolling plain of heather, with the long, vivid green stretches of the Crowborough golf course, all dotted with the players. A little to the south, through an opening in the woods, we could see a section of the main line from London to Brighton. In the immediate foreground, under our very noses, was a small enclosed yard, in which stood the car which had brought us from the station.

An ejaculation from Challenger caused us to turn. He had read his telegrams and had arranged them in a little methodical pile upon his desk. His broad, rugged face, or as much of it as was visible over the matted beard, was still deeply flushed, and he seemed to be under the influence of some strong excitement.

"Well, gentlemen," he said, in a voice as if he was addressing a public meeting, "this is indeed an interesting reunion, and it takes place under extraordinary—I may say unprecedented—circumstances. May I ask if you have observed anything upon your journey from town?"

"The only thing which I observed," said Summerlee with a sour smile, "was that our young friend here has not improved in his manners during the years that have passed. I am sorry to state that I have had to seriously complain of his conduct in the train, and I should be wanting in frankness if I did not say that it has left a most unpleasant impression in my mind."

"Well, well, we all get a bit prosy sometimes," said Lord John. "The young fellah meant no real harm. After all, he's an International, so if he takes half an hour to describe a game of football he has more right to do it than most folk."

"Half an hour to describe a game!" I cried indignantly. "Why, it was you that took half an hour with some long-winded story about a buffalo. Professor Summerlee will be my witness."

"I can hardly judge which of you was the most utterly wearisome," said Summerlee. "I declare to you, Challenger, that I never wish to hear of football or of buffaloes so long as I live."

"I have never said one word to-day about football," I protested.

Lord John gave a shrill whistle, and Summerlee shook his head sadly.

"So early in the day too," said he. "It is indeed deplorable. As I sat there in sad but thoughtful silence—"

"In silence!" cried Lord John. "Why, you were doin' a music-hall turn of imitations all the way—more like a runaway gramophone than a man."

Summerlee drew himself up in bitter protest.

"You are pleased to be facetious, Lord John," said he with a face of vinegar.

"Why, dash it all, this is clear madness," cried Lord John. "Each of us seems to know what the others did and none of us knows what he did himself. Let's put it all together from the first. We got into a first-class smoker, that's clear, ain't it? Then we began to quarrel over friend Challenger's letter in the *Times*."

"Oh, you did, did you?" rumbled our host, his eyelids beginning to droop.

"You said, Summerlee, that there was no possible truth in his contention."

"Dear me!" said Challenger, puffing out his chest and stroking his beard. "No possible truth! I seem to have heard the words before. And may I ask with what arguments the great and famous Professor Summerlee proceeded to demolish the humble individual who had ventured to express an opinion upon a matter of scientific possibility? Perhaps before he exterminates that unfortunate nonentity he will condescend to give some reasons for the adverse views which he has formed."

He bowed and shrugged and spread open his hands as he spoke with his elaborate and elephantine sarcasm.

"The reason was simple enough," said the dogged Summerlee. "I contended that if the ether surrounding the earth was so toxic in one quarter that it produced dangerous symptoms, it was hardly likely that we three in the railway carriage should be entirely unaffected."

The explanation only brought uproarious merriment from Challenger. He laughed until everything in the room seemed to rattle and quiver.

"Our worthy Summerlee is, not for the first time, somewhat out of touch with the facts of the situation," said he at last, mopping his heated brow. "Now, gentlemen, I cannot make my point better than by detailing to you what I have myself done this morning. You will the more easily condone any mental aberration upon your own part when you realize that even I have had moments when my balance has been disturbed. We have had for some years in this household a housekeeper—one Sarah, with whose second name I have never attempted to burden my memory. She is a woman of a severe and forbidding aspect, prim and demure in her bearing, very impassive in her nature, and never known within our experience to show signs of any emotion. As I sat alone at my breakfast—Mrs. Challenger is in the habit of keeping her room of a morning—it suddenly entered my head that it would be entertaining and instructive to see whether I could find any limits to this woman's imperturbability. I devised a simple but effective experiment. Having upset a small vase of flowers which stood in the centre of the cloth, I rang the bell and slipped under the table. She entered and, seeing the room empty, imagined that I had withdrawn to the study. As I had expected, she approached and leaned over the table to replace the vase. I had a vision of a cotton stocking and an elastic-sided boot. Protruding my head, I sank my teeth into the calf of her leg. The experiment was successful beyond belief. For some moments she stood paralyzed, staring down at my head. Then with a shriek she tore herself free and rushed from the room. I pursued her with some thoughts of an explanation, but she flew down the drive, and some minutes afterwards I was able to pick her out with my field-glasses traveling very rapidly in a south-westerly direction. I tell you the anecdote for what it is worth. I drop it into your brains and await its germination. Is it illuminative? Has it conveyed anything to your minds? What do *you* think of it, Lord John?"

Lord John shook his head gravely.

"You'll be gettin' into serious trouble some of these days if you don't put a brake on," said he.

"Perhaps you have some observation to make, Summerlee?"

"You should drop all work instantly, Challenger, and take three months in a German watering-place," said he.

"Profound! Profound!" cried Challenger. "Now, my young friend, is it possible that wisdom may come from you where your seniors have so signally failed?"

And it did. I say it with all modesty, but it did. Of course, it all seems obvious enough to you who know what occurred, but it was not so very clear when everything was new. But it came on me suddenly with the full force of absolute conviction.

"Poison!" I cried.

Then, even as I said the word, my mind flashed back over the whole morning's experiences, past Lord John with his buffalo, past my own hysterical tears, past the outrageous conduct of Professor Summerlee, to the queer happenings in London, the row in the park, the driving of the chauffeur, the quarrel at the oxygen warehouse. Everything fitted suddenly into its place.

"Of course," I cried again. "It is poison. We are all poisoned."

"Exactly," said Challenger, rubbing his hands, "we are all poisoned. Our planet has swum into the poison belt of ether, and is now flying deeper into it at the rate of some millions of miles a minute. Our young friend has expressed the cause of all our troubles and perplexities in a single word, 'poison.'"

We looked at each other in amazed silence. No comment seemed to meet the situation.

"There is a mental inhibition by which such symptoms can be checked and controlled," said Challenger. "I cannot expect to find it developed in all of you to the same point which it has reached in me, for I suppose that the strength of our different mental processes bears some proportion to each other. But no doubt it is appreciable even in our young friend here. After the little outburst of high spirits which so alarmed my domestic I sat down and reasoned with myself. I put it to myself that I had never before felt impelled to bite any of my household. The impulse had then been an abnormal one. In an instant I perceived the truth. My pulse upon examination was ten beats above the usual, and my reflexes were increased. I called upon my higher and saner self, the real G. E. C., seated serene and impregnable behind all mere molecular disturbance. I summoned him, I say, to watch the foolish mental tricks which the poison would play. I found that I was indeed the master. I could recognize and control a disordered mind. It was a remarkable exhibition of the victory of mind over matter, for it was a victory over that particular form of matter which is most intimately connected with mind. I might almost say that mind was at fault and that personality controlled it. Thus, when my wife came downstairs and I was impelled to slip behind the door and alarm her by some wild cry as she entered, I was able to stifle the impulse and to greet her with dignity and restraint. An overpowering desire to quack like a duck was met and mastered in the same fashion.

"Later, when I descended to order the car and found Austin bending over it absorbed in repairs, I controlled my open hand even after I had lifted it and refrained from giving him an experience which would possibly have caused him to follow in the steps of the housekeeper. On the contrary, I touched him on the shoulder and ordered the car to be at the door in time to meet your train. At the present instant I am

most forcibly tempted to take Professor Summerlee by that silly old
beard of his and to shake his head violently backwards and forwards.
And yet, as you see, I am perfectly restrained. Let me commend my
example to you."

"I'll look out for that buffalo," said Lord John.

"And I for the football match."

"It may be that you are right, Challenger," said Summerlee in a
chastened voice. "I am willing to admit that my turn of mind is critical
rather than constructive and that I am not a ready convert to any new
theory, especially when it happens to be so unusual and fantastic as this
one. However, as I cast my mind back over the events of the morning,
and as I reconsider the fatuous conduct of my companions, I find it
easy to believe that some poison of an exciting kind was responsible for
their symptoms."

Challenger slapped his colleague good-humouredly upon the
shoulder. "We progress," said he. "Decidedly we progress."

"And pray, sir," asked Summerlee humbly, "what is your opinion as to
the present outlook?"

"With your permission I will say a few words upon that subject." He
seated himself upon his desk, his short, stumpy legs swinging in front
of him. "We are assisting at a tremendous and awful function. It is, in
my opinion, the end of the world."

The end of the world! Our eyes turned to the great bow-window
and we looked out at the summer beauty of the country-side, the
long slopes of heather, the great country-houses, the cozy farms, the
pleasure-seekers upon the links.

The end of the world! One had often heard the words, but the
idea that they could ever have an immediate practical significance,
that it should not be at some vague date, but now, to-day, that was
a tremendous, a staggering thought. We were all struck solemn
and waited in silence for Challenger to continue. His overpowering
presence and appearance lent such force to the solemnity of his
words that for a moment all the crudities and absurdities of the man
vanished, and he loomed before us as something majestic and beyond
the range of ordinary humanity. Then to me, at least, there came
back the cheering recollection of how twice since we had entered the
room he had roared with laughter. Surely, I thought, there are limits

to mental detachment. The crisis cannot be so great or so pressing after all.

"You will conceive a bunch of grapes," said he, "which are covered by some infinitesimal but noxious bacillus. The gardener passes it through a disinfecting medium. It may be that he desires his grapes to be cleaner. It may be that he needs space to breed some fresh bacillus less noxious than the last. He dips it into the poison and they are gone. Our Gardener is, in my opinion, about to dip the solar system, and the human bacillus, the little mortal vibrio which twisted and wriggled upon the outer rind of the earth, will in an instant be sterilized out of existence."

Again there was silence. It was broken by the high trill of the telephone-bell.

"There is one of our bacilli squeaking for help," said he with a grim smile. "They are beginning to realise that their continued existence is not really one of the necessities of the universe."

He was gone from the room for a minute or two. I remember that none of us spoke in his absence. The situation seemed beyond all words or comments.

"The medical officer of health for Brighton," said he when he returned. "The symptoms are for some reason developing more rapidly upon the sea level. Our seven hundred feet of elevation give us an advantage. Folk seem to have learned that I am the first authority upon the question. No doubt it comes from my letter in the *Times*. That was the mayor of a provincial town with whom I talked when we first arrived. You may have heard me upon the telephone. He seemed to put an entirely inflated value upon his own life. I helped him to readjust his ideas."

Summerlee had risen and was standing by the window. His thin, bony hands were trembling with his emotion.

"Challenger," said he earnestly, "this thing is too serious for mere futile argument. Do not suppose that I desire to irritate you by any question I may ask. But I put it to you whether there may not be some fallacy in your information or in your reasoning. There is the sun shining as brightly as ever in the blue sky. There are the heather and the flowers and the birds. There are the folk enjoying themselves upon the golf-links and the laborers yonder cutting the corn. You tell us that they and we may be upon the very brink of destruction—that this sunlit day may be that day of doom which the human race has so long awaited. So far as we know, you found this tremendous judgment upon what? Upon some abnormal lines in a spectrum—upon rumours from Sumatra—upon some curious personal excitement which we have discerned in each other. This latter symptom is not so marked but that you and we could, by a deliberate effort, control it. You need not stand on ceremony with us, Challenger. We have all faced death together before now. Speak out, and let us know exactly where we stand, and what, in your opinion, are our prospects for our future."

It was a brave, good speech, a speech from that staunch and strong spirit which lay behind all the acidities and angularities of the old zoologist. Lord John rose and shook him by the hand.

"My sentiment to a tick," said he. "Now, Challenger, it's up to you to tell us where we are. We ain't nervous folk, as you know well; but when it comes to makin' a week-end visit and finding you've run full butt into the Day of Judgment, it wants a bit of explainin'. What's the danger, and how much of it is there, and what are we goin' to do to meet it?"

He stood, tall and strong, in the sunshine at the window, with his brown hand upon the shoulder of Summerlee. I was lying back in an armchair, an extinguished cigarette between my lips, in that sort of half-dazed state in which impressions become exceedingly distinct. It may have been a new phase of the poisoning, but the delirious promptings had all passed away and were succeeded by an exceedingly languid and, at the same time, perceptive state of mind. I was a spectator. It did not seem to be any personal concern of mine. But here were three strong men at a great crisis, and it was fascinating to observe them. Challenger bent his heavy brows and stroked his beard before he answered. One could see that he was very carefully weighing his words.

"What was the last news when you left London?" he asked.

"I was at the *Gazette* office about ten," said I. "There was a Reuter just come in from Singapore to the effect that the sickness seemed to be universal in Sumatra and that the lighthouses had not been lit in consequence."

"Events have been moving somewhat rapidly since then," said Challenger, picking up his pile of telegrams. "I am in close touch both with the authorities and with the press, so that news is converging upon me from all parts. There is, in fact, a general and very insistent demand

that I should come to London; but I see no good end to be served.
From the accounts the poisonous effect begins with mental excitement;
the rioting in Paris this morning is said to have been very violent, and
the Welsh colliers are in a state of uproar. So far as the evidence to hand
can be trusted, this stimulative stage, which varies much in races and in
individuals, is succeeded by a certain exaltation and mental lucidity—I
seem to discern some signs of it in our young friend here—which, after
an appreciable interval, turns to coma, deepening rapidly into death. I
fancy, so far as my toxicology carries me, that there are some vegetable
nerve poisons—"

"Datura," suggested Summerlee.

"Excellent!" cried Challenger. "It would make for scientific
precision if we named our toxic agent. Let it be daturon. To you, my
dear Summerlee, belongs the honour—posthumous, alas, but none
the less unique—of having given a name to the universal destroyer,
the Great Gardener's disinfectant. The symptoms of daturon, then,
may be taken to be such as I indicate. That it will involve the whole
world and that no life can possibly remain behind seems to me to
be certain, since ether is a universal medium. Up to now it has been
capricious in the places which it has attacked, but the difference is
only a matter of a few hours, and it is like an advancing tide which
covers one strip of sand and then another, running hither and thither
in irregular streams, until at last it has submerged it all. There are laws
at work in connection with the action and distribution of daturon
which would have been of deep interest had the time at our disposal
permitted us to study them. So far as I can trace them"—here he
glanced over his telegrams—"the less developed races have been the
first to respond to its influence. There are deplorable accounts from
Africa, and the Australian aborigines appear to have been already
exterminated. The Northern races have as yet shown greater resisting
power than the Southern. This, you see, is dated from Marseilles at
nine-forty-five this morning. I give it to you verbatim:—

"'All night delirious excitement throughout Provence. Tumult of
vine growers at Nîmes. Socialistic upheaval at Toulon. Sudden illness
attended by coma attacked population this morning. *Peste foudroyant.*
Great numbers of dead in the streets. Paralysis of business and
universal chaos.'

"An hour later came the following, from the same source:—

"'We are threatened with utter extermination. Cathedrals and churches full to overflowing. The dead outnumber the living. It is inconceivable and horrible. Decease seems to be painless, but swift and inevitable.'

"There is a similar telegram from Paris, where the development is not yet as acute. India and Persia appear to be utterly wiped out. The Slavonic population of Austria is down, while the Teutonic has hardly been affected. Speaking generally, the dwellers upon the plains and upon the seashore seem, so far as my limited information goes, to have felt the effects more rapidly than those inland or on the heights. Even a little elevation makes a considerable difference, and perhaps if there be a survivor of the human race, he will again be found upon the summit of some Ararat. Even our own little hill may presently prove to be a temporary island amid a sea of disaster. But at the present rate of advance a few short hours will submerge us all."

Lord John Roxton wiped his brow.

"What beats me," said he, "is how you could sit there laughin' with that stack of telegrams under your hand. I've seen death as often as most folk, but universal death—it's awful!"

"As to the laughter," said Challenger, "you will bear in mind that, like yourselves, I have not been exempt from the stimulating cerebral effects of the etheric poison. But as to the horror with which universal death appears to inspire you, I would put it to you that it is somewhat exaggerated. If you were sent to sea alone in an open boat to some unknown destination, your heart might well sink within you. The isolation, the uncertainty, would oppress you. But if your voyage were made in a goodly ship, which bore within it all your relations and your friends, you would feel that, however uncertain your destination might still remain, you would at least have one common and simultaneous experience which would hold you to the end in the same close communion. A lonely death may be terrible, but a universal one, as painless as this would appear to be, is not, in my judgment, a matter for apprehension. Indeed, I could sympathize with the person who took the view that the horror lay in the idea of surviving when all that is learned, famous, and exalted had passed away."

"What, then, do you propose to do?" asked Summerlee, who had for once nodded his assent to the reasoning of his brother scientist.

"To take our lunch," said Challenger as the boom of a gong sounded through the house. "We have a cook whose omelettes are only excelled by her cutlets. We can but trust that no cosmic disturbance has dulled her excellent abilities. My Scharzberger of '96 must also be rescued, so far as our earnest and united efforts can do it, from what would be a deplorable waste of a great vintage." He levered his great bulk off the desk, upon which he had sat while he announced the doom of the planet. "Come," said he. "If there is little time left, there is the more need that we should spend it in sober and reasonable enjoyment."

And, indeed, it proved to be a very merry meal. It is true that we could not forget our awful situation. The full solemnity of the event loomed ever at the back of our minds and tempered our thoughts. But surely it is the soul which has never faced Death which shies strongly from it at the end. To each of us men it had, for one great epoch in our lives, been a familiar presence. As to the lady, she leaned upon the strong guidance of her mighty husband and was well content to go whither his path might lead. The future was our Fate. The present was our own. We passed it in goodly comradeship and gentle merriment. Our minds were, as I have said, singularly lucid. Even I struck sparks at times. As to Challenger, he was wonderful! Never have I so realized the elemental greatness of the man, the sweep and power of his understanding. Summerlee drew him on with his chorus of subacid criticism, while Lord John and I laughed at the contest and the lady, her hand upon his sleeve, controlled the bellowings of the philosopher. Life, death, fate, the destiny of man—these were the stupendous subjects of that memorable hour, made vital by the fact that as the meal progressed strange, sudden exaltations in my mind and tinglings in my limbs proclaimed that the invisible tide of death was slowly and gently rising around us. Once I saw Lord John put his hand suddenly to his eyes, and once Summerlee dropped back for an instant in his chair. Each breath we breathed was charged with strange forces. And yet our minds were happy and at ease. Presently Austin laid the cigarettes upon the table and was about to withdraw.

"Austin!" said his master.

"Yes, sir?"

"I thank you for your faithful service." A smile stole over the servant's gnarled face.

"I've done my duty, sir."

"I'm expecting the end of the world to-day, Austin."

"Yes, sir. What time, sir?"

"I can't say, Austin. Before evening."

"Very good, sir."

The taciturn Austin saluted and withdrew. Challenger lit a cigarette, and, drawing his chair closer to his wife's, he took her hand in his.

"You know how matters stand, dear," said he. "I have explained it also to our friends here. You're not afraid are you?"

"It won't be painful, George?"

"No more than laughing-gas at the dentist's. Every time you have had it you have practically died."

"But that is a pleasant sensation."

"So may death be. The worn-out bodily machine can't record its impression, but we know the mental pleasure which lies in a dream or a trance. Nature may build a beautiful door and hang it with many a gauzy and shimmering curtain to make an entrance to the new life for our wondering souls. In all my probings of the actual, I have always found wisdom and kindness at the core; and if ever the frightened mortal needs tenderness, it is surely as he makes the passage perilous from life to life. No, Summerlee, I will have none of your materialism, for I, at least, am too great a thing to end in mere physical constituents, a packet of salts and three bucketfuls of water. Here—here"—and he beat his great head with his huge, hairy fist—"there is something which uses matter, but is not of it— something which might destroy death, but which death can never destroy."

"Talkin' of death," said Lord John. "I'm a Christian of sorts, but it seems to me there was somethin' mighty natural in those ancestors of ours who were buried with their axes and bows and arrows and the like, same as if they were livin' on just the same as they used to. I don't know," he added, looking round the table in a shamefaced way, "that I wouldn't feel more homely myself if I was put away with my old .450 Express and the fowlin'-piece, the shorter one with the rubbered stock, and a clip or two of cartridges—just a fool's fancy, of course, but there it is. How does it strike you, Herr Professor?"

"Well," said Summerlee, "since you ask my opinion, it strikes me as an indefensible throwback to the Stone Age or before it. I'm of the twentieth century myself, and would wish to die like a reasonable civilized man. I don't know that I am more afraid of death than the rest of you, for I am an oldish man, and, come what may, I can't have very much longer to live; but it is all against my nature to sit waiting without a struggle like a sheep for the butcher. Is it quite certain, Challenger, that there is nothing we can do?"

"To save us—nothing," said Challenger. "To prolong our lives a few hours and thus to see the evolution of this mighty tragedy before we are actually involved in it—that may prove to be within my powers. I have taken certain steps—"

"The oxygen?"

"Exactly. The oxygen."

"But what can oxygen effect in the face of a poisoning of the ether? There is not a greater difference in quality between a brick-bat and a gas than there is between oxygen and ether. They are different planes of matter. They cannot impinge upon one another. Come, Challenger, you could not defend such a proposition."

"My good Summerlee, this etheric poison is most certainly influenced by material agents. We see it in the methods and distribution of the outbreak. We should not *a priori* have expected it, but it is undoubtedly a fact. Hence I am strongly of opinion that a gas like oxygen, which increases the vitality and the resisting power of the body, would be extremely likely to delay the action of what you have so happily named the daturon. It may be that I am mistaken, but I have every confidence in the correctness of my reasoning."

"Well," said Lord John, "if we've got to sit suckin' at those tubes like so many babies with their bottles, I'm not takin' any."

"There will be no need for that," Challenger answered. "We have made arrangements—it is to my wife that you chiefly owe it—that her boudoir shall be made as airtight as is practicable. With matting and varnished paper."

"Good heavens, Challenger, you don't suppose you can keep out ether with varnished paper?"

"Really, my worthy friend, you are a trifle perverse in missing the point. It is not to keep out the ether that we have gone to such trouble. It is to keep in the oxygen. I trust that if we can ensure an atmosphere hyper-oxygenated to a certain point, we may be able to retain our senses. I had two tubes of the gas and you have brought me three more. It is not much, but it is something."

"How long will they last?"

"I have not an idea. We will not turn them on until our symptoms become unbearable. Then we shall dole the gas out as it is urgently needed. It may give us some hours, possibly even some days, on which we may look out upon a blasted world. Our own fate is delayed to that extent, and we will have the very singular experience, we five, of being, in all probability, the absolute rear guard of the human race upon its march into the unknown. Perhaps you will be kind enough now to give me a hand with the cylinders. It seems to me that the atmosphere already grows somewhat more oppressive."

III. SUBMERGED

The chamber which was destined to be the scene of our unforgettable experience was a charmingly feminine sitting-room, some fourteen or sixteen feet square. At the end of it, divided by a curtain of red velvet, was a small apartment which formed the Professor's dressing-room. This in turn opened into a large bedroom. The curtain was still hanging, but the boudoir and dressing-room could be taken as one chamber for the purposes of our experiment. One door and the window frame had been plastered round with varnished paper so as to be practically sealed. Above the other door, which opened on to the landing, there hung a fanlight which could be drawn by a cord when some ventilation became absolutely necessary. A large shrub in a tub stood in each corner.

"How to get rid of our excessive carbon dioxide without unduly wasting our oxygen is a delicate and vital question," said Challenger, looking round him after the five iron tubes had been laid side by side against the wall. "With longer time for preparation I could have brought the whole concentrated force of my intelligence to bear more fully upon the problem, but as it is we must do what we can. The shrubs will be of some small service. Two of the oxygen tubes are ready to be turned on at an instant's notice, so that we cannot be taken unawares. At the same time, it would be well not to go far from the room, as the crisis may be a sudden and urgent one."

There was a broad, low window opening out upon a balcony. The view beyond was the same as that which we had already admired from the study. Looking out, I could see no sign of disorder anywhere. There was a road curving down the side of the hill, under my very eyes. A cab from the station, one of those prehistoric survivals which are only to be found in our country villages, was toiling slowly up the hill. Lower down was a nurse girl wheeling a perambulator and leading a second child by the hand. The blue reeks of smoke from the cottages gave the whole widespread landscape an air of settled order and homely comfort. Nowhere in the blue heaven or on the sunlit earth was there any foreshadowing of a catastrophe. The harvesters were back in the fields once more and the golfers, in pairs and fours, were still streaming round the links. There was so strange a turmoil within my own head, and such a jangling of my overstrung nerves, that the indifference of those people was amazing.

"Those fellows don't seem to feel any ill effects," said I, pointing down at the links.

"Have you played golf?" asked Lord John.

"No, I have not."

"Well, young fellah, when you do you'll learn that once fairly out on a round, it would take the crack of doom to stop a true golfer. Halloa! There's that telephone-bell again."

From time to time during and after lunch the high, insistent ring had summoned the Professor. He gave us the news as it came through to him in a few curt sentences. Such terrific items had never been registered in the world's history before. The great shadow was creeping up from the south like a rising tide of death. Egypt had gone through its delirium and was now comatose. Spain and Portugal, after a wild frenzy in which the Clericals and the Anarchists had fought most desperately, were now fallen silent. No cable messages were received any longer from South America. In North America the southern states, after some terrible racial rioting, had succumbed to the poison. North of Maryland the effect was not yet marked, and in Canada it was hardly perceptible. Belgium, Holland,

and Denmark had each in turn been affected. Despairing messages were flashing from every quarter to the great centres of learning, to the chemists and the doctors of world-wide repute, imploring their advice. The astronomers too were deluged with inquiries. Nothing could be done. The thing was universal and beyond our human knowledge or control. It was death—painless but inevitable—death for young and old, for weak and strong, for rich and poor, without hope or possibility of escape. Such was the news which, in scattered, distracted messages, the telephone had brought us. The great cities already knew their fate and so far as we could gather were preparing to meet it with dignity and resignation. Yet here were our golfers and laborers like the lambs who gambol under the shadow of the knife. It seemed amazing. And yet how could they know? It had all come upon us in one giant stride. What was there in the morning paper to alarm them? And now it was but three in the afternoon. Even as we looked some rumour seemed to have spread, for we saw the reapers hurrying from the fields. Some of the golfers were returning to the club-house. They were running as if taking refuge from a shower. Their little caddies trailed behind them. Others were continuing their game. The nurse had turned and was pushing her perambulator hurriedly up the hill again. I noticed that she had her hand to her brow. The cab had stopped and the tired horse, with his head sunk to his knees, was resting. Above there was a perfect summer sky—one huge vault of unbroken blue, save for a few fleecy white clouds over the distant downs. If the human race must die to-day, it was at least upon a glorious death-bed. And yet all that gentle loveliness of nature made this terrific and wholesale destruction the more pitiable and awful. Surely it was too goodly a residence that we should be so swiftly, so ruthlessly, evicted from it!

But I have said that the telephone-bell had rung once more. Suddenly I heard Challenger's tremendous voice from the hall.

"Malone!" he cried. "You are wanted."

I rushed down to the instrument. It was McArdle speaking from London.

"That you, Mr. Malone?" cried his familiar voice. "Mr. Malone, there are terrible goings-on in London. For God's sake, see if Professor Challenger can suggest anything that can be done."

"He can suggest nothing, sir," I answered. "He regards the crisis as universal and inevitable. We have some oxygen here, but it can only defer our fate for a few hours."

"Oxygen!" cried the agonized voice. "There is no time to get any. The office has been a perfect pandemonium ever since you left in the morning. Now half of the staff are insensible. I am weighed down with heaviness myself. From my window I can see the people lying thick in Fleet Street. The traffic is all held up. Judging by the last telegrams, the whole world——"

His voice had been sinking, and suddenly stopped. An instant later I heard through the telephone a muffled thud, as if his head had fallen forward on the desk.

"Mr. McArdle!" I cried. "Mr. McArdle!"

There was no answer. I knew as I replaced the receiver that I should never hear his voice again.

At that instant, just as I took a step backwards from the telephone, the thing was on us. It was as if we were bathers, up to our shoulders in water, who suddenly are submerged by a rolling wave. An invisible hand seemed to have quietly closed round my throat and to be gently pressing the life from me. I was conscious of immense oppression upon my chest, great tightness within my head, a loud singing in my ears, and bright flashes before my eyes. I staggered to the balustrades of the stair. At the same moment, rushing and snorting like a wounded buffalo, Challenger dashed past me, a terrible vision, with red-purple face, engorged eyes, and bristling hair. His little wife, insensible to all appearance, was slung over his great shoulder, and he blundered and thundered up the stair, scrambling and tripping, but carrying himself and her through sheer will-force through that mephitic atmosphere to the haven of temporary safety. At the sight of his effort I too rushed up the steps, clambering, falling, clutching at the rail, until I tumbled half senseless upon by face on the upper landing. Lord John's fingers of steel were in the collar of my coat, and a moment later I was stretched upon my back, unable to speak or move, on the boudoir carpet. The woman lay beside me, and Summerlee was bunched in a chair by the window, his head nearly touching his knees. As in a dream I saw Challenger, like a monstrous beetle, crawling slowly across the floor, and a moment later I heard the gentle hissing of the escaping oxygen. Challenger

breathed two or three times with enormous gulps, his lungs roaring as
he drew in the vital gas.

"It works!" he cried exultantly. "My reasoning has been justified!"
He was up on his feet again, alert and strong. With a tube in his hand
he rushed over to his wife and held it to her face. In a few seconds she
moaned, stirred, and sat up. He turned to me, and I felt the tide of life
stealing warmly through my arteries. My reason told me that it was but
a little respite, and yet, carelessly as we talk of its value, every hour of
existence now seemed an inestimable thing. Never have I known such
a thrill of sensuous joy as came with that freshet of life. The weight fell
away from my lungs, the band loosened from my brow, a sweet feeling
of peace and gentle, languid comfort stole over me. I lay watching
Summerlee revive under the same remedy, and finally Lord John
took his turn. He sprang to his feet and gave me a hand to rise, while
Challenger picked up his wife and laid her on the settee.

"Oh, George, I am so sorry you brought me back," she said, holding
him by the hand. "The door of death is indeed, as you said, hung with
beautiful, shimmering curtains; for, once the choking feeling had
passed, it was all unspeakably soothing and beautiful. Why have you
dragged me back?"

"Because I wish that we make the passage together. We have been
together so many years. It would be sad to fall apart at the supreme
moment."

For a moment in his tender voice I caught a glimpse of a new
Challenger, something very far from the bullying, ranting, arrogant
man who had alternately amazed and offended his generation. Here in
the shadow of death was the innermost Challenger, the man who had
won and held a woman's love. Suddenly his mood changed and he was
our strong captain once again.

"Alone of all mankind I saw and foretold this catastrophe," said he with
a ring of exultation and scientific triumph in his voice. "As to you, my
good Summerlee, I trust your last doubts have been resolved as to the
meaning of the blurring of the lines in the spectrum and that you will no
longer contend that my letter in the *Times* was based upon a delusion."

For once our pugnacious colleague was deaf to a challenge. He could
but sit gasping and stretching his long, thin limbs, as if to assure himself
that he was still really upon this planet. Challenger walked across to the

oxygen tube, and the sound of the loud hissing fell away till it was the most gentle sibilation.

"We must husband our supply of the gas," said he. "The atmosphere of the room is now strongly hyper-oxygenated, and I take it that none of us feel any distressing symptoms. We can only determine by actual experiments what amount added to the air will serve to neutralize the poison. Let us see how that will do."

We sat in silent nervous tension for five minutes or more, observing our own sensations. I had just begun to fancy that I felt the constriction round my temples again when Mrs. Challenger called out from the sofa that she was fainting. Her husband turned on more gas.

"In pre-scientific days," said he, "they used to keep a white mouse in every submarine, as its more delicate organization gave signs of a vicious atmosphere before it was perceived by the sailors. You, my dear, will be our white mouse. I have now increased the supply and you are better."

"Yes, I am better."

"Possibly we have hit upon the correct mixture. When we have ascertained exactly how little will serve we shall be able to compute how long we shall be able to exist. Unfortunately, in resuscitating ourselves we have already consumed a considerable proportion of this first tube."

"Does it matter?" asked Lord John, who was standing with his hands in his pockets close to the window. "If we have to go, what is the use of holdin' on? You don't suppose there's any chance for us?"

Challenger smiled and shook his head.

"Well, then, don't you think there is more dignity in takin' the jump and not waitin' to be pushed in? If it must be so, I'm for sayin' our prayers, turnin' off the gas, and openin' the window."

"Why not?" said the lady bravely. "Surely, George, Lord John is right and it is better so."

"I most strongly object," cried Summerlee in a querulous voice. "When we must die let us by all means die, but to deliberately anticipate death seems to me to be a foolish and unjustifiable action."

"What does our young friend say to it?" asked Challenger.

"I think we should see it to the end."

"And I am strongly of the same opinion," said he.

"Then, George, if you say so, I think so too," cried the lady.

"Well, well, I'm only puttin' it as an argument," said Lord John. "If you all want to see it through I am with you. It's dooced interestin', and no mistake about that. I've had my share of adventures in my life, and as many thrills as most folk, but I'm endin' on my top note."

"Granting the continuity of life," said Challenger.

"A large assumption!" cried Summerlee. Challenger stared at him in silent reproof.

"Granting the continuity of life," said he, in his most didactic manner, "none of us can predicate what opportunities of observation one may have from what we may call the spirit plane to the plane of matter. It surely must be evident to the most obtuse person" (here he glared a Summerlee) "that it is while we are ourselves material that we are most fitted to watch and form a judgment upon material phenomena. Therefore it is only by keeping alive for these few extra hours that we can hope to carry on with us to some future existence a clear conception of the most stupendous event that the world, or the universe so far as we know it, has ever encountered. To me it would seem a deplorable thing that we should in any way curtail by so much as a minute so wonderful an experience."

"I am strongly of the same opinion," cried Summerlee.

"Carried without a division," said Lord John. "By George, that poor devil of a chauffeur of yours down in the yard has made his last journey. No use makin' a sally and bringin' him in?"

"It would be absolute madness," cried Summerlee.

"Well, I suppose it would," said Lord John. "It couldn't help him and would scatter our gas all over the house, even if we ever got back alive. My word, look at the little birds under the trees!"

We drew four chairs up to the long, low window, the lady still resting with closed eyes upon the settee. I remember that the monstrous and grotesque idea crossed my mind—the illusion may have been heightened by the heavy stuffiness of the air which we were breathing—that we were in four front seats of the stalls at the last act of the drama of the world.

In the immediate foreground, beneath our very eyes, was the small yard with the half-cleaned motor-car standing in it. Austin, the chauffeur, had received his final notice at last, for he was sprawling beside the wheel, with a great black bruise upon his forehead where it had struck the step or mud-guard in falling. He still held in his hand the nozzle of the hose with which he had been washing down his machine. A couple of small plane trees stood in the corner of the yard, and underneath them lay several pathetic little balls of fluffy feathers, with tiny feet uplifted. The sweep of death's scythe had included everything, great and small, within its swath.

Over the wall of the yard we looked down upon the winding road, which led to the station. A group of the reapers whom we had seen running from the fields were lying all pell-mell, their bodies crossing each other, at the bottom of it. Farther up, the nurse-girl lay with her head and shoulders propped against the slope of the grassy bank. She had taken the baby from the perambulator, and it was a motionless bundle of wraps in her arms. Close behind her a tiny patch upon the roadside showed where the little boy was stretched. Still nearer to us was the dead cab-horse, kneeling between the shafts. The old driver was hanging over the splash-board like some grotesque scarecrow, his arms dangling absurdly in front of him. Through the window we could dimly discern that a young man was seated inside. The door was swinging open and his hand was grasping the handle, as if he had attempted to leap forth at the last instant. In the middle distance lay the golf links, dotted as they had been in the morning with the dark figures of the golfers, lying motionless upon the grass of the course or among the heather which skirted it. On one particular green there were eight bodies stretched where a foursome with its caddies had held to their game to the last. No bird flew in the blue vault of heaven, no man or beast moved upon the vast countryside which lay before us. The evening sun shone its peaceful radiance across it, but there brooded over it all the stillness and the silence of universal death—a death in which we were so soon to join. At the present instant that one frail sheet of glass, by holding in the extra oxygen which counteracted the poisoned ether, shut us off from the fate of all our kind. For a few short hours the knowledge and foresight of one man could preserve our little oasis of life in the vast desert of death and save us from participation in the common catastrophe. Then the gas would run low, we too should lie gasping upon that cherry-coloured boudoir carpet, and the fate of the human race and of all earthly life would be complete. For a long time, in a mood which was too solemn for speech, we looked out at the tragic world.

"There is a house on fire," said Challenger at last, pointing to a column of smoke which rose above the trees. "There will, I expect, be many such—possibly whole cities in flames—when we consider how many folk may have dropped with lights in their hands. The fact of combustion is in itself enough to show that the proportion of oxygen in the atmosphere is normal and that it is the ether which is at fault. Ah, there you see another blaze on the top of Crowborough Hill. It is the golf clubhouse, or I am mistaken. There is the church clock chiming the hour. It would interest our philosophers to know that man-made mechanisms has survived the race who made it."

"By George!" cried Lord John, rising excitedly from his chair. "What's that puff of smoke? It's a train."

We heard the roar of it, and presently it came flying into sight, going at what seemed to me to be a prodigious speed. Whence it had come, or how far, we had no means of knowing. Only by some miracle of luck could it have gone any distance. But now we were to see the terrific end of its career. A train of coal trucks stood motionless upon the line. We held our breath as the express roared along the same track. The crash was horrible. Engine and carriages piled themselves into a hill of splintered wood and twisted iron. Red spurts of flame flickered up from the wreckage until it was all ablaze. For half an hour we sat with hardly a word, stunned by the stupendous sight.

"Poor, poor people!" cried Mrs. Challenger at last, clinging with a whimper to her husband's arm.

"My dear, the passengers on that train were no more animate than the coals into which they crashed or the carbon which they have now become," said Challenger, stroking her hand soothingly. "It was a train of the living when it left Victoria, but it was driven and freighted by the dead long before it reached its fate."

"All over the world the same thing must be going on," said I as a vision of strange happenings rose before me. "Think of the ships at sea—how they will steam on and on, until the furnaces die down or until they run full tilt upon some beach. The sailing ships too—how they will back and fill with their cargoes of dead sailors, while their timbers rot and their joints leak, till one by one they sink below the surface. Perhaps a century hence the Atlantic may still be dotted with the old drifting derelicts."

"And the folk in the coal-mines," said Summerlee with a dismal chuckle. "If ever geologists should by any chance live upon earth again they will have some strange theories of the existence of man in carboniferous strata."

"I don't profess to know about such things," remarked Lord John, "but it seems to me the earth will be 'To let, empty,' after this. When once our human crowd is wiped off it, how will it ever get on again?"

"The world was empty before," Challenger answered gravely. "Under laws which in their inception are beyond and above us, it became peopled. Why may the same process not happen again?"

"My dear Challenger, you can't mean that?"

"I am not in the habit, Professor Summerlee, of saying things which I do not mean. The observation is trivial." Out went the beard and down came the eyelids.

"Well, you lived an obstinate dogmatist, and you mean to die one," said Summerlee sourly.

"And you, sir, have lived an unimaginative obstructionist and never can hope now to emerge from it."

"Your worst critics will never accuse you of lacking imagination," Summerlee retorted.

"Upon my word!" said Lord John. "It would be like you if you used up our last gasp of oxygen in abusing each other. What can it matter whether folk come back or not? It surely won't be in our time."

"In that remark, sir, you betray your own very pronounced limitations," said Challenger severely. "The true scientific mind is not to be tied down by its own conditions of time and space. It builds itself an observatory erected upon the border line of present, which separates the infinite past from the infinite future. From this sure post it makes its sallies even to the beginning and to the end of all things. As to death, the scientific mind dies at its post working in normal and methodic fashion to the end. It disregards so petty a thing as its own physical dissolution as completely as it does all other limitations upon the plane of matter. Am I right, Professor Summerlee?"

Summerlee grumbled an ungracious assent.

"With certain reservations, I agree," said he.

"The ideal scientific mind," continued Challenger—"I put it in the third person rather than appear to be too self-complacent—the ideal scientific mind should be capable of thinking out a point of abstract knowledge in the interval between its owner falling from a balloon and reaching the earth. Men of this strong fibre are needed to form the conquerors of nature and the bodyguard of truth."

"It strikes me nature's on top this time," said Lord John, looking out of the window. "I've read some leadin' articles about you gentlemen controllin' her, but she's gettin' a bit of her own back."

"It is but a temporary set-back," said Challenger with conviction. "A few million years, what are they in the great cycle of time? The vegetable world has, as you can see, survived. Look at the leaves of that plane tree. The birds are dead, but the plant flourishes. From this vegetable life in pond and in marsh will come, in time, the tiny crawling microscopic slugs which are the pioneers of that great army of life in which for the instant we five have the extraordinary duty of serving as rear guard. Once the lowest form of life has established itself, the final advent of man is as certain as the growth of the oak from the acorn. The old circle will swing round once more."

"But the poison?" I asked. "Will that not nip life in the bud?"

"The poison may be a mere stratum or layer in the ether—a mephitic Gulf Stream across that mighty ocean in which we float. Or tolerance may be established and life accommodate itself to a new condition. The mere fact that with a comparatively small hyper-oxygenation of our blood we can hold out against it is surely a proof in itself that no very great change would be needed to enable animal life to endure it."

The smoking house beyond the trees had burst into flames. We could see the high tongues of fire shooting up into the air.

"It's pretty awful," muttered Lord John, more impressed than I had ever seen him.

"Well, after all, what does it matter?" I remarked. "The world is dead. Cremation is surely the best burial."

"It would shorten us up if this house went ablaze."

"I foresaw the danger," said Challenger, "and asked my wife to guard against it."

"Everything is quite safe, dear. But my head begins to throb again. What a dreadful atmosphere!"

"We must change it," said Challenger. He bent over his cylinder of oxygen.

"It's nearly empty," said he. "It has lasted us some three and a half hours. It is now close on eight o'clock. We shall get through the night comfortably. I should expect the end about nine o'clock to-morrow morning. We shall see one sunrise, which shall be all our own."

He turned on his second tube and opened for half a minute the fanlight over the door. Then as the air became perceptibly better, but our own symptoms more acute, he closed it once again.

"By the way," said he, "man does not live upon oxygen alone. It's dinner time and over. I assure you, gentlemen, that when I invited you to my home and to what I had hoped would be an interesting reunion, I had intended that my kitchen should justify itself. However, we must do what we can. I am sure that you will agree with me that it would be folly to consume our air too rapidly by lighting an oil-stove. I have some small provision of cold meats, bread, and pickles which, with a couple of bottles of claret, may serve our turn. Thank you, my dear—now as ever you are the queen of managers."

It was indeed wonderful how, with the self-respect and sense of propriety of the British housekeeper, the lady had within a few minutes adorned the central table with a snow-white cloth, laid the napkins upon it, and set forth the simple meal with all the elegance of civilization, including an electric torch lamp in the centre. Wonderful also was it to find that our appetites were ravenous.

"It is the measure of our emotion," said Challenger with that air of condescension with which he brought his scientific mind to the explanation of humble facts. "We have gone through a great crisis. That means molecular disturbance. That in turn means the need for repair. Great sorrow or great joy should bring intense hunger—not abstinence from food, as our novelists will have it."

"That's why the country folk have great feasts at funerals," I hazarded.

"Exactly. Our young friend has hit upon an excellent illustration. Let me give you another slice of tongue."

"The same with savages," said Lord John, cutting away at the beef. "I've seen them buryin' a chief up the Aruwimi River, and they ate a hippo that must have weighed as much as a tribe. There are some of them down New Guinea way that eat the late-lamented himself, just by way of a last tidy up. Well, of all the funeral feasts on this earth, I suppose the one we are takin' is the queerest."

"The strange thing is," said Mrs. Challenger, "that I find it impossible to feel grief for those who are gone. There are my father and mother at Bedford. I know that they are dead, and yet in this tremendous universal tragedy I can feel no sharp sorrow for any individuals, even for them."

"And my old mother in her cottage in Ireland," said I. "I can see her in my mind's eye, with her shawl and her lace cap, lying back with closed eyes in the old high-backed chair near the window, her glasses and her book beside her. Why should I mourn her? She has passed and I am passing, and I may be nearer her in some other life than England is to Ireland. Yet I grieve to think that that dear body is no more."

"As to the body," remarked Challenger, "we do not mourn over the parings of our nails nor the cut locks of our hair, though they were once part of ourselves. Neither does a one-legged man yearn sentimentally over his missing member. The physical body has rather been a source of pain and fatigue to us. It is the constant index of our limitations. Why then should we worry about its detachment from our psychical selves?"

"If they can indeed be detached," Summerlee grumbled. "But, anyhow, universal death is dreadful."

"As I have already explained," said Challenger, "a universal death must in its nature be far less terrible than a isolated one."

"Same in a battle," remarked Lord John. "If you saw a single man lying on that floor with his chest knocked in and a hole in his face it would turn you sick. But I've seen ten thousand on their backs in the Soudan, and it gave me no such feelin', for when you are makin' history the life of any man is too small a thing to worry over. When a thousand million pass over together, same as happened to-day, you can't pick your own partic'lar out of the crowd."

"I wish it were well over with us," said the lady wistfully. "Oh, George, I am so frightened."

"You'll be the bravest of us all, little lady, when the time comes. I've been a blusterous old husband to you, dear, but you'll just bear in mind that G. E. C. is as he was made and couldn't help himself. After all, you wouldn't have had anyone else?"

"No one in the whole wide world, dear," said she, and put her arms round his bull neck. We three walked to the window and stood amazed at the sight which met our eyes.

Darkness had fallen and the dead world was shrouded in gloom. But right across the southern horizon was one long vivid scarlet streak, waxing and waning in vivid pulses of life, leaping suddenly to a crimson zenith and then dying down to a glowing line of fire.

"Lewes is ablaze!"

"No, it is Brighton which is burning," said Challenger, stepping across to join us. "You can see the curved back of the downs against the glow. That fire is miles on the farther side of it. The whole town must be alight."

There were several red glares at different points, and the pile of *débris* upon the railway line was still smoldering darkly, but they all seemed mere pin-points of light compared to that monstrous conflagration throbbing beyond the hills. What copy it would have made for the *Gazette*! Had ever a journalist such an opening and so little chance of using it—the scoop of scoops, and no one to appreciate it? And then, suddenly, the old instinct of recording came over me. If these men of science could be so true to their life's work to the very end, why should not I, in my humble way, be as constant? No human eye might ever rest upon what I had done. But the long night had to be passed somehow, and for me at least, sleep seemed to be out of the question. My notes would help to pass the weary hours and to occupy my thoughts. Thus it is that now I have before me the notebook with its scribbled pages, written confusedly upon my knee in the dim, waning light of our one electric torch. Had I the literary touch, they might have been worthy of the occasion. As it is, they may still serve to bring to other minds the long-drawn emotions and tremors of that awful night.

IV. A DIARY OF THE DYING

How strange the words look scribbled at the top of the empty page of my book! How stranger still that it is I, Edward Malone, who have written them—I who started only some twelve hours ago from my rooms in Streatham without one thought of the marvels which the day was to bring forth! I look back at the chain of incidents, my interview with McArdle, Challenger's first note of alarm in the *Times,* the absurd journey in the train, the pleasant luncheon, the catastrophe, and now it has come to this—that we linger alone upon an empty planet, and so sure is our fate that I can regard these lines, written from mechanical professional habit and never to be seen by human eyes, as the words of one who is already dead, so closely does he stand to the shadowed borderland over which all outside this one little circle of friends have already gone. I feel how wise and true were the words of Challenger when he said that the real tragedy would be if we were left behind when all that is noble and good and beautiful had passed. But of that there can surely be no danger. Already our second tube of oxygen is drawing to an end. We can count the poor dregs of our lives almost to a minute.

We have just been treated to a lecture, a good quarter of an hour long, from Challenger, who was so excited that he roared and bellowed as if he were addressing his old rows of scientific sceptics in the Queen's Hall. He had certainly a strange audience to harangue: his wife perfectly acquiescent and absolutely ignorant of his meaning, Summerlee seated in the shadow, querulous and critical but interested, Lord John lounging in a corner somewhat bored by the whole proceeding, and myself beside the window watching the scene with a kind of detached attention, as if it were all a dream or something in which I had no personal interest whatever. Challenger sat at the centre table with the electric light illuminating the slide under the microscope which he had brought from his dressing room. The small vivid circle of white light from the mirror left half of his rugged, bearded face in brilliant radiance and half in deepest shadow. He had, it seems, been working of late upon the lowest forms of life, and what excited him at the present moment was that in the microscopic slide made up the day before he found the amœba to be still alive.

"You can see it for yourselves," he kept repeating in great excitement. "Summerlee, will you step across and satisfy yourself upon the point? Malone, will you kindly verify what I say? The little spindle-shaped things in the centre are diatoms and may be disregarded since they are probably vegetable rather than animal. But the right-hand side you will see an undoubted amœba, moving sluggishly across the field. The upper screw is the fine adjustment. Look at it for yourselves."

Summerlee did so and acquiesced. So did I and perceived a little creature which looked as if it were made of ground glass flowing in a sticky way across the lighted circle. Lord John was prepared to take him on trust.

"I'm not troublin' my head whether he's alive or dead," said he. "We don't so much as know each other by sight, so why should I take it to heart? I don't suppose he's worryin' himself over the state of *our* health."

I laughed at this, and Challenger looked in my direction with his coldest and most supercilious stare. It was a most petrifying experience.

"The flippancy of the half-educated is more obstructive to science than the obtuseness of the ignorant," said he. "If Lord John Roxton would condescend—"

"My dear George, don't be so peppery," said his wife, with her hand on the black mane that drooped over the microscope. "What can it matter whether the amœba is alive or not?"

"It matters a great deal," said Challenger gruffly.

"Well, let's hear about it," said Lord John with a good-humoured smile. "We may as well talk about that as anything else. If you think I've been too off-hand with the thing, or hurt its feelin's in any way, I'll apologize."

"For my part," remarked Summerlee in his creaky, argumentative voice, "I can't see why you should attach such importance to the creature being alive. It is in the same atmosphere as ourselves, so naturally the poison does not act upon it. If it were outside of this room it would be dead, like all other animal life."

"Your remarks, my good Summerlee," said Challenger with enormous condescension (oh, if I could paint that over-bearing, arrogant face in the vivid circle of reflection from the microscope mirror!)—"your remarks show that you imperfectly appreciate the situation. This specimen was mounted yesterday and is hermetically sealed. None of our oxygen can reach it. But the ether, of course, has penetrated to it, as to every other point upon the universe. Therefore, it has survived the poison. Hence, we may argue that every amœba outside this room, instead of being dead, as you have erroneously stated, has really survived the catastrophe."

"Well, even now I don't feel inclined to hip-hurrah about it," said Lord John. "What does it matter?"

"It just matters this, that the world is a living instead of a dead one. If you had the scientific imagination, you would cast your mind forward from this one fact, and you would see some few millions of years hence—a mere passing moment in the enormous flux of the ages—the whole world teeming once more with the animal and human life which will spring from this tiny root. You have seen a prairie fire where the flames have swept every trace of grass or plant from the surface of the earth and left only a blackened waste. You would think that it must be forever desert. Yet the roots of growth have been left behind, and when you pass the place a few years hence you can no longer tell where the black scars used to be. Here in this tiny creature are the roots of growth of the animal world, and by its inherent development, and evolution, it will surely in time remove every trace of this incomparable crisis in which we are now involved."

"Dooced interestin'!" said Lord John, lounging across and looking through the microscope. "Funny little chap to hang number one among the family portraits. Got a fine big shirt-stud on him!"

"The dark object is his nucleus," said Challenger with the air of a nurse teaching letters to a baby.

"Well, we needn't feel lonely," said Lord John laughing. "There's somebody livin' besides us on the earth."

"You seem to take it for granted, Challenger," said Summerlee, "that the object for which this world was created was that it should produce and sustain human life."

"Well, sir, and what object do you suggest?" asked Challenger, bristling at the least hint of contradiction.

"Sometimes I think that it is only the monstrous conceit of mankind which makes him think that all this stage was erected for him to strut upon."

"We cannot be dogmatic about it, but at least without what you have ventured to call monstrous conceit we can surely say that we are the highest thing in nature."

"The highest of which we have cognizance."

"That, sir, goes without saying."

"Think of all the millions and possibly billions of years that the earth swung empty through space—or, if not empty, at least without a sign or thought of the human race. Think of it, washed by the rain and scorched by the sun and swept by the wind for those unnumbered ages. Man only came into being yesterday so far as geological times goes. Why, then, should it be taken for granted that all this stupendous preparation was for his benefit?"

"For whose then—or for what?"

Summerlee shrugged his shoulders.

"How can we tell? For some reason altogether beyond our conception—and man may have been a mere accident, a by-product evolved in the process. It is as if the scum upon the surface of the ocean imagined that the ocean was created in order to produce and sustain it or a mouse in a cathedral thought that the building was its own proper ordained residence."

I have jotted down the very words of their argument, but now it degenerates into a mere noisy wrangle with much polysyllabic scientific jargon upon each side. It is no doubt a privilege to hear two such brains discuss the highest questions; but as they are in perpetual disagreement, plain folk like Lord John and I get little that is positive from the exhibition. They neutralize each other and we are left as they found us. Now the hubbub has ceased, and Summerlee is coiled up in his chair, while Challenger, still fingering the screws of his microscope, is keeping up a continual low, deep, inarticulate growl like the sea after a storm. Lord John comes over to me, and we look out together into the night.

There is a pale new moon—the last moon that human eyes will ever rest upon—and the stars are most brilliant. Even in the clear plateau air of South America I have never seen them brighter. Possibly this etheric change has some effect upon light. The funeral pyre of Brighton is still blazing, and there is a very distant patch of scarlet in the western sky, which may mean trouble at Arundel or Chichester, possibly even at Portsmouth. I sit and muse and make an occasional note. There is a sweet melancholy in the air. Youth and beauty and chivalry and love—is this to be the end of it all? The starlit earth looks a dreamland of gentle peace. Who would imagine it as the terrible Golgotha strewn with the bodies of the human race? Suddenly, I find myself laughing.

"Halloa, young fellah!" says Lord John, staring at me in surprise. "We could do with a joke in these hard times. What was it, then?"

"I was thinking of all the great unsolved questions," I answer, "the questions that we spent so much labor and thought over. Think of

Anglo-German competition, for example—or the Persian Gulf that my old chief was so keen about. Whoever would have guessed, when we fumed and fretted so, how they were to be eventually solved?"

We fall into silence again. I fancy that each of us is thinking of friends that have gone before. Mrs. Challenger is sobbing quietly, and her husband is whispering to her. My mind turns to all the most unlikely people, and I see each of them lying white and rigid as poor Austin does in the yard. There is McArdle, for example, I know exactly where he is, with his face upon his writing desk and his hand on his own telephone, just as I heard him fall. Beaumont, the editor, too—I suppose he is lying upon the blue-and-red Turkey carpet which adorned his sanctum. And the fellows in the reporters' room—Macdonna and Murray and Bond. They had certainly died hard at work on their job, with note-books full of vivid impressions and strange happenings in their hands. I could just imagine how this one would have been packed off to the doctors, and that other to Westminster, and yet a third to St. Paul's. What glorious rows of head-lines they must have seen as a last vision beautiful, never destined to materialize in printer's ink! I could see Macdonna among the doctors—"Hope in Harley Street"—Mac had always a weakness for alliteration. "Interview with Mr. Soley Wilson." "Famous Specialist says 'Never despair!' " "Our Special Correspondent found the eminent scientist seated upon the roof, whither he had retreated to avoid the crowd of terrified patients who had stormed his dwelling. With a manner which plainly showed his appreciation of the immense gravity of the occasion, the celebrated physician refused to admit that every avenue of hope had been closed." That's how Mac would start. Then there was Bond; he would probably do St. Paul's. He fancied his own literary touch. My word, what a theme for him! "Standing in the little gallery under the dome and looking down upon that packed mass of despairing humanity, groveling at this last instant before a Power which they had so persistently ignored, there rose to my ears from the swaying crowd such a low moan of entreaty and terror, such a shuddering cry for help to the Unknown, that—" and so forth.

Yes, it would be a great end for a reporter, though, like myself, he would die with the treasures still unused. What would Bond not give, poor chap, to see "J. H. B." at the foot of a column like that?

But what drivel I am writing! It is just an attempt to pass the weary time. Mrs. Challenger has gone to the inner dressing-room, and the Professor says that she is asleep. He is making notes and consulting books at the central table, as calmly as if years of placid work lay before him. He writes with a very noisy quill pen which seems to be screeching scorn at all who disagree with him.

Summerlee has dropped off in his chair and gives from time to time a peculiarly exasperating snore. Lord John lies back with his hands in his pockets and his eyes closed. How people can sleep under such conditions is more than I can imagine.

Three-thirty a.m. I have just wakened with a start. It was five minutes past eleven when I made my last entry. I remember winding up my watch and noting the time. So I have wasted some five hours of the little span still left to us. Who would have believed it possible? But I feel very much fresher, and ready for my fate—or try to persuade myself that I am. And yet, the fitter a man is, and the higher his tide of life, the more must he shrink from death. How wise and how merciful is that provision of nature by which his earthly anchor is usually loosened by many little imperceptible tugs, until his consciousness has drifted out of its untenable earthly harbor into the great sea beyond!

Mrs. Challenger is still in the dressing room. Challenger has fallen asleep in his chair. What a picture! His enormous frame leans back, his huge, hairy hands are clasped across his waistcoat, and his head is so tilted that I can see nothing above his collar save a tangled bristle of luxuriant beard. He shakes with the vibration of his own snoring. Summerlee adds his occasional high tenor to Challenger's sonorous bass. Lord John is sleeping also, his long body doubled up sideways in a basket-chair. The first cold light of dawn is just stealing into the room, and everything is grey and mournful.

I look out at the sunrise—that fateful sunrise which will shine upon an unpeopled world. The human race is gone, extinguished in a day, but the planets swing round and the tides rise or fall, and the wind whispers, and all nature goes her way, down, as it would seem, to the very amœba, with never a sign that he who styled himself the lord of creation had ever blessed or cursed the universe with his presence. Down in the yard lies Austin with sprawling limbs, his face glimmering white in the dawn, and the hose nozzle still projecting from his dead hand. The whole of human

kind is typified in that one half-ludicrous and half-pathetic figure, lying so
helpless beside the machine which it used to control.

* * *

Here end the notes which I made at the time. Henceforward events
were too swift and too poignant to allow me to write, but they are too
clearly outlined in my memory that any detail could escape me.

Some chokiness in my throat made me look at the oxygen cylinders,
and I was startled at what I saw. The sands of our lives were running very
low. At some period in the night Challenger had switched the tube from
the third to the fourth cylinder. Now it was clear that this also was nearly
exhausted. That horrible feeling of constriction was closing in upon me. I
ran across and, unscrewing the nozzle, I changed it to our last supply. Even
as I did so my conscience pricked me, for I felt that perhaps if I had held
my hand all of them might have passed in their sleep. The thought was
banished, however, by the voice of the lady from the inner room crying:—

"George, George, I am stifling!"

"It is all right, Mrs. Challenger," I answered as the others started to
their feet. "I have just turned on a fresh supply."

Even at such a moment I could not help smiling at Challenger, who
with a great hairy fist in each eye was like a huge, bearded baby, new
wakened out of sleep. Summerlee was shivering like a man with the
ague, human fears, as he realized his position, rising for an instant
above the stoicism of the man of science. Lord John, however, was as
cool and alert as if he had just been roused on a hunting morning.

"Fifthly and lastly," said he, glancing at the tube. "Say, young fellah,
don't tell me you've been writin' up your impressions in that paper on
your knee."

"Just a few notes to pass the time."

"Well, I don't believe anyone but an Irishman would have done that.
I expect you'll have to wait till little brother amœba gets grown up
before you'll find a reader. He don't seem to take much stock of things
just at present. Well, Herr Professor, what are the prospects?"

Challenger was looking out at the great drifts of morning mist which
lay over the landscape. Here and there the wooded hills rose like conical
islands out of this woolly sea.

"It might be a winding sheet," said Mrs. Challenger, who had entered in her dressing-gown. "There's that song of yours, George, 'Ring out the old, ring in the new.' It was prophetic. But you are shivering, my poor dear friends. I have been warm under a coverlet all night, and you cold in your chairs. But I'll soon set you right."

The brave little creature hurried away, and presently we heard the sizzling of a kettle. She was back soon with five steaming cups of cocoa upon a tray.

"Drink these," said she. "You will feel so much better."

And we did. Summerlee asked if he might light his pipe, and we all had cigarettes. It steadied our nerves, I think, but it was a mistake, for it made a dreadful atmosphere in that stuffy room. Challenger had to open the ventilator.

"How long, Challenger?" asked Lord John.

"Possibly three hours," he answered with a shrug.

"I used to be frightened," said his wife. "But the nearer I get to it, the easier it seems. Don't you think we ought to pray, George?"

"You will pray, dear, if you wish," the big man answered, very gently. "We all have our own ways of praying. Mine is a complete acquiescence in whatever fate may send me—a cheerful acquiescence. The highest religion and the highest science seem to unite on that."

"I cannot truthfully describe my mental attitude as acquiescence and far less cheerful acquiescence," grumbled Summerlee over his pipe. "I submit because I have to. I confess that I should have liked another year of life to finish my classification of the chalk fossils."

"Your unfinished work is a small thing," said Challenger pompously, "when weighed against the fact that my own *magnum opus*, 'The Ladder of Life,' is still in the first stages. My brain, my reading, my experience—in fact, my whole unique equipment—were to be condensed into that epoch-making volume. And yet, as I say, I acquiesce."

"I expect we've all left some loose ends stickin' out," said Lord John. "What are yours, young fellah?"

"I was working at a book of verses," I answered.

"Well, the world has escaped that, anyhow," said Lord John. "There's always compensation somewhere if you grope around."

"What about you?" I asked.

"Well, it just so happens that I was tidied up and ready. I'd promised Merivale to go to Tibet for a snow leopard in the spring. But it's hard on you, Mrs. Challenger, when you have just built up this pretty home."

"Where George is, there is my home. But, oh, what would I not give for one last walk together in the fresh morning air upon those beautiful downs!"

Our hearts re-echoed her words. The sun had burst through the gauzy mists which veiled it, and the whole broad Weald was washed in golden light. Sitting in our dark and poisonous atmosphere that glorious, clean, wind-swept countryside seemed a very dream of beauty. Mrs. Challenger held her hand stretched out to it in her longing. We drew up chairs and sat in a semicircle in the window. The atmosphere was already very close. It seemed to me that the shadows of death were drawing in upon us—the last of our race. It was like an invisible curtain closing down upon every side.

"That cylinder is not lastin' too well," said Lord John with a long gasp for breath.

"The amount contained is variable," said Challenger, "depending upon the pressure and care with which it has been bottled. I am inclined to agree with you, Roxton, that this one is defective."

"So we are to be cheated out of the last hour of our lives," Summerlee remarked bitterly. "An excellent final illustration of the sordid age in which we have lived. Well, Challenger, now is your time if you wish to study the subjective phenomena of physical dissolution."

"Sit on the stool at my knee and give me your hand," said Challenger to his wife. "I think, my friends, that a further delay in this insufferable atmosphere is hardly advisable. You would not desire it, dear, would you?"

His wife gave a little groan and sank her face against his leg.

"I've seen the folk bathin' in the Serpentine in winter," said Lord John. "When the rest are in, you see one or two shiverin' on the bank, envyin' the others that have taken the plunge. It's the last that have the worst of it. I'm all for a header and have done with it."

"You would open the window and face the ether?"

"Better be poisoned than stifled."

Summerlee nodded his reluctant acquiescence and held out his thin hand to Challenger.

"We've had our quarrels in our time, but that's all over," said he. "We were good friends and had a respect for each other under the surface. Good-bye!"

"Good-bye, young fellah!" said Lord John. "The window's plastered up. You can't open it."

Challenger stooped and raised his wife, pressing her to his breast, while she threw her arms round his neck.

"Give me that field-glass, Malone," said he gravely.

I handed it to him.

"Into the hands of the Power that made us we render ourselves again!" he shouted in his voice of thunder, and at the words he hurled the field-glass through the window.

Full in our flushed faces, before the last tinkle of falling fragments had died away, there came the wholesome breath of the wind, blowing strong and sweet.

I don't know how long we sat in amazed silence. Then as in a dream, I heard Challenger's voice once more.

"We are back in normal conditions," he cried. "The world has cleared the poison belt, but we alone of all mankind are saved."

V. THE DEAD WORLD

I remember that we all sat gasping in our chairs, with that sweet, wet south-western breeze, fresh from the sea, flapping the muslin curtains and cooling our flushed faces. I wonder how long we sat! None of us afterwards could agree at all on that point. We were bewildered, stunned, semi-conscious. We had all braced our courage for death, but this fearful and sudden new fact—that we must continue to live after we had survived the race to which we belonged—struck us with the shock of a physical blow and left us prostrate. Then gradually the suspended mechanism began to move once more; the shuttles of memory worked; ideas weaved themselves together in our minds. We saw, with vivid, merciless clearness, the relations between the past, the present, and the future—the lives that we had led and the lives which we would have to live. Our eyes turned in silent horror upon those of our companions and found the same answering look in theirs. Instead of the joy which men might have been expected to feel who had so narrowly escaped an imminent death, a terrible wave of darkest depression submerged us. Everything on earth that we loved had been washed away into the great, infinite, unknown ocean, and here were we marooned upon this desert island of a world, without companions, hopes, or aspirations. A few years' skulking like jackals among the graves of the human race and then our belated and lonely end would come.

"It's dreadful, George, dreadful!" the lady cried in an agony of sobs. "If we had only passed with the others! Oh, why did you save us? I feel as if it is we that are dead and everyone else alive."

Challenger's great eyebrows were drawn down in concentrated thought, while his huge, hairy paw closed upon the outstretched hand of his wife. I had observed that she always held out her arms to him in trouble as a child would to its mother.

"Without being a fatalist to the point of non-resistance," said he, "I have always found that the highest wisdom lies in an acquiescence with the actual." He spoke slowly, and there was a vibration of feeling in his sonorous voice.

"I do *not* acquiesce," said Summerlee firmly.

"I don't see that it matters a row of pins whether you acquiesce or whether you don't," remarked Lord John. "You've got to take it, whether you take it fightin' or take it lyin' down, so what's the odds whether you acquiesce or not?

"I can't remember that anyone asked our permission before the thing began, and nobody's likely to ask it now. So what difference can it make what we may think of it?"

"It is just all the difference between happiness and misery," said Challenger with an abstracted face, still patting his wife's hand. "You can swim with the tide and have peace in mind and soul, or you can thrust against it and be bruised and weary. This business is beyond us, so let us accept it as it stands and say no more."

"But what in the world are we to do with our lives?" I asked, appealing in desperation to the blue, empty heaven.

"What am I to do, for example? There are no newspapers, so there's an end of my vocation."

"And there's nothin' left to shoot, and no more soldierin', so there's an end of mine," said Lord John.

"And there are no students, so there's an end of mine," cried Summerlee.

"But I have my husband and my house, so I can thank heaven that there is no end of mine," said the lady.

"Nor is there an end of mine," remarked Challenger, "for science is not dead, and this catastrophe in itself will offer us many most absorbing problems for investigation."

He had now flung open the windows and we were gazing out upon the silent and motionless landscape.

"Let me consider," he continued. "It was about three, or a little after, yesterday afternoon that the world finally entered the poison belt to the extent of being completely submerged. It is now nine o'clock. The question is, at what hour did we pass out from it?"

"The air was very bad at daybreak," said I.

"Later than that," said Mrs. Challenger. "As late as eight o'clock I distinctly felt the same choking at my throat which came at the outset."

"Then we shall say that it passed just after eight o'clock. For seventeen hours the world has been soaked in the poisonous ether. For that length of time the Great Gardener has sterilized the human mould which had grown over the surface of His fruit. Is it possible that the work is incompletely done—that others may have survived besides ourselves?"

"That's what I was wonderin'" said Lord John. "Why should we be the only pebbles on the beach?"

"It is absurd to suppose that anyone besides ourselves can possibly have survived," said Summerlee with conviction. "Consider that the poison was so virulent that even a man who is as strong as an ox and has not a nerve in his body, like Malone here, could hardly get up the stairs before he fell unconscious. Is it likely that anyone could stand seventeen minutes of it, far less hours?"

"Unless someone saw it coming and made preparation, same as old friend Challenger did."

"That, I think, is hardly probable," said Challenger, projecting his beard and sinking his eyelids. "The combination of observation, inference, and anticipatory imagination which enabled me to foresee the danger is what one can hardly expect twice in the same generation."

"Then your conclusion is that everyone is certainly dead?"

"There can be little doubt of that. We have to remember, however, that the poison worked from below upwards and would possibly be less virulent in the higher strata of the atmosphere. It is strange, indeed, that it should be so; but it presents one of those features which will afford us in the future a fascinating field for study. One could imagine, therefore, that if one had to search for survivors one would turn one's eyes with best hopes of success to some Tibetan village or some Alpine farm, many thousands of feet above the sea level."

"Well, considerin' that there are no railroads and no steamers you might as well talk about survivors in the moon," said Lord John. "But what I'm askin' myself is whether it's really over or whether it's only half-time."

Summerlee craned his neck to look round the horizon. "It seems clear and fine," said he in a very dubious voice; "but so it did yesterday. I am by no means assured that it is all over."

Challenger shrugged his shoulders.

"We must come back once more to our fatalism," said he. "If the world has undergone this experience before, which is not outside the range of possibility; it was certainly a very long time ago. Therefore, we may reasonably hope that it will be very long before it occurs again."

"That's all very well," said Lord John, "but if you get an earthquake shock you are mighty likely to have a second one right on the top of it. I think we'd be wise to stretch our legs and have a breath of air while we have the chance. Since our oxygen is exhausted we may just as well be caught outside as in."

It was strange the absolute lethargy which had come upon us as a reaction after our tremendous emotions of the last twenty-four hours. It was both mental and physical, a deep-lying feeling that nothing mattered and that everything was a weariness and a profitless exertion. Even Challenger had succumbed to it, and sat in his chair, with his great head leaning upon his hands and his thoughts far away, until Lord John and I, catching him by each arm, fairly lifted him on to his feet, receiving only the glare and growl of an angry mastiff for our trouble. However, once we had got out of our narrow haven of refuge into the wider atmosphere of everyday life, our normal energy came gradually back to us once more.

But what were we to begin to do in that graveyard of a world? Could ever men have been faced with such a question since the dawn of time?

It is true that our own physical needs, and even our luxuries, were assured for the future. All the stores of food, all the vintages of wine, all the treasures of art were ours for the taking. But what were we to *do*? Some few tasks appealed to us at once, since they lay ready to our hands. We descended into the kitchen and laid the two domestics upon their respective beds. They seemed to have died without suffering, one in the chair by the fire, the other upon the scullery floor. Then we carried in poor Austin from the yard. His muscles were set as hard as a board in the most exaggerated rigor mortis, while the contraction of the fibres had drawn his mouth into a hard sardonic grin. This symptom was prevalent among all who had died from the poison. Wherever we went we were confronted by those grinning faces, which seemed to mock at our dreadful position, smiling silently and grimly at the ill-fated survivors of their race.

"Look here," said Lord John, who had paced restlessly about the dining-room whilst we partook of some food, "I don't know how you fellows feel about it, but for my part, I simply *can't* sit here and do nothin'."

"Perhaps," Challenger answered, "you would have the kindness to suggest what you think we ought to do."

"Get a move on us and see all that has happened."

"That is what I should myself propose."

"But not in this little country village. We can see from the window all that this place can teach us."

"Where should we go, then?"

"To London!"

"That's all very well," grumbled Summerlee. "You may be equal to a forty-mile walk, but I'm not so sure about Challenger, with his stumpy legs, and I am perfectly sure about myself." Challenger was very much annoyed.

"If you could see your way, sir, to confining your remarks to your own physical peculiarities, you would find that you had an ample field for comment," he cried.

"I had no intention to offend you, my dear Challenger," cried our tactless friend, "You can't be held responsible for your own physique. If Nature has given you a short, heavy body you cannot possibly help having stumpy legs."

Challenger was too furious to answer. He could only growl and blink and bristle. Lord John hastened to intervene before the dispute became more violent.

"You talk of walking. Why should we walk?" said he.

"Do you suggest taking a train?" asked Challenger, still simmering.

"What's the matter with the motor-car? Why should we not go in that?"

"I am not an expert," said Challenger, pulling at his beard reflectively. "At the same time, you are right in supposing that the human intellect in its higher manifestations should be sufficiently flexible to turn itself to anything. Your idea is an excellent one, Lord John. I myself will drive you all to London."

"You will do nothing of the kind," said Summerlee with decision.

"No, indeed, George!" cried his wife. "You only tried once, and you remember how you crashed through the gate of the garage."

"It was a momentary want of concentration," said Challenger complacently. "You can consider the matter settled. I will certainly drive you all to London."

The situation was relieved by Lord John.

"What's the car?" he asked.

"A twenty-horse Humber."

"Why, I've driven one for years," said he. "By George!" he added. "I never thought I'd live to take the whole human race in one load. There's just room for five, as I remember it. Get your things on, and I'll be ready at the door by ten o'clock."

Sure enough, at the hour named, the car came purring and crackling from the yard with Lord John at the wheel. I took my seat beside him, while the lady, a useful little buffer state, was squeezed in between the two men of wrath at the back. Then Lord John released his brakes, slid his lever rapidly from first to third, and we sped off upon the strangest drive that ever human beings have taken since man first came upon the earth.

You are to picture the loveliness of Nature upon that August day, the freshness of the morning air, the golden glare of the summer sunshine, the cloudless sky, the luxuriant green of the Sussex woods, and the deep purple of heather-clad downs. As you looked round upon the many-coloured beauty of the scene all thought of a vast catastrophe would have passed from your mind had it not been for one sinister sign—the solemn, all-embracing silence. There is a gentle hum of life which pervades a closely-settled country, so deep and constant that one ceases to observe it, as the dweller by the sea loses all sense of the constant murmur of the waves. The twitter of birds, the buzz of insects, the far-off echo of voices, the lowing of cattle, the distant barking of dogs, roar of trains, and rattle of carts—all these form one low, unremitting note, striking unheeded upon the ear. We missed it now. This deadly silence was appalling. So solemn was it, so impressive, that the buzz and rattle of our motor-car seemed an unwarrantable intrusion, an indecent disregard of this reverent stillness which lay like a pall over and round the ruins of humanity. It was this grim hush, and the tall clouds of smoke which rose here and there over the country-side from smoldering buildings, which cast a chill into our hearts as we gazed round at the glorious panorama of the Weald.

And then there were the dead! At first those endless groups of drawn and grinning faces filled us with a shuddering horror. So vivid and mordant was the impression that I can live over again that slow descent of the station hill, the passing by the nurse-girl with the two babes, the sight of the old horse on his knees between the shafts, the cabman twisted across his seat, and the young man inside with his hand upon the open door in the very act of springing out. Lower down were six reapers all in a litter, their limbs crossing, their dead, unwinking eyes gazing upwards at the glare of heaven. These things I see as in a photograph. But soon, by the merciful provision of nature, the over-excited nerve ceased to respond. The very vastness of the horror took away from its personal appeal. Individuals merged into groups, groups into crowds, crowds into a universal phenomenon which one soon accepted as the inevitable detail of every scene. Only here and there, where some particularly brutal or grotesque incident caught the attention, did the mind come back with a sudden shock to the personal and human meaning of it all.

Above all, there was the fate of the children. That, I remember, filled us with the strongest sense of intolerable injustice. We could have wept— Mrs. Challenger did weep—when we passed a great council school and saw the long trail of tiny figures scattered down the road which led from it. They had been dismissed by their terrified teachers and were speeding for their homes when the poison caught them in its net. Great numbers of people were at the open windows of the houses. In Tunbridge Wells there was hardly one which had not its staring, smiling face. At the last instant the need of air, that very craving for oxygen which we alone had been able to satisfy, had sent them flying to the window. The sidewalks too were littered with men and women, hatless and bonnetless, who had rushed out of the houses. Many of them had fallen in the roadway. It was a lucky thing that in Lord John we had found an expert driver, for it was no easy matter to pick one's way. Passing through the villages or towns we could only go at a walking pace, and once, I remember, opposite the school at Tonbridge, we had to halt some time while we carried aside the bodies which blocked our path.

A few small, definite pictures stand out in my memory from amid that long panorama of death upon the Sussex and Kentish high roads. One was that of a great, glittering motor-car standing outside the inn at the village of Southborough. It bore, as I should guess, some pleasure party upon their return from Brighton or from Eastbourne. There were three gaily dressed women, all young and beautiful, one of them with a Peking spaniel upon her lap. With them were a rakish-looking elderly man and a young aristocrat, his eyeglass still in his eye, his cigarette burned down to the stub between the fingers of his begloved hand. Death must have come on them in an instant and fixed them as they sat. Save that the elderly man had at the last moment torn out his collar in an effort to breathe, they might all have been asleep. On one side of the car a waiter with some broken glasses beside a tray was huddled near the step. On the other, two very ragged tramps, a man and a woman, lay where they had fallen, the man with his long, thin arm still outstretched, even as he had asked for alms in his lifetime. One instant of time had put aristocrat, waiter, tramp, and dog upon one common footing of inert and dissolving protoplasm.

I remember another singular picture, some miles on the London side of Sevenoaks. There is a large convent upon the left, with a long, green slope in front of it. Upon this slope were assembled a great number of school children, all kneeling at prayer. In front of them was a fringe of nuns, and higher up the slope, facing towards them, a single figure whom we took to be the Mother Superior. Unlike the pleasure-seekers in the motor-car, these people seemed to have had warning of their danger and to have died beautifully together, the teachers and the taught, assembled for their last common lesson.

My mind is still stunned by that terrific experience, and I grope vainly for means of expression by which I can reproduce the emotions which we felt. Perhaps it is best and wisest not to try, but merely to indicate the facts. Even Summerlee and Challenger were crushed, and we heard nothing of our companions behind us save an occasional whimper from the lady. As to Lord John, he was too intent upon his wheel and the difficult task of threading his way along such roads to have time or inclination for conversation. One phrase he used with such wearisome iteration that it stuck in my memory and at last almost made me laugh as a comment upon the day of doom.

"Pretty doin's! What!"

That was his ejaculation as each fresh tremendous combination of death and disaster displayed itself before us. "Pretty doin's! What!" he cried, as we descended the station hill at Rotherfield, and it was still "Pretty doin's! What!" as we picked our way through a wilderness of death in the High Street of Lewisham and the Old Kent Road.

It was here that we received a sudden and amazing shock. Out of the window of a humble corner house there appeared a fluttering handkerchief waving at the end of a long, thin human arm. Never had the sight of unexpected death caused our hearts to stop and then throb so wildly as did this amazing indication of life. Lord John ran the motor to the curb, and in an instant we had rushed through the open door of the house and up the staircase to the second-floor front room from which the signal proceeded.

A very old lady sat in a chair by the open window, and close to her, laid across a second chair, was a cylinder of oxygen, smaller but of the same shape as those which had saved our own lives. She turned her thin, drawn, bespectacled face toward us as we crowded in at the doorway.

"I feared that I was abandoned here forever," said she, "for I am an invalid and cannot stir."

"Well, madam," Challenger answered, "it is a lucky chance that we happened to pass."

"I have one all-important question to ask you," said she. "Gentlemen, I beg that you will be frank with me. What effect will these events have upon London and North-Western Railway shares?"

We should have laughed had it not been for the tragic eagerness with which she listened for our answer. Mrs. Burston, for that was her name, was an aged widow, whose whole income depended upon a small holding of this stock. Her life had been regulated by the rise and fall of the dividend, and she could form no conception of existence save as it was affected by the quotation of her shares. In vain we pointed out to her that all the money in the world was hers for the taking and was useless when taken. Her old mind would not adapt itself to the new idea, and she wept loudly over her vanished stock. "It was all I had," she wailed. "If that is gone I may as well go too."

Amid her lamentations we found out how this frail old plant had lived where the whole great forest had fallen. She was a confirmed invalid and an asthmatic. Oxygen had been prescribed for her malady, and a tube was in her room at the moment of the crisis. She had naturally inhaled some as had been her habit when there was a difficulty with her breathing. It had given her relief, and by doling out her supply she had managed to survive the night. Finally she had fallen asleep and been awakened by the buzz of our motor-car. As it was impossible to take her on with us, we saw that she had all necessaries of life and promised to communicate with her in a couple of days at the latest. So we left her, still weeping bitterly over her vanished stock.

As we approached the Thames the block in the streets became thicker and the obstacles more bewildering. It was with difficulty that we made our way across London Bridge. The approaches to it upon the Middlesex side were choked from end to end with frozen traffic which made all further advance in that direction impossible. A ship was blazing brightly alongside one of the wharves near the bridge, and the air was full of drifting smuts and of a heavy acrid smell of burning. There was a cloud of dense smoke somewhere near the Houses of Parliament, but it was impossible from where we were to see what was on fire.

"I don't know how it strikes you," Lord John remarked as he brought his engine to a standstill, "but it seems to me the country is more cheerful than the town. Dead London is gettin' on my nerves. I'm for a cast round and then gettin' back to Rotherfield."

"I confess that I do not see what we can hope for here," said Professor Summerlee.

"At the same time," said Challenger, his great voice booming strangely amid the silence, "it is difficult for us to conceive that out of seven millions of people there is only this one old woman who by some peculiarity of constitution or some accident of occupation has managed to survive this catastrophe."

"If there should be others, how can we hope to find them, George?" asked the lady. "And yet I agree with you that we cannot go back until we have tried."

Getting out of the car and leaving it by the curb, we walked with some difficulty along the crowded pavement of King William Street and entered the open door of a large insurance office. It was a corner house, and we chose it as commanding a view in every direction. Ascending the stair, we passed through what I suppose to have been the board-room, for eight elderly men were seated round a long table in the centre of it. The high window was open and we all stepped out upon the balcony. From it we could see the crowded city streets radiating in every direction, while below us the road was black from side to side with the tops of the motionless taxis. All, or nearly all, had their heads pointed outwards, showing how the terrified men of the city had at the last moment made a vain endeavor to rejoin their families in the suburbs or the country. Here and there amid the humbler cabs towered the great brass-spangled motor-car of some wealthy magnate, wedged hopelessly among the dammed stream of arrested traffic. Just beneath us there was such a one of great size and luxurious appearance, with its owner, a fat old man, leaning out, half his gross body through the window, and his podgy hand, gleaming with diamonds, outstretched as he urged his chauffeur to make a last effort to break through the press.

A dozen motor-buses towered up like islands in this flood, the passengers who crowded the roofs lying all huddled together and across each others' laps like a child's toys in a nursery. On a broad lamp pedestal in the centre of the roadway, a burly policeman was standing, leaning his back against the post in so natural an attitude that it was hard to realize that he was not alive, while at his feet there lay a ragged newsboy with his bundle of papers on the ground beside him. A paper-cart had got blocked in the crowd, and we could read in large letters, black upon yellow, "Scene at Lord's. County Match Interrupted."

This must have been the earliest edition, for there were other placards bearing the legend, "Is It the End? Great Scientist's Warning." And another, "Is Challenger Justified? Ominous Rumours."

Challenger pointed the latter placard out to his wife, as it thrust itself like a banner above the throng. I could see him throw out his chest and stroke his beard as he looked at it. It pleased and flattered that complex mind to think that London had died with his name and his words still present in their thoughts. His feelings were so evident that they aroused the sardonic comment of his colleague.

"In the limelight to the last, Challenger," he remarked.

"So it would appear," he answered complacently. "Well," he added as he looked down the long vista of the radiating streets, all silent and all choked up with death, "I really see no purpose to be served by our staying any longer in London. I suggest that we return at once to Rotherfield and then take counsel as to how we shall most profitably employ the years which lie before us."

Only one other picture shall I give of the scenes which we carried back in our memories from the dead city. It is a glimpse which we had of the interior of the old church of St. Mary's, which is at the very point where our car was awaiting us. Picking our way among the prostrate figures upon the steps, we pushed open the swing door and entered. It was a wonderful sight. The church was crammed from end to end with kneeling figures in every posture of supplication and abasement. At the last dreadful moment, brought suddenly face to face with the realities of life, those terrific realities which hang over us even while we follow the shadows, the terrified people had rushed into those old city churches which for generations had hardly ever held a congregation. There they huddled as close as they could kneel, many of them in their agitation still wearing their hats, while above them in the pulpit a young man in lay dress had apparently been addressing them when he and they had been overwhelmed by the same fate. He lay now, like Punch in his booth, with his head and two limp arms hanging over the ledge of the pulpit. It was a nightmare, the grey, dusty church, the rows of agonized figures, the dimness and silence of it all. We moved about with hushed whispers, walking upon our tip-toes.

And then suddenly I had an idea. At one corner of the church, near the door, stood the ancient font, and behind it a deep recess in which there hung the ropes for the bell-ringers. Why should we not send a message out over London which would attract to us anyone who might still be alive? I ran across, and pulling at the list-covered rope, I was surprised to find how difficult it was to swing the bell. Lord John had followed me.

"By George, young fellah!" said he, pulling off his coat. "You've hit on a dooced good notion. Give me a grip and we'll soon have a move on it."

But, even then, so heavy was the bell that it was not until Challenger and Summerlee had added their weight to ours that we heard the roaring and clanging above our heads which told us that the great clapper was ringing out its music. Far over dead London resounded our message of comradeship and hope to any fellow-man surviving. It cheered our own hearts, that strong, metallic call, and we turned the more earnestly to our work, dragged two feet off the earth with each upward jerk of the rope, but all straining together on the downward heave, Challenger the lowest of all, bending all his great strength to the task and flopping up and down like a monstrous bull-frog, croaking with every pull. It was at that moment that an artist might have taken a picture of the four adventurers, the comrades of many strange perils in the past, whom Fate had now chosen for so supreme an experience. For half an hour we worked, the sweat dropping from our faces, our arms and backs aching with the exertion. Then we went out into the portico of the church and looked eagerly up and down the silent, crowded streets. Not a sound, not a motion, in answer to our summons.

"It's no use. No one is left," I cried.

"We can do nothing more," said Mrs. Challenger. "For God's sake, George, let us get back to Rotherfield. Another hour of this dreadful, silent city would drive me mad."

We got into the car without another word. Lord John backed her round and turned her to the south. To us the chapter seemed closed. Little did we foresee the strange new chapter which was to open.

VI. THE GREAT AWAKENING

And now I come to the end of this extraordinary incident, so overshadowing in its importance, not only in our own small, individual lives, but in the general history of the human race. As I said when

I began my narrative, when that history comes to be written, this occurrence will surely stand out among all other events like a mountain towering among its foothills. Our generation has been reserved for a very special fate since it has been chosen to experience so wonderful a thing. How long its effect may last—how long mankind may preserve the humility and reverence which this great shock has taught it—can only be shown by the future. I think it is safe to say that things can never be quite the same again. Never can one realize how powerless and ignorant one is, and how one is upheld by an unseen hand, until for an instant that hand has seemed to close and to crush. Death has been imminent upon us. We know that at any moment it may be again. That grim presence shadows our lives, but who can deny that in that shadow the sense of duty, the feeling of sobriety and responsibility, the appreciation of the gravity and of the objects of life, the earnest desire to develop and improve, have grown and become real with us to a degree that has leavened our whole society from end to end? It is something beyond sects and beyond dogmas. It is rather an alteration of perspective, a shifting of our sense of proportion, a vivid realization that we are insignificant and evanescent creatures, existing on sufferance and at the mercy of the first chill wind from the unknown. But if the world has grown graver with this knowledge it is not, I think, a sadder place in consequence. Surely we are agreed that the more sober and restrained pleasures of the present are deeper as well as wiser than the noisy, foolish hustle which passed so often for enjoyment in the days of old—days so recent and yet already so inconceivable. Those empty lives which were wasted in aimless visiting and being visited, in the worry of great and unnecessary households, in the arranging and eating of elaborate and tedious meals, have now found rest and health in the reading, the music, the gentle family communion which comes from a simpler and saner division of their time. With greater health and greater pleasure they are richer than before, even after they have paid those increased contributions to the common fund which have so raised the standard of life in these islands.

There is some clash of opinion as to the exact hour of the great awakening. It is generally agreed that, apart from the difference of clocks, there may have been local causes which influenced the action of the poison. Certainly, in each separate district the resurrection was practically simultaneous. There are numerous witnesses that Big Ben pointed to ten minutes past six at the moment. The Astronomer Royal has fixed the Greenwich time at twelve past six. On the other hand, Laird Johnson, a very capable East Anglia observer, has recorded six-twenty as the hour. In the Hebrides it was as late as seven. In our own case there can be no doubt whatever, for I was seated in Challenger's study with his carefully tested chronometer in front of me at the moment. The hour was a quarter-past six.

An enormous depression was weighing upon my spirits. The cumulative effect of all the dreadful sights which we had seen upon our journey was heavy upon my soul. With my abounding animal health and great physical energy any kind of mental clouding was a rare event. I had the Irish faculty of seeing some gleam of humor in every darkness. But now the obscurity was appalling and unrelieved. The others were downstairs making their plans for the future. I sat by the open window, my chin resting upon my hand and my mind absorbed in the misery of our situation. Could we continue to live? That was the question which I had begun to ask myself. Was it possible to exist upon a dead world? Just as in physics the greater body draws to itself the lesser, would we not feel an overpowering attraction from that vast body of humanity which had passed into the unknown? How would the end come? Would it be from a return of the poison? Or would the earth be uninhabitable from the mephitic products of universal decay? Or, finally, might our awful situation prey upon and unbalance our minds? A group of insane folk upon a dead world! My mind was brooding upon this last dreadful idea when some slight noise caused me to look down upon the road beneath me. The old cab horse was coming up the hill!

I was conscious at the same instant of the twittering of birds, of someone coughing in the yard below, and of a background of movement in the landscape. And yet I remember that it was that absurd, emaciated, superannuated cab-horse which held my gaze. Slowly and wheezily it was climbing the slope. Then my eye traveled to the driver sitting hunched up upon the box and finally to the young man who was leaning out of the window in some excitement and shouting a direction. They were all indubitably, aggressively alive!

Everybody was alive once more! Had it all been a delusion? Was it conceivable that this whole poison belt incident had been an elaborate

dream? For an instant my startled brain was really ready to believe it.
Then I looked down, and there was the rising blister on my hand where
it was frayed by the rope of the city bell. It had really been so, then.
And yet here was the world resuscitated—here was life come back in an
instant full tide to the planet. Now, as my eyes wandered all over the great
landscape, I saw it in every direction—and moving, to my amazement,
in the very same groove in which it had halted. There were the golfers.
Was it possible that they were going on with their game? Yes, there was a
fellow driving off from a tee, and that other group upon the green were
surely putting for the hole. The reapers were slowly trooping back to
their work. The nurse-girl slapped one of her charges and then began to
push the perambulator up the hill. Everyone had unconcernedly taken up
the thread at the very point where they had dropped it.

I rushed downstairs, but the hall door was open, and I heard the
voices of my companions, loud in astonishment and congratulation,
in the yard. How we all shook hands and laughed as we came together,
and how Mrs. Challenger kissed us all in her emotion, before she finally
threw herself into the bear-hug of her husband.

"But they could not have been asleep!" cried Lord John. "Dash it
all, Challenger, you don't mean to believe that those folk were asleep
with their staring eyes and stiff limbs and that awful death grin on
their faces!"

"It can only have been the condition that is called catalepsy," said
Challenger. "It has been a rare phenomenon in the past and has
constantly been mistaken for death. While it endures, the temperature
falls, the respiration disappears, the heartbeat is indistinguishable—in
fact, it *is* death, save that it is evanescent. Even the most comprehensive
mind"—here he closed his eyes and simpered—"could hardly conceive a
universal outbreak of it in this fashion."

"You may label it catalepsy," remarked Summerlee, "but, after all,
that is only a name, and we know as little of the result as we do of the
poison which has caused it. The most we can say is that the vitiated
ether has produced a temporary death."

Austin was seated all in a heap on the step of the car. It was his
coughing which I had heard from above. He had been holding his head
in silence, but now he was muttering to himself and running his eyes
over the car.

"Young fat-head!" he grumbled. "Can't leave things alone!"

"What's the matter, Austin?"

"Lubricators left running, sir. Someone has been fooling with the car. I expect it's that young garden boy, sir."

Lord John looked guilty.

"I don't know what's amiss with me," continued Austin, staggering to his feet. "I expect I came over queer when I was hosing her down. I seem to remember flopping over by the step. But I'll swear I never left those lubricator taps on."

In a condensed narrative the astonished Austin was told what had happened to himself and the world. The mystery of the dripping lubricators was also explained to him. He listened with an air of deep distrust when told how an amateur had driven his car and with absorbed interest to the few sentences in which our experiences of the sleeping city were recorded. I can remember his comment when the story was concluded.

"Was you outside the Bank of England, sir?"

"Yes, Austin."

"With all them millions inside and everybody asleep?"

"That was so."

"And I not there!" he groaned, and turned dismally once more to the hosing of his car.

There was a sudden grinding of wheels upon gravel. The old cab had actually pulled up at Challenger's door. I saw the young occupant step out from it. An instant later the maid, who looked as tousled and bewildered as if she had that instant been aroused from the deepest sleep, appeared with a card upon a tray. Challenger snorted ferociously as he looked at it, and his thick black hair seemed to bristle up in his wrath.

"A Pressman!" he growled. Then with a deprecating smile: "After all, it is natural that the whole world should hasten to know what I think of such an episode."

"That can hardly be his errand," said Summerlee, "for he was on the road in his cab before ever the crisis came."

I looked at the card: "James Baxter, London Correspondent, *New York Monitor*."

"You'll see him?" said I.

"Not I."

"Oh, George! You should be kinder and more considerate to others. Surely you have learned something from what we have undergone."

He tut-tutted and shook his big, obstinate head.

"A poisonous breed! Eh, Malone? The worst weed in modern civilization, the ready tool of the quack and the hindrance of the self-respecting man! When did they ever say a good word for me?"

"When did you ever say a good word to them?" I answered. "Come, sir, this is a stranger who has made a journey to see you. I am sure that you won't be rude to him."

"Well, well," he grumbled, "you come with me and do the talking. I protest in advance against any such outrageous invasion of my private life." Muttering and mumbling, he came rolling after me like an angry and rather ill-conditioned mastiff.

The dapper young American pulled out his notebook and plunged instantly into his subject.

"I came down, sir," said he, "because our people in America would very much like to hear more about this danger which is, in your opinion, pressing upon the world."

"I know of no danger which is now pressing upon the world," Challenger answered gruffly.

The pressman looked at him in mild surprise.

"I meant, sir, the chances that the world might run into a belt of poisonous ether."

"I do not now apprehend any such danger," said Challenger.

The pressman looked even more perplexed.

"You are Professor Challenger, are you not?" he asked.

"Yes, sir; that is my name."

"I cannot understand, then, how you can say that there is no such danger. I am alluding to your own letter, published above your name in the London *Times* of this morning."

It was Challenger's turn to look surprised.

"This morning?" said he. "No London *Times* was published this morning."

"Surely, sir," said the American in mild remonstrance, "you must admit that the London *Times* is a daily paper." He drew out a copy from his inside pocket. "Here is the letter to which I refer."

Challenger chuckled and rubbed his hands.

"I begin to understand," said he. "So you read this letter this morning?"

"Yes, sir."

"And came at once to interview me?"

"Yes, sir."

"Did you observe anything unusual upon the journey down?"

"Well, to tell the truth, your people seemed more lively and generally human than I have ever seen them. The baggage man set out to tell me a funny story, and that's a new experience for me in this country."

"Nothing else?"

"Why, no, sir, not that I can recall."

"Well, now, what hour did you leave Victoria?"

The American smiled.

"I came here to interview you, Professor, but it seems to be a case of 'Is this nigger fishing, or is this fish niggering?' You're doing most of the work."

"It happens to interest me. Do you recall the hour?"

"Sure. It was half-past twelve."

"And you arrived?"

"At a quarter-past two."

"And you hired a cab?"

"That was so."

"How far do you suppose it is to the station?"

"Well, I should reckon the best part of two miles."

"So how long do you think it took you?"

"Well, half an hour, maybe, with that asthmatic in front."

"So it should be three o'clock?"

"Yes, or a trifle after it."

"Look at your watch."

The American did so and then stared at us in astonishment.

"Say!" he cried. "It's run down. That horse has broken every record, sure. The sun is pretty low, now that I come to look at it. Well, there's something here I don't understand."

"Have you no remembrance of anything remarkable as you came up the hill?"

"Well, I seem to recollect that I was mighty sleepy once. It comes back to me that I wanted to say something to the driver and that I couldn't make him heed me. I guess it was the heat, but I felt swimmy for a moment. That's all."

"So it is with the whole human race," said Challenger to me. "They have all felt swimmy for a moment. None of them have as yet any comprehension of what has occurred. Each will go on with his interrupted job as Austin has snatched up his hose-pipe or the golfer continued his game. Your editor, Malone, will continue the issue of his papers, and very much amazed he will be at finding that an issue is missing. Yes, my young friend," he added to the American reporter, with a sudden mood of amused geniality, "it may interest you to know that the world has swum through the poisonous current which swirls like the Gulf Stream through the ocean of ether. You will also kindly note for your own future convenience that to-day is not Friday, August the twenty-seventh, but Saturday, August the twenty-eighth, and that you sat senseless in your cab for twenty-eight hours upon the Rotherfield hill."

And "right here," as my American colleague would say, I may bring this narrative to an end. It is, as you are probably aware, only a fuller and more detailed version of the account which appeared in the Monday edition of the *Daily Gazette*—an account which has been universally admitted to be the greatest journalistic scoop of all time, which sold no fewer than three-and-a-half million copies of the paper. Framed upon the wall of my sanctum I retain those magnificent headlines:—

TWENTY-EIGHT HOURS' WORLD COMA

UNPRECEDENTED EXPERIENCE

CHALLENGER JUSTIFIED

OUR CORRESPONDENT ESCAPES

ENTHRALLING NARRATIVE

THE OXYGEN ROOM

WEIRD MOTOR DRIVE

DEAD LONDON

REPLACING THE MISSING PAGE

GREAT FIRES AND LOSS OF LIFE

WILL IT RECUR?

Underneath this glorious scroll came nine-and-a-half columns of narrative, in which appeared the first, last, and only account of the history of the planet, so far as one observer could draw it, during one long day of its existence. Challenger and Summerlee have treated the matter in a joint scientific paper, but to me alone was left the popular account. Surely I can sing "Nunc Dimittis." What is left but anti-climax in the life of a journalist after that!

But let me not end on sensational headlines and a merely personal triumph. Rather let me quote the sonorous passages in which the greatest of daily papers ended its admirable leader upon the subject—a leader which might well be filed for reference by every thoughtful man.

"It has been a well-worn truism," said the *Times*, "that our human race are a feeble folk before the infinite latent forces which surround us. From the prophets of old and from the philosophers of our own time the same message and warning have reached us. But, like all oft-repeated truths, it has in time lost something of its actuality and cogency. A lesson, an actual experience, was needed to bring it home. It is from that salutary but terrible ordeal that we have just emerged, with minds which are still stunned by the suddenness of the blow and with spirits which are chastened by the realization of our own limitations and impotence. The world has paid a fearful price for its schooling. Hardly yet have we learned the full tale of disaster, but the destruction by fire of New York, of Orleans, and of Brighton constitutes in itself one of the greatest tragedies in the history of our race. When the account of the railway and shipping accidents has been completed, it will furnish grim reading, although there is evidence to show that in the vast majority of cases the drivers of trains and engineers of steamers succeeded in shutting off their motive power before succumbing to the poison. But the material damage, enormous as it is both in life and in property, is not the consideration which will be uppermost in our minds to-day. All this may in time be forgotten. But what will not be forgotten, and what will and should continue to obsess our imaginations, is this revelation of the possibilities of the universe, this destruction of our ignorant self-complacency, and this demonstration of how narrow is the path of our material existence and what abysses may lie upon either side of it. Solemnity and humility are at the base of all our emotions to-day. May they be the foundations upon which a more earnest and reverent race may build a more worthy temple."

NYARLATHOTEP

H.P. LOVECRAFT

The stories of H.P. Lovecraft (1890–1937) abound with extradimensional entities whose emergence onto our own plane of existence portends the end of life as we know it. This dream-like prose-poem first appeared in the December 1920 issue of the United Amateur. Over the remainder of Lovecraft's writing career—in his own tales and in the stories of colleagues who riffed on his creations in their weird fiction—Nyarlathotep became a signature monster in the shared world of cosmic horror stories by Lovecraft and others dubbed the Cthulhu Mythos.

Nyarlathotep . . . the crawling chaos . . . I am the last . . . I will tell the audient void. . . .

I do not recall distinctly when it began, but it was months ago. The general tension was horrible. To a season of political and social upheaval was added a strange and brooding apprehension of hideous physical danger; a danger widespread and all-embracing, such a danger as may be imagined only in the most terrible phantasms of the night. I recall that the people went about with pale and worried faces, and whispered warnings and prophecies which no one dared consciously repeat or acknowledge to himself that he had heard. A sense of monstrous guilt was upon the land, and out of the abysses between the stars swept chill currents that made men shiver in dark and lonely places. There was a daemoniac alteration in the sequence of the seasons—the autumn heat lingered fearsomely, and everyone felt that the world and perhaps the universe had passed from the control of known gods or forces to that of gods or forces which were unknown.

And it was then that Nyarlathotep came out of Egypt. Who he was, none could tell, but he was of the old native blood and looked like a Pharaoh. The fellahin knelt when they saw him, yet could not say why. He said he had risen up out of the blackness of twenty-seven centuries, and that he had heard messages from places not on this planet. Into the lands of civilisation came Nyarlathotep, swarthy, slender, and sinister, always buying strange instruments of glass and metal and combining them into instruments yet stranger. He spoke much of the sciences—of electricity and psychology—and gave exhibitions of power which sent his spectators away speechless, yet which swelled his fame to exceeding magnitude. Men advised one another to see Nyarlathotep, and shuddered. And where Nyarlathotep went, rest vanished; for the small hours were rent with the screams of nightmare. Never before had the screams of nightmare been such a public problem; now the wise men almost wished they could forbid sleep in the small hours, that the shrieks of cities might less horribly disturb the pale, pitying moon as it glimmered on green waters gliding under bridges, and old steeples crumbling against a sickly sky.

I remember when Nyarlathotep came to my city—the great, the old, the terrible city of unnumbered crimes. My friend had told me of him, and of the impelling fascination and allurement of his revelations, and I burned with eagerness to explore his uttermost mysteries. My friend said they were horrible and impressive beyond my most fevered imaginings; that what was thrown on a screen in the darkened room prophesied things none but Nyarlathotep dared prophesy, and that in the sputter of his sparks there was taken from men that which had never been taken before yet which shewed only in the eyes. And I heard it hinted abroad that those who knew Nyarlathotep looked on sights which others saw not.

It was in the hot autumn that I went through the night with the restless crowds to see Nyarlathotep; through the stifling night and up the endless stairs into the choking room. And shadowed on a screen, I saw hooded forms amidst ruins, and yellow evil faces peering from behind fallen monuments. And I saw the world battling against blackness; against the waves of destruction from ultimate space; whirling, churning; struggling around the dimming, cooling sun. Then the sparks played amazingly around the heads of the spectators, and hair stood up on end whilst shadows more grotesque than I can tell came out and squatted on the heads. And when I, who was colder and more scientific than the rest, mumbled a trembling protest about "imposture" and "static electricity," Nyarlathotep drave us all out, down the dizzy stairs into the damp, hot, deserted midnight streets. I screamed aloud that I was *not* afraid; that I never could be afraid; and others screamed with me for solace. We sware to one another that the city *was* exactly the same, and still alive; and when the electric lights began to fade we cursed the company over and over again, and laughed at the queer faces we made.

I believe we felt something coming down from the greenish moon, for when we began to depend on its light we drifted into curious involuntary formations and seemed to know our destinations though we dared not think of them. Once we looked at the pavement and found the blocks loose and displaced by grass, with scarce a line of rusted metal to shew where the tramways had run. And again we saw a tram-car, lone, windowless, dilapidated, and almost on its side. When we gazed around the horizon, we could not find the third tower by the river, and noticed that the silhouette of the second tower was ragged at the top. Then we split up into narrow columns, each of which seemed drawn in a different direction. One disappeared in a narrow alley to the left, leaving only the echo of a shocking moan. Another filed down a weed-choked subway entrance, howling with a laughter that was mad. My own column was sucked toward the open country, and presently felt a chill which was not of the hot autumn; for as we stalked out on the dark moor, we beheld around us the hellish moon-glitter of evil snows. Trackless, inexplicable snows, swept asunder in one direction only, where lay a gulf all the blacker for its glittering walls. The column seemed very thin indeed as it plodded dreamily into the gulf. I lingered behind, for the black rift in the green-litten snow was frightful, and I thought I had heard the reverberations of a disquieting wail as my companions vanished; but my power to linger was slight. As if beckoned by those who had gone before, I half floated between the titanic snowdrifts, quivering and afraid, into the sightless vortex of the unimaginable.

Screamingly sentient, dumbly delirious, only the gods that were can tell. A sickened, sensitive shadow writhing in hands that are not hands, and whirled blindly past ghastly midnights of rotting creation, corpses of dead worlds with sores that were cities, charnel winds that brush the pallid stars and make them flicker low. Beyond the worlds vague ghosts of monstrous things; half-seen columns of unsanctified temples that rest on nameless rocks beneath space and reach up to dizzy vacua above the spheres of light and darkness. And through this revolting graveyard of the universe the muffled, maddening beating of drums, and thin, monotonous whine of blasphemous flutes from inconceivable, unlighted chambers beyond Time; the detestable pounding and piping whereunto dance slowly, awkwardly, and absurdly the gigantic, tenebrous ultimate gods—the blind, voiceless, mindless gargoyles whose soul is Nyarlathotep.